SHADOW

of the

LANTERN BEARER

www.chrisrunderwood.com

First paperback edition March 2020

Cover art by Adrian Regalado

ISBN: 9781654762940

◆ THE GOLDEN REMNANT SAGA: BOOK ONE ◆

SHADOW
of the
LANTERN BEARER

CHRIS R. UNDERWOOD

To the lands of Ashash

The Golden Remnant

IN THE YEAR 422 POST OUTBREAK

RED EXPANSE

To the lands of Ashash

Beckoning Idol

Gaptooth

WINDLESS PEAKS

Lastwater Lake

Lake of Solitude

Hark's Camp

Valley of Tears

DUSKWODE

Ruin of Vale City

Vale of Twelve

Baybury

RATWOOD

Ruined Fortress
of Madia

Hale's Crossing

NOTTE'S
MIRE

THE NECK

Bay of
Barbarians

Locket

DROWNING SEA

To Sundar

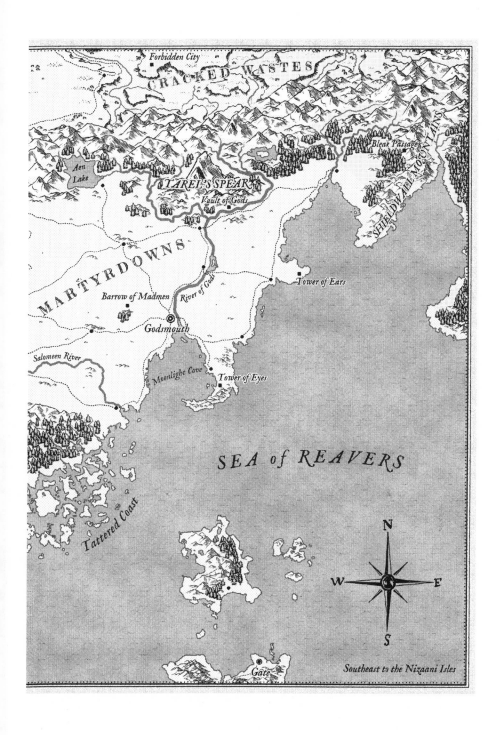

PART I
RUIN

CHAPTER

1

IT WAS THREE DAYS until Lampnight, and Mertyn Walter was scheduled to die.

Half the population of Hale's Crossing had turned out to watch, along with representatives from several of the nearby fishing villages. Everyone was dressed in their brightest colors: reds and blues and golds, with some of the women wearing silver bracelets or silk head scarves. Many of the younger children wore freshly made flower chains in their hair.

Kole Felmen stood apart from them all. He was thankful that the boiled leather mask he wore kept out the worst of the swamp stink from nearby Notte's Mire. What it didn't keep out was the heat.

It was not yet midday, but already he was broiling in the leather cloak and full-face hood. His breathing echoed in his own ears, fogging up the hood's scratched glass lenses. Sweat matted his hair to his forehead. The oppressive humidity did nothing to calm his hammering heart.

He had never killed a man before.

Kole tugged nervously on his new calfskin gloves. Da had assured him that they'd fit better once they'd been broken in, but Kole wasn't convinced. He could barely squeeze his fingers into them.

He could feel his da watching him now, along with the rest of the town. Da was standing off to the side, also garbed in the protective gear of a headsman. His gloved hands were clasped in front of him. A talisman against sorcery hung from his neck, just like the one Kole wore. Kole couldn't make out his da's eyes through the hood, but when he glanced anxiously at him, Da just gave him a slow nod.

Just like we practiced, Kole could hear his da saying. *One strike, delivered with all your strength. He'll thank you for it.*

Kole tightened his fingers around the hilt of the heavy sword. Its rounded point had sunk into the soft dirt at his feet.

He had wielded the sword before, of course. Against tree stumps. And dummies made of reeds. And once against the half-rotted corpse of a deer that had sunk to its belly on the outskirts of the swamp. Before Kole and his da hauled it out the deer had been so badly trapped even the swamp cats couldn't get to it.

Kole had developed the muscles to swing the headsman's sword. Now, at seventeen, his da had decided it was time he developed the stomach.

Swallowing, Kole stared through his fogged-up lenses at the condemned man beside him. A cloth gag was stuffed in Mertyn Walter's mouth and his wrists were tied together behind his back. His ankles, too, were tied, though he wouldn't be running anywhere anytime soon. An hour ago Kole had fed the man a cocktail of sedatives Ma had prepared. Now the fisherman's eyes were lidded, his body slumped and unmoving against the large, flat-topped headstone. The stone was scored with cuts and stained brown with the blood of those who had taken his place before.

The man was so still that Kole could almost imagine he was already dead.

But Kole had seen the dead before. He'd handled them, carried them, burned their bodies. As the only corpse draggers within twenty miles of Hale's Crossing, Kole and his da dealt with the bodies of almost everyone in the region who died. Sometimes animals as well, like when a rabid dog had got at Farmer Estmond's sheep. The dead were impure—dangerous, even—so only the impure could handle them.

Kole knew well what a dead man looked like. And Mertyn Walter was not dead. Not yet.

A foul wind blew off the swamp, stinking enough that Kole could smell it even through his hood. Gasps of disgust rose from the crowd of townsfolk standing apart from Kole and the condemned man. Several of them breathed through scented handkerchiefs.

It was still a few minutes until noon, but when the crowd started grumbling impatiently, Townmaster Haddin stepped forward and cleared his throat. He was dressed in his feastday best, wearing a wide-brimmed hat and a jacket that he couldn't possibly buckle over his belly. From his pocket he produced a sheet of parchment, which he unfolded and held at arm's length.

Squinting, he read, "On this day at noon, the Elder Council condemns Mertyn Walter to death. With a strike of the headsman's blade, this poor wretch's soul will be set free from the corruption of his tainted body. May the Watcher of Souls guide him safely to the Beyond."

Townmaster Haddin lowered the paper. A baby in the crowd let out a cry and was quickly shushed by its mother. The only other sounds were the croaking of distant frogs and the incessant chirping of a thousand crickets.

Licking his lips, the townmaster looked over at the condemned man, then turned to address the crowd. "Mertyn was a good man. He worked hard every day of his life. I always knew that if there was something that needed to be done, I could count on Mertyn. No matter the task, no matter the hour. A good man. He loved his family, too. Don't let the horrors of the last few days make you forget that. Those girls were everything to him, and Ana…" The townmaster's voice cracked. He touched his fist to his lips. "I remember when he married Ana, out there by the sea. A spring day, it was, raining like the gods were trying to drown us all. But Mertyn's smile kept us all warm. I've never seen a man so happy as the day he took Ana as his wife.

"It's not fair what happened to Ana. Or those girls. Or Mertyn himself. He didn't ask to…to get sick. But he did, and then he did what he did to Ana and the girls, and so here we are." The townmaster paused. "It ends here. Mertyn didn't infect anyone else. We still don't know where he picked up the plague, but we'll find out. The council thinks it was a rat bite, and I'm inclined to agree. If that's the case, we'll catch the rat before anyone else comes to harm. There's no need for panic. And I don't want to hear any more gossip about Ana and the girls, about what they looked like after…after…" He trailed off.

Kole didn't need to hear the gossip. It'd been him and Da who'd burned the bodies. Well, *body*, really. Kole had never seen anything like it before. Three people—a woman and two young girls—fused together in a tangle of flesh and limbs. Bound together by flesh-bending sorcery.

In truth, it was worse than the rumors. Because when he and Da had come to take the bodies away, they hadn't quite been dead yet.

They'd looked it, all right. But when he and Da, in their protective gear, had started moving the merged bodies, Ana's eyes had opened. She began to whisper, except the words came from the mouth of one of the girls, a mouth that was fused with another's thigh.

Kole couldn't hear the whispers, but Da was closer. Da had sent Kole home to fetch a new breathing filter for his hood. When he returned, the thing that had once been Ana and her daughters was dead.

Kole didn't know whether they'd finally succumbed or if Da had taken pity on them and helped them along. He hadn't asked.

Growing queasy at the memory of Mertyn's family, Kole looked out at the crowd. The townmaster's speech had at least drawn the attention away from Kole, for which he was thankful. The townsfolk stood clustered together in the middle of the muddy field. In the distance, beside the old stone bridge that stretched across Duskwatch River, was the cluster of simple wooden houses and shops that made up Hale's Crossing. Aside from the old guildhall, only two buildings in the town stood more than a single story high: the townmaster's house and the Empty Net, the town's only inn.

Movement within the crowd pulled Kole's attention away from the town. He caught sight of Darvin Rike, the huntsman's son, along with two of his friends. Darvin was grinning as he showed his friends the contents of a small sack. The dark-haired boy had a few inches on Kole, with muscles trained on his father's hunting bow.

Suddenly, Darvin seemed to sense Kole looking at him, though surely he couldn't see Kole's eyes through the fogged lenses. With a smirk, the huntsman's son pulled the sack closed and gestured to his friends. The three of them melted back into the crowd.

The townmaster squinted up at the sun, then turned and called out to Kole. "That'll do. Headsman, proceed."

Kole's heart lurched, his palms suddenly damp within his gloves. The eyes of the town were on him again. With trembling hands, Kole pulled the tip of the sword out of the mud and turned to the headstone.

Mertyn Walter had always been a thin man—now he was like skin draped over a skeleton. The fisherman must've only been infected a few days ago, a week at most, but the sorcerer's plague had practically eaten him alive. He was dressed now in soiled rags, still bruised from the beating he'd taken when the posse of locals caught him. If it hadn't been for the townmaster's intervention, they might have killed him on the spot.

Mertyn's eyelids twitched as Kole approached. Kole paused, watching, but the sedatives appeared to be keeping the man subdued. His breaths were slow and shallow, barely visible.

Kole's gaze moved to the back of the man's neck. The points of his vertebrae poked against his skin. Kole tried to recall what his da had taught him. He had to bring the sword down in the right place. Too high and the sword would catch the man's skull. Too low and the strike might be slowed by the bulk of Mertyn's neck muscles.

He glanced over at his da again, but the older headsman just stood impassively now, watching. This would be Kole's first great test. He was a Felmen, born into an impure family. He would never be allowed to be a fisherman, or a smith, or an innkeeper. Even the tanners would be hesitant to work with him. He was destined to make his living as a corpse dragger, a body burner, a headsman. If he couldn't even do that…

He found himself wishing his sister was here. Arabeth would give him a kick and tell him to get on with it.

Through his gag, Mertyn murmured something, his eyes still closed. The sedatives wouldn't keep him unconscious much longer. And Kole could feel the townsfolk getting restless.

Gripping the sword in both hands, he hefted it above his head. It was heavier than he remembered. Taking a deep breath, he focused on a small mole on the back of Mertyn's neck. That would be his target.

Don't look at the sword, Da's voice rang in his head. *Look where you want it to land.*

Except he could hardly see the mole now. His lenses were fogging up worse than ever. He was breathing too fast. He squinted through the mist on the glass, his muscles tensing.

Something smashed into the side of Kole's head, splattering gunk across one of the lenses. He staggered into Mertyn's unconscious form, knocking the condemned man off the headstone and nearly dropping the sword.

Fruit flies buzzed around his head. Distantly, he heard laughter.

With a gloved hand he quickly wiped the muck off his hood. He was just in time to see a second rotten apple fly out of the crowd toward him.

He tried to dodge the apple, but his bulky protective gear made movement cumbersome. The apple splattered against his shoulder, the sweet stink of it reaching him even through his hood.

"Darvin Rike!" the townmaster roared. "Get out of here or I'll have you and your friends searching for bog iron until you're as gray as me!"

Kole heard more laughter, and then hurried footsteps squelching in the mud. He could just make out the three figures running back toward the town.

He was glad his hood hid the burning in his cheeks. Darvin never passed up an opportunity to make Kole's life miserable. He just hadn't expected Darvin to do it when he had an actual sword in his hands.

Planting his sword in the mud, he searched through the misted lenses for the unconscious Mertyn. More by feel than sight, he found the man and hauled him back onto the headstone.

Panting, Kole picked up the sword and raised it above his head once more.

There was so much fog he couldn't see the man's mole. Gods, he couldn't even tell where the man's neck began. Flies still buzzed around Kole's head.

Cursing, he lowered the sword once more, put his back to the crowd, and lifted his hood. He couldn't execute a man if he couldn't even see him.

The fresh air was welcome, even if it stank of swamp and rotten fruit. He stuck his hand inside the hood and wiped the lenses with his gloved fingers. He could hear the crowd murmuring among themselves. A few were laughing softly, the tension broken by Darvin's apple-throwing.

As he glanced over his shoulder at Darvin and his friends high-tailing it back to town, Kole caught sight of another figure standing near the trunk of a lone, withered tree.

It was a woman, though he didn't recognize her from Hale's Crossing or any of the surrounding villages. She was dressed in traveler's clothes: a thin gray cloak over a simple tunic, with trousers tucked into a pair of riding boots. Her dark hair was cropped almost to the skin at the sides, a fashion that clearly marked her as an outsider.

She was standing well away from the whispering townsfolk—most of them seemed not to have noticed her. She stared at the proceedings with an intensity that made Kole shiver despite the heat.

In the distance, past Darvin's gang, Kole could just make out three more figures on horseback making their way into town, leading another pair of horses behind them. A merchant and his guards, maybe? Then where was his wagon?

Over the sound of the crowd's murmurings, another sound reached Kole's ears, dragging his attention away from the strangers. Still trying to clean his lenses, he glanced down at the headstone.

Mertyn's eyes were open and staring. Not at Kole—at something far away. A faint ring of red rimmed his irises.

His gag had come loose. It dangled about his neck. Cold clutched at Kole's guts.

The man was muttering as fast as an Ashashi, though the language was like nothing Kole had ever heard before. It was more than words—it was filled with clicks and humming and sounds that he didn't know a man could make. All of it was strung together in a surprisingly melodic way, like all of creation was singing through this wasted old fisherman.

As he spoke, something trailed from the corners of Mertyn's lips. Like smoke of the purest red. The thin trails danced in the breeze, dispersing in the air.

Sorcery. Mertyn was performing sorcery.

With a jolt of horror, Kole realized his hood was still raised. He jerked it back down over his face. Had he inhaled? Had he breathed in the contagion?

Blood pounded in his ears. Frozen in place, he watched as Mertyn's sing-song mutterings reached a crescendo. The man's shoulders began to contort unnaturally. His skin seemed suddenly fluid, and he began to slide free of his bonds.

With shaking hands, Kole shoved the gag back in the man's mouth and tightened it around the back of his head. Mertyn continued to mumble around the gag, but the red smoke ceased to trail from his lips. The man's shoulders returned to their usual form.

Panting, Kole turned toward the crowd.

The townsfolk were staring with a mixture of confusion and curiosity. They had grown silent once more. But there were no screams, no cries of, "Sorcery!"

They didn't see, Kole realized. They were too far back, and he'd been standing partly between the crowd and Mertyn. The whole thing had taken no more than a couple of seconds. Their own murmurings had drowned out Mertyn's whispers. They hadn't seen the man's body contort as he worked his sorcery upon himself.

"Kole?" Da called, his voice muffled by his hood. He was approaching.

Kole swallowed, staring first at the townsfolk, then at Da. "He nearly got the gag loose," he said quietly enough that his voice wouldn't carry to the crowd. "The sedatives are wearing off."

"Let's be quick, then." With a nod, Da backed off again, giving Kole some space.

Kole turned back toward Mertyn, getting into position and raising his sword above his head once more. It trembled in his hands.

I didn't breathe it in, he told himself. *I'm fine. I'm not infected.*

Mertyn turned his head to look up at Kole. Around the gag, he smiled a madman's smile.

Kole brought the sword down.

The blade bit deep into Mertyn's neck. But the blow landed too low. Mertyn's eyes rolled back in his head, a choking sound escaping his lips. He began to twitch and shudder.

No. No, no, no.

Kole pulled on the sword, trying to lift it for another swing. But the blade had cut deep. It was stuck in the man's spine. With each jerk of the sword, Mertyn made another choking gasp.

Quiet groans rose from the gathered townsfolk. Kole turned to see several of them looking away. The baby started crying again.

He heard footsteps squelching in the mud. Turning, he saw Da approaching.

Shame twisted his stomach into knots. Swallowing bile, he stopped pulling on the sword.

Da laid a hand on his shoulder, gently pushing him aside. As Kole stumbled away, Da took the sword by the hilt. His legs felt weighed down by stones.

Planting one foot on the headstone, Da jerked the sword free of Mertyn's neck. He raised it high above his head.

As the sword fell, Kole looked back toward the stunted tree across the field. The strange woman was nowhere to be seen.

Steel rang against the headstone, and Mertyn's soul was finally set free of his sorcery-plagued body.

CHAPTER
2

KOLE STARED INTO the blazing fire, watching Mertyn Walter's body burn.

With a grunt, Da set the two buckets of water down and tossed him a bar of soap. Kole caught it without taking his eyes from the pyre.

Stripping off his gloves, Da began to unbuckle the straps on his leather coat. Wordlessly, Kole did the same. Both of them had already taken off their hoods and set them aside for cleaning.

Sweat matted Da's hair to his narrow, lined face. There were beads of moisture in his thin beard. The air was finally starting to cool in the late afternoon, though the heat of the fire was intense. They were in the muddy field not far from the headstone, where the wind would carry the smoke away from the town.

The two of them sat down on a dead log. Kole cupped his hands in his bucket and splashed the cool well water on his face. He felt as unclean as if he'd taken a dip in a tub of sheep shit. He scrubbed fiercely at himself with the soap.

He could feel Da's eyes on him, but he didn't face him. He just watched the fire, watched the sparks of orange dance amid the smoke, carrying Mertyn's soul up into the sky and out to the Beyond. Out of the corner of his eye he saw Da stripping off his undershirt.

"Did I ever tell you about my first execution?" Da asked as he splashed himself with water.

Kole shook his head.

"It was a bandit captain who used to rob tax collectors on the High Road. Went by the name Black Fist or some such. Wasn't enough just to rob them, either. He and his gang left a lot of bodies behind."

Kole looked up. "How old were you?"

"Your age. Maybe a little older. I threw up twice before I even got to the headstone. No one saw that, luckily. Anyway, I go up there, and I'm shaking. Shaking hard. Takes me a while to get my nerve." A smile pulled at the corner of Da's lips. "And while I'm plucking up the courage, the slippery bastard gets his ankles loose. Next thing I know the man I'm supposed to kill is running around like a bloody chicken."

"He escaped?"

Da shook his head, his smile becoming a grin. "Of course not. Your grandpa would've flayed me alive if I'd let that happen. I did the only thing I could think of. I chased the man. I chased old Black Fist, or whatever his name was, all around the field." He lifted his hands above his head like he was holding a sword.

Da began to laugh, and the image made Kole chuckle as well. He couldn't believe he hadn't heard this story before.

"He slipped, finally," Da said. "I was so addled I didn't even think to take him back to the headstone. I just did it right there, in the mud. Took me four swings before his head finally came off." He chuckled, shaking his head. "I still think about that day. But you know what?"

"What?"

"It never got any worse than that. That was the worst execution I ever did. After that, every time went a little better."

Kole eyed his da suspiciously. "How much of that story was true?"

Da shrugged innocently. "Most of it." He held out a finger. "Don't you breathe a word of it to your sister. She doesn't respect me enough as it is."

Slapping his hand over his heart, Kole said, "I'll take it with me to the pyre."

The words had been meant in jest, but as he spoke them he thought again of the mad smile that Mertyn had given him just before he died. He thought of the red smoke coming from the man's lips as he tried to use his sorcery to escape his bonds.

I didn't breathe it in, he told himself forcefully. *I'm not going to become like him. I'm not going to end up on that same headstone, waiting for the sword to fall.*

But he started scrubbing himself again anyway.

Da eyed him. "You all right, boy?"

Kole nodded.

"Are you thinking about Mertyn's family?"

After a moment's hesitation, Kole nodded again.

"Me too," Da said. "I've seen a lot of things in my time. Nothing like that."

"What the townmaster was saying… Are they sure no one else got infected?"

"Is that what you're worried about?" Da reached over and laid a hand on his shoulder. "It's all right. People are on the lookout, now. If anyone else starts showing signs, we'll find out soon. We can put an end to it before anyone else gets hurt."

Somehow, that didn't reassure him. He slipped out from beneath his father's hand.

Da stared into the fire. "We were lucky, you know. Lucky that Mertyn's wife and daughters were the only victims. If anyone else had been around while Mertyn was working his sorcery, they might have become infected as well. Before long the plague could have spread all through Hale's Crossing. We could've had a whole town full of mad sorcerers."

Kole nodded. "Doesn't feel lucky, though."

"No. No it doesn't."

"How could he do what he did? How could he do that to his family?"

"Mertyn wasn't in his right mind, boy. You know that."

Kole fell silent.

You're not infected, he told himself. *You'd know if you were.*

Da was looking at him again. "It's a mercy, what we do. You understand that, right?"

It was a speech Kole had heard many times before. "That's not how they see it."

"They?"

Kole jerked his head past the fire, toward the town. Da frowned and nodded slowly.

"No," he agreed. "But we do it anyway. Because someone has to."

"Even if they hate us for it?"

"Are you getting worked up about the Rike boy throwing those apples?" Da asked. "Don't give him space in your head. The Rike family are trouble, always have been. You remember Darvin's uncle. He was a piece of work. A thief and a murderer."

"It's not just Darvin Rike. It's the whole town."

"They're just scared, Kole. They don't understand."

"They could at least pay us for what we do."

"They do pay us," Da said.

"Yeah?" Kole nodded toward Da's pocket. "How much was in that pouch the townmaster threw at your feet?"

"Enough."

"They were short, weren't they?"

Da shrugged, like it didn't matter. "Times are tough for everyone."

"Ma is going to kill you."

"Why do you think I haven't gone home yet?"

The fire was slowly dying. Mertyn's body was little more than a skeleton now, the taint burned away in the heat of the fire.

After a lot of scrubbing, Kole was finally starting to feel clean again as well. He pulled on a fresh tunic.

"You did good today," Da said. Taking the coin pouch out of his pocket, he fished out a silver coin and four copper pennies and handed them to Kole. "Go take the rest of the afternoon off. I'll deal with the fire."

He looked down at the coins. They were uneven and roughly minted—Remnant coins usually were, unlike the coins he'd seen Ashashi merchants trade in. Each depicted a portrait of the Moonlit Tyrant, a crown of stars above his head. Kole glanced at the pouch in Da's hand—it looked much emptier now.

"The coppers will be enough." Kole tried to hand the silver coin back, but Da wouldn't take it.

"A headsman deserves a decent purse," Da said. "Especially his first time out."

Kole hesitated. "I didn't even finish, though."

"He was finished. I just hurried things along. Keep the silver. Spend it. You earned it. Now get out of here."

"I need to enter Mertyn's name into the records." Kole said.

"I've got it. Go on. Go do your drawings or something."

Kole hesitated, but he wasn't about to pass up a few hours of free time. He stood, then turned back to Da.

"I saw a woman today. Someone from out of town. She was watching the execution."

Da nodded. "I saw her too."

"Who was she? I heard one of the merchants talking last week about Hallowed Order knights outside Baybury. You think she's one of them?"

"Didn't look like any knight I ever saw."

"Well, she's not here to fish."

"You worry too much, boy. She probably got lost on her way to the Neck. Now get out of here before I find some work for you to do." He looked around and pointed. "For a start, the sword will need sharpening—"

Kole threw up his hands. "I'm going, I'm going."

Just upriver from Hale's Crossing was an ancient statue carved from unnaturally white stone. At some point in the last four hundred years, the top half of the statue had been sheared off. It lay at the bottom of the river now, the details worn smooth by the water's flow. What remained of the statue's lower half showed thin robes clinging to the hips of a youthful, feminine figure. Strangling vines had grown up around her legs and the statue's base, digging in so tight they'd started to wear away at the stone as well. Flowers of pure white sprouted from the cracks in the stone.

A few months ago, Kole had cleared enough of the weeds around the statue's base to reveal what might've once been an inscription, but the words had been worn away almost to nothing. Kole could read—Ma had made it a point to teach him—but the knowledge of who this mysterious woman had been was forever lost to him, stolen away by the ravages of time. Was she a prophet? Or maybe a sorceress, before sorcery itself became a plague that destroyed the ancient empire from the inside out.

Or maybe she was a representation of one of the old gods, those jealous gods who had grown angered by humanity's quest for forbidden knowledge, until they turned their gift to humanity into a blight.

In some ways, Kole was glad he didn't know the statue's identity. It left him something to wonder about. A mystery, like one of the tales the bards sometimes spun when they made the journey this far out west.

Kole liked coming to the statue, especially near sunset. He sat down in the grass, leaned against the ruined stone, and looked south toward the Drowning Sea. Nowhere else had a better view.

Half a dozen other villages hugged the northern coast of the sea. Most of the fishing boats had already returned to their villages for the night, but a few stragglers still bobbed in the water, their nets cast, hoping for one last catch before sunset.

The fisherfolk had been grumbling about their catches for years now. Every year was worse than the last, to hear them tell it. Many put the blame on the ancient whale that supposedly roamed the Drowning Sea. According to legend it had been trapped there ever since the mad sorcerers of the past tore the land apart and flooded the ancient city that once stood on the banks of the sea.

Kole had never seen the mysterious whale, or spoken to anyone who had. He suspected the fisherfolk were just getting grumpier and more gullible as they got older.

Kole opened his leather pack and took out his sketchbook and charcoal. Despite careful rationing, the sketchbook only had a few blank pages left and the charcoal was halfway to being a nub. The silver coin Da had given him would buy replacements, but only if he could convince Mrs. Tannith at the general store to sell to the likes of him.

Still, Kole had to clear his head, even if it meant sacrificing another precious page of the sketchbook. He flipped through until he found a clean page near the back. Staring out at the crystal-blue waters that stretched away before him, he let the day's stresses settle in his mind.

Bringing charcoal to paper, he began to sketch the strange woman he'd seen watching the execution.

The cloak had concealed the woman's build, but the way she stood made him think she wasn't a merchant. And she was certainly no refugee. In the last year, two Sundarin families had settled in Hale's Crossing after making the long journey north from their own lands, running from some civil war they seemed reluctant to talk about. But they'd arrived as thin, worn people, their backs bent by the weight of their packs.

The woman at the execution had been straight-backed, casually strong and full of purpose. A hunter? A warrior of some kind?

Whatever she was, Kole wondered if she'd find much hospitality in Hale's Crossing. Everyone was terrified by what had happened to Mertyn and his family, and many didn't believe the council's claim that a plague rat was responsible for Mertyn's infection. Any stranger to town could be carrying the plague, and no one would know until it was too late.

Gods, he couldn't get the image of Mertyn's family out of his head. He closed his eyes and saw it again—that mass of flesh and limbs and horrified eyes.

And then the faces changed: they became Da and Ma and his sister. Kole imagined himself standing over them. He imagined his own eyes wide and mad, his irises rimmed with red. He heard the musical gibberish spilling from his lips. It wasn't enough to drown out the screams of his family as their bodies knitted together.

"Whatcha drawing?"

Kole jumped. The gurgling of the river had covered the sound of his sister's approach. He glanced down at his sketchbook.

His drawing of the woman at the execution had morphed into something different. A horrible reflection of what he'd seen at Mertyn's house. The sketch of Mertyn's family sprawled across the whole page, limbs reaching in every direction.

He slapped the sketchbook closed as Arabeth dropped into the grass beside him. He clenched his fingers around the book to keep his hand from shaking.

Arabeth brushed back her tangle of black hair. There were leaves caught in it, but she didn't seem to notice. "You're not obsessively drawing pictures of Kateen Miller again, are you?"

"I haven't done that for years," he said. "And it wasn't obsessive."

Arabeth shrugged. She was a waif of a girl, paler even than the Sundarins who'd settled in town. She rubbed her bare feet against the ground, wiggling her toes into the dirt.

"What were you drawing, then?" she asked.

"It's not finished yet."

"You always say that."

He glanced at her, then out at the Drowning Sea. Off to the west he could see the sun slowly sinking below the wild forests that stretched all the way to the Windless Peaks in the north. The last fishing boats had made their way back to shore, leaving the sea to its quiet solitude.

"You're out early," he said. Arabeth normally slept until sundown. Her condition made sunlight too painful to bear, so she spent most of her waking hours roaming the town at night.

She shrugged again. "Heard Darvin and his friends used you for target practice today."

"Joke's on them. They could've made cider out of those apples."

"So say I know where a bucket of rotten fish heads could be found. And say I know that Darvin's going to be away for a while. What would you say to sneaking into his house and stuffing said fish heads into his mattress?"

Despite himself, Kole grinned at the thought. "Tempting."

"Not good enough? All right. Let's do one better. We wait until he goes to use the outhouse tonight, then we dump the whole bucket on him."

"You have an evil mind."

"It's settled, then." She sprang to her feet, weeds still clinging to her dress. "Let's go before they toss out the fish heads."

He hesitated, then shook his head. "Another time."

"There might not be another time. This bucket is ripe. It's overflowing. It's perfect."

"Forget about Darvin. I already have."

She crossed her arms and pouted. "You're no fun."

"Sit down, kid. Enjoy the view for a while."

With a dramatic sigh, she plopped herself down next to him again.

"What was it like?" she asked him after a few seconds.

"What was what like?"

"You know." She stuck her tongue out and dragged her thumb across her throat.

"Oh. I don't...I don't really know." The shame of his failure still gnawed at his gut. He was supposed to give Mertyn a clean death, not prolong his suffering. He sighed. "It was Mertyn lying there. But it wasn't. Not really. Not anymore." He glanced at the sparse woods that surrounded them, though he knew there was no one there. "He tried to do a...a spell or something before he died."

Arabeth's eyes grew wide. "What kind of spell?"

"I think he was trying to escape. His gag came loose for a second." He shook his head. "He gave me this look just before I swung the sword. It was..."

"What?"

"Excited," Kole said. "Like he was the luckiest man in all the Golden Remnant. I don't think I've ever seen anyone that happy before."

"Weird," Arabeth breathed. She was staring far out over the sea, at the orange light glittering on the surface of the water.

Kole suddenly heard Ma's voice in his head, berating him for filling Arabeth's head with nonsense. The girl was prone to flights of fancy as it was. If she started having nightmares, he'd be the one to pay for it.

She should be scared. If Mertyn's family had been more scared, they might still be alive.

He pushed the thought aside. If Kole was infected, he'd know. He wouldn't be like Mertyn. At the first sign of corruption, he'd do something about it. He would...he would...

He didn't know what he'd do. Or rather, he knew what he should do. He was just afraid to do it.

"Hey, kid," he said. "Close your eyes and hold out your hand."

She narrowed her eyes suspiciously at him. "I'm not falling for that. You're going to put a frog in my hand."

"Do I look like I have a frog?"

"Maybe you're hiding it."

"Just close your eyes. It's not a trick, I promise. You can push me in the river if it is."

Arabeth peered at the river, pursed her lips, and nodded sharply. "Deal." She screwed up her eyes and held out a hand.

He dropped the silver coin into her upturned palm. She opened her eyes.

"See?" he said. "Not a frog."

"Maybe you got Mertyn to transform a frog into a coin before you took his head."

"It's just a coin. But look. Silver. Not bad, huh? My first pay as a headsman."

"Show off." She held the coin to catch the last rays of the fading sunlight. "What are you going to buy?"

"Nothing. I'm giving it to you."

The suspicious eyes returned. "Why?"

"Stop looking at me like that. It's not a trap. Just keep it safe for me, all right? The town shorted Da on the fee. You know how tight things are getting. Ma and Da barely have two coppers to rub together these days. That'll keep you...keep us from going hungry a few days, at least."

"Why don't you keep it? Or give it to Da?"

"Da won't take it. And I... Look, just hold onto it for me. All right?"

She eyed him a moment longer, then frowned and made the coin disappear into the folds of her dress. "You know, Darvin has a gold coin. His friends do too."

"What? Who told you that?"

"Kateen Miller."

"You talk to Kateen Miller?"

Arabeth bobbed her head. "She's my friend."

"They don't make friends with us. We're Felmen."

"Well, she's my friend. And she says Darvin has a gold coin."

Kole shook his head. "Darvin's lying to her."

"No! Kateen saw it with her own eyes. Held it, too. It was heavy, so it had to be gold. It was an old coin, she said." Arabeth patted the ruined statue behind them. "Like this lady. Had a picture of a lantern on it."

Kole was skeptical. He'd heard the local story that old lady Ganner had once fished an ancient gold coin out of the Drowning Sea, but that seemed about as likely as all the fisherfolks' talk of trapped whales. The only thing of interest he'd ever seen come out of the sea was a vase of startlingly blue glass that had washed up on the shore years back. It now sat on the shelf behind the bar at the Empty Net, gathering dust.

"Where in the nine hells would Darvin Rike get a gold coin?" Kole said.

"One of the strangers gave it to him."

"You mean the strangers that arrived today?"

Arabeth nodded. "There's a whole bunch of them. Four or five. Got horses and everything."

"I saw. One of them was watching the execution. What are they? Merchants?"

Eyes shining, she shook her head. "They're freebooters."

Of course. Suddenly things started to make sense. The strangers weren't merchants or Hallowed Order knights. They were treasure hunters, tomb robbers, scavengers who made their fortune plundering the ruins of the past. It would explain why the woman he'd seen looked so hard-bitten.

He was still confused, though. "What are they doing here? Are they going to swim to the bottom of the Drowning Sea?"

"Kateen says that Darvin says that the freebooters think there's treasure in the swamp."

"There's nothing in the swamp. If there was, we'd know about it."

"Not if it's hidden. The swamp's big. When was the last time someone went in deep?"

"There's no reason to go deep."

"Well, maybe there is. Kateen says the freebooters hired Darvin and his friends. They're mounting an expedition into the swamp. They need…I don't know…porters and stuff, I suppose."

"And they're paying a gold piece?"

"Two. One now, and one when they get back. And a share of the treasure as well, Kateen says."

Kole shook his head at the madness of it all. There would be no treasure. All the wealth of the old city was deep beneath the Drowning Sea—everyone knew that. Notte's Mire stretched for nearly thirty miles. It held nothing but leeches and leatherbacks and swamp cats. Darvin and his friends would return damp, miserable, and empty-handed—assuming they didn't fall into some sinkhole, never to emerge again.

At least they'd still have their gold coins, he supposed.

A thought occurred to him then. A mad thought. He dismissed it at first, but it circled his head and returned, like a persistent mosquito.

"This expedition," he said slowly, "how long is it supposed to take?"

"A few days, I think," Arabeth said. "A week, maybe. Plenty of time to sneak fish heads into Darvin's mattress."

A week. That would be long enough. Long enough for him to start showing signs if he really was infected.

If Kole joined the expedition, he would be out of town. Away from the townsfolk. Away from Ma and Da and Arabeth.

And if he did begin to…change…the freebooters would see it. They spent their lives raiding the ruins of the old world. Surely they knew about sorcery. They would be vigilant. If he changed, they could put an end to it before he harmed anyone.

Arabeth rapped on the side of his head with her knuckles. "Kole. Kole. Are you listening?"

Kole blinked, bringing the world back into focus. When had it got dark? The sun had set so quickly.

"Yeah," Kole said. "I mean no. I wasn't listening. What did you say?"

"Ma told me she didn't want us out too late tonight. Which means I have to go home so I can sneak out again later. You coming?"

Nodding dumbly, he pushed himself to his feet and retreated back into his thoughts.

They only had a half moon and the fading twilight to illuminate their way back to town, but Kole had walked this same path many times, and Arabeth seemed to have a cat's ability to see in the dark. As they passed beneath an overhanging bank studded with glow worms, Kole warred with himself, selfish fear competing with concern for his family.

He thought of the near-empty purse Da had taken home to Ma, and he thought of gold coins clutched in Darvin Rike's greedy hand. He thought of the mad smile on Mertyn's face just before Kole had swung the sword, and he thought of that deer, half sunk into the mire, starved to death.

By the time their home came into view on the north-eastern outskirts of Hale's Crossing, he'd made his decision.

CHAPTER
3

IN THE LIGHT of the early morning, Kole made his way into the heart of Hale's Crossing.

He kept his head down, watching his feet and avoiding the rotten planks of the boardwalk. Most of the townsfolk who were up and about this early were too distracted by their own business to pay Kole any attention, but he didn't want to push his luck. After the business with Mertyn Walter, they would be even less tolerant of Kole and his family.

Mrs. Tannith, the proprietor of the general store, was out washing grime off the shop's leaded windows. A gang of fisherfolk, their nets slung over their shoulders, were heading down to the shore while loudly discussing their predictions for the day's weather. They cast suspicious glares at the cloudless sky, each trying to outdo each other with their predictions of doom.

Kole hovered beneath the eave of the candlemaker's shop until the fishing gang had passed, then hurried on through town. Turne, the rat-catcher, was already at work, undoubtedly at the behest of the council. He had an empty cage in one hand, and his terrier trotted along beside him, nails clicking against the boardwalk.

A couple of young women were stringing up colored lanterns across the main boardwalk in preparation for Lampnight. Food for the festival was already being stockpiled in the ancient stone guildhall, though rumors abounded that it would be a meager feast this year. He'd heard through Arabeth that a caravan full of supplies from out east had gone missing on the way here. Townmaster Haddin was fending off townsfolk every hour demanding to know when the caravan would arrive.

At last Kole came to the Empty Net. The bulk of the inn's lower story was made of stone brick, while the upper story was wood topped with a steep slated roof. Expansions had been made to the inn since it was built—a separate wing sprawled out to one side, wrapping around the veranda that stretched out to the boardwalk.

A boy—one of the Paleth brothers—was hauling water around the side of the inn toward the stables. Kole caught a glimpse of a spotted mare out back grazing on some hay.

Just as he was about to step up onto the veranda, the inn door creaked open. He froze as the strange woman who'd been watching the execution stepped through the doorway, a large book tucked under one arm and a hunk of bread in the other hand.

Up close, she was taller than he'd thought. She wore a clean green tunic, though her riding boots were still dirty with dried mud. Her hair was braided along the top, though the sides of her head had been cropped close enough that Kole could see her scalp. There was something there, beneath the dark fuzz: a series of runic symbols tattooed in blue ink. He'd never seen their like before.

The woman paused in the doorway, casting an eye over him. She had a hard face, lined by wear, not laughter.

For a moment, Kole thought she might recognize him, like he recognized her. But he'd been dressed in his protective gear during the execution. Even when he'd lifted his hood she would've been too far away to make out the details of his face. To her, he was just some village boy. Maybe she even thought he was working here, like the Paleth brother hauling water to the stables.

A second passed, then the woman stepped out of the doorway and made her way to one of the two tables set out on the veranda. She opened her heavy book on the table, settled into a creaking chair, and tore a bite out of her bread.

Kole took a deep breath. *Do it, or go home.*

He couldn't afford to dither. Da needed him to head to one of the nearby villages today. A farmer's sow out in Fairhill had produced a litter of stillborn piglets, and someone had to dispose of them. One stillborn piglet the farmer might've dealt with himself, but a whole litter meant they could be tainted somehow. Kole would be leaving within the hour—by the time he got back, the freebooters might already be gone.

Gathering his nerve, Kole stepped onto the veranda and approached the woman. She didn't look up from her book.

"Excuse me," he said.

The woman took another bite of her bread, her eyes swiveling to meet his. She stared at him in silence.

Kole swallowed. "I heard you're mounting an expedition into the swamp. And that you're paying for folk to come with you."

He paused expectantly, and she just continued to stare at him.

"I…um…I want to come," he finished lamely.

For several seconds she just chewed her bread. Then, swallowing, she jerked her head toward the inn door. "Talk to Angok. He does the hiring."

"Angok." He nodded and turned toward the door. Pausing, he glanced back. "How will I know…?"

"The Sundarin with the beard."

"Beard. All right. Thank you."

The woman didn't acknowledge him. She was back to reading her book. Kole glanced at the text over her shoulder, but he couldn't read it. It was written in some foreign alphabet. The edges of the pages were decorated with patterns of blue and red. Some of the patterns, he noticed, bore a passing resemblance to the runes tattooed on the woman's scalp.

The woman glanced up at him once more, her brow creasing into a frown. Realizing he was lingering, Kole nodded once more and then pushed open the inn door.

No fire had been lit inside, so the only light came streaming in through the small windows on the eastern side of the building. The stone floor of the taproom was still muddy with the footprints of last night's patrons. The scent of stale ale hung thick in the air, mixed with the faint stink of old smoke.

Most of the tables were empty. Tucked into one corner, taking his breakfast, was a merchant from Baybury, one who made the journey here every few weeks. There were a couple of old locals as well, fisherfolk no longer strong enough to haul nets or row boats. The old men were casting suspicious glances at the tavern's other occupants.

A man sat near the windows, muttering to himself. On the table in front of him were pieces of parchment of all shapes and sizes—one large piece draped over the edges of the table, while others were little more than scraps. All the parchment looked aged, the ink so faded that the man seemed to be having trouble reading it. He shifted the scraps about, peering at them and them putting them aside one by one.

At first Kole thought the man was ancient, older even than the fisher-folk in the corner. But on a second glance he decided the man was no more than fifty. His face was lined and weathered, but not much more than Da's. It was the hair that had confused Kole at first. It was shockingly white and badly tangled. A flat-topped red cap was perched atop the man's head, and a pair of spectacles clung to the tip of the man's crooked nose.

Across the table from the white-haired man was a woman. She sat with her head resting on the table, snoring loudly. One hand was curled protectively around a tankard, while the other clutched the hilt of a curved knife that had its point jammed into the table. A scrap of torn white cloth was caught between the knife and the table.

The sleeping woman's dark hair was divided into dozens of locks, each woven with beads and flashes of silver jewelry. The locks had all been gathered together at the back of her head and tied with a ribbon of red silk. He couldn't see her face, but her hair made Kole guess she was Nizaani—one of the mysterious far travelers that could supposedly sail through the eye of a storm and come out dry on the other side.

The final freebooter was leaning against the bar, talking to Mr. Godett, the innkeeper. The Sundarin freebooter was a bear of a man, towering a head above Mr. Godett. Curls of red hair fell down to his shoulders, and his beard was the bushiest Kole had ever seen. He was dressed in the pale skin of some animal Kole didn't recognize.

"And we'll need fodder for the horse as well," the Sundarin was saying to the innkeeper, a hint of his lilting accent creeping into his voice. "Enough for a week, if you can manage it."

Nodding, Mr. Godett dipped his pen into a bottle of ink and scratched something on the paper in front of him.

Without looking up from his parchment, the white-haired man at the table barked at the Sundarin. "Forget the horse. Can't bring a horse into a swamp."

"We're going to have to if you want to drink anytime in the next week," the Sundarin said. "Didn't you hear what the man said? The water in there isn't potable. Even your filters won't be enough. And we can't carry a week's water on our backs. Not with everything else."

"Make the porters carry it."

"We're bringing a horse," the Sundarin said firmly. "Just one. Mugsy is tough and well-trained. She can make the journey."

"She'll sink, more like," the white-haired man grumbled, but he said nothing more.

Mr. Godett hesitated over his paper, then glanced at the Sundarin. "So was that fodder or no fodder?"

"Fodder," the Sundarin said. "You have oats? She likes oats."

Mr. Godett started to nod, then his gaze slid past the Sundarin and landed on Kole, standing just inside the doorway. His face darkened.

"Oi!" He waved his pen at Kole. "Out of here, you. You ain't allowed in here."

Kole flinched, then lifted his chin. "I'm here to talk to the strangers." He looked at the Sundarin, who had a confused expression on his face. "Are you Angok?"

"I am," the Sundarin said.

"The lady outside said—"

"You got wax in your ears, boy?" Mr Godett barked. "These folks don't want you making them sick. Go on. Get."

The slumped Nizaani woman snorted in her sleep, disturbed by the shouting. She murmured something Kole couldn't make out and then went quiet again.

Angok raised an eyebrow at Kole, then lifted his hand to cut off Mr. Godett. "It's all right, innkeep. I've got a strong constitution. Besides, the lad doesn't look ill to me."

"He's not ill," Mr. Godett whispered loud enough for Kole to hear. "He's...he's a Felmen."

"A what?"

"He's a corpse man. Him and his whole family. Very sorry, sir. I'll get him out of here."

He picked up a broom and started to lift the hinged bar top, but the Sundarin put his hand on it, keeping the innkeeper trapped behind the bar.

"Corpse man, huh?" Angok gave Kole an appraising look. "That was you out there yesterday? Executing the sorcerer?"

Kole shuffled nervously. "That's right."

Angok nodded to himself, though Kole couldn't say what for. A curious smile split the Sundarin's red beard in two. "And what did you want to talk to me about, young Mister...Felmen, was it?"

"I heard you were hiring people to come with you into Notte's Mire."

The white-haired man spoke up again without so much as a glance in Kole's direction. "Got enough hirelings already."

"Now, hold on, Quintus." Angok pushed himself away from the bar with his hip and strolled across the tavern toward Kole. For the first time,

Kole noticed a bone-handled dagger sheathed at the Sundarin's side. It was the length of Kole's forearm.

He forced himself to meet the Sundarin's green eyes as the giant stopped in front of him and folded his arms across his massive chest.

"This isn't going to be some feastday frolic, lad. We don't give out gold for nothing. I'm sure you know better than I what kinds of things are in that swamp. Maybe there's things in there you've never even dreamed of. We're going in deep. Deeper than anyone in this town has gone before. We'll be in there days. Weeks, maybe. And there'll be no rests. No breaks. Everyone who comes with us will be carrying sixty pounds of supplies. All day, every day. And even when we camp, we'll be on alert. Everyone takes watches."

Angok took a step closer, staring down at Kole. "And at the end of all that, there's no guarantee you'll make it back to your nice little village in one piece. Maybe you'll be lucky and just lose a finger to swamprot. Maybe some piece of an old ruin will fall on you and take your arm. You'd better hope you don't lose a leg, because none of us can carry you home."

Kole swallowed and said nothing.

"Now, you look like a strong lad," Angok said. "Been swinging that headsman's sword around, I suppose. And maybe we could do with one more strong lad. But I need you to know what you're asking for. My friends aren't nice people. Quintus, here?" He gestured to the white-haired man. "I don't think he's ever felt affection for anyone a day in his life. If he had to choose between saving you and saving one of his books, well, it wouldn't even be a choice. And you see the snoring Nizaani? I don't even know her real name. We call her Catgut."

"Why?" Kole interrupted.

Angok paused, looking a little thrown off. "You know, I don't remember. All I know about her is she spent half her life climbing the masts of a Nizaan corsair ship, and now she's the best second-story woman I know. Don't ever get too close to her, even when she's asleep. Your innkeep here found that out the hard way."

Kole glanced at the scrap of torn white cloth caught beneath the point of the Nizaani's knife, then looked over at Mr. Godett, who was cleaning a glass and scowling. His sleeve was torn, part of it missing.

"You met Mara outside, didn't you?" Angok continued. "She cares for her gods and no one else. Piety is no virtue, she convinced me of that." The Sundarin stood up straight and pointed his thumb at his own chest. "And me, well, I'm all right. But that doesn't mean I won't leave you in a ditch if it comes down to you or me. If I were you I'd stay here. Lopping off heads is fine work, lad. Don't let these small-minded fools tell you otherwise." He gestured over his shoulder at Mr. Godett, whose scowl deepened.

Angok stared down at him. "I look at you, lad, and I think maybe I see someone who might amount to something. Not like the others we hired. Those gold coins I gave them are going to be the best things that ever happen to any of them. Maybe you'll be different. Maybe you'll find a woman one day. Or a man. Or a fish, maybe. I don't know what you folks are into around here. Maybe you'll have kids of your own. No need to risk all that on some foolhardy swamp run. So how about you head on home. I'm sure you've got plenty of work to be getting on with."

Kole stood his ground.

"Is the innkeep right?" Angok said. "Do you have wax in your ears? Didn't you hear what I said?"

"I heard," Kole said. "And if it's true, you'll need someone reliable. Not like Darvin Rike and his friends. When they run back to town the instant their socks get wet, you'll be glad you still have me."

The hint of a smile tugged at the corner of Angok's lips. "What's your name, lad?"

"Kole. Kole Felmen."

Angok glanced over his shoulder at the white-haired man. "Quintus?"

With a sigh, the man pushed his spectacles up on his nose and peered at Kole. After a moment, he frowned, waved his fingers, and returned his attention to the table.

"Don't say I didn't warn you, Kole Felmen." Angok pulled his bulging coin purse from his belt. Tugging it open, he fished out a large coin and held it up. It glinted impossibly gold in the early morning light streaming through the windows. It was a perfect disk, not a flaw to be seen, with an image of a glowing lantern in the center.

The Sundarin started to lower it into Kole's hand, then withdrew it when Kole reached for it.

"We leave at dawn tomorrow," Angok said. "Which means you need to be here and ready an hour before dawn. Bring your best boots, a cloak, and a single change of clothing. Maybe a good knife if you have one. Nothing else. We'll supply the rest. Make sure you're all settled up with your loved ones before we go. If you die in the swamp, they won't want your restless spirit haunting them."

"Can…can that really happen?"

The Sundarin shrugged. "I'd rather not find out. Now, remember what

I said. An hour before dawn. If you don't show, I'll send Catgut to get our money back. I promise you won't enjoy the experience." He eyed Kole hard, then slowly lowered the strange gold coin into Kole's palm. "One gold coin now, and another when we return, assuming you haven't deserted. As for treasure, if we find any, me and my friends each get a full share. Hirelings get a quarter share each. Understand? How's your arithmetic, lad?"

"Good enough," Kole said. He looked at the coin, weighed it in his hand. Arabeth was right: it was heavy. He considered biting the coin—he'd heard you were supposed to do that with gold. But he didn't know what you were supposed to look for, so he kept his teeth behind his lips. He looked up at Angok. "I want the second coin now as well."

"Not a chance."

"I need to make sure my family is looked after if I die out there."

"Tell you what, lad. If you die bravely, I'll give the second coin to your family."

"And what if you don't come back?"

"I don't intend on dying out there."

"Then you'll have no trouble taking your coin back from my family if I don't hold up my end of the bargain."

Angok stared at him for a moment. Then he threw back his head and let out a booming laugh. The old fisherfolk in the corner of the tavern jumped at the sudden noise. Kole was startled as well. This man was nothing like the Sundarin refugees who'd settled in Hale's Crossing. They were dour, quiet people—he couldn't remember ever hearing one laugh.

"Clanfather's balls, lad," Angok said when his laughter subsided. "I'm glad you're coming along. I'm starting to like you." He pulled out a second gold coin, a twin of the first, and dropped it into Kole's hand. "Don't tell the other hirelings, huh? I don't want a mutiny before we even leave town."

Quintus cleared his throat loudly and shot Angok a pointed look over the rims of his spectacles. Grinning, the Sundarin slapped his heavy hand on Kole's shoulder and steered him toward the door.

"All right, get out of here. We have preparations to make. See you tomorrow, lad. Hope you've got as much nerve when we're three days into the swamp with no sign of home."

He threw open the door and pushed Kole through it. Kole opened his mouth to speak, but before he could get a word out the door was slammed in his face.

Kole looked down again at the two gold coins in his hand. Though there was ancient grime caught in the grooves and indentations, the gold shone blindingly bright in the morning light.

He turned one of the coins over and saw that there was more decoration on the other side. A blank face stared out—some kind of mask, perhaps? Around the mask were five symbols, like the five points of a star. There was writing running around the edge of the coin as well. Most of the alphabet was familiar, but the words seemed like gibberish. He rotated the coin in his hands, trying to read it.

"By the five we prosper," came a voice from beside him.

He looked up to see the strange woman—Mara, he now knew—sitting on the table outside, reading her book. She'd finished off her hunk of bread, and now a couple of sparrows were hopping about the woman's feet, pecking at the crumbs.

"What?" Kole asked.

"That's what it says on the coin. 'By the five we prosper.' It's in Old Graetian, the formal language of the Lamplight Empire." At his look of confusion, she sighed. "The empire that the Golden Remnant used to be a part of. Before the plague. It was said that you could walk from one end of the Empire to the other entirely bathed in lamplight."

"Oh. And the five?"

"The five old gods. See the symbols? The Architect, the Sage, the Cripple, the Gambler, and the Champion. It was through their power that the Empire flourished."

Kole nodded, though he didn't really understand. He knew of a lot of gods. There was Un, the god of the Drowning Sea, and his brother Ur, the god of the Sea of Reavers. Ith, of course, was the patron god of Godsmouth, who looked down from His home on the moon to ensure the Moonlit Tyrant was never overthrown.

As a corpse dragger, Kole knew plenty about the Watcher of Souls and the Worm King, each of whom had their parts to play after a person's death. The Ashashi apparently had their own God Kings they paid tribute to, while he'd heard that each of the Sundarin clans worshiped their own Clanmother and Clanfather. There was even a minor god of Hale's Crossing, Valetar, to whom a sacrifice would be made on Lampnight to keep Him appeased. The gods, everyone knew, were dangerous if not properly bribed or mollified.

It seemed odd to Kole that a whole empire might be watched over by only five gods. Perhaps they were very powerful gods.

"I take it you're coming with us, then?" the woman said.

He nodded. "My name is—"

"Tell me when we get back. I'm tired of learning the names of dead boys."

The inn door opened again and Angok stuck his head out. "Mara, we…" He paused, frowning at Kole. "You still here, lad? Don't the people in this village do any work? Mara, we're discussing final preparations. You can puzzle over your book later."

The Sundarin disappeared back inside the inn, leaving the door open. With a flicker of annoyance, Mara closed her book and stood up.

As she turned and headed for the door, Kole got another look at the tattoo on her scalp. He realized that the symbol that formed the heart of the pattern bore a strong resemblance to one of the symbols representing the old gods on the coin.

"The five gods," Kole said. "Where are they now?"

Mara paused in the doorway. She spoke without looking back at him. "Dead. All dead."

Then she strode through the door and shut it behind her.

CHAPTER
4

IT WAS AFTER DARK by the time Kole got back from Fairhill. Disposing of the litter of stillborn piglets had gone smoothly enough, but it had taken him the better part of two hours to locate the correct farm. Most of the locals he'd asked for directions had been reluctant to talk to him once they realized what he was.

Finally, one old lady with milky white eyes had overheard him trying to get some directions out of a pair of farmhands. She'd pushed her basket full of eggs into his hand, then taken him by the arm and started hobbling slowly down the dirt road. "Help me with those, there's a good boy. The old Gladen farm is on my way. I'll show you."

At first, Kole had been too shocked to say anything. It had been a long time since someone not part of his family had willingly touched him. He realized she must be half-blind—she hadn't seen the corpse-handling gloves and apron slung over his shoulder.

When he tried to tell her, though, she just patted his arm and shushed him. "Don't you worry about me, boy. Look at this old skin of mine. After all I've put it through, it's tough as leather. You couldn't corrupt me if you tried."

So he'd let her lead him slowly along the road, and then down a muddy track, until finally he caught sight of a small farmhouse hidden behind a copse of trees. It wasn't until after she'd wandered off again, basket in hand, that he realized he hadn't asked her name.

While Kole built a pyre for the piglets and cleansed the corner of the field the sow had given birth in, Farmer Gladen had looked on, gossiping the whole time with one of his sons. Mertyn Walter's infection and the fate of his family was apparently the talk of every village within two days of Hale's Crossing, though in the version Farmer Gladen had heard, Mertyn had used his sorcery to curse the land itself before he was caught and executed. That, Gladen suspected, was the reason for the stillbirths.

"It's bad news, all right," Farmer Gladen had said around the stem of his pipe while the pyre burned. "Bad news indeed."

Gladen was still talking about it by the time Kole was done. The old farmer had started wondering aloud if the Hallowed Order knights who were supposedly camped near Baybury could be convinced to come and perform some sort of purification ceremony to cleanse the land of the curse Mertyn had laid upon it.

"Been too long since the Hallowed Order were out this way," Farmer Gladen said while his son nodded in agreement. "Ain't no wonder we're having sorcery trouble."

It was a relief when Kole could finally collect his meager pay and depart for home. He was sick to death of hearing about Mertyn bloody Walter. And as exciting as it would be to see a Hallowed Order knight in the flesh, the heroes of the Outbreak were unlikely to travel all the way out here to deal with a single dead sorcerer.

His family had eaten dinner and settled down for the night by the time Kole finally returned to their small home on the outskirts of Hale's Crossing. Arabeth was already out doing whatever she did all night, and Ma and Da were in bed.

Kole stood outside their room for a minute, watching the light from the candle flickering through the crack beneath the door. He could hear them speaking softly inside, though he couldn't make out the words.

He rested his hand on his coin purse, felt the weight of the two gold coins within. If he told Ma and Da what he'd agreed to, they would be furious. Arabeth was always getting into trouble—Kole was supposed to be the sensible one. The one to be counted on.

He couldn't bear to see the look on Da's face when Kole told him he might be infected. Da would blame himself. He'd say he should've been the one to execute Mertyn. And Ma…Ma wouldn't say anything. And that would be worse, somehow.

The murmuring in Ma and Da's room went quiet. There was the creak of a mattress, and then the candlelight was snuffed out. Kole stood in the dark before his parents' door a few moments longer. Then he turned and made his way to the room he and Arabeth shared.

His sleep was restless and plagued by nightmares. He dreamed of climbing the skeleton of a dead god, trying to reach its grinning skull so he could pry the gold coins out of its eyes. He dreamed of squealing piglets dragging themselves out of the pyre he'd thrown them in, the flesh melting off their bones.

He dreamed that he could see the fabric of the world laid out before him, every weave, every stitch. And he saw that if he reached out, if he had the courage, he could make everything so much better. He could strip Arabeth's affliction away, let her experience the warmth of the sunshine without pain. He could give life to those stillborn piglets. He could sweep the clouds from the eyes of that old lady who'd led him to the Gladen farm, so that she might see clearly as she once had. It would be so easy.

Reality was but a drawing, a sketch. And it could be redrawn however he wanted it.

Kole awoke well before dawn and knew he wouldn't be able to get back to sleep. He rolled over, peering into the gloom at the bed opposite. Arabeth was still out on one of her nightly adventures. The house was quiet.

He pulled himself out of bed and dressed in silence. After lighting a candle, he collected a change of clothes into a bundle and then tore a scrap of paper out of his sketchbook. He wrote a note telling Ma and Da not to worry and tucked it under his blanket where they wouldn't find it until after he was long gone.

Kole hesitated, then tucked his sketchbook and charcoal into the bundle with his clothes. Angok had told him not to bring anything else, but the sketchbook wouldn't weigh him down, and he would kick himself if there really was something to be found in the swamp and he didn't have his sketchbook with him to draw it.

Finally, he took his entire coin purse and tucked it under Arabeth's pillow. As soon as she found the gold coins, she would know what he'd done. With any luck, he'd be too far gone by then for anyone to follow.

He stepped out into the tiny kitchen, breathing in the familiar smell of his home. His hands shook a little as he clutched his bundle under one arm.

It wasn't too late to back out. He could go to the inn, return the coins, apologize for wasting the freebooters' time. He could be back here before dawn. He could be back before anyone even knew he was gone.

The image of Mertyn's mad grin flashed once more before Kole's eyes.

He rubbed his throat and pictured himself lying on the headstone, grinning that same grin at whoever had been sent to take his head. Would it be Da who did it? Could he bring himself to cut off his own son's head?

Kole lit a candle at the small shrine to Valetar they maintained near the hearth—an offering of light so that the minor god would watch over his family while he was gone.

And then Kole stepped out into the predawn twilight and pulled the door closed behind him.

The freebooters were loading up their packhorse by lantern light when Kole returned to the Empty Net. Most of the town was still dark and silent. The only other movement was a cat out prowling for rats and a pair of fisherfolk getting their gear together so they could get the best fishing spot for the day. Stars shone down from a clear and cloudless sky, promising a hot, still day.

The freebooters talked in hushed voices as they packed. A water barrel was already strapped to the back of the dappled packhorse, and Mara and Angok were loading up the saddlebags with supplies that had been piled on the boardwalk in front of the inn. Quintus, the white-haired sage, was sitting on the stairs to the veranda, holding a lantern in one hand while he inspected a map he'd laid over his knee. Mr. Godett stood in the doorway, still in his sleep clothes, yawning and watching.

The Nizaani woman, Catgut, was lacing up a pair of boots that stretched nearly to her knees. Now that she was awake, Kole got a better look at her. Even in the lantern light he could tell she was stunningly beautiful. She was small and slender, not much bigger than Arabeth. There was an athleticism to her, though—her figure-hugging clothes made that clear.

A pair of daggers were sheathed in a strap that ran across her chest. There was another sheath at her side, the hilt of a short sword protruding from it.

As Kole approached he realized the other freebooters were armed as well. Angok had an axe with a wickedly curved blade tucked into one side of his belt, and a sword was sheathed on the other side. He was busy strapping a small round shield to the packhorse's flank. Inside the notched metal rim of the shield was a design, white on blue, of some sort of tusked beast rearing on two legs.

When Mara turned to heave a sack onto the packhorse's back, Kole caught sight of a war hammer hanging from her belt. The head had a curved spike on one side. It looked as well-used as Angok's shield.

The only weapon Quintus bore was a small belt knife, though perhaps he had a crossbow hidden under the flat-topped cap that was perched atop his head.

Catgut was the first to catch sight of Kole as he approached. Dark, almond eyes flashed up to find him in the darkness. She seemed to have no trouble seeing him, even though he carried no light. She didn't move, but there was danger in her stillness. She reminded Kole of a coiled snake. A shiver ran down his spine.

"Which one is this?" Catgut said, her voice silken.

Angok glanced up, peering into the dark. "That you, young corpse dragger? What was your name again?"

"Kole Felmen." He came forward until he was within the pool of lantern light.

"Felmen." Angok nodded. "That's right. Congratulations. You're the first one here. That means you get the lightest pack. Get this on, see how it feels."

Angok picked up one of four overladen backpacks resting against the veranda and tossed it to Kole. It slammed into his chest, knocking the wind out of him as he tried to catch it. He staggered back, caught his heel on a raised plank, and toppled onto the boardwalk.

Catgut let out a soft laugh. Cheeks burning, Kole scrambled to his feet, his tail bone aching.

"Sorry, lad," Angok said, rubbing the back of his neck. "I'll warn you next time."

Kole stuffed his sketchbook and clothing into one of the outer pockets. The pack was made of some sort of waxed canvas and each of the pockets could be cinched tight to keep the water out. He slipped the pack onto his back. Almost immediately the straps began to bite painfully into his shoulders. He had to lean forward to keep from being pulled backward by the weight of the pack. How was he supposed to wear this for a week?

Catgut sprang to her feet and sauntered over to him. "Do not look so worried, little fisherboy. It will get lighter as we drink all our water and eat all our food. One day, perhaps, when the food runs out, you will be wishing it was a little heavier, yes?"

"Leave the poor lad alone, Catgut," Angok said.

"I am only giving him perspective." The Nizaani woman pursed her lips as she examined him, then grabbed hold of a couple of straps and yanked on something. One strap tightened, then the other. "Here, tie this one across your chest. Like this. See?"

As soon as it was done, the pack felt a little better. It was still threatening to make him topple over backward, but the straps no longer cut into him as much, and the weight felt better distributed across his whole torso.

"Thank you," Kole said, testing the weight on his shoulders.

"If you sink into the swamp," Catgut said, "cut this strap and throw us the pack. We cannot afford to lose supplies."

With a smile, she spun around and returned to her step, the light shining from her bejeweled hair.

"Don't listen to her," Angok said to Kole. "She's just joking. I think. It's hard to tell sometimes."

Familiar voices came from somewhere down the boardwalk, loud and raucous in the silence of the town. Kole recognized the voices before their owners appeared out of the darkness.

Darvin Rike and his two friends, Tilda and Wolfun, were laughing and joking together like they were about to embark on a great adventure. Their giddy enthusiasm only faded when Darvin's gaze landed on Kole. The laughter died in his throat, and a moment later his friends went quiet as well.

"What's he doing here?" Darvin said, not taking his eyes off Kole.

"The same thing you are," Angok replied. The Sundarin gestured to the remaining packs. "Get them on. We're about to move out."

Darvin narrowed his beady eyes at Kole. Tilda's pinched features tightened into a look of disgust, while Wolfun, the well-muscled fisherboy on Darvin's right, puffed out a chest as if he expected a fight to break out at any moment.

"He can't come with us," Darvin said. "Don't you know what he is?"

"He's a lad with a strong back," Angok said. "That's all I need from him. From any of you."

"He's tainted."

"Hate to break this to you, lad, but me and my friends here have dealt with more dead things in the last month than young Felmen has in his whole life. If that's a deal breaker for you, we'll have to find some other porters. Of course, if you're out, we'll be needing that gold back. Catgut?"

With a grin, the slender Nizaani woman snatched a dagger from one of the sheaths strapped across her chest. She sauntered forward, casually waving the point at the three young townsfolk. Their eyes went wide.

Darvin jabbed a finger toward Kole. "He can't even kill a sorcerer right. Had to get his da to do it for him. You're making a mistake."

"Aye, maybe," Angok said. "My mistake to make, though. Now, are you coming, or are you giving me my gold back?"

Catgut was now only a few feet away from them. Tilda and Wolfun started to back away, but Darvin stood his ground. Glaring at Kole, he said, "Fine. We're coming." He eyed his friends. "We're all coming."

Angok clapped his hands together. "Well, that's settled. Catgut, down."

The Nizaani twirled her knife in her fingers and slid it smoothly back into its sheath. As she wandered away, Darvin and his friends moved to pick up their packs.

"Better watch your step, corpse dragger," Darvin muttered to Kole as he passed. "Lot of sinkholes in the swamp."

Kole said nothing in response.

The three of them got their packs on and adjusted with some help from Catgut. To Kole's private satisfaction, all of them were visibly uncomfortable with the weight of the packs. Tilda began to complain, but Darvin told her to shut up. The girl gave him a nasty scowl. She was the only ugly daughter out of five beautiful siblings, a fact she seemed perversely proud of.

The freebooters finished loading up the packhorse, who was looking about as uncomfortable as Kole felt. Mara stroked the horse's nose and whispered something in her ear.

"Don't worry about Mugsy," Angok said. "She's well-trained. She'll manage."

Mara nodded. "She has a brave heart."

With a grunt to announce that he was ready, Quintus folded his map and stood up. He cast a critical gaze over the rims of his spectacles at Kole and the other porters, then grunted again.

"Our route is prepared," the sage said, then he frowned at the packhorse. "Let us depart before this nag collapses of exhaustion."

"How long will it take us to find the ruin?" Mara asked.

"Two days. No more."

Catgut raised her eyebrows. "He said that last time," she whispered loudly to her companions.

"If you're referring to our journey to the Altar of the Once-Chosen," Quintus snapped, "that was an aberration. I had to translate the directions from a dialect that was barely known even at the height of—"

"Easy, Quintus," Angok said, getting between the sage and Catgut. "You have our full faith. If you say it'll take two days, then two days it will take. Right, Catgut?"

Catgut shrugged. "Time is but a river; it is not within man's power to grasp."

"Catgut," Angok said warningly.

"Of course, Quintus is so much more than a man." She cocked her head to the side and smiled sweetly at Quintus. "Two days. Lead us, dear sage."

Quintus's frown only deepened, but he said nothing more. With a *hmmmph*, he rolled up his map and slid it into a waxed leather map case.

The other freebooters pulled on their own backpacks, which were notably slimmer and lighter than those Kole and the others were bearing. Each of the freebooters' packs couldn't be holding more than a bedroll, a change of clothes, and maybe a few rations. Only Mara's pack seemed to have any weight to it, and from the bulge in the canvas, it appeared to be due to the book she'd been reading the day before.

"Why are your packs so thin?" demanded Wolfun, Darvin's fisherboy friend.

Angok grinned and patted the head of the axe at his belt. "If something tries to kill us, lad, you'll be glad my friends and I aren't too encumbered to use our weapons effectively. That, and it's our expedition, and we're the ones paying you, so keep your damned mouth shut."

Mara took the horse's reins and Catgut bared her teeth at Kole and the others to get them moving. Accompanied by the clopping of the pack-horse's hooves on the boardwalk, they slowly made their way out of town by the south road.

In the predawn light, Notte's Mire appeared as a black ink splotch against the landscape. The swamp clung to the edge of the Drowning Sea and stretched out to cover the horizon. Angok thrust a lit lantern into Kole's hand, but the flickering orange light inside did little to fight off the darkness.

The smell of fish gave way to the fetid stink washing off the swamp. Aside from the distant croaking of frogs, the only other sounds were the grunts of the porters and the squelch of mud trying to suck at their boots.

They passed the headstone where Mertyn Walter had met his end. Turning in place for a moment, Kole looked back past Mara and the pack-horse. Hale's Crossing was silhouetted behind them, a handful of lights burning in the darkness.

All his life he'd lived in the shadow of the town. It had never meant much to him, honestly. It had never felt like home. The likes of Darvin and his friends had seen to that. Kole and his family had always been outsiders.

Now, though, he wondered if he'd ever see Hale's Crossing again. The thought was like a lead sinker pulling on his heart.

He found himself stumbling to a halt. The column of freebooters trailed slowly past him, until only Mara and the packhorse remained between him and the town. She caught his gaze and shook her head.

"Hold to the past, boy," she said, "but not too tightly. We can only go forward."

Swallowing, Kole nodded. Turning his back on Hale's Crossing, he trudged on into the Mire.

CHAPTER

5

THAT FIRST DAY in the swamp was the most hellish Kole had ever experienced.

An hour after dawn they had passed the border of the swamp and were walking beneath the thin canopy of gnarled bog trees. By mid-morning, the air was so hot and thick he could barely breathe.

His shoulders were in agony well before midday. The pack that had seemed heavy but manageable back in town was now an intolerable burden. The straps chafed and something was scraping against his hip with every step. Worse, the weight threw off his balance as he tried to navigate the thick swamp. Vines and branches seemed to reach out and grab at the pack, frustrating any forward progress.

His boots—a pair of hand-me-downs from Da with soles so thin he could feel every root and thorn underfoot—soon became so wet he doubted they would ever dry. Often he was forced to wade through green, stinking, knee-deep water, with only shifting silt beneath his feet.

Just before noon Tilda slipped and disappeared beneath the water, sinking deep into a soft patch of silt. She would've drowned if Angok hadn't acted quickly, hooking his axe into the top of her pack and dragging her out of the muck. She had emerged screaming and crying, her hair slick with algae. They'd been forced to take a break until she'd calmed down enough to continue.

After that, a steady stream of complaints had flowed from the girl's mouth, echoed frequently by Darvin and Wolfun. The sound was worse than the buzzing insects. Kole almost wished they'd go back to spitting insults at him so at least he could listen to something other than the constant moaning.

Even the freebooters weren't above complaining. For several minutes Kole had thought the swamp was making some strange burbling sound, until he realized he was hearing Quintus's mutterings as the white-haired sage struggled through a seemingly endless patch of barbed swamp grass.

And the mosquitoes. Gods, the mosquitoes. They came in swarms, appearing out of nowhere and descending on the party, attaching themselves to any bare skin they could find. Kole would swat at himself, killing five insects at a time, only to find they'd been replaced an instant later.

The mosquitoes weren't the only creatures hungry for blood. In the afternoon Kole finally emerged from a long stretch spent wading through stagnant water and felt a slight pinch in his calf. Rolling up the wet legs of his trousers, he found a half dozen leeches clinging to him, their bodies fat with his blood. His companions all found themselves equally under attack.

Wolfun had shrieked like a baby when he realized a leech had gotten inside his trousers and attached itself to his thigh. Kole had tried to stifle his laughter, but it wasn't enough to keep Wolfun from shooting him threatening glares as Angok and Mara lit candles and burned the leeches off everyone one by one.

As the afternoon wore on and the heavy air pressed in around him, Kole became suddenly aware how lost he would be if he somehow got separated from the rest of the party. They'd spent so much time wading through swamp water he wouldn't even be able to follow his own tracks back to the others.

He had no choice but to put his faith in Quintus. The sage spent much of the journey carrying a copy of his map pinned to a board, following whatever esoteric directions he could glean from it. Kole couldn't see how the man could be so confident in his own navigation skills—there were no landmarks here, no hills, nothing but the close press of reeds and lilies and brush and trees.

Catgut spent much of the journey ranging ahead of the party, scouting their path. She was sometimes gone for an hour or more at a time, until Angok started hollering for her to come back. And each time she did—wet and muddy and covered in fresh scrapes, but always with a sly grin on her face and a navigable path for them to follow.

Whenever Catgut was off scouting, Angok took the lead, one hand resting on his axe while his eyes scanned the branches above. Kole had been worried about swamp cats, but so far he hadn't seen any—perhaps they'd all been scared off by the noise of the party's approach.

Quintus, Kole, and the other porters trailed along in Angok's footsteps. Darvin and his friends grumbled ceaselessly to each other—sometimes in hushed voices, sometimes loud enough that Angok threatened to tie them to a tree and leave them behind. That would usually shut them up for another five minutes, until one of them slipped over or got attacked by a swarm of flies, then the moaning would begin again.

Mara brought up the rear of the party, leading the packhorse. For almost the entire day, Kole never heard her speak to anyone except the horse. She whispered in the animal's ear often, though, while she helped it clamber up slippery banks and when she brushed the hookseeds out of its coat.

Kole kept his mouth shut even when the others were complaining. The freebooters didn't seem interested in including the Hale's Crossing folk in conversation, and Kole knew better than to talk to Darvin and the others. Whatever he said, he would only be giving them arrows to shoot him with.

He didn't mind, really. He had nothing to say to them anyway. Nothing they would understand.

Finally, when the sun was sinking low and shafts of orange light shone through the leafy canopy, Catgut reappeared once more and announced that she'd found a patch of solid ground suitable for setting up camp.

They traveled for another fifteen minutes until they finally reached the spot Catgut had found. To Kole's eyes, it didn't look much more solid than the rest of the swamp they'd spent the day trudging through, but by then he could've fallen asleep on his feet. Kole and the other porters staggered over to the shelter offered by the tall bog tree that loomed over the clearing and collapsed to the ground without taking off their packs. Darvin immediately started pulling off his soaking wet boots.

"Oi!" Angok gave Darvin a light kick in the thigh. "We don't rest until camp is set up."

"Gods," Darvin groaned. "Give us a minute to catch our breath, will you? We've been carrying these packs all day."

"And you'll be carrying them again tomorrow. And the day after that, probably. But only if we make it through the night. You lot are clearing the campsite. See if you can't find some wood that's dry enough to burn as well. Fire ought to keep away any curious swamp cats." He gave Darvin another kick. "Go on. Get moving."

Groaning, they all stripped off their packs and pulled themselves to their feet. With the weight gone, Kole almost felt like he could float away. He took a long swig from his waterskin and then staggered off after Darvin and the others.

The fire, when Darvin finally got it going, was a sad, sickly thing, not much brighter than what they could get from their lanterns. Darvin had refused to let Kole help build the fire—they wanted a campfire, not a corpse pyre, he said. Still, the sight of the small flame crackling to life brought warmth to Kole's heart.

The mood in camp seemed to improve almost instantly. Kole stripped off his socks and boots, setting them next to the fire to dry. He sat down with his bare feet pointed toward the flames. One by one the other porters did the same.

Catgut took a battered tin pot out of one of the packs, filled it with water from the barrel they'd taken off the packhorse, and set it above the fire. When it started to bubble, Catgut took out a strange packet of dried herbs and sprinkled a few into the boiling water.

"Is that some kind of soup?" Kole asked.

"Don't worry about her," Angok said. "She's just making one of her foul-smelling Nizaani teas."

Catgut grinned at him. "It is the only thing that can overwhelm the stink of the bear fat you grease your beard with, Sundarin."

Angok dug through the supplies. "Well, let's see what Mr. Godett managed to source for our dinner. Oh, good, looks like we have salted herring, salted broadhead, and a little salted crab to round it all out." Angok looked at Kole and the others. "Don't you people eat anything but fish?"

"We're a fishing village," Tilda grumbled.

Angok grunted, apparently unsatisfied, but he began portioning out the food. There was some bread as well, though it had had been badly crushed on the journey. Kole was just glad it wasn't soaking wet. The packs he and the other porters bore were remarkably watertight.

Quintus took his dinner with a frown, then cast a jealous eye at the unloaded packhorse, who was feasting on some oats. "I think I'll swap with the nag. I despise seafood."

"All right, folks," Angok said when everyone was eating. "Listen up. In case you haven't noticed yet, we're in hostile territory now. If you thought today was dangerous, tonight is going to be even worse. Night is when people get complacent. Especially when they're as exhausted as we all are.

So from now on, we're pairing up. Everyone gets a new best friend. I'll look after Quintus. Mara and Catgut, you're now bonded at the hip." He pointed at Kole and then at Darvin. "You two are together. And so are you two." He gestured to Tilda and Wolfun. "Until we get out of this damned swamp, you never let your new partner out of your sight. You'll be on watch together. You'll sleep next to each other. If one of you needs to take a shit, you shit together. Got it?"

Darvin turned his gaze on Kole and his face twisted up in disgust. He opened his mouth to complain, but Angok cut him off.

"No arguments, fisherboy."

"I'm a hunter, not a fisher," Darvin snapped back. "And why don't you get stuck with the corpse dragger?"

"Because I'm paying you to do what I say. We've been over this." Angok strode over and jabbed a finger into Darvin's chest. "And if I catch you shirking your duty, *hunter*, I'll hang you upside down from a branch as bait for the swamp cats."

Darvin shot Kole a sullen scowl. Kole gave him a small grin back. Darvin's face darkened, but he kept his mouth shut. Angok stared hard at them a moment longer, then turned to address the group again.

"All right. Now that that's out of the way, let's put our feet up, huh?" He dropped down next to Quintus, who was sitting on a fallen log, his nose once more in his map. Angok rolled up the legs of his trousers and scratched at the insect bites covering his skin. "Things could be worse. We've still got a little blood left. Everyone's still alive. And look at this place. It's kind of beautiful, isn't it?" He looked up at the canopy and gestured around himself. When no one replied, he elbowed Quintus in the ribs. "Don't you think, Quintus? Beautiful, right?"

"I would rather return to the flooded catacombs of Atun-Ra than spend another day in this fetid pit," the sage replied.

"I agree," Catgut added. "At least the catacombs did not smell this bad."

Angok's hands fell. "You lot are the worst."

The freebooters fell into silence. A choir of frogs croaked somewhere nearby, loud enough to drown out the crackling of the tiny fire Darvin had managed to build.

Kole ate his salted fish and stared into the dancing flames, trying to ignore the ache in his muscles and the itching of mosquito bites. Despite the sticky heat—and despite the dark looks Darvin kept sending in his direction—he felt strangely at peace. The day had been painful and exhausting and miserable, and tomorrow would be more of the same. But now, for a few hours, he could relax, and somehow that made it a little better.

The knots that had been tied in his gut ever since the execution of Mertyn Walter were slowly starting to loosen. His thoughts were clear. He had shown no signs that he'd been infected by Mertyn's sorcery. He'd heard that the mad never knew they were mad, of course, but surely if he'd been acting strangely, someone would have said something.

No, he couldn't be infected. He'd gotten lucky. He'd made a stupid mistake, lifting his hood at the execution—a mistake he would never make again.

In a few more days he'd be back home. Ma and Da would give him hell, but he could deal with that. Gods, maybe he'd even bring home some treasure. They couldn't stay mad at him if he returned with a chest full of gold and jewels.

Of course, he still didn't really believe there was any treasure to find out here. That didn't matter. He couldn't wait to get back home and tell Arabeth all about his adventure. He could always embellish a little if it turned out he'd spent a week trudging through the swamp for nothing. Arabeth was always more interested in a good story than the truth.

The thought of her wide, shining eyes and all the questions she would ask made him smile to himself. Maybe all this would be worth it just for that look on his sister's face.

As he took the last bite of his bread and chased it down with a drink from his waterskin, Kole took a look around the camp, imprinting it in his mind. He looked at Catgut stretched out on the ground, her arms folded behind her head as she stared up at the darkening sky through the thin canopy. He watched while Angok pointed at the map over the shoulder of an annoyed Quintus. There were crumbs stuck in the Sundarin's red beard. He looked at Darvin and his friends murmuring to each other, and at Mara sitting alone with her strange tome open across her knees. A deep frown creased the woman's forehead, as if she were straining to understand something.

Later, when he had some time alone, Kole would sketch this scene. Their first night in the swamp. The first night of his adventure.

He frowned as a thought occurred to him. Perhaps it was something he should have wondered about before, but until now he'd been so worried about being infected that he simply hadn't cared about the answer. Now, though, his curiosity was getting the better of him.

"What are we actually looking for out here?" Kole asked.

He hadn't addressed the question to anyone in particular. Quintus didn't look up from his map, but Angok stopped harassing the sage and glanced over at Kole. After a beat, Kole realized that Darvin and his friends had fallen silent to listen to the answer as well.

"Treasure," Angok said after a moment's hesitation.

"What, just sitting out here in the swamp?" Kole said.

"Are you simple? No, corpse dragger." The Sundarin glanced at Quintus, but the sage was pointedly staying out of the conversation. Angok sighed and looked across the fire to Mara. "You want to take this, Mara? You know more about this ruin than me."

Mara's eyes flicked up from her book and glanced around the campfire, as if she'd only just realized everyone else was there. In the deepening night, her eyes seemed to glow orange in the firelight.

She closed her book with a thud. "We seek the lost idol of Gnothea, the giant statue that formed the body of the greatest temple in the western Lamplight Empire. Centuries ago, before the Outbreak, it used to overlook the city that now lies at the bottom of the Drowning Sea. Pilgrims and holy men from all over the Empire and beyond would travel here to bow down before the majesty of this depiction of the Architect, Lady of Silver and youngest of the five old gods. Accounts from the time claim the statue stood five hundred feet high, and that it took a host of the Empire's greatest silver sorcerers two decades to complete."

Kole frowned. "If it's that high, we'd be able to see it from town."

Mara nodded. "It was long assumed to have been destroyed at the height of the Outbreak, when infected sorcerers ran rampant across the Empire." She glanced at the swamp trees that stretched above them. "This used to be a forest, the great garden of the Architect, tended by sorcerers skilled in coaxing life from the earth. The forest was said to be a wonder every bit the equal of the idol itself. It stretched for miles, but no one could ever lose their way or die within its borders, for every creek bubbled with the purest water and luscious fruit hung from the branches of every tree. But when the plague struck and the sorcerers lost their minds, a warband of deranged Silvers tore at the land itself. The Sea of Reavers burst its banks and flooded this land, until the forest became a swamp and the Drowning Sea swallowed the ancient city that the idol used to watch over. After that, there are no more accounts of the idol of Gnothea. Most believe it was destroyed when the land was riven."

"But you don't?"

Mara's lips tightened. "Quintus doesn't."

Darvin spoke up. "And if it's still around, you think it'll have treasure in it?"

The woman paused for a second, then gave a short nod. "The Architect was the god of civilization, of trade and wealth and prosperity. Pilgrims brought jewelry and artifacts and precious metals in the hopes that She would grant them prosperity in the future. The priests who dwelt there collected it all. If the idol still exists, and if it has not been plundered, there will be treasure there."

Darvin and his friends exchanged excited looks. Kole had to admit that the thought of all that wealth thrilled him a little as well. Still, he couldn't help but look at the twisted boughs around him and think of the forest that Mara said was once here. What would it have been like to live in those times, when sorcery was something to be loved, not feared? Did the people who lived then have any concept of how fortunate they were? Did they have any inkling of the fate that would soon befall them?

"Well, there you go," Angok said. "Let the thought of an armful of gems keep you going tomorrow. Finish up and let's head to bed. We'll be up at dawn, so sleep while you can. We've got four pairs, so we'll have four watches. Quintus and I will take first watch, then Mara and Catgut." He pointed at Wolfun and Tilda. "You're third, and the hunter and the corpse dragger are on last watch. Keep the fire going, and try to make sure we don't all get eaten by leatherbacks, huh?"

Through his thin bedroll, Kole could feel every root and stone. Even so, he was asleep within minutes. Darvin was snoring even before that. The huntsman's son hadn't said a word to Kole as they'd bedded down beside each other, which was about the best Kole could've hoped for.

It felt like he'd only been asleep for a few seconds before he heard someone talking to him. "Corpse dragger! Corpse dragger, get your ass up. Don't make me find a stick to poke you with."

Blearily, Kole opened his eyes. Through the canopy above he could see stars twinkling. A figure stood over him, silhouetted by the dim light given off by the nearly burnt-out fire behind him.

It took Kole a few seconds to realize where he was. It was the croaking of the frogs that reminded him. Groaning, he pulled off his blanket and sat up. Every muscle ached. He felt like he'd fallen off a ship and been dashed against the rocks again and again.

Darvin was standing over him, trying to wake him without touching him. In the dim firelight Kole could make out the shapes of several other people lying on bedrolls not far away.

Kole dragged his hand across his face. "What time is it?"

"Watch time. Come on. Wolfun and Tilda have already gone back to bed, and I don't want that stinking Sundarin to yell at us for shirking our duty."

With another groan, Kole dragged himself out of bed, fed a few more sticks into the fire, and staggered over to the fallen log they'd been using for a seat. Putting his back to the fire, he rubbed his eyes and stared out into the darkness. After a few seconds, Darvin sat down as well, as far away from him as he could manage without actually sitting in the mud.

They sat in silence for an hour. Kole couldn't stop yawning. His eyes were so heavy he could barely keep them open.

Finally, in an attempt to keep himself awake, he tried to strike up a conversation with Darvin.

"What are you going to spend your treasure on?"

Darvin shot him a withering look. "None of your business."

Kole sighed and said nothing. He didn't know what he'd been expecting.

They sat silently a few more seconds. Then Darvin spoke again.

"You may have fooled the Sundarin into being your new best friend," he said, "but I know what you are. You and your whole family."

Kole's jaw tightened. Gods, even all the way out here Darvin wouldn't let him forget who he was. "What in the hells is your problem with me, Darvin? Everyone else in town is happy just keeping their distance, but you…"

"My problem? I'm not the one who gets paid to cut people's heads off."

"We don't do it for fun. No more than you and your da kill deer for fun."

"Don't you dare try to compare my family to yours. My da is a hunter. Yours is a murderer. He murdered my uncle."

Kole was speechless for a moment, trying to figure out what Darvin was talking about. Though he'd only been twelve at the time, he remembered Darvin's uncle, all right. Everyone did.

"Your uncle was the murderer," Kole said. "He robbed and killed a merchant."

"My uncle never killed nobody," Darvin said with a sneer. "The merchant was dead when he found him. My uncle tried to explain that, but the council wouldn't listen, and your da was all too happy to take his head and collect the silver." Darvin spat. "My uncle never even had a chance to clear his name."

Kole opened his mouth, but the words died in his throat. Darvin's uncle had always been a known troublemaker, even more so than the rest of the Rike family. He was a thief and a conman, everyone knew that. No one had been surprised when he'd been caught raiding that wagon, the merchant lying dead in the driver's seat with an arrow in his chest.

Still, Kole could hear the righteous fury in Darvin's voice. As if he really believed what he was saying.

"You're serious?" Kole asked. "You think he was innocent."

"My uncle was no killer. Not that that mattered to your da."

Kole went quiet for a minute. "Even if my da tried to stop the execution, do you think the council would have listened? Do you think anyone in town cares what a Felmen thinks?"

With a grunt, Darvin picked up a stick and hurled it into the darkness. There was a soft *plop* as it hit water, and for a moment the frogs quietened. They started croaking again a moment later.

Kole and Darvin remained silent for several more minutes. Then, as the sky slowly began to lighten, Darvin said, "Baybury."

"What?"

"When I get my treasure, I'm going to Baybury. I have cousins there. I'm going to buy a house. And hire servants. And I'm never going to go hunting ever again." He picked up another stick and stabbed it into the soft dirt. "I hate hunting."

Kole was shocked to realize he was feeling...sympathy? Nine hells, he couldn't believe he'd ever feel sympathy for Darvin bloody Rike.

As dawn approached, the shapes of trees and shrubs slowly began to appear out of the darkness. The fire was all but burned out now, the last of the firewood gone. Kole could hear the others in the camp snoring and shuffling beneath their blankets. He wasn't looking forward to waking everyone when dawn came. They'd almost certainly be as grumpy as he felt.

With a groan, Kole stood up and stretched his arms above his head. Gods, he was stiff. He wasn't sure he could even get his pack on, let alone carry it.

As he turned in place, he caught sight of a slumped shadow about twenty feet outside camp, down near the swamp water. At first glance he took it for a shrub, but then he paused and took another look.

"Hey," he whispered to Darvin. "You see that?"

"See what?" Darvin frowned. "Wait, is that...?"

Licking his lips, Kole slowly made his way around the edge of the camp. Darvin followed a few steps behind. The shape lay motionless in the mud. As they got closer, Kole saw something sticking out from the shadow, trailing in the stagnant water.

A foot.

Mud squelched behind Kole as Darvin came to a halt. "No," the boy breathed.

Swallowing, Kole staggered forward and crouched down. His hand trembled a little as he reached out.

"No," Darvin said again. "Don't touch her. Don't...don't..."

Kole laid his hand on a cold, stiff shoulder and rolled the body over. Tilda's bulging, bloodshot eyes stared sightlessly up at the predawn sky.

"Wake everyone up." Kole's voice sounded like it was coming from far away. "She's dead."

CHAPTER

6

ANGOK WAS FURIOUS.

"You stupid, bumbling, fish-brained idiots." The Sundarin loomed over them, his beard quivering with rage. "What did I say? What was the one thing I told you to remember at all costs?"

No answer was forthcoming. Most of Angok's fury was directed at Wolfun, though his piercing green eyes sent plenty of glares toward both Kole and Darvin as well. Behind him, the other three freebooters were breaking down camp and loading the packhorse in silence.

Angok shook his head in disbelief. "By the Clanmother's grace. I told you to stick together. No matter what! Where in the hells were you?" he roared at Wolfun.

The broad-shouldered fisherboy stared at the Sundarin's boots. "She said she'd just be a second," he mumbled.

"What?"

The boy swallowed and spoke again, louder. "She said she'd just be a second. It was the end of our watch. I went to wake Darvin, and she said she'd just be a second."

"Then why didn't you go look for her when she didn't come back? Clanfather's balls, she was within spitting distance of your bedroll."

The boy mumbled something else, too quiet for even Kole to hear. Angok jabbed him in the shoulder. "Speak up, fisherboy."

"I fell asleep!" Wolfun snapped back, his face screwed up. "All right? I was tired. If you hadn't pushed us so hard yesterday—"

"I told you to stay alert! I warned you something like this would happen if you let your exhaustion get the better of you. But did you listen? No. You fell asleep. Your friend went off to take a piss by herself. And while you were snuggled up safe and sound, a mire serpent came out of the water and stuck its fangs in her. Now look at her. Look at her!"

The boy twisted away, refusing to look at the body of the girl laid out before them. But Kole looked. In the light of the morning she looked even worse than she had in the predawn darkness.

The fang marks were clearly visible on her bare left foot. The skin there had gone a nasty shade of purple, and a web of veins bulged black around the puncture marks.

The girl's face and neck were so badly swollen she was almost unrecognizable. Bloody foam still clung to the corners of her mouth. Kole had heard that the venom of a mire serpent was so fast-acting that the victim often didn't have time to shout before their throat swelled up. She would have been dead within minutes of being bitten, suffocating just a few feet from the rest of the camp.

Darvin spoke up. "We should go back to town. Her body... We have to take her back."

"Back?" Angok shook his head. "We don't go back until we find the idol. I told you that before we left. I told you this was dangerous. I told you that you could die out here. I... Corpse dragger, what in the hells are you doing?"

Kole had rolled Tilda's body gently onto her side so that he could position her blanket beneath her. He lowered her into the center of it and began to carefully wrap her body, using the blanket as a shroud.

"We can't burn her body here," Kole said. "We won't be able to find enough dry firewood."

"Who said anything about burning? We leave her."

Leave her? Kole glared up at the Sundarin. "She'll be torn apart by swamp cats and leatherbacks if we don't wrap and bury her. That's if the insects don't make a home of her first."

"She's dead. She won't care. We're not wasting time on this."

Darvin stepped forward, his hands clenched into fists. But another voice rang out first.

"Angok," Mara said sharply. "Let the boy bury her."

The Sundarin whirled toward the woman. He opened his mouth to argue, but she just stared at him with cold, hard eyes.

Exhaling sharply, he threw up his hands and turned back toward Kole and the others. "Fine. Fine. We leave in half an hour, whether or not she's in the ground." He jerked a finger toward the girl's pack. "Dump anything we don't need out of her pack. You three are carrying the rest. The horse shouldn't have to suffer for your stupidity. She's got enough to carry as it is."

The only tools they had to dig the grave were a pick-axe and a small shovel that was little more than a trowel. And their hands, of course.

The mud was frustratingly difficult to dig in—it seemed to resist any attempts to make a hole. Kole and the other two boys knelt in the mud, pawing at the ground as best they could.

Catgut disappeared to scout their route even before the freebooters had finished breaking camp. Angok stood around sullenly, tightening straps on the packhorse. Quintus ate his breakfast in silence, seemingly unconcerned by everything that had happened.

Kole had ritually wrapped the dead girl's body head to toe, tying the blanket in place with a rope from one of the packs. Angok had complained loudly about sacrificing the rope, but Mara shot him another glare and he'd gone silent once more.

Now Mara was standing over the girl's body, head bowed and hands folded in front of her. Every now and then Kole thought he saw the woman's lips moving as if in prayer, but he couldn't hear her speaking.

Finally, when Angok's half hour was nearly up, the three boys looked at each other and silently decided the hole was finished. In truth, it wasn't really a hole at all—just a gash in the mud a foot deep.

Kole knew it wouldn't be enough to keep out predators. The swamp cats would have the girl dug up before nightfall. But this was as much a symbolic gesture as it was practical. The girl deserved respect in death. She needed to be given at least the basic funerary rites before her soul moved to the Beyond.

Putting down the shovel, Kole moved to the head-end of the girl's wrapped body. He laid his hands on her shoulders. She'd already gone stiff. Even through the blanket, she seemed colder than the air around her.

Kole looked at Darvin. "Help me with her legs."

The huntsman's son flinched. He glanced over at Mara, but the woman simply stared back at him, expressionless.

Swallowing, Darvin's shoulders slumped. He nodded once, then slowly made his way to the girl's feet.

He gingerly touched her blanket-wrapped ankles, then jerked his hand back as if she was burning hot.

"She's covered," Kole said. "You won't be tainted."

Darvin swallowed again, then took hold of her ankles. Kole met the other boy's eyes, and together they lifted her into the hole they'd dug.

As soon as she was in the hole, Darvin snatched his hands back and wiped his palms on his tunic. He stopped when he saw the look Mara was giving him.

Kole spoke a few words, beseeching the Watcher of Souls to protect the girl's soul on its journey to the Beyond as Darvin and Wolfun each dropped a copper coin into the grave. The Watcher of Souls was usually depicted as a magpie, or a flock of magpies. Like most gods, She needed to be bribed and appeased if She was to do Her duty.

With the girl's soul departed, her body became the domain of the Worm King, who claimed all dead things, both human and animal. Kole offered no prayers for Him. He wouldn't hear them, deaf and blind as He was.

They had enough time to shovel a thin layer of mud over the top of the girl before Angok told them it was time to head out. The Sundarin had calmed down by then, his voice sombre rather than angry. As the porters were pulling on their packs—now heavier than ever—Angok laid a hand on Darvin's shoulder and pressed something into the boy's hand. Kole caught a glimpse of gold as the Sundarin released Darvin.

"Make sure the girl's family gets that," Angok said. "And you three stick together now, all right? I don't want to be burying another one of you."

Darvin nodded. One by one, the party passed by the girl's grave, then headed out into the swamp once more.

The second day was worse than the first. The clouds of insects were thicker and more persistent. Carpets of tangleweed covered the surface of the mire, fighting them as they forced their way onward. Just before midday they had to backtrack for an hour and find an alternate route when Catgut reported a nest of more than thirty leatherbacks in their path, all looking very hungry.

But though the going was tough, the complaining dwindled to almost nothing. Even Quintus's grumbling had quieted, though Kole suspected that had less to do with Tilda's death and more to do with his interest in his maps.

When they found a spot to take their noonday break, Kole approached Mara, who was applying some sort of cream to a series of insect bites along the horse's flank. The woman gave no sign that she'd heard the squelching of Kole's approaching boots.

He held out a small cloth-wrapped package. "Oatcake?"

Mara didn't glance back. "For me or the horse?"

"Whoever wants it more."

She turned and took the package from Kole. She unwrapped it, glanced at the horse, then took a bite of the oatcake herself.

"Quintus is right," she said around a hunk of the sticky oatcake. "Mugsy already eats better than us."

Kole reached out slowly and gave the horse a gentle pat on the nose. It stared at him impassively.

"You were saying something this morning, while we were preparing the grave," Kole said. "A prayer or something."

Mara hesitated. "Not a prayer. Just a hope."

"What kind of hope?"

"In the Elder Days, long before the rise of the Lamplight Empire, certain philosophers envisioned death as the space between two moments. Like the silence between one drum beat and the next. Or a breath fully exhaled, before the next is drawn. I hoped…I hoped that was so for your friend. I hoped the gods would make it so, if they still could."

Kole didn't really understand what she was saying, but he nodded anyway. "The old gods, you mean?"

"Yes."

"Did they answer?"

Surprisingly, Mara smiled at that—a small, sad smile. It was the first time he'd seen her smile, he realized. It made her seem younger than she'd appeared at first.

For some reason he thought of that broken statue near the river outside Hale's Crossing, half consumed by strangling vines, half worn smooth by the river's flow.

"No," she said. "I told you, the old gods are dead."

"Then why talk to them? Why hope that they can help?"

"Perhaps they too are caught between one moment and the next. Perhaps they wait to inhale once again."

Her eyes took on a faraway look. With one hand she brushed her hair back, her fingers absentmindedly trailing along the pattern tattooed on her scalp.

Kole glanced down at the pack sitting near Mara's feet. The side of it bulged with the heavy book it contained.

"Your book," he said. "What does it say?"

Before she could answer, Angok's voice rang out. "Pack it up, folks. Lunch is over. We don't stop again until we make camp."

"Thanks for the oatcake," Mara said, slinging her pack over her shoulder and taking the horse by the reins. The horse snorted and gave Kole a weary stare as it trudged past.

Groaning, Kole pulled on his own pack once again and followed after.

"All right, folks," Angok said after they'd made camp that evening. "I know it's been a rough journey so far. I have a little good news for us, though. Quintus thinks we're within a couple of miles of the idol of Gnothea. If it still stands—and if we don't get turned around—we should arrive before noon tomorrow."

He swung his pack off his back and opened a pocket on the side. "Now, I was going to save this until after the delve. But I think we could all use a little pick-me-up." He pulled out a strangely shaped bottle of white glass. It was formed into a ring, with a long neck stretching out the top. Angok shook the bottle. Liquid sloshed inside. "What do you say we crack this open?"

"What is it?" Darvin asked warily.

"Nizaani sugarale. Favored drink of corsairs and pirate-hunters from the Shimmering Isles to the sugar fields of Nizaan. So I'm told, anyway. I don't sail well."

Angok sank his teeth into the cork, pulled it free, and spat it into the swamp. He took a swig and smacked his lips.

"There. Much better." He started to hand it to Darvin, then pulled it back. "Just a sip, mind. If anyone gets drunk I'll stick their head in swamp water until they sober up."

He handed the bottle to Darvin, who sniffed it suspiciously. Tentatively, the huntsman's son took a sip.

"Not bad, right, lad?" Angok said.

"Sweet," Darvin said, blinking a few times. "Very sweet."

"Exactly. Well, don't hog it all yourself. Pass it on, lad."

When the bottle made its way around the party and arrived at Kole, he started to pour a little into a tin cup.

"Clanfather's balls, lad," Angok said. "Just drink from the bottle."

Kole hesitated, glancing at Darvin and his fisherboy friend. Wolfun frowned, but after a moment's hesitation, Darvin just gave a little shrug and looked away.

Kole brought the bottle to his lips. Darvin hadn't been kidding. The sugarale was so sweet it was almost sour. It didn't really taste like anything, but it had a burning heat to it, stronger than any ale or beer he'd had in town.

He passed it on to Catgut, who winked at him and gulped down almost all the remaining sugarale in the space of a second. She handed the near-empty bottle back to Angok. The Sundarin shook the bottle and frowned at how little was left. He finished it off and then addressed the party again.

"You fisherfolk types might not know this," he said, "but in Sundar, my people have a grand tradition of epic romance poetry. To raise our spirits, I'd like to weave you all a tale of the lost lovers Ilik and Injuk, who were swallowed by the great whale Siar-mika only to—"

"Please, no," Catgut groaned loudly, throwing back her head to beseech the sky.

"Champion, lend me strength," Mara muttered.

"Again with the whale story," Quintus said. "Was that the only poem you learned before you migrated north in search of warmer climes?"

Angok scowled. "Well, the fisherfolk haven't heard it."

"Lucky devils," Catgut said.

"Fine," Angok snapped. "What do you all propose we do, then? Sit around moping?"

For a few seconds, no one said anything. Then Darvin spoke up.

"You could show us how to use that sword."

Wolfun perked up at that, and even Kole found himself sitting forward a little more. The Sundarin rested the heel of his hand on the sword's pommel and frowned, considering.

"I don't know," Angok said. "I'm not sure any of you even know which end to hold."

Maybe it was the sugarale, but Kole found himself speaking up. "I do. I know how to wield a sword."

Angok scoffed. "You mean that sharpened iron bar you village headsmen swing about? That's not a sword. Well, it's a sword in the same way that both you and Mugsy are pack animals, I suppose."

"Show us your sword, then," Wolfun said.

"Lad." Angok shook his head and patted the hilt. "I don't draw this sword unless I intend to use it."

"Except," Catgut chipped in, "when he thinks he can impress a fair maiden with it."

"That still counts as using it." The Sundarin cocked his head to the side, then shrugged. "Very well. You've twisted my arm."

He wrapped his fingers around the hilt and drew it in one smooth motion. It made no more than a whisper as the sharpened steel cleared the simple leather sheath. Firelight caught the edge of the blade, causing it to burn with an orange glow.

Angok was right; it was nothing like the headsman's sword Kole had spent so many hours practicing with. It was thinner—no more than three fingers wide—and shorter as well. The short hilt was clearly meant to be gripped by only a single hand, and it ended in a pommel that looked much more scuffed and worn than the blade.

The Sundarin held the sword with casual ease, swiping it through the air. It looked almost weightless.

"I prefer an axe, honestly," Angok said, touching the head of the axe tucked into his belt. "But for some things you just can't beat a sword." He held up the sword, examining it. "Forged in the Drakeshead Ward of Godsmouth. Nothing fancy, but it's solid. Reliable."

"Have you ever killed anyone with it?" Wolfun asked, excitement creeping into his voice.

Scowling, Angok lowered the sword. "What kind of fish-brained question is that?"

"I was only asking," the fisherboy muttered.

Angok glared at him for a few seconds longer, then returned his gaze to the sword. "I killed a boy with it, once. No older than you. Skinnier, though, so skinny I could see his bones poking against his skin. Can't have eaten in weeks. I was out on the road, eating an apple, and he just comes bursting out of the woods, knife in hand, crazed hunger in his eyes." He sighed and lowered the sword. "I would've given him the apple."

He fell quiet, and no one else spoke. The fire cracked and popped as insects danced in its light.

The Sundarin suddenly shook his head and thrust the sword back into its sheath. "Anyway, it's not for killing men. Not unless I don't have a choice. But there are other things that sometimes need killing. Things that lurk in the lost places of the world."

"Like what?" Kole asked.

"Like ratmen, for starters."

Darvin laughed, and Angok frowned at him.

"Something funny, lad?"

"Come on," Darvin said. "Ratmen? Next you'll be telling us you're scared of the merfolk that live at the bottom of the Drowning Sea."

"Ratmen aren't some fishwives' tale, lad. You never hear of the Ratwood, out by the Tattered Coast? They don't call it that because it's full of cuddly bunnies."

Darvin looked at Catgut. "He's just trying to scare us, right?"

The Nizaani shrugged.

"If you don't believe me, lad," Angok said, "then that's just fine. I suppose you won't want me showing you a thing or two about swordsmanship, in that case." He started to turn away.

"Wait!" Darvin jumped up, nearly knocking Wolfun's dinner of salted fish out of his hand. "Teach us."

The Sundarin glanced at him and raised an eyebrow.

Darvin paused. "Please."

Angok clapped his hands together. "That's more like it. All right. What about you, corpse dragger? You want to learn how to use a real sword?"

Kole hesitated for a second. He knew instantly that Da wouldn't approve. He was a headsman, not a warrior. The role of a headsman was to end a man's life in the cleanest, most merciful way possible. It was a service he carried out for the benefit of the whole community—whether or not the community respected that. He did not kill for the sake of killing. He did not kill out of greed or anger.

So Da always told him, anyway.

But Kole had seen the way Angok's sword had cut through the air. He'd seen the way the Sundarin handled it. There was an allure there that he couldn't deny. Like everyone else in Hale's Crossing, he'd grown up on old tales from the Elder Days, tales of heroic swordsmen and -women striking out across the land, cutting down demons and bringing justice wherever they walked.

They were just stories, he knew. If people like that had once existed, they didn't anymore. But look where he was now. Deep in Notte's Mire, adventuring with a band of freebooters. There was danger out here—not ratmen, perhaps, but other perils. Tilda's death this morning had proved that.

Kole put down his dinner and stood up. Angok gave him a wink and a grin.

"All right," Angok said, sheathing his weapon. "These are your swords."

He picked up a trio of thin, crooked branches from the pile of firewood and tossed one each to Kole, Darvin, and Wolfun. The Sundarin picked up a fourth for himself and gripped it in both hands.

"Let's begin."

CHAPTER
7

KOLE REGRETTED HIS DECISION to join the sword training as soon as he started pulling on his pack the next morning. Not only were his muscles still aching from two days of trudging through the swamp, now he was covered head-to-toe in welts as well.

Angok's teaching style differed substantially from Da's. It consisted mostly of hitting his students with a stick while barking instructions at them. "Keep those elbows bent! Eyes up! Move those feet! Keep your guard up! Clanfather's balls, look at me, not at my blade!"

And it had only got worse after Catgut decided they were putting on such a pitiful showing that she should join in as well.

At least Kole was able to derive some small satisfaction from the groans and winces coming from Darvin and Wolfun as they pulled on their own packs. Kole had performed marginally better than the other two boys—mostly, he assumed, due to his familiarity with the headsman's sword. Darvin was sporting a nasty purple bruise on his left cheek after he'd stumbled on a root while Angok was swinging at him. It had been after that strike that Mara had suggested they all head to bed.

At least the training had distracted Kole for an hour from the memory of Tilda's swollen corpse.

Quintus seemed unusually animated as they set off in the morning light. "Not far now," he kept saying whenever Angok asked him how much longer it would be until they reached the idol of Gnothea. "We're close. Very close."

They'd been walking for a couple of hours when Kole suddenly stopped. From behind him, Darvin cursed. "Don't just stop like that. I'm right behind you."

Kole turned in place. "Do you hear that?"

"Hear what?"

"It's quiet."

Darvin frowned, then cocked his head to the side. The squelching of the rest of the party's footsteps quietened as Angok paused to look back at them.

It had taken Kole a while to notice, but now that he had it was obvious. For two days they'd been surrounded by the croaking of frogs and the buzzing of flies, the chirping of crickets and the calls of the birds filling the trees above. Now there was…nothing. Nothing but the sounds of the party—the wet sounds of mud and the heavy breathing of men and women struggling through the unforgiving mire.

"Like I said," Quintus muttered as he eyed the position of the sun and then scribbled something onto his map with a stick of charcoal, "we are close."

Angok eyed the surrounding swamp suspiciously, one hand resting on the head of his axe. "All right, folks. Let's keep it moving. Eyes open, huh?"

Kole began to follow once again. He put his boot down in a muddy puddle that was too wide to step over.

The puddle had no bottom.

He lurched forward, his stomach leaping into his throat. He grabbed for a thin tree branch. As soon as his fingers wrapped around it, the rotten branch snapped. The weight of his pack threw him forward and he toppled toward the black sinkhole below.

Someone grabbed his wrist just before his head went into the algae-slicked water. His fall was halted with a jerk that threatened to tear his arm from his shoulder. The hand gripping his wrist tugged, pulling him back so both of them went splashing into shallower waters.

The hand released him. Kole wiped the muck from his face. He found himself staring at Darvin. The boy was sitting in the fetid swamp water beside him. Darvin stared back at Kole, then glanced down at his hand. The hand that had touched Kole's bare wrist.

With a scowl, Darvin pulled himself out of the water. "Watch where you're putting your feet, Felmen," he snapped. "I don't want to have to carry your pack, too."

He tried to wipe the mud from his tunic, only to smear it further. With a grunt, he turned away.

"Darvin," Kole said.

The boy stopped. "What?"

"Thanks."

Darvin stared at him as if he was going to say something else. Then, with another grunt, he stomped away after the others. Kole picked himself out of the mud and followed.

They walked for another two hours through the eerily silent swamp. As the morning wore on, Quintus began to consult some device he kept in a small wooden box. At first Kole thought it was a compass, but when his curiosity got the better of him and he tried to catch a glimpse of it, all he could see was a small glass ball inside the velvet-lined box. For a second, Kole thought he could make out some sort of pale liquid—or maybe smoke—swirling inside the ball. But Quintus snapped the box closed as soon as he noticed Kole looking.

The sage glared at him over the rims of his spectacles. "How am I supposed to find anything with you looming over me and blocking all my light?"

Kole mumbled an apology and backed off. Quintus continued to glare at him until he was at the back of the column with the packhorse. Only then did the sage turn away and open his box once more.

"Is he always like that?" Kole asked Mara.

"Only when he is in the field," she replied. "When he is cloistered in his study, he is much grumpier."

Reeds rustled nearby, loud in the silence of the swamp. Mara moved a hand to the handle of her war hammer.

The reeds parted. It was only Catgut returning from another scouting excursion. The party came to a halt.

The Nizaani had an odd look in her eyes. Mara seemed to see it too. "What is it?"

"I have found…something," Catgut said.

"Something?" Quintus hurried over, heedless of the mud splashing onto his cloak. "You've found the idol?"

Catgut shook her head. "No. But there is something. A marker, perhaps."

"A marker? What kind of marker? No, wait, don't bother answering. Your wild guesses will only corrupt my own investigations. Lead us there."

The Nizaani cocked her head to the side, causing jewels to dance in her hair. "I did not hear a please, Master Sage."

Quintus's eyes narrowed and his face took on a look like he'd just swallowed a fish bone. He glanced at Angok, who shrugged.

"Wouldn't kill you," the Sundarin said.

Quintus's scowl deepened. "Please," he spat.

With a grin, Catgut spun around and beckoned to the party. "Since you asked so nicely."

Two pillars stood alone together in the swamp. Each was about seven feet across and stretched at least ten feet into the air, one reaching a little higher than the other.

The swamp had not been kind to the pillars. One was bent at an angle, and both were nearly drowning in strangling vines and thornweeds. Still, in the gaps between the foliage, Kole could see unnaturally white stone shot through with veins of gold and blue.

There were no seams that Kole could see, no joins where one stone had been set atop another. The stone was smooth and untouched by tools. Both pillars had rounded tops that brushed the branches of overhanging swamp trees.

As soon as he laid eyes on the pillars, Quintus started hurrying toward them. Catgut threw out an arm to stop him, then pointed to the top of the shorter pillar.

"What do you see, Master Sage?"

"I can't see anything from all the way over here," Quintus snapped. "Let me take a closer look."

Catgut shrugged and released him. "As you wish. When they spit out your bones, I would like to use them for an art piece I have planned. With your permission, of course."

"My bones?" Quintus said as he strode forward, clearly paying more attention to the pillars than Catgut. "What are you yammering about?"

"The nest of hanging snakes wrapped around the head of that pillar, of course. I am sure a man of your keen intelligence and perception spotted them there among the vines."

Quintus froze, lifting his head toward the top of the pillar. Now that Catgut had pointed them out, Kole could see them as well: great, thick coils laid one atop another, the same color and shape as the thick vines that surrounded them. Each was as thick as Kole's forearm. It was impossible to tell where snake one ended and the next began. Straining his eyes, he could see the shine of black reptilian eyes staring back at him, and the flickering of forked tongues tasting the air.

The snakes were otherwise motionless, clinging to the pillar and awaiting the approach of prey. Quintus staggered back toward the rest of the party.

"Are you having second thoughts, Master Sage?" Catgut asked.

"I am just considering the implications."

"What implications?" Angok asked. "They're snakes. It all seems pretty simple to me."

Quintus shot Angok a withering glare. "The only simple thing here is you. Think, for once in your life."

Kole stared at the fat-bodied snakes, an unbidden question forming on his lips. "What do they eat?"

Without glancing back, Quintus pointed at Kole. "You see, Angok? Even the village children have grasped the pertinent question. In the last three hours, how many creatures have you seen? How many wrens? How many horned turtles? We have heard neither mating call nor cry of alarm. Even the cursed crickets are quiet here. I saw a single swamp rodent an hour ago. That is it. Something is keeping the animals away. But if there is no prey..."

"What do the snakes eat?" Angok finished.

Quintus raised his arms. "At last the man begins to understand. Truly it is a momentous day."

"All right, Quintus," Angok said warningly. "We're all very impressed by your mental acumen, but if you're not careful me and Catgut are going to share our own gifts with you."

"I will enjoy him trying to heckle us without a tongue," Catgut said with a smile. She had wandered over to the packhorse and was pulling a bow case and a quiver of arrows from among the supplies.

"What are you doing?" Quintus asked.

"I shall kill the snakes and allow you to approach the pillars safely. You are most welcome."

"Can't you people go an hour without trying to kill something?"

As the freebooters bickered among themselves, Kole splashed through muddy water until he reached a semi-solid patch of ground. He took off his pack and stretched his aching muscles. The heat, at least, wasn't quite so bad today. The blisters on his feet had burst the previous day, and he hoped it wouldn't be long until they formed callouses. One thing was for sure: when he returned home he would never again complain about having to wear the protective gear of a headsman. Compared to the weight of the pack, it would be like a silk robe.

Lowering himself gingerly onto a tree stump, he took a long drink from his waterskin and then opened one of the pockets on his pack. He'd been worrying about the state of his sketchbook ever since he nearly fell into that bottomless sinkhole, but the pack had kept most of the water out. Aside from a little dampness in the corner, the sketchbook was otherwise undamaged.

He brought out his charcoal intending to sketch the twin pillars set in front of him. He didn't know what their significance was, but they were clearly ancient—perhaps even older than the broken statue near the river outside Hale's Crossing.

When he set charcoal to paper, though, it wasn't the scene in front of him that he began to draw. It was the scene from their first night in the swamp, the whole party sitting around the campfire together.

He found himself focusing most on Tilda, who was now lying in a shallow grave several miles to the north. In the sketch, she was off to the side, staring into the fire, a village girl who'd found herself far from home. In truth, Kole didn't know much about her—the only times she'd spoken to him were when she'd been helping Darvin torment him. Kole would be lying if he said he liked her. But she had been on this journey with them, and now she wasn't, and that sense of loss lingered.

A shadow fell across Kole's sketchbook. He looked up to find Darvin standing over him, staring down at the page. Kole felt the sudden urge to slap the sketchbook closed. He instinctively clutched it a little tighter, as if Darvin was going to rip it out of his hands and throw it into the mud.

But Darvin just stood there, studying the picture.

"It's Lampnight tomorrow," Darvin said. "Tilda's going to miss the feast."

Kole said nothing. After a moment, Darvin spoke again.

"Do you remember last Lampnight, when she set a dozen live chickens loose in the guildhall?" He gave a crooked smile. "And one of them flew at Townmaster Haddin, and spooked him so much he fell out of his chair. You remember that?"

Kole shook his head. "I wasn't there."

Understanding dawned on Darvin's face. "Oh. Right." He paused, then looked over at the arguing freebooters. "I'm starting to think there might not be any treasure."

"At least you've got that nice lump on your face to show for it all."

Darvin touched the bruise he'd taken during sword training the previous night. "Just didn't want to show the rest of you up," he said with a grin. "I could've taken the Sundarin if I really wanted to."

"Ask him for a rematch. He's not doing anything now."

"Maybe later." Darvin glanced down at Kole's sketchbook again. "Do you think… Could I have that picture? It's just that it looks exactly like her. Every time I think about her, I see her all swollen up, like she was when we found her. I want to remember what she was like before."

Kole was caught off guard. No one had ever asked him for one of his sketches before—not even Arabeth. And Darvin's tone was so…respectful. Like he was talking to an equal. Some suspicious part of him wondered if this was a trick.

"Uh…sure." Kole carefully tore the page from its binding and handed it to Darvin.

The boy looked down at it for several seconds, then folded it and put it into his pocket. "Thanks."

He hesitated a moment longer, then nodded once more and walked back toward the rest of the group.

Kole stared as Darvin walked away, still confused by the conversation. Shaking his head, he glanced back down at his sketchbook and turned the page.

He found himself staring at the picture he'd drawn the other day—the twisted sketch of Mertyn's family merged together by his terrible sorcery. Kole stared at their screaming mouths and their pleading eyes.

But there was something else in the picture as well. Something he hadn't noticed before. Something in the way the lines of charcoal were scribbled across the page.

The lines wavered about, as if he'd been shaking when he drew them. But now it seemed to him that there was something unnatural about the squirming lines. They weren't random, not entirely.

It was like there was some message hidden there, in the movement of the lines. He peered closer, trying to make sense of it. Because there was sense there—he was sure of that now. He could almost read it. He just had to—

The twang of a bowstring snapped him out of his trance. Across the clearing, an arrow sank into the flesh of a hanging snake. The creature uncoiled from the pillar and splashed into a puddle of shallow water, still writhing. Catgut nocked another arrow.

Kole slammed his sketchbook shut, nearly knocking it into the mud. His heart was slapping against the inside of his chest. His hands shook violently.

He needed to get himself under control. The exhaustion of the last few days was wearing at him. Playing tricks with his mind. What he thought he'd seen…he hadn't. That was all there was to it.

Trembling, he opened his sketchbook once more, turning to the picture he'd drawn of Mertyn's family. With his eyes he traced the lines of the sketch.

There was nothing there. No hidden language. No secrets. Nothing but the horrific sketch.

Exhaling, he closed the sketchbook again. He just needed some sleep. That was all. And maybe something to eat. Come to think of it, his stomach was beginning to gnaw at him. He might as well have lunch while he had the chance. It would be a while until Catgut had cleared the nest of snakes.

He returned his sketchbook to his pack, then got up and splashed back toward the others. Darvin and Wolfun were already raiding the rations while Mara tried to encourage the packhorse to eat a handful of oats from her hand. The horse seemed a little jumpy—its tail swished nervously with every twang of Catgut's bowstring.

Since the sinkhole incident, he'd taken to testing the murky water ahead of him with a branch before he took each step. The water here was getting deeper as he walked—now it was almost past his knees. He was just about to take another route toward the others when his branch hit something solid beneath the thin layer of mud.

He paused, looking over at the pillars again as another large snake splashed into the mud, an arrow through its head. The creature twisted in its death throes, joining its writhing companions. As he studied the shape of the pillars, something shifted in his mind, and he suddenly saw the pillars differently.

Kole glanced down at the water in front of him. He stabbed the branch into the water once more.

It sank through a few inches of mud and then stopped suddenly, hitting something that felt like smooth stone. Slowly, trying not to stir up the murky water too much, he began to scrape away the mud from the swamp floor.

Something glimmered beneath the water. Something gold.

He looked up. "They aren't pillars."

No one paid him any attention. Mara had managed to calm the packhorse enough to get it to take a few bites, but it still stomped its feet nervously. Darvin and his friend were tearing into some salted fish, while Quintus stood nearby, scribbling something down in a small leather-bound journal. While Catgut sent arrow after arrow into the snakes coiled around the top of the pillar, Angok stood nearby, axe in hand, ready to hack the head off any serpent that survived an arrow and tried to slither toward them.

"Hey!" Kole shouted. "They aren't pillars."

This time he got the party's attention. Catgut lowered her bow, and even Quintus looked up from his notes to shoot a glare in his direction.

"They aren't pillars," Kole said again. "They're fingers." He tapped his branch against the smooth plate of gold beneath the water. "And I think I just found the eye."

CHAPTER
8

"IT APPEARS THE BOY is right," Quintus said, staring down into the water. "The idol of Gnothea is beneath our feet."

They were all standing in the knee deep water, gathered around the large plate of gold that appeared to form the iris of the statue's eye. With branches and a small shovel they'd managed to clear away a little more of the mud, revealing more of the same white stone that formed the statue's fingers.

Kole struggled to comprehend the size of the statue that was buried below them. Just the golden iris was several feet across. The head must be colossal—not to mention the rest of it.

"How could something that big just sink into the earth?" Kole wondered aloud.

"More importantly," Angok said, "how are we going to get inside?"

"An excavation," Catgut said. "There is no other way."

Angok blinked at her. "Did you swallow some swamp water? Do you realize how big this idol is?" He lifted the small shovel they'd been using to scrape away the mud. "You want me to dig it out with this?"

"Think bigger, my bear-loving friend." She gestured to Kole and the other porters. "We simply hire the rest of the Hale's Crossing to assist us. Or perhaps we locate some out-of-work miners in need of an opportunity."

"Do you understand logistics, Catgut? I suppose being raised by pirates you don't learn that kind of stuff. Let me break it down for you. We're in a swamp. We're two and a half days from civilization, if you can call Hale's Crossing civilization." He glanced at the porters. "No offense, lads. But think about it, Catgut. We can barely sustain ourselves out here. If we didn't have Quintus's filters we would have run out of water already. We'd need hundreds of people working years to even start to excavate the idol. How are we supposed to feed them? Clanfather's balls, how are we supposed to pay them?"

Darvin thrust a broken branch into the water, tapping it against the golden iris. "Why don't we just dig this up? There's a lot of gold here. Better than going home empty-handed."

"We're not going anywhere," Quintus said. "And we're not digging up the eye. We have to get into the temple."

"I admire your persistence, Quintus," Angok said, "but we're currently thin on solutions. Maybe we ought to return to town until we can come up with a plan. We know where this place is now. We can find it again if we need to. I... Quintus, are you even listening?"

The sage was staring off toward the two great stone fingers reaching into the sky. His gaze snapped back, but his stare settled on Kole, not Angok.

"How could it just sink?" Quintus muttered. "How indeed?" He frowned, then turned his eyes on Mara. "Describe to me again the idol of Gnothea, as depicted in the ancient accounts you found."

The woman frowned back at him. "Describe what, exactly?"

"What did it look like? Describe the statue to me."

"The idol depicted the Architect as a middle-aged woman, dressed in great sweeping robes, with a chain of coins about her neck. She overlooked the city, offering it protection and prosperity."

"And her hands? What of her hands?"

"One is extended toward the city, the other grasps a staff. The staff represents—"

"Yes, yes." Quintus waved away her words. "That doesn't matter. Her other hand, the one that is extended. Like this?" He held out his arm, palm forward, as if warding someone away.

Mara shook her head. She reached out and turned the sage's hand to the side, until it seemed more like he was reaching out to grasp someone's hand.

Quintus looked at his hand, then at the white stone fingers emerging from the swamp. He nodded, then hurried away from the group, splashing through the water toward the stone fingers.

"Quintus," Angok said. "Where are you...? Forget it. Remember, those snakes over there are dead, but they're still venomous!"

Without glancing back, Quintus raised a hand, waving away Angok's concerns. The Sundarin sighed. "If he steps on a dead snake and gets himself bitten, I'm not sucking the poison out."

"I still think we should dig up the eye," Darvin said.

"No one's digging up anything," Angok said firmly. "We're after better treasure than a little gold plating."

"Not to mention," Mara said, "it is blasphemy of the highest order to desecrate the idol of a god."

"Sure." Angok shrugged. "That too, I suppose."

From over near the stone fingers, Quintus gave a shout of excitement. He hurried away from the fingers—not back toward the party, but over to where they'd left their packs. He started rummaging through the supplies.

"If you're looking for antivenom," Angok called, "we don't have any, because you insisted we couldn't afford it."

The sage ignored him. He pulled a small object wrapped in linen from one of the packs and then splashed back toward the fingers.

"What is he up to?" Angok muttered.

Catgut shrugged. "One should not strive to understand the mind of a madman, lest one becomes mad oneself."

Kole watched as Quintus moved to the larger of the two fingers and crouched beside it. With a small dagger, the sage sawed through a couple of thick vines, revealing a section of the white stone surface. Seemingly satisfied, he sheathed his dagger and unwrapped the object he'd taken from the packhorse's saddlebag. It was hard to make out from where Kole was standing, but it looked like a small ball of glass or crystal—not so different from whatever Kole had glimpsed inside that wooden box Quintus had been carrying.

Angok grunted something under his breath when he saw what Quintus was doing. He started striding toward the sage. "Quintus!" he hissed. "Do you really think you should be doing that in front of the—"

Quintus pulled his arm back and smashed the glass ball against the stone finger.

A deep *whump* reverberated through Kole's chest. His ears popped and he felt momentarily dizzy. The packhorse let out a frightened whinny.

As the glass shattered, a thin cloud of something silvery puffed into the air. A symbol—some sort of rune?—suddenly shone silver on the surface of the stone finger. As the sparkling mist dispersed, Quintus pushed his hand against the symbol.

The swamp water all around Kole began to tremble. He felt something vibrating deep beneath the earth.

"Sweet Clanmother's mercy," Angok cursed. "Everyone out of the water, quick!"

Catgut was already moving. Mara shoved Darvin and Wolfun toward solid ground. Kole staggered after them as fast as the muddy water would allow.

As he ran, the water began to pull at him like the current of a fast-flowing river. Against his better judgment he glanced back to see a whirlpool forming where they'd been standing.

The party reached the flat patch of muddy ground where the pack-horse was hitched to a tree. The poor mare was dancing about nervously, pulling at the rope that held her in place. Mara went to the beast, putting a hand against the horse's neck and muttering in her ear.

"Look!" Quintus called over the sound of sucking water. "It rises!"

Panting, Kole looked back and stared, stunned. With a grinding of stone and a quaking of the earth, a great mound of white stone was rising out of the muddy pit.

The idol's head did not emerge directly from the ground, like a horned turtle peeking out of its shell. Rather, it twisted up out of the mud, a sleeping god pulling itself awake. The white, veined stone shifted and contorted like it was liquid, and Kole was suddenly reminded of the warping Mertyn's flesh had exhibited when the infected sorcerer had tried to escape from his bonds.

As the head rose out of the earth, mud and algae and great clumps of waterweed clung to it. But as all that began to fall away, Kole realized something was wrong. This wasn't the statue Mara had described—a benevolent middle-aged woman offering wealth and civilization to the people of that ancient empire. It had been twisted. Defaced.

Mara saw it too and gasped. She curled her fingers so only her thumb and forefinger were extended, then drew a large circle in the air in front of her, as if warding herself against what she was seeing.

The head that was rising out of the swamp was not human. Perhaps it had once been—there was something in the golden eyes that hinted at that. Those eyes were open wide as if in ecstasy.

The lower half of the statue's face was protruding and flattened. Any hint of a nose had been smoothed away, leaving only slits for nostrils. The surface now suggested scales instead of skin.

With a final groan, the great head came to a halt, standing upright atop a long, sinewy neck. Whatever shoulders the statue bore were still buried beneath the mud. Swamp water dripped from the elongated cheekbones and from the curve of the long, slit-like mouth.

"What have they done?" Mara breathed.

Angok cleared his throat. "Is the Architect…is she supposed to look like a snake?"

The ground began to rumble once more. With a horrific squeal, the statue's mouth began to open.

The snake-Architect's jaw unhinged, dropping open unnaturally wide. Great stone fangs sliced down from the statue's upper jaw. Waterweed dangled from one fang. As the lower jaw reached the swamp floor and stopped, Kole saw that the thing even had a huge forked tongue inside its mouth. Darkness filled the back of the statue's throat, hiding whatever lay within.

And then the swamp was silent once again. The statue grew still, molten stone becoming fixed once more. Kole waited and stared, half-expecting it to begin moving again. But though the great golden eyes stared down at him, it remained still.

"Ah," Quintus muttered as he rejoined the group. "Fascinating."

"Fascinating?" Mara said. "This is blasphemy."

"The most interesting things always are. I knew a group of sorcerers must have been involved somehow. The position of the statue's fingers made that clear. Some Silvers must have altered the position of the idol's hand before they plunged it into the earth, hiding it from view. Of course, those sorcerers must have left a set of runes in place to allow entrance to the temple."

Kole was staring at Quintus with wide eyes. Darvin and Wolfun were backing away slowly.

"Sorcery," Darvin said. "You used sorcery to…to do that!" He jabbed a finger toward the great snake-like head.

Angok raised his hands. "It's all right, lads."

"He's infected!" Wolfun pointed at Quintus.

"Don't be ridiculous," Quintus snapped, shaking his head. "Do I look mad to you? Well, boy?"

The fisherboy hesitated, then shook his head, unsure.

"Of course not," Quintus said. "I'm as much a sorcerer as you are. The mechanism for raising the idol was already in place. Come, I'll show you the runes if it will calm you."

The sage reached out to grab the boy's arm, but Darvin and Wolfun both flinched back. The fisherboy's meaty hands tightened into fists. "I...I saw it, though. You used sorcery."

Quintus sighed. "I applied a small amount of raw source to the runes in order to activate them." He held up a finger. "Pure source. A few untainted vessels still remain from before the Outbreak. There is nothing to be concerned about."

"Speak for yourself, Quintus," Mara said. She was still staring at the deformed idol. "I am extremely concerned."

"About what? This?" The sage gestured to the great head and shrugged. "During the chaos of the Outbreak many abandoned the Five and turned to the worship of ancient, primitive gods. Clearly a group of mad sorcerers turned to some serpentine deity and usurped the idol of Gnothea for their own use. Distasteful, yes, but hardly something to worry about. Likely all this snake business is simply surface dressing. I suspect the temple's interior and contents will be largely intact."

"Unless it has flooded," Catgut said.

"Yes, well, let us hope that even while mad, the sorcerers were wise enough to keep the temple watertight. In any case, we won't know until we enter. I propose we do so immediately. Presumably the temple can be accessed through the idol's mouth. We do not have enough supplies to linger on the temple's doorstep fretting about blasphemy."

"I do not like this, Quintus," Mara said, her eyes roaming across the statue's open mouth. "I do not like this one bit."

Kole had to agree with her, though he didn't voice his opinion. He doubted the freebooters had much interest in it.

He still felt uneasy standing this close to Quintus after what he'd seen the man do. That silvery mist that had escaped the glass sphere bore a remarkable resemblance to the red smoke that Kole had seen curling from the corners of Mertyn's lips.

Quintus could claim that the source—or whatever it was that the sphere contained—he could claim it was pure all he liked. But how did he know? What if it was the same contagious sorcery that could pass from person to person? Gods, Kole had only just narrowly escaped infection himself. He didn't want to risk a second exposure.

He could tell Darvin and Wolfun were feeling the same way, despite Quintus's attempts at reassurance. They had edged away from the group and Wolfun was cracking his knuckles nervously.

Even setting aside the risk of infection, a deep sense of unease had taken root in Kole's gut. He couldn't keep his eyes from returning to that huge, snake-like head—the visage of a god defaced by infected sorcerers. And Quintus expected them to just walk into its open mouth, into whatever was inside?

Maybe the sage was mad after all.

A faint hope blossomed in Kole's mind: perhaps he wouldn't have to enter. He and the other two boys from Hale's Crossing were here as porters. There would be no need to haul all their supplies into this ancient temple. Besides, they would only get in the freebooters' way. Surely Quintus and the others would want them to stay out here and guard the packhorse.

But that hope was dashed when Angok began rummaging through the supplies and returned carrying three hooded lanterns. The Sundarin pushed one into Kole's hands and passed the other two to Darvin and Wolfun.

"Good news, lads," Angok said. "You don't have to wear those packs for a while."

PART II
DESCENT

CHAPTER
9

NGOK PULLED A SHIRT of chain mail over his head and then cinched his belt around it. After testing the position of his sword and sliding his axe into the belt, he took his battered round shield and strapped it to his left arm.

Mara was putting on a similar mail shirt. Her war hammer leaned against her leg, its head in the mud at her feet.

Catgut wore only a pair of bracers and a plate of boiled leather over her upper torso. She pulled her locks of bejeweled black hair into a bun at the back of her head, then worked her daggers about in their sheaths, loosening them.

Quintus was the only one of the freebooters who seemed both unarmed and unarmored, apart from a belt knife and a small satchel at his hip. While the others armed themselves, he breathed on his spectacles and wiped them off on a teal handkerchief that was patterned with embroidered flowers.

"Listen up," Angok said to Kole and the other boys. "You've all been promoted from porters to lantern bearers. Congratulations. When we go in, you have one job and one job only. Any guesses as to what that job is?"

"Bear the lanterns," Kole said.

Angok pointed at Kole. "I knew we were paying you for something. Your job is to keep those lanterns burning and bring the light where we need it. Sounds easy, right? Hopefully it will be. Now, I'm reminded of something Quintus told me once. About a creature they have up near the

City of Rivers, across the Ashashi deserts. It's called a…a…" He turned. "Quintus, what's it called? That big gray thing that likes splashing about in the water."

The sage raised an eyebrow. "An elephant?"

"No, no, no. I know what an elephant is. The other one."

"A hippopotamus?"

"That's the one. See, lads, these hippopotamus things are huge. Great big beasts with great big teeth. Get between one of them and its offspring, you'll have a bad time. But those big teeth of theirs get covered in all sorts of gunk. And the hippopotamus has these big stumpy legs that can't reach its mouth. So what do they do? They open up wide, and along comes a bird. This bird perches in the beast's mouth and eats all the gunk out of its teeth. Now, at any moment, the beast could snap its jaws closed and eat that bird whole."

"They're herbivorous," Quintus said.

"What?"

"They don't eat birds. They eat grass."

Angok shook his head at the sage. "You're ruining my story. The point is the bird and the beast need each other. The bird needs to eat, and the hippopotamus needs its teeth cleaned. So they have to trust each other. What's that called again, Quintus?"

"Symbiosis," the sage said.

"Exactly. Symbiosis. When we're in that temple, we have to be symbiotic as well. Like as not, that temple is empty. It's probably been sealed for centuries. Anyone who was in there before it closed is long dead. But there's always a chance that it's not empty. There's a chance that there's something dangerous in there. Some dark creatures are drawn to places like this."

"Like ratmen," Darvin said flatly.

Angok's eyes narrowed slightly. "That's right. Like ratmen. What I'm saying is this: if there is something down there, we need to be symbiotic. Me and Catgut and Mara, we can't fight in the dark. We need you to bring the light. And you need us to stand between you and whatever foul things we find down there. If you let the light burn out, if you drop your lantern, if you turn and run, we'll get cut down in the dark. And if we die, you'll die too."

He gave the three of them a long stare, as if daring them to scoff at his intensity. None of them did, not even Darvin. Kole felt queasy. His gaze kept being drawn toward the scratches and scuff marks on Angok's shield.

The blue background and the rearing white beast painted onto the shield had clearly been retouched, but beneath the paint Kole could see a set of long, deep scratch marks, bigger even that what a swamp cat could do.

He'd been a fool to come with the freebooters. He'd known that even before he left, and it had only become clearer when he'd found Tilda's swollen body. Now he'd seen the defaced idol of a dead god rise from the swamp, and his companions were arming themselves as they prepared to enter its gaping mouth. This went beyond foolishness—it was madness.

What would happen if he refused to enter? What would the freebooters do? They wouldn't kill him, would they? They were tough, but they didn't seem as cruel as that.

Certainly he would lose any claim to the treasure—and he realized with surprise that he now believed there was treasure to be found down there. There had to be *something*, surely.

Was that treasure worth his life? He supposed that depended on how much treasure there was. As he gazed upon the face of the snake-Architect, he imagined some great horde of riches contained within, a pile of jewels and coins from a decadent empire.

What could he do with wealth like that? What could he change?

He could change the lives of everyone in his family. They could move to Baybury, or Locket, or even Godsmouth. They could leave behind their lives as corpse draggers and become anything they wanted to be. They could be merchants. Perhaps they could even raise themselves to nobility. They wouldn't have to be ostracized anymore. They wouldn't have to be alone.

Perhaps they could even find some treatment for Arabel's condition. Ma and Da had once—at great expense—been able to arrange for a traveling physik to examine her. But the physik had been unable to offer any treatment for her sunlight sensitivity, or even an explanation for it.

Surely, though, there were many great physiks in a city like Godsmouth. Their services would not be cheap, but with a coin purse full of ancient gold, few doors would be closed to them.

Kole imagined Arabeth standing outside in the noonday sun, the light in her hair. He imagined her smiling.

Could he let that chance fade away—however slim it was? Could he turn back now, when he was so close, after all he'd gone through to get here?

Darvin glanced at his lantern, then at Catgut. "If she isn't using her bow, maybe I could. I'm a pretty good shot."

"We don't need an archer. We need lantern bearers. That's your job." Angok drew his axe from his belt. "Ready, lads?"

Kole glanced at Darvin and Wolfun. He saw his own uncertainty reflected in their faces, the same warring doubts. He'd never noticed how small the two of them looked, how young. Kole wondered if he looked the same.

He swallowed and lifted his lantern. "Ready."

Catgut was going in first, and Kole would be right behind her.

"Two steps," the Nizaani said to him. "That is the distance you will maintain. One step and you will be breathing down my neck. Three steps and the light becomes too poor. You will hold the lantern up. Higher."

She touched the flat of her sword to his elbow, forcing the lantern up above his head. He knew it wouldn't be long until his shoulder began to ache.

"Good. Like so." She turned away. "Two steps. Follow me."

She stepped into the idol's gaping serpentine mouth. Taking a deep breath, Kole stared up at the great stone fangs overhead, then followed Catgut inside.

The smooth white stone beneath his feet was slick with algae. Kole's boots threatened to slip with every step, but Catgut seemed to have no such trouble. She prowled forward, slightly crouched, her sword held ahead of her.

As Kole followed, his lantern cast flickering orange light along the ridged roof of the snake-woman's mouth. Catgut lightly prodded the edge of the huge forked tongue with the point of her sword, as if testing for seams. Satisfied, she stepped up onto the tongue and followed it deeper inside.

The rest of the party followed along behind Kole. Angok was at his back, shield in one hand and axe in the other. The Sundarin was uncharacteristically silent. Behind him came Quintus and the other two porters, with Mara at the rear, her hammer held in both hands.

The packhorse was the luckiest of all of them—she got to remain outside, hitched to a tree next to some oats and fresh water. Kole hoped that Catgut had successfully exterminated all the hanging snakes in the area. Or if she had not, that Mugsy was watchful and had a good kick.

As they reached the back of the gaping mouth, Catgut slowed and peered forward.

"Stairs," she whispered over her shoulder. "Single file. Do nothing to distract me."

She crouched down low and started forward. Kole looked over her head and caught sight of a steep circular stairway spiraling downward. It was carved from the same white stone as the rest of the statue—although perhaps "carved" wasn't the right word. Kole had still not seen a single seam between blocks of stone, let alone a tool mark. It was like the whole place had been crafted by pouring molten stone into a gigantic mold.

A damp, stale scent wafted out of the dark stairwell, stronger even than the stink of the swamp outside. He could hear dripping from somewhere far below, echoing up the stairwell. How far down did it stretch?

Catgut moved slowly. She tapped the stairs ahead of her gently with her sword, head cocked as if listening to the sound the stone made. Only when she was satisfied did she move to the next step and repeat the process.

Once they'd descended half a turn into the stairwell, she began examining the walls as well, and then the sloping ceiling. The stairwell was narrow, only three feet wide, the stairs curling tightly around a central pillar. The stairs were steep as well, with nothing but the bare stone wall to hang onto as they slowly descended.

The ceiling was too low to keep the lantern as high as Catgut had demanded. Every time they took another step down she hissed instructions back at him, telling him to move the lantern here and there.

A few steps behind, Kole could hear Angok grumbling as the low ceiling forced him to stoop. The footsteps and whispers of the others followed, echoing strangely in the tight stairwell.

"What's taking so long?" he heard Wolfun whisper.

It was Quintus who answered. "Remember that this is a ruin, boy, one exposed to the twin destructive forces of water and time. We do not know for sure that everything is entirely stable."

Swallowing, Kole glanced up at the low ceiling bathed in flickering lantern light. He could see no cracks, no dripping water.

"In addition," Quintus continued, "it seems likely this temple was host to a cabal of mad sorcerers sometime during the Outbreak. Silvers, in particular, tended to develop a deep paranoia as their insanity manifested."

"Who are these Silvers you keep talking about?" Darvin asked.

"Sorcerers gifted with the Lore of Silver. They used their sorcery to work metal, stone, and other matter. This idol was originally built by Silvers before the Outbreak. And others reworked the idol into this serpentine image after they became corrupted. In their madness, many corrupted Silvers became convinced that their refuges would be attacked and destroyed. Perhaps not an unreasonable concern, given the attempts to contain the Outbreak by quarantining infected sorcerers. As such, it is common to find traps in the strongholds of those sorcerers, many of them still functional even centuries later."

"Found one," Catgut called back. She tapped the stair in front of her with her sword. "This is a pressure plate. I would advise no one step on it, unless they want to find out what comes out of these holes."

She gestured to four small holes set into the outer wall of the stairwell. They were arranged vertically, the lowest at ankle-height while the highest was at Kole's eye level. Kole doubted he would have noticed them had Catgut not pointed them out.

Catgut took a piece of chalk out of her pocket and drew a large X on the trapped stair. "I have marked the plate. We continue."

She stepped over the marked stair and continued probing ahead of her. As Kole followed, he glanced into the highest of the four holes. His lantern light glinted from the point of something sharp and metallic. Swallowing, Kole watched where Catgut stepped and put his feet exactly where hers had been.

He didn't know how far they descended down that spiraling staircase. In that darkness, the only way of tracking time was by watching their candles burn down. Their travel was slower even than their treks through the deepest and thickest parts of the swamp. Soon, even the threat of traps was not enough to keep the tedium at bay, though Catgut seemed to have inexhaustible patience. She never hurried, never stopped examining every crack, every corner.

Just as Kole was replacing his candle, Catgut identified another trapped stair, with a similar arrangement of holes in the wall alongside. She marked it with chalk as she had the first, then continued.

Kole had grown so used to the narrow staircase that he was caught by surprise when it ended. He'd started to wonder if it continued on forever, spiraling down into the dark hells at the center of the world.

And then, suddenly, there was a doorway. A tattered blue rag hung from hooks above the doorway, and Kole realized it must have once been a curtain. The air felt still and heavy. It left a taste in the back of Kole's throat: dust and decay. The sound of dripping was louder here, echoing like the doorway opened into a huge cavern.

Catgut took extra care examining the doorway for traps. He could hear Angok shuffling impatiently behind him.

"What is it?" the Sundarin hissed. The stairwell's tight spiral kept him from seeing what was happening.

"We found a doorway," Kole said.

"A doorway to what?"

Kole shrugged. He couldn't make out much past Catgut.

Finally, the Nizaani straightened, seemingly satisfied that the doorway held no hidden surprises.

"Everyone remain here," she called. "The boy and I will scout ahead. Come, boy."

She gestured to Kole and then turned and slipped through the doorway. Licking his lips, Kole followed, holding his lantern high.

Vast. That was the first word that entered his head as he stepped into the chamber.

He'd thought, after spending so long in the claustrophobic confines of the stairwell, that it would be a relief to be out of it. He was wrong.

The white stone floor stretched out in every direction, reaching beyond the glow of his lantern. At the edge of the light on either side of him were two curving white pillars that seemed far too thin to support any kind of weight. They stretched upward, disappearing into the dark. Only when he strained his eyes did he imagine he could make out a vaulted ceiling high above him.

At least in the stairwell he'd been bounded by walls and surrounded by companions. Out here, where his lantern failed to penetrate the endless dark, anything could be hiding.

He glanced back. Kole inhaled sharply as his lantern illuminated dozens of gigantic figures standing on either side of the doorway he'd come through.

Catgut's soft-soled shoes whispered against the stone floor as she spun back toward him. "What is it?"

As Kole realized what he was looking at, he exhaled slowly, trying to calm his hammering heart. The wall was crafted from the same veined stone that formed the floor and the pillars. Dozens of figures had been sculpted in high relief upon the wall—men, women and children, all larger than life.

Many were dressed in strange clothes with high collars and broad-brimmed hats fitted with great feathers. Some clutched books, while others appeared to be in discussion with one another. One woman with a hairstyle that reminded Kole of a beehive passed a handful of coins to a trio of young children. On either side of the doorway pairs of armored horses reared. Atop them sat warriors with flowing hair and swords lifted high in the air.

"The sculptures," Kole said. "They just…they caught me by surprise."

As he lowered his lantern and the shadows shifted across the surface of the relief, he noticed that there was something carved at the feet of the figures. He'd taken it at first for some decorative pattern, but as he looked closer he realized what it truly was.

Snakes. A thousand stone snakes, a sea of them, carved into the base of the relief. Some of them stretched up, coiling around the legs of the figures. Now that he was looking more closely, he saw more of them among the carvings—what he'd first thought was a scarf was really a serpent curled tight about a rotund man's neck. As he swept his lantern around, he saw the figure of a young woman reclining on a couch as two large snakes slithered suggestively along her legs, forked tongues licking thighs.

The artistry of the snakes seemed cruder than whatever hand had crafted the figures. It was as if the serpents had been added later, twisting the original artwork just as the visage of the Architect had been twisted into her serpentine form.

"We are not here to admire the artwork," Catgut said. "Two steps, boy. Come."

Shuddering, Kole forced himself to turn away from the snake-infested relief and hurry off after the Nizaani. She was creeping directly away from the door, sword in hand. Her head never stopped moving—Kole could tell she was studying not just the floor at her feet but also peering into the darkness at the edge of the lantern light.

Motes of dust floated in the air, disturbed by their movement. They passed between the two narrow pillars and continued on.

At the edge of the light, off to his left, Kole caught sight of a row of wooden pews, facing in the same direction he and Catgut were walking. He lifted the lantern and spotted more pews to his right.

Catgut slowed. He returned his attention forward again and saw a railing ahead of him, carved from the same white stone as the rest of the temple. There were more pillars reaching up from it, stretching into the darkness above.

Without leaning on the railing, Catgut peered out over it, looking first down and then up. She gestured to him.

"Light," she whispered.

He came forward, holding the lantern out over the railing. The darkness stretched away below him. He looked up. What he'd thought was a ceiling overhead seemed to be another floor like the one they were on. It stretched out a little further than their own floor and then ended. There had to be another ceiling even higher up.

"We are on a mezzanine," Catgut whispered, peering down. By the way the sound reverberated, the chamber had to be huge. "There is another below us. Perhaps more."

Kole strained his eyes, but apparently the Nizaani's night sight was better than his. "How far down does it go?"

She took a piece of chalk out of her pocket and tossed it over the edge. After several seconds, he heard the soft clatter of the chalk hitting stone.

"Too far to climb," she said simply.

"I didn't realize that was an option we were considering."

She stepped back from the edge and started following the railing around. "Come. We must find more stairs down."

A little further on, they came to a section of the floor that had crumbled away. Catgut got down on her belly and wriggled along the cracked floor toward the edge. She peered up and down for a moment, then crawled back to him. "Something from above fell and took out this floor and the one below it. Possibly more. It is too unstable this way. We must try the other direction."

They turned and went back the way they'd come, following the edge of the mezzanine around. The mezzanine seemed to be arranged into sections that surrounded the great opening in the center of the chamber. The rows of pews they passed all looked inward, toward the opening.

"How did they light this place?" Kole whispered as they crept along. "It's huge."

"Shadowlight," Catgut said.

"What?"

"Some sort of sorcery. Ask Quintus."

Out of the corner of his eye, Kole saw a shape among the pews. At first he thought it was one of the relief sculptures, or maybe a fallen pillar. As he swung his lantern toward it, though, he saw it was neither.

There was someone sitting in the pews.

He froze. "Catgut," he hissed. "Someone's there."

The woman spun in the direction he'd pointed, raising her sword. The figure didn't move. The lantern light struggled to pick out the person's shape amid the darkness.

Catgut stood still for a moment, sword pointed toward the figure. She glanced around, her eyes glinting in the lantern light.

"Follow," she whispered.

She started quickly down the aisle toward the figure, and Kole had no choice but to follow or be left alone.

As he hurried after her, lantern swinging from his hand, Catgut tugged a dagger from the strap across her chest and held it loosely in her off-hand. Still the figure made no move.

As he came closer, Kole saw why. It was a man sitting there—or at least it had once been. His skin was almost black—not the dark skin tone of an Ashashi, but a black like burned meat. His shriveled flesh was pulled tight across his skull. Teeth that were almost as white as the stone beneath their feet shone brightly in the lantern light. If the man had eyes, they were as scorched black as the rest of him.

His clothes—not so different than the clothes worn by the characters in the wall relief—seemed melted to him, though they were not nearly as charred as the man himself.

Catgut kicked aside the pew in front of the man to give her more room as she stalked toward him. Slowly, she reached out and nudged the man with the flat of her sword.

His arm flopped to the side. Part of his high-collared shirt began to disintegrate as it was disturbed. Dust puffed off him. He didn't smell rotten, just…stale.

With a grunt, Catgut stepped back. "Dead."

Swallowing, Kole nodded. A dead body didn't bother him—he'd seen plenty before. But what could have done this to him?

"Let us not linger," Catgut said.

"Is this sorcery?" he asked.

The Nizaani hesitated, then shook her head. "I do not know. It does not matter. He is dead. Come. We must find those stairs."

They found more bodies among the pews.

First, a woman, sitting alone in the front row. Her gown of blue silk had survived remarkably well. She wore a circlet of silver atop her blackened head, with a small red jewel set into the center. A ruby, Kole thought, though he'd never seen one before.

"Touch nothing," Catgut said. He didn't need to be told. Though he was here in search of treasure, he had no intention of stealing jewels from a corpse.

Further on they found what looked like a family: two women and a boy, maybe seven years old. The two women were both clutching the child tight. Protecting him, perhaps.

Or keeping him from getting away.

At last they came to a grand stairway leading down to the next level. A badly decayed blue carpet still clung to the center of the wide stairway. They followed it down far enough to determine the stairway was intact, then they retreated back to the spiral staircase where the rest of the party waited.

"About time," Angok grumbled when they returned. "Quintus had already given you up for dead, and I was about ready to agree with him."

Catgut rapidly relayed what they'd found. Quintus could offer no explanation for what had happened to the bodies, but he displayed no concern.

"Whatever sorcery killed them is likely long dispersed," he said. "If I had to guess, I would say they were victims of some foul sorcerous ritual. You said they were just sitting there, yes? Then unless they were sheltering here and were caught by surprise, I would suggest they were willing victims. Hold your sympathy and focus on the task at hand." He turned to Mara. "What do you know of the temple's layout?"

"From what has been described," Mara said, "I would guess we are in the four-tiered nave, formed from the body of the idol. It is here the pilgrims and worshipers would gather to reflect on the Architect's glory and to hear the Silver Bell ring. On the bottom level will be archways leading to smaller chapels dedicated to the other four gods, as well as the entrance hall."

"And the repository?" Quintus said. "The archives?"

"Deeper still, below the idol itself, and above the catacomb levels."

"Then that is where we must go. Let us hope the snake worshipers confined their debauchery to the upper levels, and that the repository remains intact."

CHAPTER
10

THEY DESCENDED THROUGH the great dark silence.

No one spoke above a whisper as they made their way down the grand, sweeping staircase leading to the next tier of the nave. Even with the combined light of all three lanterns, they couldn't see more than fifty feet ahead of them.

As they came to the second level, they caught sight of more blackened figures sitting in pews. Here, they were mostly gathered in groups of five or six, all still, all staring straight into the great opening in the center of the temple.

They continued on down past another mezzanine floor filled with pews. The dripping grew louder as they descended.

And then the stairways came to an end—not on a mezzanine this time, it seemed, but a ground floor. There were no pews here. As Kole stepped forward with the lantern, he saw that the floor was no longer the same veined white stone that formed the walls and pillars of the temple. There was a pattern in it—not etched or carved, but infused within the floor itself, as if the temple's creators had somehow managed to coax inks of black and blue and gold into the pale stone. Here, in the small bubble of light that surrounded them, he could only guess at the pattern's true form—a sunburst, perhaps? But even with the fraction of it he could see, he recognized the intricate detail in the pattern, like the finest lacework he had ever seen.

"The entrance hall should be directly opposite us," Mara whispered, "past the chancel. The base of the temple is octagonal, with the chapels to the other gods found at the four diagonals. The western wing leads to the chapter house and the quarters for the priests and novices. To the east is the library, the refectory, and the priests' offices, along with the entrance to the lower levels."

"Then we go east," Catgut said. "Follow behind and do not stray. Boy, we go ahead."

Their footsteps echoed through the towering nave. They kept the wall within the light's reach as they passed alongside thin, towering pillars. Kole knew those pillars must be holding up the three tiers of mezzanines above them, but he could not see how it was possible. The weight of all that stone…

As they moved, their light exposed more of the pattern worked into the stone floor, but still Kole was no closer to understanding its full significance. He could only ever see slivers of it at a time, as beautiful as those slivers were.

He began to notice cracks in the floor as they followed the temple wall around. At first there were just a couple, stretching away into the darkness ahead of him. But as they continued, the floor became splintered and riven with fractures that radiated out like spiderwebs. Catgut hesitated, studying the cracks for a moment before continuing on.

A light glinted ahead of them, and Kole stopped with a start. "There's a light," he hissed.

The rest of the party came to a halt. Kole heard Angok's knuckles crack as he tightened his hand around the handle of his axe.

"Wait." Catgut stalked forward and slipped into the shadow of a pillar off to their right. He could just make out her shape in the darkness, peering ahead.

There was silence for several seconds. The small light ahead of them remained where it was.

"Boy," Catgut hissed. "Cover your lantern."

Kole did what she said, lowering the hood on his lantern. Most of the light from the lantern disappeared, leaving him in near-darkness.

The light ahead also disappeared.

A soft laugh near Kole's shoulder made him jump. It took him a moment to realize it was Catgut. She had crept back over to him so silently he hadn't heard her approach.

Trying to calm his breathing, he clumsily lifted the hood of his lantern. Catgut's grinning face appeared out of the darkness near him. Ahead, the light returned.

"Not a light," he said. "A reflection."

"Indeed," Catgut said. "Do not look so embarrassed, boy. Caution is what keeps one's head attached to one's shoulders. Come. Let us see what a mirror is doing here."

She hissed to the others, then they started forward again.

It was not, it turned out, a mirror. It was a bell.

The bell stood three times Kole's height. Though its surface was marred with scratches and white dust, the silver beneath shone through in patches.

The huge bell lay in a crater on the temple floor, amid piles of debris and chunks of smashed stone flooring.

The remains of a broken chain hung down from the top of the bell, trailing along the floor beside it. From somewhere high above, drips of water were trickling down, falling onto the bell and filling the crater with puddles of murky water.

"The Silver Bell," Mara said as the rest of the party approached. "The Voice of the Architect. Its sound used to ring over the lost city."

"I hate bells," Angok said. "They remind me of herding yaks. All day long the bells around their necks would ring." He crouched down by the heavy broken chain, then looked up into the darkness. "Something blew this chain apart. Long time ago, by the look of it."

Kole noticed that Darvin wasn't looking at the bell. He was off to the side, shining his lantern into the dark near the center of the temple floor.

"Hey," Darvin said. "There's something else over here."

"We're wasting time," Quintus muttered. "We should be heading to the repository. We need to find the arcanum."

Ignoring the sage's grumbling, Angok went to join Darvin. "What is it, lad?"

"I don't know. But look. Do you see it? There."

Peering into the dark, Angok grunted. "What in the nine hells...? Quintus, you might want to look at this."

With a grunt of annoyance, Quintus reluctantly shuffled over to Angok. Kole and the others followed.

As the darkness retreated before their lights, Kole caught sight of a group of rounded shadows half sunken into a large crack that had spread from the crater. The mounds were not the polished white of the stone beneath them. Instead, the lantern light fell on a rough, leathery surface, cream spotted with brown.

There were three of them, each about two feet high. One looked sunken in on itself, like a ball of butter left out in the sun. The other two sagged to the side, as if unable to hold up their own weight. Still, even decayed as they were, they looked almost like...

"Eggs," he breathed.

Angok grunted and glanced around at the darkness pressing in around them. "Quintus," he whispered. "Why are there eggs here?"

The sage hurried forward to examine the half-decayed eggs. Sliding his knife from its sheath, he crouched and prodded the nearest of the eggs. It didn't crack—rather, it sagged a little more. A faint stink of sulfur wafted from it. Quintus pressed his handkerchief across his mouth and nose.

"Uncalcified," Quintus muttered. "Leathery texture. Reptilian, perhaps."

"You mean serpentine," Catgut said.

"I cannot say."

"He cannot say," the Nizaani muttered. "We delve into an ancient temple corrupted by snake worshipers, and he believes it is a gecko that has hatched its spawn here."

Quintus shook his head. "These eggs have not hatched. They were never fertilized. They have been here some time."

"Not four centuries, though," Angok said. "Not since the Outbreak. They're more recent than that."

The sage straightened and said nothing.

"W...what does it mean?" Wolfun stammered, staring wide-eyed at the eggs.

"What do you think it means?" Darvin snapped at him. "There's something down here."

Wolfun shook his head. "So we're leaving, right?"

"This changes nothing," Quintus said.

"Nothing?" Wolfun's voice rose. He gestured wildly at the eggs. "Gods damn you all. How is this nothing?"

"Keep your voice down, lad," Angok said. "Quintus is right. We factor this into our plan. We do this delve quickly and quietly. But we do it still."

The fisherboy shook his head violently. "You do it, then. First Tilda, and now...now this! I've had enough of this shit. I'm getting out of here."

He stormed away from Angok, the lantern swinging wildly in his hand. His pounding footsteps echoed through the nave.

"Corpse dragger!" Angok hissed. "Stop him."

Kole was already moving to block Wolfun's exit. "Hey! Angok's right. You can't go off alone. If something's out there..."

"Out of my way," Wolfun spat, trying to give Kole a wide berth.

"Wait!" Without thinking, Kole reached out and grabbed the boy's arm.

Wolfun let out a shriek that seemed deafening in the silence of the temple. He yanked his arm free of Kole's grasp and stumbled back, catching his heel on a crack in the ground. He splashed into a puddle of water near the fallen bell and his lantern dropped from his grip. The candle inside flickered out as one of the panels cracked.

As the boy inhaled to shout, Darvin suddenly appeared on top of him. Darvin slammed his knee into Wolfun's chest, forcing him to the stone floor with a gasp. Darvin's free hand closed over the fisherboy's mouth.

"Shut your damned mouth," Darvin whispered through clenched teeth. "Shut it before I shut it for you. You're going to get us all killed."

The fisherboy's wide eyes darted from Darvin to Kole to the cluster of freebooters quietly approaching. Catgut and Mara both had their backs to the light, peering into the dark, while Angok stared down at the fisherboy, axe in hand.

"Your friend's right, lad. When I die, it's going to be on top of a mountain, as close to the sun as I can get. I won't let you get me killed down here. And I won't let you get everyone else killed either. No one goes off on their own. No one leaves. No one makes a sound. We're going down into the repository together, and we're coming back up together. Is that clear?"

Wolfun shoved Darvin's hand away from his mouth. He glared at all of them, but finally he gave a single curt nod of his head.

"Then get that lantern lit," Angok said. He glanced over his shoulder at Mara and Catgut. "Are we all right?"

"I perceive nothing," Catgut said.

Angok nodded. "Maybe we're alone down here after all." He turned back to the fisherboy. "You panic again, you'll find this axe in your spine. That goes for everyone here. Understood?" Silence answered him. "Good. Then let's keep moving."

Darvin stood up and offered a hand to his friend. Wolfun ignored it, pulling himself out of the puddle and brushing himself off. In silence, he relit his lantern from Darvin's candle and turned away.

Kole shot Darvin a look. Darvin just shook his head.

"He's just scared," Darvin whispered.

"You need to keep an eye on him," Kole said.

"He's fine." Darvin's voice was hard. "I'll handle it." He looked up at the darkness above them, then over at the clutch of decayed eggs. "It's just this place, is all."

Kole nodded. He knew what Darvin meant. Something was wrong here. Deeply wrong.

With one last look at the huge, rotted eggs, Kole moved to rejoin Catgut. As he passed Angok, he paused.

"Are you sure this treasure is worth the risk?" he asked the Sundarin. "We could always just loot the bodies in the pews and get out of here. I saw plenty of jewelry."

"Didn't expect to hear you advocating for robbing the dead, corpse dragger."

"Neither did I, until I saw those eggs."

"I told you all before we entered there could be things down here," Angok said.

"Then why stay? Why risk it?" Kole gestured to Darvin's friend. "He's not entirely wrong. You know that."

The Sundarin gave him a tight smile. There was something else there, as well—fear, maybe? Sadness? "You'll need someone reliable."

"What?"

"That's what you told me back at the inn. You said I'd need someone reliable. Not like them." He jerked his thumb toward Darvin and Wolfun. "'When they run back to town the instant their socks get wet, you'll be glad you still have me.' That's what you said. But did you mean it? The dark, it…does things to people. I need you to keep those two from losing their heads. Can you do that for me, lad?"

Kole exhaled deeply. What would Da say, if he were here?

He would have told Kole he was a damned fool for ever entering the swamp in the first place. That was certain. But now that he was here…

His mind returned to Tilda lying dead in the swamp a few feet from their camp, her face swollen beyond recognition. All his life, Da had talked about the responsibility their family had to the safety and well-being of the village. Even though many in the town feared them, maybe even hated them, they still had a job to do. The dead had to be burned, and those corrupted by sorcery had to be given a merciful end. Da didn't do it for the purse. He did it because someone had to.

Though Kole had nodded his head whenever Da had tried to tell him that, he wasn't sure he'd ever really understood.

He was beginning to.

He nodded slowly. "All right. I can do that."

"Good lad." Angok paused. "And to answer your question: yes. This treasure is worth the risk."

"Why? How much is it worth?"

The Sundarin's bushy red eyebrows lowered. "Everything, maybe."

Kole opened his mouth to ask what in the hells that was supposed to mean, but before he could, Catgut hissed to him.

"Stop gossiping with the bear-lover, boy. I need my light. The passage-way is over here."

Angok shot him a grin that seemed sinister in the lantern light. He jerked his head toward Catgut, and Kole reluctantly began to follow the Nizaani once again.

The vast archway led into a large, open passage formed by rows of the same great slender pillars Kole had seen earlier. Other sections of the temple lay to the left and right, beyond the pillars, unconstrained by doors or walls. Mara whispered that the temple's public library was located off to their left, while the refectory and all its many nooks and crannies could be found to the right. Kole could see nothing but darkness.

"Something occurs to me," Quintus said as they made their way quickly but quietly down the main passage, "Let us assume for the moment that those eggs did belong to some sort of monstrous serpent. Snakes, I recall, are said to have poor hearing. However, they are remarkably skilled at detecting and analyzing earthly vibrations."

"And what does that mean for us, exactly?" Angok whispered.

"It means we should walk softly."

"The Sundarin may struggle with that," Catgut said over her shoulder.

Angok grunted. "When I was a boy, I was light-footed enough to sneak up on a herd of mammoths in open ground. Managed to jump on the calf and ride it for twenty miles until it finally collapsed of exhaustion."

Catgut shrugged, unimpressed. "I imagine you were smaller then." She glanced back at them all. "Perhaps everyone should take their boots off."

Angok scoffed. "I do not want to fall into a pit trap while barefoot."

"Agreed," Quintus said.

Catgut narrowed her eyes. "I will identify any pit traps before you fall."

"That's what you said last time."

"You were not supposed to wander off on your own!"

"I wasn't wandering," Angok said. "I was guarding our backs!"

Mara hissed at them and Angok and Catgut fell silent.

At last the row of pillars ended and they came to a large door of wood and iron set into a wall of white stone. The door seemed much more practical and less ornate than anything else Kole had seen in the temple thus far. There was no relief carved into the wall here, though Kole's light fell on some tattered scraps on the floor that might have once been tapestries.

"If our information is correct," Mara said quietly, "this should lead down beneath the idol, to the repository level. Access was restricted to priests and selected novices."

Gesturing to Kole to follow, Catgut approached the doorway and peered at the cracks around the door. Carefully, she tested the handle. The door swung open.

At a nod from Catgut, Kole thrust his lantern forward, casting light down a short passageway that became another stairwell spiraling down into the dark. Catgut stepped carefully forward and started tapping her short sword against the top stair.

Kole's heart sank. It was going to be another long descent.

CHAPTER
11

MERCIFULLY, THE STAIRWELL to the repository was far shorter than the one that had spiraled down from the statue's serpentine head above ground. Catgut searched every step, but she found no traps, and they made it to the bottom of the stairwell intact.

By now, Kole had completely lost track of time. He had no idea if night had fallen. They had not yet stopped for food, but his stomach was so tied up in knots he wasn't sure he could eat anyway.

The stairwell ended in a doorway that opened into the center of a large square chamber. Passageways branched off in each direction. Though the walls and floor were crafted of the same smooth white stone as the temple above, the chamber appeared far less opulent than the nave. In fact, it reminded him a little of the old guildhall in the center of Hale's Crossing.

"Does anyone smell that?" Darvin whispered as the party gathered at the bottom of the stairs. "Something stinks down here."

He was right. A smell lingered in the air—a smell Kole had had plenty of experience with. "Something dead."

"Could be whatever laid those eggs," Angok suggested. "I'd rather we didn't have to find out. Smells like it's coming from somewhere over there." He peered down the passageway to their left. "Mara, where are we going?"

"Down here, I believe." She gestured to the archway to the right.

Angok nodded. "Away from the stink. Good. Let's go."

They made their way slowly and carefully down the passageway, but Kole could sense a growing excitement from Quintus. His footsteps had become more purposeful, and he kept having to slow down so as not to overtake Catgut and Kole.

"Patience, Master Sage," Catgut whispered.

Though the passage was not as grand as those upstairs, it was easily wide enough for them to travel two abreast. At intervals along the passage, sculptures stood tall on stone plinths, posturing proudly. A few had fallen, the shattered fragments strewn across the floor.

Some of the intact statues seemed like soldiers or military officers, resplendent in strange plated armor and fine uniforms. Others were more simply adorned, and made Kole think of priests or scholars. Still more held strange objects in their hands: devices whose purpose he could not fathom. As he crept along behind Catgut, his lantern light fell on each sculpture in turn, casting the details into sharp relief. Kole was thankful that there were no snakes to be found slithering up the legs of any of them.

In between the sculptures were doors—dozens of doors. Several hung open, and in one case the door had been broken entirely off its hinges and lay splintered on the floor inside the doorway. Kole shone his light into each of the open doorways and caught glimpses of long rooms stretching beyond the reach of his light. Towering shelves stretched to the ceiling, each packed tight with tomes and manuscripts. There were more books in a single room than he'd ever seen in his life.

Many of the shelves he glimpsed had toppled over, spilling their contents onto the floor. One room seemed to hold artwork and artifacts— he caught glimpses of lacquered urns and paintings whose subjects he couldn't discern.

They passed other passageways and stairs branching off the main passage, disappearing out into darkness. At first Kole had thought this level was small compared to those above, but he was starting to realize just how vast and sprawling it really was. He didn't realize this many books existed in the world, let alone within a few dozen miles of Hale's Crossing.

"How big is this place?" Darvin muttered, mirroring Kole's own thoughts.

"The repository level spreads out well beyond the footprint of the temple," Mara said. "It was said to be the largest of its kind in the western empire. We are in the archival wing, where the collected knowledge of church and state was gathered, along with a handful of culturally relevant artifacts."

"I thought we were after treasure," Wolfun grumbled. "Not books."

"We'll go find the treasury when we're done here, lad," Angok said.

"We just have a stop to make first. And if I hear another complaint, I'll throw you into the catacombs."

Wolfun shot Angok a glare. He opened his mouth as if to argue, then turned sullenly and kept walking.

Catgut interrupted. "There are doors ahead. Is this the place?"

Kole's light fell on a large pair of arched doors that filled the passageway. The banding was silver and ornate, seemingly untouched by time.

Mara and Quintus hurried forward. "Yes," Mara said. "I think this is it."

Quintus started for the doors, but Catgut grabbed him. "Let me, Master Sage."

On each door was a large handle and a lock mechanism in the shape of a hammer. Catgut spent a few seconds examining the lock and the cracks around the doors, then she gingerly tested a handle.

"Locked," she said.

"This may be good news," Quintus said. "Perhaps the snake-worshipers that took over here did not bother to ransack the arcanum."

Catgut crouched before the door and pulled a set of long metal probes from some pocket hidden beneath her jacket. Carefully, she slid two of the probes into the keyhole.

"Let us hope the mechanism is not frozen," she said. "Bring the light over here, boy."

As Kole lowered the lantern, the Nizaani began to work. He could hear the soft scraping of her probes, but there was otherwise no sign that she was making progress. He stared back the way they'd come, toward the stairwell.

"I keep thinking about those eggs," Kole said. "The size of them. For something to lay them, it would have to be…"

"Monstrous," Angok finished for him. He shrugged. "There are plenty of monsters in this world, lad. Just one more thing our ancestors left for us to enjoy."

Kole frowned. "What do you mean? What do our ancestors have to do with anything?"

It was Mara who answered. "The world was not always haunted by monsters, save those who wear a human guise. Beasts, yes, even those as strange as Quintus's hippopotamus or Angok's mammoth. But the ratmen, the devil bird of the Windless Peaks, the burrowing horrors that plague the Caravan Lords of the Ashashi, even the Choir of the Undying that plague the eastern wildlands, they are all perversions of the natural order, the like of which has not been seen since the Elder Days, when demons raided humanity relentlessly. They are abominations given life by our ancestors."

"Through sorcery," Kole said. The sickening image of Mertyn Walter's family flashed before his eyes.

Mara nodded. "Just as those gifted with the Lore of Silver could reshape stone and metal as they saw fit, those who knew the Lore of Flesh could reshape the living. Maybe even the dead too, so the stories say. Before the plague, most Flesh sorcerers were healers, gardeners, preservers of the natural order. The forest that used to surround the idol was coaxed into being by Flesh sorcerers. Life itself was their canvas.

"And then, of course, came the Outbreak. The Gift of Flesh spread among the population as quickly as any of the other sorceries, driving already skilled sorcerers wild and turning ordinary people into vessels of terrible power. Most of those infected individuals who were not sorcerers before the plague used their newfound power to destroy their friends and neighbors in a fit of madness, wielding their sorcery in its raw, untethered form. Those who had developed their talent through years of training, however, often turned their power to more…productive uses. The natural world became a laboratory for them. In their madness, they gave life new forms. Creatures and men were twisted and deformed, until they barely resembled what they had once been."

"The plague is not entirely to blame," Quintus added. "There are numerous reports claiming that in the last days of the Empire some Flesh sorcerers were already pushing the bounds of their craft. It is believed that the Choir of the Undying began as some sort of botched attempt to create a servant race."

Kole's mind whirled. "How do you know all this? You're treasure hunters, aren't you?"

Mara opened her mouth, but it was Angok who spoke first. "You pick things up when you spend too much time in old ruins. Mara just likes to pontificate. Are you nearly finished with that lock, Catgut?"

The Nizaani glanced back. "This is an ancient lock of the finest design. It has not been touched in centuries. The bolt is rusted and the tumblers are frozen. On top of that, I am attempting to pick it in the dark."

"All right, all right. Just tell me how much longer."

There was a click, then a thunk. Catgut pocketed her probes and stood, grinning.

"If you were nearly done," Angok said, "why be an ass about it?"

"I merely wanted you to appreciate my masterful handling of such a difficult task."

"I'll masterfully handle you right into a wall if you're not careful," Angok said. "Is it safe to open?"

"I believe so."

Angok nodded. "One way to be sure. Back up, everyone."

Kole and the others stepped aside, and Angok slid his axe into his belt. With his shield up, the Sundarin pushed on the handle. It turned, but the door only groaned softly.

"Put your back into it, bear-lover," Catgut said.

With a scowl, Angok put his shoulder against the door and shoved. Rusted hinges squealed in protest as the door ground open.

Kole cringed at the sound. He raised his lantern and glanced around, half-expecting something to come roaring out of the darkness toward them.

Darvin and Wolfun were nervously looking around as well, and even stoic Mara had her hammer in both hands, though her face betrayed no fear. Angok stepped back and drew his axe.

"Why do you all look so nervous?" Quintus snapped. "I already told you snakes have poor hearing."

"And what of geckos?" Catgut asked.

The sage shot her a withering look. "I'll have to consult my books." He hurried forward, peering through the open door. The rest of the party followed.

Lantern light spilled into a grand chamber that stood two stories high, the vaulted ceiling held aloft by slender pillars. In the center of the room stood a series of tables and high-backed chairs, hemmed in by towering shelves. At the far end of the room, where the light only just reached, Kole could see a staircase leading up to the second floor, where more shelves covered every wall.

A sweet musk wafted out of the chamber. With a noise of excitement, Quintus scurried through the doors, the rest of the party following close behind him.

There were books here: thousands of them. Kole's lantern light shone from waxy leather-bound spines and bundles of loose parchment.

But the shelves had more than tomes and manuscripts. The wall to Kole's left held nothing but rolled scrolls, untold hundreds of them lying stacked atop one another. Another shelf had been fitted with racks to hold hundreds of small glass spheres, much like the one he'd seen Quintus smash against the idol's great stone finger. As his light glinted from the spheres, he glimpsed wisps of smoke swirling in each—some silvery, some red, others black or golden or blue.

Sorcery, Kole thought. A shiver ran down his spine.

"It's intact," Quintus breathed as he stood in the center of the chamber and turned in place, staring at the shelves all about him. "It's all intact." He snapped his fingers at Wolfun. "Light! Bring me light. We must search!"

"Search for what?" the fisherboy asked as he hurried forward with his lantern, but Quintus was already ascending the staircase to the upper level, muttering to himself as he scanned the shelves.

Angok stared after them, shaking his head. "He's like a little boy trying to find his midsummer gift. All right, everyone. Let's take a water break, then we'll help the old man search." He turned to Darvin. "You and I will scour the lower level. Mara, where do you think we should start? Mara?"

Mara had wandered away from the others to stand at the foot of the stairs. On the landing halfway up was a statue: a woman draped in modest robes, her hands clasped in front of her. The statue stared imposingly down toward the bottom of the stairs, where Mara stood, unmoving.

Angok grunted. "Never mind. I can see you're busy." He settled down in an ancient chair and opened his waterskin.

Kole watched Mara while he unwrapped some hard cheese and took a bite. It seemed like she was having a profound moment, and Kole wasn't sure he should intrude. After a minute, though, his curiosity got the better of him. He returned the rest of his cheese to his pack and quietly joined her in looking up at the sculpture. The figure reminded him of the broken statue that stood near the river outside Hale's Crossing.

Mara surprised him by speaking first. "Here, at least, she stands uncorrupted."

"Is this the Architect?" Kole asked.

She nodded. "Imperious, isn't she?" There was reverence in her voice.

Before he could answer, he sensed Catgut approaching him.

"Enough statue-gazing, boy," the Nizaani said. "We must scout."

"Again?"

"This chamber is a dead end. If there is something alive in this place, I do not want to run into it here. Foreknowledge is the sharpest weapon. Come."

He glanced at Mara, half hoping she would demand they stay, but the woman was already turning away to light her own candle. Reluctantly, Kole lifted his lantern and followed Catgut back through the double doors.

She paused as she closed the doors, head cocked to one side. Glancing back at him, she said, "Remove your boots."

He looked down at them. "Really?"

"You sound like a stampeding wildebeest. Perhaps the Sundarin doesn't mind alerting every snake in the temple, but I do. Boots off."

Grumbling to himself, Kole pulled off his boots and socks. He hoped Quintus and the others found whatever it was they were looking for soon. All he wanted to do was get some treasure and get out of here. With each passing minute he felt more sympathetic to Wolfun's desire to leave.

Leaving his boots behind, Kole followed behind Catgut, bare feet padding against the cold stone floor. He felt strangely vulnerable without his boots on. Maybe it was all the talk of snakes. He kept glancing down at the floor, half-expecting to see a coiled serpent ready to bite his ankles.

They made the long trek back down the passage until they came once again to the central chamber and its spiraling staircase. The smell of decay hit Kole once again. It made him think of the stillborn piglets he'd disposed of up in Fairhill, and Farmer Gladen's prophecies of doom. The old man would have a heart attack if he knew what lay buried here in the swamp.

With whispers and gestures, Catgut directed Kole to shine his light through each of the archways leading off the central chamber. One archway led to another long passage similar to the one they'd already been down, while another held a stairway descending even further below ground. The walls of the stairway were carved into relief, but the figures standing here were more somber than those in the nave.

"Catacombs," Catgut whispered as she stared down the stairs.

"We're not going down there, are we?"

To his relief, Catgut shook her head. "It would be unwise. Let us... Wait. Bring the light over here."

As Kole brought the light closer, Catgut crouched at the top of the stairs and lifted something off the floor with the tip of her sword. It dangled down from the blade, a scrap of something golden and translucent. At first Kole thought it was some ancient silk or a long piece of unusually thin parchment. Then he saw the faint pattern on its surface. A pattern of scales.

Catgut lifted the scrap higher, but it began to break up and disintegrate. Fragments and dust floated down and settled on the stairs.

Kole swallowed. "Snakes shed their skin, don't they?"

"I believe so," she whispered.

"That had to come from a big one. As big as the ones you killed outside."
Catgut stood. "The skin cannot be old. Weeks or months at most."

Kole nodded. There was no question now: something was down here, and still alive. "I thought the temple was sealed. What does the snake eat?"

"Not us," Catgut said. "Not if we are careful. Silence from now on. Let us find the source of this smell."

They moved to the final archway, from which the stink of decay wafted. A short way down the passage, a set of stairs descended a few feet before continuing on. Catgut moved more quickly now, only giving the stairs a cursory search for traps as they made their way down.

The passage here was unusually bare compared to the more richly adorned halls they'd traveled before. There was something austere about the place.

No doors led off the passage, but shortly they reached another archway that opened up into a small room lined with chairs. As they entered the room, Kole saw that the chairs were made of white stone, though they seemed as delicate as the pillars that held the ceiling aloft. There was no other furniture in the room, no artwork.

But the smell of decay grew stronger. At the far end of the unadorned room was a simple wooden door. It hung open on broken hinges. As they carefully approached, Kole saw that there was something black smeared around the bottom of the doorway.

Catgut gestured to Kole, and he half-lowered the hood of his lantern to dim the light. The lantern trembled in his hand. His own breathing sounded deafeningly loud in his ears, no matter how quiet he tried to be.

Crooking a finger at him to follow, Catgut raised her sword and approached the doorway. Her slippered feet didn't make a whisper against the stone floor. She peered inside for a moment, then slipped through. Kole followed, the stink becoming overwhelming.

They were on the edge of a tall, circular room. The floor was almost entirely covered in black smears and rotting animal parts. In the dim light, Kole saw feathers, beaks, claws. Patches of animal fur.

And bones. Thousands of tiny bones.

A pair of steps led down to the sunken floor of the room. A thin layer of murky fluid coated the floor. Below the surface, Kole caught sight of a large gold disk set into the stone. It shone brightly even through the fetid liquid and the scraps of rotting flesh.

The stink threatened to turn Kole's stomach. He'd smelled death before, but this...

Catgut put her arm across her mouth to breathe through her sleeve, and Kole lifted the collar of his tunic up to his nose. What was this place? A feeding room? A latrine?

A drip fell from the ceiling, shimmering briefly in the lantern light. Kole glanced up and saw a large circular opening in the ceiling directly above the gold disk in the floor. Some kind of chute? He lifted his lantern to try to get a better look.

With a hiss, Catgut grabbed his arm and forced the lantern back down. Her fingers darted out and slipped the hood fully down over the lantern. In the sudden near-darkness, her silhouette pointed toward the room's only flat wall.

Just above head height, a large ornate stone lattice was set into the wall. Kole got the impression that there was another room beyond the lattice, but it seemed to have been designed so that little could be seen through the holes.

A light appeared on the other side of the lattice—the flickering light of a candle. Over the sound of Kole's pounding heart, he heard footsteps and shuffling.

Catgut touched his shoulder, gently nudging him back out the door. He nodded though he knew she could barely see him. Together they crept back into the antechamber and out toward the passage. When they were far enough from the bone-filled chamber that the light wouldn't be noticed, Kole lifted the lantern's hood again.

"Who was that?" Kole whispered. "That wasn't a snake. Snakes don't hold candles."

"We return to the others," Catgut said. "Quick and quiet. Move."

Kole steadied the lantern in both hands to keep it from rattling as they hurried quietly back to the library at the end of the passage. He kept glancing back at the darkness that followed them, but he couldn't hear or see anything.

The closed pair of library doors finally loomed ahead of them, a little candlelight escaping through the crack between them. Catgut creaked one door open just enough for the two of them to slip through, then she pushed it closed behind them.

Angok leaned over the second floor railing and called down to them. "Find anything?"

"We are not alone," Catgut said.

The Sundarin instantly straightened. His hand went to the axe at his belt. On the bottom floor, Mara and Darvin turned toward them.

"Were you followed?" Angok asked.

"No," Catgut said. "We were undetected. There is a round chamber down the western passage. That is the source of the smell."

"The evaluation chamber?" Mara asked.

The Nizaani shrugged. "Perhaps."

"It is where novices undertook their final evaluation before being raised to the cloth. The sun's light travels down the mirrored shaft of the Architect's staff to the chamber. There the novice stands, in the fullness of the divine light, while a priestly conclave interrogates the novice on matters both theological and personal."

"Not any more," Catgut said. "Now it is a pit for beasts to eat and shit. We saw a light coming from the neighboring room. Someone was there."

Angok frowned deeply. "Quintus. Have we found anything yet?"

The sage emerged from behind a shelf. "No. And I never will if you keep interrupting me."

Kole glanced around. "Where's Wolfun?"

"What?" Quintus looked back down the aisle. "He's...hmmm." The sage disappeared behind the shelves and then reappeared once more, holding a lantern. "He seems to be gone."

With a growl, Angok drew his axe and stomped down the stairs. "You didn't notice your lantern bearer wandering off?"

Quintus shrugged. "The lantern was still here."

"Clanfather's great sagging balls." He looked at Catgut. "Could it have been the fisherboy you saw?"

"Perhaps."

He grunted. "Better fetch him before he gets himself killed. Mara, you stay here and watch Quintus. Find that damned book." He jerked his head at Darvin. "You're with me, lad. Catgut?"

"This way." The Nizaani slipped back through the door. Swallowing, Kole followed.

CHAPTER
12

ATGUT LED THE WAY down the passage with Kole close behind her. Darvin and Angok followed.

The sound of the Sundarin's footsteps behind him reminded Kole that his boots were back outside the library. He thought about asking Catgut if he could go back for them, considering all the noise Angok was making.

He decided to keep his mouth shut.

"What does that fish-brained moron think he's doing?" Angok grumbled. "When I find him I'm going to wring his fat little neck."

"Quiet," Catgut hissed. She paused at a side passage, cocked her head to the side, then gestured with her sword. "This way."

Kole's stomach was in knots. He was already picturing what they would find—another dead body, swollen with snake venom. He glanced at Darvin, but the boy's face was a dark mask.

Catgut slowed and made a patting motion. "Dim the lights."

Kole and Darvin lowered the hoods on their lanterns. As Kole's eyes adjusted to the dark, he saw what Catgut had seen: a trickle of candlelight from the crack beneath a large door to their left. Catgut tugged a dagger from its sheath and held it in her off-hand as she approached the door.

Jerking his head at Darvin to follow him, Angok formed up on the other side of his door, axe in one hand and shield in the other.

"When we open the door," Catgut whispered, "give us light."

A soft clink came from inside the room. The candlelight flickered beneath the door.

Catgut put a hand on the door handle and glanced at Angok. Baring his teeth, the Sundarin nodded.

Catgut flung open the door. Fingers trembling, Kole jerked up the hood on his lantern. A heartbeat later, Darvin did the same.

By then, Catgut had already dived into the room. Angok rushed in two steps behind her, shield raised. Kole and Darvin followed.

There was a squeal of surprise, then a loud clatter of something hitting the floor. Angok lowered his shield.

They were in a large, comfortable chamber, the remains of a pale blue carpet still on the floor. A chandelier hung from the high ceiling, though Kole could see nowhere on it that candles could be set. Around the walls of the chamber were several identical cabinets with glass tops. Several of the cabinets had obviously been looted, the tops smashed. Fragments of glass were scattered around them, glittering like stars in the lantern light. Other cabinets were still intact, and in each Kole could see rods and scepters. Some were silver and of simple design, while others were inlaid with gold. Still others were fitted with jewels of red and blue and purple.

The wall at the far end of the room was not entirely solid. It formed a large lattice, through which wafted the stink of the round assessment chamber beyond. Facing the lattice were five high-backed chairs that were each extravagant enough to be thrones. Behind the chairs, in the center of the room, stood a life-sized silver statue of the Architect. In her hands she held a silver scepter topped with what looked like a spherical ruby.

And standing there, beside the Architect, was Wolfun. He stared at the four of them with a shocked expression on his face. A lit candle sat on a cabinet beside him, mounted unceremoniously on the pointed helm of an ancient stone statuette.

At Wolfun's feet was a sack. A dozen scepters of silver and gold spilled from the opening.

"Idiot," Darvin muttered.

"I ought to cut off your head and make your skull into a lantern," Angok said. "At least then you'd do your damned job."

The fisherboy ducked down and started hurriedly shoving the scepters back into the sack. "It's not like that grumpy bastard needed someone to hold his lantern. He didn't even notice me going."

Angok thrust his axe into his belt and stomped forward. Wolfun straightened, clutching the sack full of scepters in front of him. Even at his full height he was dwarfed by the Sundarin.

With a growl, Angok snatched the sack out of his hands.

"Hey!" the fisherboy whined. "Those are mine. I found them."

"A quarter share. That's what you get. Not whatever you get your grubby hands on. A quarter share." Angok shook the sack in his face. "And we don't divide it up until we're out of here."

"You haven't even tried to look for treasure yet!" Wolfun protested. "I didn't risk my life to look at dusty old books."

Catgut rolled her eyes at Kole as the two argued. She gestured to him and returned to the door, peeking out through the opening.

Kole started to follow her, but as he turned away he felt something tugging at him, like a fish hook in his mind. He paused, then glanced at the silver statue of the Architect standing in the center of the room.

The tugging sensation was an odd feeling—like nothing he'd ever felt before. It was gentle, subtle. But insistent. He could feel it in his head, in his gut. His feet carried him toward the statue.

The Architect appeared stern in this depiction, commanding and judgmental. She gripped the scepter in both hands, as if ready to either touch it to Kole's shoulder or hit him over the head.

Except there was something strange about her. Kole held the lantern up, peering deep into her eyes. The detail was extraordinary—each individual eyelash had been carved. He could even make out the striations of her irises, the tiny flaws. And the pupil.

A long, slitted pupil. A serpent's pupil.

Kole swallowed. The statue was still pulling at him. But the longer he stared, the less it seemed he was drawn to her face. His gaze dropped lower, to where the hem of her robe gathered around her feet.

There was something carved there into the robe. A line of symbols, each circular, and yet each subtly different. At first he thought they were simply decoration, a little detailing around the hem of the robe. But no— there was meaning there. He could almost sense it. He peered close, drawn in by the symbols.

He blinked, and he could still see them. Golden afterimages of the symbols flashed across his eyes, twisting and writhing. They remained even when he opened his eyes once again.

His heart began to hammer, but he couldn't tear his eyes away. As he scanned the line of symbols, he began to notice strange inconsistencies, symbols that seemed somehow out of place, though he couldn't explain how he knew that. It was like reading a note that had been altered—words squeezed in where they shouldn't be, letters replaced to subtly change the original meaning of the text.

"Felmen," a voice came to him from far away. "Felmen!"

Kole jerked back from the statue and spun around, panting. Darvin was standing next to him, staring and frowning. Angok and Wolfun were still arguing while Catgut guarded the door.

"What's the matter?" Darvin said.

Kole shook his head, blinking away the symbols that felt seared into his retinas. "Nothing. It's just...can you feel that?"

Darvin's frown deepened. "Feel what?"

He tried to find the words to explain, but he couldn't. Even now the sense of being pulled toward the statue was rapidly fading, and with it the memory. He felt himself grasping for the feeling, as if he was trying to recall a dream.

"All right, enough!" Angok barked, cutting short his argument with Wolfun. He picked up the candle Wolfun had set down and pushed it back into his hands. "No more out of you, fisherboy. Let's get back to the arcanum and see if Quintus and Mara are done yet."

"But there's still more treasure here," Wolfun said, gesturing to the display cases that he hadn't yet looted.

"Books first," Angok said firmly. "Then treasure." He bundled up the sack of scepters and stuffed it into his belt. "I'll hold onto this."

He headed to the door where Catgut was still keeping watch. Darvin glanced at Kole one last time, then the two of them followed the freebooters.

"Anything?" Angok murmured to Catgut.

"We appear to be clear," the Nizaani replied. "Let us try not to stomp so loudly on our way back, yes?"

She opened the door and slipped out, with Angok and Darvin following. As Kole was about to step through, he heard a hollow *thunk* from behind him. A freezing feeling suddenly lanced through his head. The circular symbols appeared in his vision once more, flaring gold.

He spun around to see Wolfun grappling with the scepter clutched in the Architect's hands. He'd tried to pull it free; instead, her arms had bent on some hidden joints, so now the scepter was tilted to the side, nearly horizontal.

Somewhere beneath Kole's feet, he could feel the vibration of some ancient mechanism. The fisherboy felt it too. He released the scepter and staggered back, eyes wide.

A faint light appeared through the lattice on the far side of the room. It was a cold, blue light—moonlight, Kole realized. He remembered what

Mara had said, about how the temple's novices were given their final assessment. Somewhere far above them, at the surface of the swamp, something had opened, allowing light to shine down into the assessment room.

But it was not the moonlight that drew Kole's eye. He stared at the statue of the Architect, at the symbols engraved around the hem of her robe. Before, he'd felt something leaking from them, like light through a keyhole. Now it was as if the door had been flung open wide, and the light inside was brighter than the sun. The symbols burned with a golden light, as dazzling and shifting as sunlight off the water.

"What in the hells was that noise?" Angok's voice was distant. "If you've broken something…"

Kole heard the Sundarin approach and then stop. He didn't turn around. He was staring at the Architect. A faint haze of golden smoke was rising off her, like steam on a hot summer's day.

Sorcery.

He suddenly became aware that the light of his lantern was changing as well. The candle flame blazed strong, taking on a sickly yellow tone, as if responding to the sorcery leeching from the statue of the Architect.

A soft squealing sound echoed through the grate. It was quiet at first, so quiet Kole didn't even notice it. It grew louder and louder.

Then there was a sickening splat and the squealing suddenly ceased. A moment later, he heard another screech slowly growing louder.

"Clanmother shield us," Angok breathed. The Sundarin pushed past Kole and rushed to the lattice just as there was another soft thud, and then another.

Kole didn't want to look. He wanted to turn and run. But he followed Angok anyway, woodenly stepping past the line of thrones and peering through the holes of the lattice.

He was staring into the round assessment chamber. A familiar, suffocating stink wafted up from the thin layer of dark fluid that covered the floor. Faint moonlight now filled the chamber, streaming down through the hole above. The golden disk set into the floor below shone brightly in the pale light.

As Kole watched, something that might have been a frog came tumbling out of the hole. It hit the floor hard and was still. A moment later, a squealing rat hit the floor next to it.

"What…what's happening?" Kole said.

"Feeding time," Angok murmured.

For a moment, the moonlight streaming into the assessment room was occluded. Kole heard something heavy scratching at the walls of the shaft.

A swamp cat fell through the hole and slammed into the floor, sending dark fluid splattering around it. The large, sleek creature gave a pitiful whine and then went still.

Kole flinched back from the lattice, turning away from the horror of it all. He stared at the faint yellow mist rising off the Architect.

"She's calling them," he whispered. "She's calling them to her."

Catgut and Darvin had reappeared in the room, drawn by the sound of the animals. Wolfun was staring wide-eyed at the statue of the Architect. His mouth moved but no sound emerged.

For a few seconds, everything fell silent once more. No more animals came tumbling down the shaft. Though the Architect was still giving off her strange sorcerous miasma, Kole almost allowed himself to believe that it might be over.

Then he heard the squawking. And the flapping. Swallowing, he turned back toward the assessment chamber and stared through the lattice.

A flurry of birds came pouring out of the shaft, shrieking wildly as they swarmed into the chamber. Wrens and stilt-walkers and herons and hawks and even a marsh owl swooped into the room in a great swirling morass of wings and feathers, each competing with the other to screech the loudest. Their combined calls hammered into Kole's skull and went echoing down the passages of the temple's underlevels.

Angok tugged his axe from his belt and spun away from the grate. His sudden movement shocked Kole out of his stupor. He staggered after the Sundarin as the giant stomped toward the door.

"Move," Angok barked. "Back to the arcanum. We're leaving."

Wolfun gaped, staring first at the statue and then toward the cacophony of the birds. "I...I didn't..."

"Move!" Angok roared, shoving the fisherboy toward the door.

Catgut grabbed Darvin by the shoulder and hauled him into the passage. Kole's bare feet slapped against the stone floor as they all took off running.

The lantern swung wildly in Kole's hand as he followed the Sundarin. Shadows jerked and danced across the white walls.

The screeching of the birds followed them down the side passage, back toward the main corridor. But there was something else as well. A faint rumbling that Kole could feel through his feet.

Ahead, Catgut reached the main corridor. She burst out into it, glanced toward the central chamber, and froze in her tracks. Darvin and Wolfun stumbled to a halt behind her. The Nizaani slowly shifted her feet and brought her sword and dagger up in a fighting stance.

Eyes wide, Darvin and the fisherboy began to back away. Catgut hissed over her shoulder. "Do not move."

Angok and Kole reached the intersection alongside them. Kole looked in the direction Catgut was staring. His mouth went dry.

A dozen pairs of huge, pale eyes stared back at him from the edge of the lantern light. Forked tongues darted out, tasting the air. He wondered if they could taste the sudden terror that had gripped his heart.

The snakes were huge. Each was a coil of black scales and sinewy muscle as wide as Angok's thigh. They filled the passage, lying atop one another like some great wave of black oil frozen in time. Their scales glistened in the dancing lantern light.

"Slowly," Catgut whispered. "We move slowly toward the arcanum. Perhaps they will go to their food."

Somehow, Kole knew everyone was thinking the same thing as him: *Perhaps we are the food.*

"Slowly," Catgut said again. Without taking her eyes off the snakes, she shifted her foot back.

Hissing, the tide of snakes surged forward.

With a roar, Angok shoved Kole back and charged in alongside Catgut, his shield raised. Catgut's hand flashed and a handle of a dagger suddenly appeared in the center of a snake's head. Twisting, the snake fell. The rest of the snakes swarmed over their dead brother, moving with unnatural speed.

Catgut had just enough time to pull a second dagger from its sheath. Then the snakes were on top of them.

A serpent reared back and struck at Angok, fangs bared. He swung his shield around and Kole heard a hollow thud as the snake's fangs met wood instead of flesh. Bellowing in a language Kole didn't understand, Angok brought his axe down and cleaved the snake's head from its body. A second snake was striking at him before the first one was even dead.

Catgut was a blur of flashing steel. Kole had never seen anyone move so fast. It was a dance in which each of her arms were independent and yet synchronized, twisting and striking and retreating. Gods, she nearly seemed like a snake herself.

Footsteps pounded away from Kole. He tore his eyes from the scene in front of him to see Wolfun sprinting back down the passage, his candle flame disappearing into the darkness.

Kole felt his own heart quake. Darvin stood beside him, lantern quivering in his hand, eyes darting between the snakes and the retreating fisherboy. He took a step back, turning to run.

"Hold!" Angok shouted over his shoulder as he slashed with his axe at another snake. "You run, we all die! Hold!"

And somehow, he did. With the hissing, and the shouting, and the sound of steel meeting flesh, every fiber of Kole's being screamed at him to run. But he didn't. He stood, holding the lantern aloft.

He could see his own fear reflected in Darvin's eyes. But the other boy, too, held his ground.

A snake lunged high, jaws snapping toward Angok's axe arm. The Sundarin had to twist and jerk back to avoid the bite. Swinging, he caught the snake's head against the blade of his axe and drove it into the wall. The clang of steel on stone rang down the passage.

From beneath the mass of headless, writhing snake bodies at Angok's feet, Kole caught sight of serpentine eyes flashing yellow in the lantern light. A forked tongue darted out, then the snake's jaw opened wide, lunging for the Sundarin's ankles.

"At your feet!" Kole shouted.

Angok stepped back quickly. The snake's fangs found only air. With a grunt, Angok slammed his shield down, striking the snake with the rim and pinning it to the floor. As it writhed, trapped, the Sundarin lifted his axe and brought it down hard, severing its head from its body.

But now Catgut was out of position, without anyone to guard her side. She seemed to realize it just as a snake lunged forward, coiling around her calf.

She cried out, slashing with her dagger at one snake while she hacked with her sword at the flesh of the huge snake wrapped around her leg. Dark blood spurted from the snake. But it was not enough to stop it from sinking its fangs into her leg.

"No!" Angok roared. Surging forward, he slashed at the serpent, his axe sinking deep into its flesh. In its death spasm, it released Catgut and twisted about on the floor. Angok kicked it away and drove back another snake that was trying to strike.

Catgut's dagger dropped to the floor with a clatter of steel. Putting a hand against the wall to steady herself, she continued fighting. Her face was set into a grim mask as her sword flashed out again and again. Kole's eyes were drawn to the red stain blossoming around the ragged holes in her breeches.

From somewhere far down the passage, toward the central chamber, there came a rumbling sound, and then a rattle. Through Kole's bare feet, he thought he could sense some distant vibration.

The remaining snakes appeared to sense it as well. All at once they squirmed back from Angok and Catgut, falling back from the flashing sword and the hacking axe. With a final, defiant hiss, they turned and slithered rapidly back into the darkness, leaving the thrashing bodies of their dead fellows behind.

Kole was panting, though the fight must have lasted less than a minute and all he'd done was hold a damned lantern. The tips of his fingers were tingling. Shaking, he tried to calm his breathing.

Catgut's face glistened with sweat. She turned toward Angok with glazed eyes and opened her mouth to speak.

Angok caught her as her knees buckled. Her head drooped forward into his chest.

"Help me!" Angok yelled.

Kole jerked forward, though his feet felt like they were fused to the stone. He took Catgut's weight over his shoulder. She was murmuring something, but either she was speaking gibberish or it was a language he didn't understand.

"What do we do?" Darvin asked, his voice breaking.

Angok's face was flushed, his eyes wide as he stared down at Catgut. Letting Kole take her weight fully, he stood and glanced back in the direction the snakes had gone.

"Back to the arcanum. We get everyone and we get out."

Darvin swallowed and stared at Catgut. "Is...is she...?"

"Move." Angok shoved Darvin with his shield. "Back to the others. While we have—"

A scream echoed down the passage. Wolfun's scream. A moment later came a woman's shout, followed by the squelching, crunching sound of something heavy hitting flesh.

"Ancestors' blood," Angok breathed, staring down the passage. "With me!"

He charged toward the sound of battle. Darvin stood frozen in place for a moment. He turned his wide eyes toward Kole. There was a question there. Kole was asking the same question himself.

Follow? Or run?

There was another clatter of steel as Catgut's sword slipped from her grip and hit the ground. Kole stared down at it, then thrust his lantern into

Darvin's free hand.

"Hold this."

Kole pulled Catgut over his shoulder. She'd lost consciousness entirely now. Crouching, he snatched up her sword. It felt unfamiliar in his grasp, the hilt slick with sweat. Black blood stained the blade, thick and oily and utterly unnatural.

He met Darvin's eyes. Swallowing, the other boy gave a slight nod.

They took off after Angok.

CHAPTER

13

HOUTS AND THUDS and hissing echoed down the passage toward them. As they ran, Kole could make out a pair of flickering candle flames in the distance, casting a pool of dim light that illuminated the open doors of the arcanum.

Quintus stood just outside the doorway, a lantern in one hand and something tucked under the other. He looked as grumpy and put-out as a fisherman inspecting a disappointing day's haul.

Hunched back against the passage wall, closer to Kole and Darvin, was Wolfun. His legs poked out from behind a plinth, jerking erratically as if he wanted to get up and run but couldn't find the strength. The dim light of his candle wavered.

And there, between Quintus and the fisherboy, were Angok and Mara. A fresh wave of the huge black serpents seemed to have surged out of a side passage. The two freebooters stood at the intersection in the pool of dim light, keeping the snakes from surrounding them entirely. Angok was fending off the striking snakes with his shield while his axe rose and fell, rose and fell.

Mara stood beside him, her hammer whirling in both hands. Her face was fixed and stern, eyes darting across the mass of snakes with cold distaste. Kole had thought her hammer would be a savage, brutal weapon, but she wielded it with precision, each blow well-timed and exact. Snakes struck at her, but her hammer swings caught them in the air, crushing their skulls one by one and sending the dead serpents whipping away.

And yet there were always more. With each snake that died, another two came surging out of the darkness of the side passage. Kole had never heard of snakes working together like this. Not this many at once.

"Light!" Quintus shouted over the din of fighting. "Bring more light! The serpents recoil from it."

Kole ran forward on legs he could no longer feel, Catgut's limp body draped over his shoulder. After a moment's hesitation, Darvin followed, a lantern in each hand.

As Darvin brought the light to bear, it almost seemed like the snakes did recoil. Their hisses grew more angry as they twisted, turning their large, pale eyes away from the lantern light.

"Push them!" Angok shouted, and together he and Mara stepped toward the tide of serpents, their weapons never slowing. The snakes twisted over each other, seemingly torn between the hunger to strike and the urge to retreat from Darvin's light.

"Now, Quintus!" Mara called over her shoulder. "While it's clear."

With a curt nod, the sage hurried along behind them as the two warriors held back the tide of snakes. He kicked at the cowering Wolfun as he passed.

"Up, boy."

The fisherboy just shook, frozen in place. His eyes were wide and unseeing. Quintus kicked him again, harder this time.

"Up, you sniveling wretch. Or shall we leave you for the serpents?"

That seemed to reach him. Blinking and crying, Wolfun rose to his feet.

"Come," Quintus said to Angok and Mara. "I have it. It is time to leave."

"Working on it," Angok growled back through gritted teeth as he kicked one snake away from him and sank his axe into the head of another.

"We should not delay."

"You want to swap places?" the Sundarin snapped back. "I'll hold the book and you can fight the snakes."

Quintus frowned, as if a thought had just occurred to him. "Why is the Nizaani not fighting? Where is…? Oh."

The sage finally seemed to notice Catgut slung over Kole's shoulder. His eyebrows lowered—the only sign of emotion to cross his face.

He tucked the book he was carrying under his other arm and reached out, lifting Catgut's head up by the chin. He stared at her for a moment, then released her, grunting. His eyebrows lowered even further.

"If we have to run," he said, looking into Kole's eyes, "you should leave her."

"I can carry her," Kole said.

Quintus opened his mouth as if to argue, then shut it again and gave a single nod. Behind, Mara and Angok slowly began to back toward them, striking at the snakes as they followed.

"Fighting retreat," Angok said. "Just like the Altar of the Once-Chosen."

Mara shook her head as she crushed a snake beneath her hammer. "We can't. It's too far. We will tire before we get back to the stairs."

"What, then?"

"Quintus," Mara said. "Oil."

"Hmm? Oh, yes, very well." The sage rummaged through his satchel for a few moments, then pulled out a small glass vial. He lifted it high above his head. "Ready?"

"This is a bad idea," Angok warned.

"You have a better one?" Mara asked.

"I'm sure I'll think of one once we're out of here. All right. On three."

Mara nodded. "One. Two. Three!"

As one, they surged forward, hammer crushing and axe slashing. With a roar, Angok slammed his shield into two striking snakes and shoved them back.

And then, an instant later, Angok and Mara fell back in unison. Serpents struck at the air where they'd been standing an instant before. A few feet of space opened up between the freebooters and the snakes. Coiling, the serpents prepared to pursue.

Quintus threw the vial. It sailed past Angok and Mara and shattered in front of the snakes. Clear fluid splashed across the floor, accompanied by a sweet, pungent scent. The serpents recoiled for a moment, then began to slither forward once more.

Turning, the sage snatched one of the lanterns from Darvin's hand and threw it at the pool of oil. The lantern's housing smashed as it hit the stone floor. The candle flame caught.

Fire suddenly filled the passageway, blazing hot. Kole flinched back from the sudden heat of it. He'd never seen oil erupt into flame with that much ferocity before.

"Stop your gaping and run!" Angok roared. Mara shoved Darvin down the passage as Quintus began to run ahead, pulling Wolfun with him.

Half-blind from the fire, Kole turned and followed.

Catgut wheezed and moaned as she bounced on his shoulder. Panting, he gripped her legs tight to keep her from falling off.

The light from behind him was already fading. He risked a glance over his shoulder and saw that what had been a blazing inferno seconds ago was now almost burnt out. The tide of snakes swarmed over the dwindling flames and gave chase.

Angok pounded along beside him, chain mail rattling. At the head of the pack, Quintus and Wolfun were pulling away. Kole could make out the fisherboy's candle flickering, threatening to extinguish itself as they ran. Beyond, he could see the opening to the wide central chamber, and the large stone column in the center that held the spiraling staircase.

Over the hissing of the pursuing snakes and the slapping of his bare feet on the stone, Kole heard a heavy, scraping sound from somewhere up ahead. Like leather dragged across stone. Despite the wave of snakes behind him, Kole slowed as he approached the archway to the central chamber.

Quintus and Wolfun were already through the doorway and running for the stairs when the creature emerged from behind the stairwell, wearing the darkness as a cloak. It moved like a great shadow rippling across the blackness beyond.

At first Kole thought it was another snake. It slithered like one, its long, fat body undulating as it scraped along the stone floor. Its black scales glistened as if wet in the candlelight. Muscles contracted and expanded as the huge, slithering thing pulled its great weight along.

But though it had a serpent's tail, a serpent's movement, it was something else. Something monstrous.

It reached out with a long, coiling arm, wrapping claws as long as a headsman's sword around the stairwell. The scrape of claws on stone sent a quiver up Kole's spine.

As the huge thing pulled itself forward, Quintus and the fisherboy came stumbling to a halt. Angok spat a curse and Mara whispered, "Champion protect us."

"What in the hells is that thing?" Darvin shrieked.

The creature turned its head toward Darvin, then returned its gaze to the two closest to it—Quintus and Wolfun. Huge white eyes stared down at them.

Though its face was scaled and black, it did not seem serpent-like. It was almost human, which somehow made it worse.

Perhaps, Kole thought, it had once *been* human.

Not anymore. Now it was swollen and monstrous, tall enough to nearly reach the chamber's ceiling. Scaly lips pulled back into a horrify-ingly wide grin, a grin that split the creature's long face in half. It was a smile of anticipation.

A hungry smile.

With a wail of unbridled terror, Wolfun went staggering back. Quintus threw himself in the opposite direction.

The abomination went for Quintus.

The muscles in its arm coiled, shoving itself away from the stairwell with enough force to make the chamber tremble. It slithered across the stone, reaching for the sage.

Mara appeared as if from nowhere, hammer flashing. In the dancing lantern light, she seemed to Kole like a warrior of holy light, some hero from ages past doing battle against a demon of shadow and smoke.

Her hammer crashed into the abomination's reaching claw. There was a sickening crunch, but the abomination gave no howl of pain, no screech of rage. In silence, it turned its grinning face on Mara.

The creature's tail whipped toward Mara. She brought her hammer up to guard.

The tail slammed into her, sending her flying into the wall. There was a sickening thud as her body hit stone.

Kole's bare feet felt frozen to the cold floor. He gaped at the monstros-ity as it turned back toward Quintus, still grinning. The sharp points of its teeth glinted in the light from Darvin's lantern.

The hissing of snakes behind grew stronger. He glanced back just as one broke free of the pack, slithering rapidly toward him. Quivering, Kole raised Catgut's sword.

With a roar, Angok stepped between him in the snake, the blade of his axe catching it just as it reared back to strike. As the serpent fell, the rest of the endless tide swarmed closer.

They're herding us, he realized in horror. *They're herding us toward their master.*

"The stairs, lad!" Angok shouted over his shoulder. "It's the only way out."

Swallowing, Kole nodded. Gripping Catgut tight, he turned back toward the chamber.

Mara lay crumpled in a heap against the wall, groaning. On the other side of the chamber stood Wolfun, candle in hand, wide eyes staring at the slithering abomination. He was groaning incoherently—the sound of a broken man.

Darvin was edging slowly around the side of the room, away from the creature. He kept shaking his head as if he couldn't believe what he was seeing.

In the shadows on the other side of the chamber, Kole saw Quintus try to dart toward one of the archways leading out of the room. He ducked beneath the creature's first strike, moving with a nimbleness Kole had never seen the sage display before. His cloak swirled behind him as he sprinted for the archway.

He reached it just as the abomination's second strike found him. A claw swept down from above and plunged straight through Quintus's left calf, pinning him to the floor. The sage howled.

Kole's stomach twisted. Slowly, the abomination began to scrape its claw along the floor, pulling Quintus back toward it. A long, split tongue squirmed out of the creature's mouth and slathered its lips.

Kole reached Darvin's side and they shared a wide-eyed look. The entrance to the stairwell was close, so close. But just as Kole took a step toward it, the abomination's long tail twisted about and slammed down in front of the opening. The creature didn't turn away from Quintus. But it knew. It knew they were trying to escape. There was a hungry intelligence behind those huge, white eyes.

The abomination lifted its claw, pulling Quintus up off the floor. His cries reached a new pitch as he dangled upside down from the claw that pierced his leg. His spectacles clattered to the floor.

As the howling filled the chamber, Mara stirred. Kole had thought her dead for certain, but now she lifted her head, blood trailing from her lips. Blinking, she stared at the dangling Quintus. Her hand groped for her hammer.

"No!" Quintus's voice rang out. Candlelight flickered across his pale, drawn face. His expression was pained, but his eyes were clear as he stared at Mara. "I don't matter. Only the book matters."

Back down the passage, Angok's axe clanged against stone again and again as he held the wave of snakes at bay. Shaking her head, Mara tried to rise.

Darvin made a run for it, heading for one of the other passages. Kole stayed where he was, frozen in place.

As the abomination slowly dangled Quintus above its waiting mouth, the sage threw the book. It hit the stone floor with a thud and slid to Mara's feet. Fumbling at his satchel, Quintus drew out a fist-sized glass sphere. Blue smoke swirled within.

"No," Mara rasped.

From the passageway behind, Angok let out a cry of pain. Kole suddenly became aware that he could no longer feel Catgut breathing.

His world was tumbling down around him. There was no escape.

This couldn't be happening. How could it have all gone so wrong? What madness had driven him into this temple, to die so far from home?

"Da," he whispered. "Ma. Arabeth. I'm sorry."

Across the chamber, the abomination unhinged its jaw. Quintus dangled above its open maw, blood streaming down his leg. He raised the sphere.

"Get the book to the Citadel," he said to Mara. "Get it home."

Despite the pain that was clear in his face, his lip quirked into what Kole realized was supposed to be a smile. It was the first one he'd ever seen the sage give.

"The path is clear," he said.

Then he hurled the sphere at the abomination's leering face.

Glass shattered. Sorcerous blue light filled the chamber, casting tendrils out in every direction. For a moment, all sound was stripped from the world, leaving Kole with nothing but the beat of his own heart.

Then the tendrils of blue light snapped back to a single point, and the world exploded.

CHAPTER

14

KOLE WAS IN DARKNESS. The deepest, purest darkness he had ever known. Where was he? Had he gone blind?

"I'm scared," he whispered.

His words vanished as soon as they were spoken, swallowed by the void.

"Ma?" he said. "Da?"

The words disappeared into the black. There was nothing—no sound, no smell, no taste. Kole couldn't even feel his own body.

"Please," Kole whimpered. "I'm scared."

And you always will be.

"Who said that?" Kole tried to turn his head, but he didn't seem to have one anymore.

Every time I step up to the headstone, every time I lift that sword, I'm scared. I'm terrified.

"Da? Da, where am I? I can't see."

You will, in time. And you'll be scared by what you see. That's all right. It doesn't matter. It only matters what you do.

"What do I do?"

There was no response.

"Da? What do I do?"

There was nothing. Nothing but the dark.

And then: pain. It was distant at first, numbed as if by one of his ma's special tinctures. Slowly, though, it began to grow. It lanced up from his leg—he had a leg, now—a jolting, agonizing pain. It dragged him out of the darkness, dragged him blinking back to life.

Thirty feet away a lantern had fallen, the candle inside flickering dimly, nearly burnt out. Thick white dust filled the air.

Lying against an archway, hand outstretched toward the fallen lantern, was a slumped figure. The figure lay there, barely moving, with only a soft groaning to indicate that they were still alive.

Darvin, Kole realized. As the name came to him, he remembered where he was. He remembered the idol of Gnothea. He remembered the passages below the buried temple. And he remembered what they'd found down here.

The chamber ceiling whirled overhead. Head pounding, he looked down at himself.

His right leg was crushed beneath a slab of white stone the width of a small tree trunk. Just past his knee, his trouser leg was flattened almost to the floor. Through the rips in the fabric he could see bloodied purple flesh.

A wave of horror overwhelmed him. "No, no, no," he rasped.

He knew in an instant that there was no saving the leg. It was utterly crushed, mangled beyond repair.

The pain in his thigh was excruciating, but he could barely feel anything at all beyond his knee. Perhaps the fallen rock had severed his lower leg entirely.

The thought made his stomach roil. Bile spilled into his throat. Moaning, he tried to roll onto his side. A jolt of agony stabbed from his crushed leg up into his spine, turning his moan into a howl.

Spots appeared in his vision. He vomited onto the floor next to him. That only brought more pain. He bit down on his hand to stifle his scream. Despair filled him, as black as the chamber around him.

He became aware of other sounds. A soft scraping. And a hissing.

Blinking the spots from his eyes, he looked over at Darvin's unconscious form again. In the darkness beyond, Kole saw a shape slithering slowly toward the boy.

The snake's tongue darted out, tasting the air. Its flesh was scored with a long, bleeding cut, but that didn't appear to be dissuading the creature. It fixed its pale eyes on Darvin and slithered toward him.

"No!" Kole shouted, hoarse. "Get away from him!"

The serpent paused, raising its head to stare at him.

Reaching about him, Kole's hand closed on a small chunk of white stone.

"Get away!" He hurled the stone at the snake.

It sailed harmlessly over the creature's head and clattered away into the dark. The snake tasted the air again. Then its eyes moved back to Darvin and it began to slither closer.

Kole let out a moan of frustration. In all his life he'd never felt so helpless. So alone. He reached for another stone, one small enough for him to throw, but all he could find were large chunks too heavy for him to lift.

"Darvin," he said. "Darvin, wake up. Get up!"

The boy gave a soft groan and then went quiet again. The snake glided closer.

With a curse, Kole cast his eyes around him, searching for something—anything. At the edge of the candlelight, half buried beneath a pile of white stone, Kole glimpsed something metallic glinting in the light of the candle.

Catgut's sword.

In desperation, he reached for it, though he knew it was too far away. As the serpent's hissing grew louder, Kole stretched out, fingers grasping against the cold stone.

A dizzying new wave of agony ripped upward from his crushed leg. He couldn't stifle his scream this time.

With the room spinning around him, Kole stared down at his mangled leg. The flesh seemed to pulse in time with his own pounding heart.

A moment of calm settled over him. It was warm, familiar, like a well-loved blanket. The pain receded into the background. He could no longer hear the snake slithering slowly toward Darvin. He could no longer hear the soft clatter of falling stones.

But he could hear the beat of his own heart, loud and yet unhurried. It was perfect—an untiring machine pumping blood to every inch of his body, as it had done since before he was born. He could feel that blood now, could feel it flowing through arteries and veins, warm and crimson.

He could hear his breathing as well. He could hear the creak of his diaphragm expanding, the popping of a thousand minuscule pockets inflating, filling his lungs with air. And he could hear Darvin's breathing as well, and the beating of the snake's heart.

No, that wasn't quite right. He couldn't hear them. He could sense them, though, like the warmth of tiny fires.

His attention floated over those other life flames, then returned to his shattered leg. He could see something in his mind's eye. Symbols, like those he'd seen carved into the hem of the Architect's robe. Symbols for each drop of blood, each scrap of torn flesh, each splinter of bone. They burned in his head, in his soul.

He frowned, puzzling over the symbols. One by one their meanings were becoming clear to him. He could see how they were all broken apart. He could see how they could all fit together once more.

I can fix this, he thought, staring down at the shifting symbols written across the fabric of reality. It would be like reassembling a letter torn into pieces. Just a puzzle. A simple thing.

He realized suddenly he was speaking aloud. The words leaving his mouth were of no language he'd ever spoken before. But they had meaning, just the same—meaning he understood. It was as if he'd always known these words, though he'd forgotten them for a time.

It was the language of creation.

The words seemed to twist and dance as they left his mouth. He could feel something warm trickling upward from the corners of his lips. A thin red veil passed across his eyes.

His broken flesh began to move. It stretched, flowed, like molten metal reshaping itself in the hands of some invisible entity. From beneath the huge chunk of white stone that had fallen on him, the bubbling flesh and bone of his leg began to flow and pool.

Even as he spoke the words that reshaped his flesh, some part of Kole was looking on with horror. In his own voice he could hear the same tuneful gibberish Mertyn Walter had spoken at the headstone. That same sorcerous language that the condemned fisherman had used to try to escape his bonds.

Sorcery. He was using sorcery. He was infected.

The terror of that realization was almost as great as the horror he'd felt staring down at his mangled leg. He was a sorcerer, now. Destined for madness.

And yet he didn't stop speaking the words that were reshaping his flesh. Not because he couldn't. But because he didn't want to. Because he didn't want to die down here, trapped beneath the earth. Because he didn't want to watch Darvin die, as Tilda had died out in the swamp. Not when he still had a chance to save him.

So he did not stop. He spoke quickly, drawing the words from some part of his brain he didn't know existed. Perhaps it had not existed until Mertyn infected him with the sorcerer's plague. He drew on the words, stringing them together, ordering reality to reshape itself as he saw fit.

And reality obeyed.

As the flesh of his leg flowed out from beneath the fallen stone, he could feel splinters of bone begin to fix themselves back together. Torn muscle knitted together as skin reformed. He could not draw back the blood that had already been spilled, but he felt networks of blood vessels reconnecting.

It hurt, but not unduly so. No more than holding your hand a little too close to a flame. The sight of the leg reforming was more horrible than anything he could feel.

And then, suddenly, it was done. He sang one last command, a mark to punctuate the end of the spell, fixing it in place. The veil of red lifted from his eyes. He stared down at what emerged from the torn leg of his trousers.

The leg that had reformed seemed thinner than the one alongside it. The flesh was pale, almost translucent. He could see veins snaking beneath the skin. A dull ache remained, like a memory of an old injury.

But when he told his toes to wiggle, they wiggled. When he told his leg to bend, it bent.

This is madness, he told himself. It had to be. He'd seen his leg crushed to pulp. He'd felt it. He could still feel it.

And yet he couldn't deny what his eyes told him. His leg was back. He'd reshaped it.

Perhaps he was already mad. Everyone knew that the sorcerer's plague took hold quickly. Once someone was infected, the power of sorcery tore their mind asunder. It drove them to great and terrible acts, until finally they destroyed themselves or were brought down by those who had once been their friends.

And yet…and yet he didn't feel mad. He felt scared. Terrified. But not mad.

If he were truly mad, though, would he even be able to tell?

A hiss brought him crashing back to reality. He tore his attention from his leg and looked over at Darvin.

The snake was at Darvin's side. Kole didn't know how much time had passed while he'd reforged his leg. In some ways it had felt like hours, but the snake had only slithered a few feet closer. Perhaps it had been distracted by his sorcerous chanting.

Not now, though. Now, the snake only had eyes for Darvin. As the boy groaned softly, the serpent reared back, jaws opening.

Kole grabbed the hilt of Catgut's sword from where it lay half-buried beneath the stone. Leaping to his feet, he charged across the distance and swung the sword at the snake.

The creature jerked back, hissing angrily at him as the sword blade whistled past. Kole staggered toward it, raising the sword once more. His reformed leg felt weak, shaky, but it held his weight, carried him forward.

"Back!" he roared, swinging the sword again.

Hissing, the snake struck at him.

His blade cleaved into the side of the snake's sinuous body. Its jaws snapped shut an inch from Kole's forearm.

Shouting wordlessly, Kole continued swinging the sword. The snake was flung into the wall, twisting and bleeding. With a final hiss, it slithered away into the darkness.

Kole swayed on his feet. He felt like he hadn't eaten a meal in three days. His hands wouldn't stop shaking.

From some distant corridor he could hear movement—the slithering of more snakes. He didn't know if the monstrosity that had attacked Quintus was still alive, but some of the serpents still were. He had to get out of here.

Summoning what strength he had left, he picked up the broken lantern and held it aloft. Shapes resolved in the darkness.

Not far away, amid the same pile of rubble that had held the sword, Kole could now make out the shape of a slender woman. Catgut must have been flung from his shoulder when the explosion—or whatever it was—had gone off. Her skull and chest were crushed by a chunk of stone the size of a large sow.

He didn't know whether she'd still been alive when the stone had crushed her. Maybe the snake bite had already killed her.

Now, though, she was dead. That he was sure of.

Swallowing, he staggered over to her and crouched at her side amid the rubble. He couldn't see her face—for that he was thankful. He thought for a moment about leaving the sword with her, but he reconsidered. He wasn't out of here yet.

He spied the leather scabbard buckled to her belt. After a moment's hesitation, he pulled on the belt, hacking through it with the sword until he finally cut the sheath free. He slid the sword into the scabbard and tucked it through his own belt.

Picking up the lantern once more, he turned in place.

"Is there anyone else here?" he called out. His voice sounded frail, hollow. "Angok? Mara?"

There was no response except the hissing of distant snakes.

Fighting down the urge to curl into a ball on the floor, Kole returned to Darvin's side.

"Darvin. Darvin, are you all right?"

The boy groaned softly and said nothing. Kole could see now he was bleeding from a large gash on his scalp.

Kole called Darvin's name again, shaking him. But still he couldn't rouse him.

A thought occurred to Kole. A mad thought, perhaps. He looked down at his own reforged leg, then at the gash on Darvin's head. The boy was badly injured. Concussed, maybe, or worse.

But what if…what if Kole could fix him? Like he'd fixed his own leg. Could he do it?

He had the power inside him. He could hear the words he'd need gathering in the back of his head.

With a sudden bolt of fear, he banished the words. What had he been thinking? He couldn't use sorcery. Not on Darvin. Maybe Kole hadn't gone mad yet, but it was only a matter of time. If he used his sorcery to fix Darvin, he would infect him. The boy might survive the temple only to face a headsman's sword when he returned to town.

Gods, maybe he already had infected Darvin. He hadn't been near Darvin when he'd spoken the incantation, but he wasn't sure how far the infectious miasma could spread.

That didn't matter now. He had to get Darvin out of here. He had to get him back to town, where they could call for a physik.

"Come on," Kole said, though he didn't know if he was talking to Darvin or himself. "We have to go before the snakes come back."

Crouching, he lifted Darvin off the floor. The boy groaned in pain, but didn't wake.

Darvin was heavier than Catgut. So heavy Kole wasn't sure his newly reforged leg could take the weight. Gritting his teeth, Kole pulled the other boy over his shoulders. He staggered, but didn't drop him.

Turning in place, he inspecting the shattered chamber.

The blast had left him disoriented, but at last he found his bearings. He could just make out the central column that held the staircase back up to the temple's upper levels. Debris surrounded it. Straining under Darvin's weight, he made his way forward, searching for the doorway.

Something squelched beneath his bare foot. Something wet and sticky. Kole stumbled back.

Chunks of flesh were scattered about the floor ahead of him, like huge fillets of fish. Raising his light higher, Kole saw their source.

What remained of the grinning abomination was slumped back against the central column, a great pile of stinking meat. The top half of the creature appeared to have exploded from the inside out, scattering gore across the floor nearby. The abomination's long, fat tail lay unmoving in front of the doorway to the stairwell.

Kole stared at the dead creature in disbelief. What had Quintus thrown at the thing to cause it to explode in such a way? It had to be more sorcery. He thought he could feel it lingering in the air. It prickled at his skin and tasted sour in the back of his throat.

Darvin groaned again. Kole stopped staring at the abomination. It was dead, that was all that mattered.

Along with Quintus. Along with everyone, maybe.

No. Not everyone. Darvin might yet be saved.

Ignoring the warm squelch of the monster's flesh underfoot, Kole staggered forward. The creature's giant tail was partially blocking the way, so he had to make his way around it to get to the doorway.

As he did so, he heard a sound coming from somewhere off to his left. At first he thought it the hissing of a snake. Then he heard it again. Not hissing, but a shaky, sobbing breath. He turned, raising his lantern.

"Hello?"

There was no response, but the sound came again. Kole cast a longing glance toward the stairwell, then steeled himself and crept slowly toward the sound.

The candlelight fell on a figure sitting hunched over in the darkness. Wet, staring eyes glinted in the light.

It was Wolfun. White dust covered him from head to toe, making him as pale as a ghost. As Kole edged closer, he could see tear streaks running through the dust on the boy's cheeks.

"Wolfun," Kole said. "It's me. It's Felmen. Are you all right? Are you hurt?"

The fisherboy didn't appear to hear him. He just stared straight ahead, past the candlelight and into the darkness.

Kole reached the boy's side. Blood trickled from one of Wolfun's ears, staining the neck of his tunic. Had he lost his hearing in the explosion? Had he lost his mind?

Grunting with the effort of holding Darvin, Kole crouched down in front of Wolfun, putting himself directly in the boy's eye line. He waved the lantern back and forth in front of the fisherboy's face.

Finally, Wolfun blinked, eyes shifting to meet his. His forehead creased in confusion.

"It was dark," the boy muttered. "So dark."

"Where's your candle?" He swept his light around until he spotted the fallen candle, still mounted to the small statuette. "There."

The boy stared at the candle but didn't move.

"Pick it up," Kole said. Maybe he was imagining it, but the hissing of snakes seemed to be growing nearer. "Come on. We have to get out of here."

Frowning in confusion, the fisherboy picked up the candle and shook the dust off it. He stared at it as if he'd never seen a candle before in his life.

Kole squashed his impatience. "Light it. Here." He held out his broken lantern. "Quickly."

With painful slowness, Wolfun lifted his candle and held the wick to Kole's flame. It caught, and the fisherboy withdrew the candle, staring at the new flame with wide eyes.

"Listen to me," Kole said. "Darvin is hurt. Everyone else is dead. Do you understand? We have to get out of the temple. We have to get home."

"Home," Wolfun echoed.

"That's right. Can you stand? I can't carry you. I have to carry Darvin."

The boy nodded, still dazed. Shakily, he rose to his feet. He had cuts and scrapes across his arms, but he didn't appear to be seriously injured.

"All right," Kole said. "That's good. Let's go. Up the stairs over there. We—"

He twisted in place, suddenly sensing that he was being watched. His lantern light glinted off a half-dozen pairs of pale, serpentine eyes coming toward them out of the darkness.

"Go!" he shouted. "Run!"

With a yelp, Wolfun took off toward the stairs. Kole staggered after him.

Hissing, the snakes gave chase.

Kole's bare feet slipped on the slick floor. Darvin's weight was badly unbalancing him. But he kept his feet and stumbled on.

Wolfun disappeared through the doorway, taking his light with him. Kole was two seconds behind.

The fisherboy was already out of sight, his panicked footfalls echoed back down the spiraling staircase. Panting, Kole began the ascent.

He didn't glance back. He couldn't risk it. But he could hear the snakes, hear them slithering up the stairs behind him. Darvin moaned with every step. Kole didn't slow. He couldn't. The muscles in his reforged leg were already aching, but he couldn't stop.

He burst out of the top of the stairwell to see Wolfun's candlelight wavering in the distance ahead of him.

"Wait!" Kole called out, his muscles burning. "Help me with Darvin!"

But if the boy heard, he didn't slow. Cursing, Kole followed him down the wide, pillar-lined corridor.

He could no longer tell if the snakes were still following him. Sound echoed strangely in the upper levels of the temple. He ran on anyway despite the aches and the fiery pain in his muscles, praying all the while that his wavering candle flame wouldn't blow out.

The archway to the nave appeared ahead of him. When he passed through it, he saw that Wolfun had gained even more ground over him. He appeared now as little more than a single flickering star amid an endless blackness.

Kole staggered on and on, across the temple floor and up the grand staircases. He ran until he could no longer feel the pain in his bones. He ran until he could no longer think of the snakes, or the dead freebooters, or the specter of his own sorcery hanging over him. All he could think of was putting one foot in front of the other.

The blackened bodies of the temple's ancient worshipers sat silently in the pews, watching him as he ascended. At last he reached the uppermost mezzanine of the four-tiered nave. He hurried after the fisherboy's disappearing candlelight, running past the figures carved into relief on the wall of the temple—ancients blind to the infestation of snakes that curled about their feet.

He came finally to the doorway at the back of the temple, to the spiraling staircase that led back to the Architect's serpentine head. Back to the surface. Back to the light.

Wolfun was already climbing the stairs ahead of him by the time Kole staggered through the doorway, gasping for breath. Kole could just make out the distant footfalls echoing above him. Kole took a moment to catch his breath, then started up after the other boy.

He'd taken two steps when a realization suddenly hit him. His stomach clenched.

"Wait!" he shouted after the fisherboy. "The traps!"

Before the words had left his mouth, he heard a crunch, followed by the sharp sudden screech of metal against stone. The footfalls stopped. Everything fell silent.

Something heavy pulled at his gut as he ascended the stairs. He didn't want to look, but he couldn't stay here, not forever.

Partway up he found Wolfun.

The boy was still standing, held in place by the steel spikes that had pinned him to the inner wall. Beneath his feet, the stair was slightly sunken, the chalk X smudged where he'd stepped on it. One spike had pierced his temple, while another had gone through the side of his chest. His hands hung limply at his sides, hovering over his fallen candle.

Kole suddenly found he didn't have any strength left. With a pitiful whimper, he slumped against the wall, dropping down onto a stair. Darvin moaned and muttered something as he hit the ground next to him, then went quiet again.

Kole put his head in his hands. He couldn't look at Wolfun. The despair that he'd been trying to push down threatened to come spilling back up. It wanted to break him, like it had broken the fisherboy.

Death. He was surrounded by it. It had been a part of his life ever since he was born, but this…this…

Blood dripped from Wolfun's fingers onto the fallen candle and snuffed out the flame. Kole looked at his own light. The candle inside the broken lantern was now little more than a puddle of wax with a wick sticking out. It wouldn't be long now until that flame burnt out too, leaving him alone in the dark with an unconscious Darvin and a dead Wolfun.

That's what you wanted, isn't it? Isn't that why you came out here?

He screwed his eyes up tight, opened them again. It was true. He'd come with the freebooters to get away from Hale's Crossing, to get away from Ma and Da and Arabeth. He'd come out here fearing he was infected with sorcery, trying to protect those he loved from suffering the same fate as Mertyn Walter's family.

Now he knew he was infected. Kole looked down at his leg, stretching it out in front of him. He could no longer remember the words he'd spoken, the spell he'd conjured to reforge his leg. It seemed to him now like a dream half-remembered upon waking. The evidence was clear, though. His leg had been crushed, and now it wasn't.

He was a sorcerer.

And yet he still didn't feel mad. The look that Mertyn Walter had given him before he died had been a look of pure joy. A madman's joyous delusion.

Kole didn't feel joy. He felt sick to his stomach. He wanted to weep. He wanted to crawl into a ball and wait for the snakes to find him. But he did not feel mad.

Perhaps the madness would come later. Perhaps it was an insidious thing, burrowing so slowly into his mind he would never notice it.

Darvin muttered something in his senseless state. "No. Da, no! I didn't do it." His words faded away into murmured rambling, then he went quiet entirely.

Kole looked down at the unconscious boy, at his bloodied scalp and his drawn, pale face. Kole had hated Darvin for so long. Now, though, he only felt pity.

He looked up at the skewered Wolfun. If Kole and Darvin died down here as well, no one back home would ever know what had happened to any of them. There would be no funeral. Just pain and lingering doubts.

Sighing, Kole stood. Mad or not, he knew what he had to do.

The steel spikes that had skewered the fisherboy blocked the stairwell, but they were old, rusted. He pulled on one, trying to force it back into its hole. He could only pull it back an inch before his strength gave out and it snapped back into place. It must've been set on a powerful spring.

Holding up the lantern to inspect each of the spikes, he decided the third one down was the most badly rusted. The spike had missed Wolfun's leg when it sprang from the wall, blunting its point instead on the stone wall opposite.

He glanced down at his bare feet, then returned to Darvin. Crouching by the boy's feet, he said, "Sorry, but I think I need these more than you right now."

Kole unlaced Darvin's boots and tugged them off. They were well-worn but sturdy. He took Darvin's socks as well, then pulled the boots on over top. They fit well enough.

Returning to the spikes, Kole braced himself against the walls as best he could. Ignoring the sight of the dead fisherboy, he gritted his teeth and brought his foot down hard on the side of the most rusted spike.

The metal groaned at his kick. Flakes of rust spilled off the pole as it bent slightly.

He slammed his foot into the spike again and again. With each kick it bent a little more. Kole realized the pole must be hollow inside. Where the rust was thickest, the metal began to crack and split.

He gave it one last kick and the spike finally broke with a tortured groan. It didn't come loose entirely, but Kole was able to crouch down and bend it by hand until there was enough space for him to crawl through.

From somewhere far below, Kole heard a scraping sound echoing up the stairwell. The sound of tortured metal had drawn something's attention.

Quickly, he snatched up Wolfun's fallen candle and wiped the blood off the wick. After lighting it on the guttering flame of his own burnt-down candle, he replaced the candle and set the lantern down on the other side of the spikes.

Grabbing Darvin under the arms, he started to drag him through the opening he'd made in the bars. Even with one of the spikes out of the way, it was a tight squeeze, made all the more awkward by having to crawl through while dragging Darvin with him. The boy moaned in pain with every twist and bump.

Another scraping sound echoed up from somewhere below, closer this time.

And then finally they were through the bars. Without stopping to catch his breath, Kole hauled Darvin back over his shoulder, picked up the lantern, and continued the ascent.

He found the second marked stair further up and stepped over it, careful not to trigger the trap. Then he staggered up and up, following the spiral until his thighs burned and his head felt light and dizzy.

And then: light. Not just the flickering orange candlelight swaying in his hand. A cold, pale light was filtering down the stairwell from up above.

Moonlight.

Hope surged in Kole's heart. Pushing his protesting muscles on, he hurried up the last few stairs.

He burst out of the stairwell onto the slick stone of the idol's great gaping mouth. Though it was nighttime, the glow of the moonlight made him squint after so many hours spent deep below the earth.

The still, silent swamp greeted him with indifference as he stumbled out of the idol's mouth. The shadowed shapes of gnarled trees stared down at him from every direction. The familiar stink of the swamp returned, though now Kole found it comforting when compared to the ancient musk he'd been breathing in the temple.

The sky above the clearing was growing gray in the east. Not far from dawn. Exhaustion suddenly pulled at his bones and scratched at his eyes as he realized he'd been awake all night. But he couldn't stop now. He'd need every hour of sunlight he could get if he was going to return to Hale's Crossing before Darvin was beyond help.

He splashed through the shallow swamp water, lantern held aloft. From the shadow of a bog tree nearby there was a whinny of panic.

"It's all right, Mugsy," he called out in the most soothing voice he could muster. "It's just me. It's Kole."

He approached the packhorse slowly, holding the lantern so it would illuminate him. As he got closer, the mare's shape resolved itself beneath the shadow of the tree she had been hitched to.

The packhorse stamped her hooves nervously, then went still. Her eye shone in the lantern light as she studied him.

The creature looked no worse for wear. The night was warm enough that she didn't seem cold, and the oats and water bucket that had been set in front of her were still half full. It seemed like she'd been asleep until he startled her.

Kole made his way out of the swamp water and set down the lantern. He looked back toward the idol's gaping mouth. No snakes emerged. Slowly, he approached the horse, hand extended. His shoulder was begging him to set Darvin down, but he was afraid if he did so he wouldn't be able to pick him up again.

The horse snorted and eyed him warily, but she allowed him to lay his hand on her nose.

"There, Mugsy," he said softly, stroking her nose. "It's all right. We're getting out of here."

Mugsy glanced at Darvin, then looked back at him.

"They…they're all dead, girl. We're all that's left. I'm sorry."

He didn't know why he was talking to the horse, but it comforted him somehow. He gave Mugsy one last pat on the nose and moved to her side.

The freebooters had taken the supplies off the packhorse before they'd gone into the temple, stacking them up beside the tree along with the packs he and the other porters had been carrying through the swamp. Carefully, Kole heaved Darvin up so he was sitting astride the horse. The boy threatened to slide off almost immediately. Kole quickly fetched a rope from the pile of supplies and tied Darvin's legs to Mugsy's harness. It wasn't pretty, but it would keep him from falling.

Working quickly, Kole affixed the half-full water barrel to Mugsy's harness and stuffed some saddlebags full of rations and oats. He put a few more candles and blankets and another rope into his pack, along with his sketchbook. He kept Catgut's sword as well, threading his belt through the scabbard so it wouldn't tangle in his legs during the journey. Almost everything else he left behind. As the sky started to lighten, he wrapped a crude bandage around Darvin's head and unhitched the packhorse.

"Come on, Mugsy," he muttered, leading the horse away from the serpentine head of the idol of Gnothea. "Let's go home."

CHAPTER
15

IT WASN'T LONG until Kole began to fear that he was lost.

The swamp was a maze of fetid water and tangleweed. So many routes were impassable, blocked by deep water or walls of brambles. There were no landmarks to speak of, no high ground to stand atop. Kole considered climbing a tree, but he didn't know if he had the strength to clamber up the gnarled branches. He didn't imagine it would help him much, in any case. As the sun rose, thick mist filled the air, concealing everything ahead of him.

At least he was no longer trying to find a single ruin in the middle of the vast swamp. Now he had only a single goal: get out. Once he was beyond the borders of the swamp, he would be able to find his way back to Hale's Crossing.

He kept the morning sun on his right side as best he could, heading north. As long as he did that, he would eventually escape the mire as long as his food and water held out that long.

Assuming nothing else took him for an easy meal, now that it was just him and the packhorse and the unconscious Darvin out here alone.

Darvin stirred from time to time, enough to mutter a few words or rave about snakes in the dark. But he soon went quiet again, slipping back below the veil of consciousness.

Kole wished he could sleep as well, just sit down with his back against a tree and rest his eyes for a minute. But he knew if he did that he would fall into a sleep so deep he wouldn't wake for hours. So instead he pressed on, through the humidity and the growing heat.

After a couple of hours, the sounds of life began to return to the swamp—the buzzing of insects and the flutter of birds in trees. He had to have traveled beyond the influence of the idol.

He shuddered as he remembered the horrible screeching of the rats falling down that hole into the assessment chamber, the panicked squawking of dozens of birds. He would never forget that sound. He would never forget any of it.

Unless the madness finally took him, he supposed. Perhaps that would be some kind of mercy.

On he staggered through the swamp, pulling the packhorse along with him. When the sun was at its zenith, he sought the shade of a copse of bog trees and took Darvin off the horse. The boy's scalp wound had stopped bleeding, but a nasty purple bruise had spread across much of his face. Kole thought he might have a fever as well, although perhaps it was just the heat of the day making Darvin hot and sweaty. Kole redressed the head wound, then splashed some fresh water on a strip he tore off a blanket and draped it around the boy's neck. It was the best he could do to cool him down, though the air was so humid he doubted it would be much help.

Propping Darvin up against a tree for a moment, Kole dribbled some water into the corner of the boy's mouth. Darvin coughed at first, but then he seemed to swallow and open his mouth for more. Kole gave him some, careful to keep him from choking on it, then drank some himself and poured out a little into a bucket for Mugsy. He couldn't think of a way to feed Darvin, so he just took a few bites of salted fish and stuffed some cheese into his pocket to eat while walking.

Heaving Darvin back onto the horse, they continued on. Mugsy gave Kole a tired look, but the horse allowed herself to be led, still munching on the stunted carrot Kole had found at the bottom of one of the saddlebags.

Kole wasn't sure if it was the heat or the exhaustion or some sorcerous madness burrowing into his brain, but sometime around mid afternoon the world seemed to slip out of focus around him. A gray haze settled over his eyes, turning his thoughts to soup.

He blinked, and suddenly it was dark. The last glimmers of orange sunlight touched the western corner of the sky. Through the canopy of leaves Kole could make out the eye of the moon glaring down at him.

Stumbling to a halt, Kole stared about himself in bewilderment. Mugsy snorted as she eyed him, her flanks glistening with sweat.

Kole rubbed at his eyes. How far had he traveled? He had no sense of where the last few hours had gone, or whether he had even been traveling in the right direction. He appeared to be pointed roughly north, but only the gods knew how far off-course he'd gone, or how much time he'd spent wandering in circles.

The dark was rapidly closing in around him. He should've been on the lookout for a good spot to camp for the night, but now it was too late. He couldn't journey through the night—even if he wasn't worried about blacking out again, he couldn't risk falling into a sinkhole or breaking Mugsy's ankle on a tree root.

He continued on another few minutes until he found a small patch of dry ground beneath a pair of skeletal trees. It would have to do. By the light of his lantern he scrounged up a few damp sticks for firewood and tried to coax a fire to life.

The flame he finally managed to create was a pitiful thing, but it was the best he could do. He hitched Mugsy to a tree, then laid Darvin out on a blanket on the flattest piece of ground he could find. The boy muttered something that Kole couldn't quite make out. It sounded scared.

Kole dribbled water into Darvin's mouth and draped a wet rag across the boy's head to try to fight the fever that burned through him. He didn't know how much good it would do.

All he wanted to do then was collapse to the ground, but he forced himself to get up again and set some oats and water in front of Mugsy. He rubbed her down as the last glimmers of daylight faded entirely.

Then, exhausted, Kole sat down with his back against a tree and Catgut's sword across his knees. He was almost too tired to eat, but he forced himself to choke down a few bites of stale bread. He needed to keep his strength up. It would be a long day tomorrow.

Mosquitoes and swamp flies danced hypnotically in the light of the small fire. The sound of crickets chirping and frogs croaking soon began to lull Kole to sleep. His head drooped down and he jerked awake again, blinking.

He couldn't sleep. It was too dangerous. Darvin couldn't take watch, so Kole had to.

He looked down at his damp, tattered clothes and the scratches across his arms. A mosquito was biting him, but he couldn't bring himself to crush it. It was just trying to survive, same as him.

"Seems a shame, doesn't it?" he said to Darvin. "We went all that way. Delved so deep. Lost so much. And with nothing to show for it."

Darvin moaned softly but said nothing.

"They were right, though. The freebooters. Gods, but they were right. There was treasure down there. Enough to make us all rich. Enough to make everyone in town rich." He looked up at the stars. "Maybe one day we'll go back. You think? Round up some people, make the journey back. Go in and finish off whatever snakes are left. Take all the bodies back so they can be burned properly. Maybe take some treasure with us on the way." He almost laughed at the absurdity of it. "That's if we can ever find it again, I guess."

Wisps of cloud drifted lazily across the night sky. Kole wasn't cold, but he hugged himself anyway.

"It was pretty amazing, though, wasn't it? The size of it. The beauty. I wish I could've seen it before. Back when it was still standing. It must have been something. To think that people made that. *Sorcerers* made that."

He looked down at his reforged leg and rubbed it gingerly. The skin seemed vaguely translucent in the firelight, and the muscles there were noticeably smaller than his other leg. There was something strange about the sensation in the leg, something raw.

Sighing, he looked away from his leg and rested his head against the tree trunk. Gods, he was tired. His eyelids had weights attached.

He had to close his eyes. Just for a minute.

He wasn't sure exactly what it was that startled him out of the deepest sleep he'd ever known. It hadn't been a sound, because he couldn't hear anything over the chirping of crickets. No, it had been something else. A scent, maybe.

Kole didn't know. All he knew was that they were not alone.

The fire had burned down to embers. In the dim orange light, Kole caught a glimpse of something lithe and sleek prowling on the edge of the camp. Eyes glinted red in the darkness.

Kole's breath caught. Trembling, he clutched the hilt of Catgut's sword.

The creature paused for a moment, as if sensing his movement. On the other side of the camp, the packhorse gave a soft snort in her sleep. Then the beast began to move again, creeping closer. A black tail twitched.

A panicked thought ran through Kole's exhausted mind. *Snake.* But no. The thing didn't move like a snake. It was more graceful than a serpent. As it stepped into the firelight, Kole could see muscles rippling as paws padded closer.

Swamp cat.

The man-sized cat twitched its whiskers, intelligent eyes darting around. It licked its lips and prowled closer. But it wasn't heading for Kole.

It was going for Darvin.

Kole surged to his feet, pulling the sword free of its scabbard. The swamp cat flinched back, eyes darting to meet his.

The sword trembled in Kole's hand as he pointed the blade toward the black swamp cat.

"Get away," he said. "Go!"

Mugsy awoke at his shout, snorting and whinnying nervously. As she spotted the swamp cat, the mare stomped her hooves on the damp ground.

The cat just stared at him. The flesh was pulled tight across the creature's ribs. With hunger in its eyes, it glanced at Darvin again.

"I'll kill you," Kole said. His voice shook.

The swamp cat stared at him a moment longer. Tentatively, it took a step toward Darvin.

Kole yelled wordlessly, swiping at the cat with his sword. The creature darted back easily out of his reach, pausing at the edge of the firelight.

Then the cat glanced toward the packhorse.

"No," Kole said. "You get away."

Eying him, the cat began to prowl toward the horse. Mugsy squealed and pulled on her tether.

Kole grabbed a drawstring bag from beside the fire and hurled it toward the swamp cat. The bag fell open and the cat snarled and darted back a few steps. A couple of packages of salted fish spilled onto the dirt.

"There!" Kole yelled. "You want food, take that! Take it and go. Go!"

The cat's eyes flashed toward him, then to the bag. Sniffing at the air, the cat slowly approached the bag.

"Just go," Kole murmured, his grip tightening around the sword. "Please. Just go."

The swamp cat gave him one last suspicious look. It licked at one of the packages that had fallen out of the bag. Then it sank its teeth into the bag and dragged it away into the dark.

Gasping for breath, Kole lowered the sword. He waited for the cat to return, but nothing else moved beyond the firelight.

The packhorse continued to shake her head, stamping and trying to pull free of her hitching. Sheathing Catgut's sword, Kole carefully approached the horse.

"It's all right, girl. The swamp cat is gone. You're all right."

Mugsy eyed him, unconvinced, but her panicked movements slowed. Kole patted the horse's flank, trying to rein in his own fear.

"We're going to get out of this," he said, more to himself than the horse.

The packhorse stared at him a moment longer, then nuzzled his shoulder. Kole smiled.

"Mara was right," he said. "You've got a brave heart."

Kole fed a few more damp twigs into the dying fire, then dragged Darvin closer to Mugsy. Sitting down on a blanket with his back to the fire, Kole stared out at the dark until the first fingers of dawn began to reach across the sky.

CHAPTER
16

KOLE'S STOMACH RUMBLED as he trudged through the swamp, pulling Mugsy along behind him. He was already starting to regret giving the swamp cat almost all the food he had left. Even the last of the bread had been in the bag the cat had dragged away, though Kole doubted the beast would find the hard loaf much to its liking.

At least the water was untouched, along with the horse's fodder. Kole had considered stealing a handful of Mugsy's oats for his breakfast, but Mugsy had given him a fierce glare as soon as he started eying them up.

Instead, he'd made do with a small package of salted fish left behind when the swamp cat dragged the rest of the food away. It had been something, at least.

To take his mind off his grumbling stomach, he thought of home. He could almost sense it now, somewhere to the north. He could taste the salt on the breeze coming off the Drowning Sea, see the light sparkling against the clear blue water.

They were good people, the people of Hale's Crossing. Small-minded, some of them. Superstitious and naive. They had not always been kind to Kole's family, but he realized now that Da was right: it wasn't malice that drove them, or even hatred. It was simply fear—fear of what they did not understand. Fear for themselves, fear for their own families. Fear that the sorcerer's plague might flare again, tearing apart Hale's Crossing like it had many other towns in the years since the Outbreak.

Kole had not truly understood that before. But he'd experienced real fear now. He'd seen what a powerful force it could be. He'd seen what it did to people—what it had done to Wolfun. Gods, that same fear had nearly broken Kole's mind as well.

If the people of Hale's Crossing experienced even a hint of that same fear when they came too close to him and his family…well, he could understand their reactions. He didn't like it. But he understood.

Their fear would only grow when they found out what he was now. What he'd become.

Sorcerer. The voice in his head was accusatory, filled with disgust.

Kole forced it away. He didn't yet know what he would do when he got back. Would he tell anyone? Would he tell Da?

He knew what that would mean. And Da would too. He would be asking his own father to kill him.

It would be better for him to simply disappear. To return to the swamp, maybe, and wait for the madness to take him.

Or maybe…maybe he wouldn't have to. He wasn't mad yet, after all. Maybe the madness wasn't some inevitable thing, a worm burrowing into his mind. Maybe it would only manifest if he used the sorcery.

That was possible, wasn't it? He'd only used it once, to reforge his leg. What if he never used it again? Not for anything. Maybe that would keep the madness at bay.

But what if you need it? What if you're hurt again, and you need to use the sorcery to survive.

Then he simply wouldn't. He would just die. Better that than becoming like Mertyn Walter.

What if it's not you that's hurt? What if it's Ma? What if it's Arabeth?

Kole's chest tightened at the thought. Could he do it? If it was Arabeth with her leg crushed beneath a rock, could he stand by and not use his sorcery to help her? Could he let her suffer that pain and do nothing?

It would help if he knew more about the sorcerer's plague, more than rumors and old superstitions.

Quintus might have known more. Or Mara. Even Angok might have had some clue. Maybe he should have asked them while he had the chance. They might not have killed him, at least not until he showed signs of infection.

Kole sighed. He had been trying not to think about the freebooters' deaths. He'd been focusing instead on getting home, taking Darvin to someone who could help.

He thought of the freebooters lying deep beneath the swamp, forgotten by all who knew them. Did they have families in some far off land? Friends? People who would miss them?

He supposed no one would be terribly surprised when the freebooters didn't return. Treasure hunting was a perilous undertaking, everyone knew that. All the easy-to-find wealth and artifacts of the old world had long since been carried off to Godsmouth or the Glimmering Isles or the Domed Cities. Anything that was left was buried deep or hidden in some dark corner of the world. Those foolhardy few who went searching for it did so at their own risk.

Despite that, Kole was still in shock. The freebooters had seemed so strong. So confident. He'd seen their chain shirts and their gleaming swords and thought they would be able to survive anything the temple could throw at them.

The pain of their passing was a small, niggling thing, buried deep in Kole's stomach. It was waiting to burst free, he knew. He'd barely known them, but he could feel the grief there nonetheless. They'd shown him respect, the kind of respect he'd never got from the people of Hale's Crossing. They had led him into danger, but Kole could not blame them for that. He had volunteered to join the expedition.

He thought of Angok's wide grin and Catgut's easy grace. He thought of Mara's lonely, mournful eyes. He even found himself missing Quintus, the cantankerous bastard.

Perhaps they'd left some information with Mr. Godett, the innkeeper of the Empty Net. Perhaps Kole could send word to their people about what had happened. It was something, at least.

Kole's stomach cramped with faint hunger pains as the day wore on. It was only an hour or two until sunset now. It would be a hungry night if he had to spend it in the swamp.

He knew he should start looking for a campsite—somewhere safer and more defensible this time. But though his bones ached and exhaustion weighed more heavily on him than any pack, he kept trudging through the mud and water, pushing on. Maybe the hunger was getting to him, but he thought the swamp was starting to thin. The ground didn't seem quite so soggy, the swarms of insects not quite so thick.

He had to be close now. He'd been traveling faster than the party had on the journey to the temple. There were fewer supplies weighing him down, fewer pauses while Quintus attempted to plot them a route to their destination. He'd traveled north for miles. Surely the swamp would end soon.

Unless he'd gotten turned around. Unless in some exhausted delirium he'd started traveling in circles.

He glanced at Darvin slumped over the neck of the packhorse. The boy's eyes were darting about behind closed eyelids. He'd been murmuring in his sleep more frequently in the last few hours. Once he even shouted loud enough to startle a nearby heron. Kole wasn't sure Darvin would survive another night in the swamp.

Setting his jaw, Kole picked up the pace. Mugsy snorted in protest, but the horse allowed him to lead her on.

As the sun sank low, Kole glimpsed an opening in the press of trees ahead of him. At first he thought it was merely a trick of the light. Just another clearing filled with reeds and fetid water.

But when he slogged through the mud and emerged from between the gnarled trees, he did not find himself at the edge of another pool of still water, or another bank lined with leatherbacks.

Instead, he found himself staring at a field of tall grass stretching away into the distance, dotted with brush. In the last light of day, Kole could see a line of mountains far to the north. The Windless Peaks.

Hope surged. Kole let out a relieved sob as he breathed in the fresh air blowing in from the west.

The loose borders of Notte's Mire spread out on either side of him, disappearing into the distance. But somewhere nearby there had to be roads. Farms.

And home.

A rush of excitement swept the exhaustion from his bones. He couldn't be far now. Though it was growing dark, he couldn't stop to camp. Not when he was so close.

"Come on, Mugsy," he said, pulling her on. "We're nearly there."

She gave him a weary look, but allowed him to lead her through the long grass.

As the night closed in, Kole lit his lantern and hurried on, hugging the border of the swamp. He must've come out a few miles east of where they'd entered Notte's Mire. The border of the swamp was patchy and ill-defined, though now at least he had some idea where he was.

Darkness fell rapidly. Kole knew he was at risk of twisting an ankle in a hidden rabbit hole, but he didn't stop. He scanned the darkening landscape constantly for some familiar landmark.

An owl hooted somewhere nearby. As he passed through a lightly wooded area on the border of the swamp, a warm breeze blew, carrying distant cries of excitement and the faint scent of woodsmoke.

There was an orange glow on the horizon. Silhouetted against it, Kole could see the shapes of low buildings.

Hale's Crossing. Relief filled Kole's heart. He had made it. He was home.

Another wave of shouts were carried by the wind. Kole tromped through the long grass toward the town, pulling Mugsy with him.

There's a bonfire, he thought. He'd arrived home in time for Lampnight after all.

But even as the thought passed through his tired mind, it rang false to him. It wasn't possible. Too many days had passed. He'd missed Lampnight. He was sure of it.

The wind gusted again, carrying the smell of smoke and ash. He heard the shouting again. The night seemed to press in around him, cold and cloying.

Those were not the raucous shouts of celebrating townsfolk.

They were shouts of terror.

CHAPTER
17

OR A MOMENT, as the screams washed over him, Kole felt his heart stop. He couldn't move. All he could do was listen, stunned.

There were other sounds mixed in with the screams. Shouts barked in a harsh, eastern accent. Wild, wordless cries. Something thudding again and again, like woodsmen felling a tree.

There were fires. The flames stretched into the sky, spreading from one building to the next. He could see movement as well, clustered figures rushing here and there, black shadows against the light of the fires behind them. For an instant Kole thought he saw someone on horseback galloping through the town. A moment later they were swallowed by smoke.

Kole shook himself out of his daze. He was having trouble understanding what he was seeing. But he couldn't just stand here. He took a step forward, pulling Mugsy with him.

He paused, glancing back at the packhorse and Darvin tied to her back. He dithered for a second, then quickly led the horse back toward the copse of trees behind him.

As the distant screams continued to fill the air, Kole hitched Mugsy to a tree. The packhorse stared at him.

"Just…just stay here," he said. "I'll be back."

He turned away, glancing down at the sword hanging from his belt. He could see the orange light of the fires reflected in the sword's pommel.

Swallowing, he picked up his lantern and hurried toward the town.

Smoke stung his eyes as he approached Hale's Crossing. He was coming at the town from the south, across the empty fields that backed onto the swamp. The stink and the mud ensured that no farmer wanted to plant crops or raise livestock here. Holding his lantern low, he passed the headstone where Mertyn Walter had met his end. The stains that marred the stone still seemed wet in the light of his lantern.

Ash and embers danced in the hot air above Kole's head. The shouts grew louder, more distinct. Between the buildings ahead, Kole caught a glimpse of a pair of shadowed figures fleeing along the boardwalk. A few seconds later came the rumbling of more footsteps on the wooden planks, then a half-dozen more figures went charging along in the same direction. One bore a lantern and another was holding aloft a makeshift torch. The smoke was too thick to make out any more about them before they disappeared out of sight once more.

Kole reached a building on the outskirts of town, the hut of a fisherfolk family. Old nets lay tangled in the grass next to the outhouse. The stink of fish was strong enough that he could smell it even over the smoke. Kole crouched and peered around the corner of the building.

Across the boardwalk and down a little way, Kole could see another cluster of houses burning. The flames had nearly consumed one wooden house entirely, and another was already beyond saving. The fire spat embers into the air, sending them dancing toward the shops on the main boardwalk.

And yet no one was rushing to put out the fire. There were no bucket gangs, no fire bells ringing. If someone didn't do something soon, the whole town would go up.

Kole was about to slip out from behind the building when he heard a shout from somewhere nearby. From a muddy side street, a figure came barreling out of the smoke. He was blackened with soot and his sleeve was blood-soaked. He glanced back behind him as he ran limping toward the boardwalk.

Kole suddenly recognized the man through the soot and filth. It was Mr. Godett, the innkeeper.

Opening his mouth, Kole started to call out to the terrified man. But before he could speak, another shout rose up from behind the innkeeper.

"Over there!"

Three more figures came running out of the smoke in pursuit of Mr. Godett. Two men and a woman, it looked like. Though all wore rags across their mouths and nose, Kole realized with a shock that he knew one of them: one of Farmer Gladen's adult sons, the one who'd watched Kole build a pyre to burn the stillborn piglets. No one could miss that unnaturally small head set atop a too-thick neck.

The Gladen son was holding a shovel like it was a club. The other two were armed as well: the man with a long staff and the woman with a carving knife. The three of them shouted indistinctly as they chased Mr. Godett.

Terror shining in his eyes, Mr. Godett glanced back at his pursuers. Instantly, Kole saw what was about to happen, though he was powerless to stop it.

Mr. Godett's foot slipped on a bucket that had been abandoned in the road. With a cry, the innkeeper splashed into the mud.

He tried to scramble to his feet, but his pursuers reached him a moment too soon. They swarmed over him like the snakes from the temple.

It was over in a second. Mr. Godett kicked out at the woman who reached him first, then the Gladen son lifted his shovel and brought it down. The hollow thunk made Kole feel sick. The innkeeper went limp, a groan escaping his lips. Before he could fall back into the mud, his attackers grabbed him under the arms and dragged him away into the smoke.

Kole stared after them, shaking. He couldn't believe what he was seeing. None of it made any sense. Unless…

His thoughts drifted back to that morning he'd spent at the Gladen Farm, burning the stillborn piglets. He thought of Farmer Gladen's ramblings about sorcery, about the curse Mertyn Walter had supposedly put on the land before he'd been executed. Nonsense, all nonsense.

But Kole had heard stories of towns put to the torch when the plague had taken hold there. Some feared that when the roots of corruption had grown too deep, it wasn't enough simply to eliminate the sorcerers that could be identified. By the time one was executed, another two might become infected. That infection could spread through the town and beyond it. To nearby villages. To an entire region. To the entire world, perhaps, as it had done during the Outbreak.

Better to put an end to it first. Better to cut out the corruption rather than let it spread.

Distant screams echoed in Kole's head. This wasn't supposed to be happening. Hale's Crossing was supposed to be safe! That promise of safety had got him through the swamp after everyone else had died. It had got him home.

How could things have turned so fast? He'd been gone less than a week. How had the people of the neighboring villages driven themselves into such a frenzy in a matter of days? Gods, many of those who lived in the nearby villages were kin to those in Hale's Crossing.

Kin. As he thought the word, a cold dread gripped his heart, greater than anything he'd felt in the bowels of the temple of Gnothea.

Where was his family? As Felmen, they would be the first target of this…this riot, or whatever it was. Everyone already believed them impure. He and Da had been in close contact with both Mertyn Walter and his family—if the rioters suspected the infection had spread, their suspicions would fall first on them.

Perhaps not without cause. Gods, was he somehow responsible for all this? Had someone found out he was infected?

Kole put the sickening thoughts out of his head. He had to find his family. That was the most important thing right now.

His house was on the north-eastern outskirts of town, near the main trade route to Baybury. To reach it, he'd have to get across town or around it.

From somewhere off to Kole's left came more shouting. He could see the glow of torches approaching through the swirling smoke. Pulling his tunic up over his mouth to filter out the worst of the ash, he slipped from the cover of the building and headed toward his home.

Smoke burned his eyes, sending tears pouring down his cheeks. He darted across the main boardwalk and then ducked behind a rainwater barrel as a mob of villagers marched past, coughing behind their face masks. The urge to cough tickled at Kole's lungs, but he managed to suppress it until the group had vanished into the smoke once more.

He hurried on through the dark, his lantern half-hooded to allow him to see in the dark alleys where the firelight didn't reach.

The Empty Net was ablaze, as was the baker's. Someone was crying in the night. Kole forced the sound out of his head, turning north instead.

From somewhere up ahead he could hear someone calling out, her voice hard and authoritative. Her words were tinged with an eastern accent. As Kole crept down a muddy alley, the words became clearer.

"Do not fear, people of Hale's Crossing! If you are untainted, you will not be harmed. Abandon your resistance and come forth!"

The only response was the continued shouting and the crackle of fire. It was coming from the direction of the town square, where the ancient guildhall and the council office stood. Kole crept forward, hoping to find a way to skirt around the square.

Wind gusted down the road, clearing the smoke for a moment. Kole froze as the town square came suddenly into view ahead of him.

At least two dozen armed villagers filled the square, swarming about like a colony of fire ants. One group threw their lit torches through the windows of Townmaster Haddin's residence, while on the other side Kole could see the Gladen son and his gang dragging Mr. Godett toward a cowering huddle of bloodied Hale's Crossing townsfolk. The captured townsfolk were being guarded by several armed men dressed in chain mail and blue surcoats. These weren't villagers, that much was clear.

The whole affair was being watched over by three figures on horseback. The horses stood still and at ease despite the fire and screaming. They were clad in patterned blue horse-trappers that fluttered wildly in the fire-breeze.

The riders were as still as their mounts. All three wore strange armor made of laced bronze plates. They wore helmets as well: strange things shaped like the skulls of gigantic birds. They were not looking in his direction, but even so Kole could sense the intensity of the gazes coming from those great, black eye holes.

The riders were armed. One had a long, hooked polearm across his saddle and a large shield hanging from his back. Another—a woman, Kole thought, perhaps the one who had spoken before—had a sheathed greatsword slung across her shoulder.

As Kole stared at the three riders standing amid the smoke, he brought to mind the rumors he'd heard in the last few weeks. Rumors that a band of Hallowed Order knights had gathered near the city of Baybury. He hadn't thought much about those rumors since entering the swamp.

Now, though, they came rushing back to him. He remembered Farmer Gladen wondering aloud if a few knights from that famous order could be convinced to cleanse the land of whatever curse Mertyn Walter had supposedly laid upon it.

The Hallowed Order. Kole had never seen one of their knights before. He'd heard the legends, though. How at the height of the Outbreak they had ridden out from the Blackspire to battle the roving bands of wild sorcerers that plagued the lands. They were the saviors that had kept the Golden Remnant from descending into madness.

They were one of the few institutions that had survived from before those turbulent times. In the centuries since, they'd acted as the last bastion against the return of the plague.

Until now, Kole had not understood exactly what that meant.

He stared at the knights, doubt creeping through his mind. The

Order's presence here didn't make sense. Mertyn Walter was already dead. If the Hallowed Order set fire to a town each time a sorcerer appeared, the Golden Remnant would be nothing but a charred wasteland.

Had the plague spread while he was gone? Had it raged out of control, until this was the only recourse?

As the fire in the townmaster's house burned brighter, Kole could make out movement on the far side of the square, where the guildhall stood. The great stone guildhall was older even than the bridge that spanned the river on the western side of town, some relic of the old empire. It was the largest building in town, taller and wider than the townmaster's residence across the way. Kole didn't know what it had originally been built for, but now it was used as a feast hall on holidays and an indoor market during the winter months when the ground outside was even more muddy than usual.

Through the haze, Kole saw a pair of Hale's Crossing townsfolk running toward the guildhall. The young woman clutched a screaming baby. A knot of armed villagers were in pursuit.

With his heart in his throat, Kole watched as the baby's father ran to the heavy oaken doors of the guildhall and started hammering on them. A few of the armed villagers who'd been swarming about the square split away, joining in the pursuit of the young family.

There was movement in one of the windows set high into the guildhall's front, then a shout from inside. One of the oak doors swung open and the family ducked quickly inside.

Shouts rose up from the pursuing villagers. Even as the door began to swing closed again, three armed villagers threw themselves against it, trying to shove it open. Screams and cries rose up from somewhere inside. Through the partly open door, Kole could see huddled shadows and flickering candlelight. Some Hale's Crossing townsfolk were holed up inside.

Two more of the armed mob charged in to add their weight to the three already leaning against the door. They shoved the door open another foot.

A figure appeared again at the high window and started pelting the attackers outside with bits of broken furniture. It did little to dissuade the raging mob.

All the while Kole crouched in the shadows, powerless. As powerless as he'd been watching the abomination in the temple dangle Quintus above its grinning maw. He wanted to help. He wanted to do…*something*. He found himself clutching at the hilt of the sword tucked into his belt, as if the weapon would be any use at all against the mob.

With a roar, the mob forced the door open further. Cheering, several of them began to rush inside.

There was a flash of steel from inside the guildhall. Something heavy struck the first villager to step through the door. A spray of blood went up and the villager staggered back, his chest cleaved open.

The second villager tried to stop, but the press of the mob behind him kept him moving forward. He let out a scream that echoed across the square before a heavy blade flashed from the darkness inside the guildhall and drove deep into the man's skull. His scream was cut short as he slumped to the ground.

Shouting, the remaining villagers stumbled back from the door, clutching their own makeshift weapons. A shadow passed across the open doorway and a figure stepped through, heavy sword still swinging.

Kole's breath caught in his throat as he took in the sight of the tall figure clad in heavy black leather. Firelight shone orange in the glass lenses set into the stiff black hood. Kole couldn't see the face of whoever wore the gear. But as the figure lifted the huge headsman's sword once more and brought it arcing toward the armed villagers, Kole had no doubts about the man's identity.

"Da," he breathed.

The mob staggered back from the swing of the headsman's sword. One was too slow. The blade struck the man's arm, hacking his forearm off at the elbow. Screaming and clutching his stump, the man collapsed to the ground.

Kole could hear Da shouting something at the townsfolk still inside the guildhall. The muffled words were drowned out by the baying of the mob. The townsfolk in the guildhall seemed to be having trouble getting the door shut again. The body of the first villager through the door was jammed somehow, keeping them from closing it.

"Seize the hall," the female Hallowed Order knight called to the villagers in the square. With her bird-skull helmet on, her voice had a metallic ring to it. "The corruption cannot be allowed to linger!"

The knight's call seemed to drive several of the mob into a frenzy. A group surged forward, weapons raised.

Da stood in front of the doorway, his heavy sword never slowing. He swung it in huge, cleaving arcs, cutting down any villager who got close.

Kole had seen Da wield that sword a thousand times, both in training and against the condemned. But he'd never seen him use the sword like this—as a true weapon. He wasn't as quick as Catgut with her flashing sword, nor as precise as Mara and her hammer strikes. He was a force of nature, a raging storm that struck down anyone foolhardy enough to venture into it.

Kole was in awe. How long could Da keep this up? Swinging that sword was exhausting. To use it like that, never letting it slow...

And yet Da kept moving, kept swinging. Two villagers came at him at once, one armed with a pitchfork, another with a woodcutting axe. Da stepped aside from the pitchfork thrust and let the weight of his sword swing carry him forward, cutting the axe-wielding woman's legs out from beneath her. He turned, still swinging, and brought the sword slashing up, breaking the pitchfork and turning one of the villager's hands to pulp.

Kole had to do something. He had to help somehow.

His hand was clenched around the hilt of Catgut's sword. Most of the mob filling the square now seemed distracted by the whirling death that was Kole's da. Heart pounding, Kole crept out of the alley, aiming to skirt around the edge of the square, using the smoke for cover. He didn't know what he planned to do if he got to the guildhall. But he couldn't just stay hidden any longer.

The helmet of the female knight turned in his direction. He froze, thinking she'd seen him moving. But no, she was saying something to the knight beside her.

Kole couldn't make out what she said. The other knight nodded, though, and reached down to draw something from a leather case attached to his saddle.

Thick smoke filled the square for a moment, turning the mob into half-formed silhouettes. Taking his opportunity, Kole hurried around the edge of the square, ducking behind the old stone well in the corner just as the smoke began to clear again.

When it did, Kole could see that Da was still fighting, though he was moving slower now. The shoulder of his leather coat was torn where a villager had struck him. At his feet lay several of the crazed mob, some still, others writhing or crawling away. Behind him, the door to the guildhall had been cleared. Da backed slowly toward it, swinging the sword at the mob to keep them from closing in.

Kole glanced back toward the knights. His heart stopped.

He saw what the knight alongside the leader had been drawing. It was a long, curved bow made from polished black wood. As Kole watched, the knight nocked an arrow with a broad point and drew it back.

"No!"

As Kole shouted, the knight loosed the arrow.

It seemed to Kole as if he could see the arrow soaring unhurried toward its target. He felt he should be able to run over to it, pluck it out of the air.

But he was moving as slowly as the arrow. So was everyone else. Da swung his sword one more time, moving as if he was underwater.

And then the arrow struck. It punched through Da's leather cloak, driving deep into his shoulder and sending him staggering back.

Perhaps the arrow had been meant for his heart. Perhaps Kole's shout had distracted the knight, sending the arrow a few inches high. Kole didn't know. He couldn't think. His mind was a blank.

Da's gloved left hand slipped from the hilt of the sword, though he held tight with his right. The rounded tip of the headsman's sword sank into the mud. Though Kole couldn't see Da's face, he could sense his pain as Da went stumbling back toward the doorway.

The three knights turned toward Kole, alerted by his shout. He could feel their eyes on him from within the shadows of their beaked helmets. Something inside him trembled at their gaze, but he continued to stare at Da across the square.

As he stumbled back, Da lost his footing and slipped to one knee. Hands reached out from the dark of the guildhall, grabbing him under the arms and hauling him through the open doorway. Da tensed in pain.

As he was dragged away, Da's hooded head turn toward Kole, as if he too had heard the shout before the arrow had struck him. Kole couldn't see Da's eyes, but he could feel them, even through the smoke and the dark.

Da shouted a single word, strained with pain and nearly swallowed by the screaming of the mob. Kole heard it nonetheless. It rang in his head, like that ancient silver bell from the temple ringing through the ages.

"Run!"

Then Da was dragged into the guildhall and the heavy door was slammed shut. The mob threw themselves against the door once more, but it held fast.

Kole stood frozen, staring at the closed door of the guildhall. His mind was stuck like a cart in the mud, the same thoughts spinning around and around.

Da was hurt. Where was Ma? Where was Arabeth? What could he do?

The leader of the knights jerked her head at the knight who'd loosed the arrow. With a nod, the knight handed her the bow and pulled on his horse's rein, turning toward Kole.

Run! Da's voice echoed in Kole's head once more.

The cart wheel of his mind skidded out of the mud. His heart gave a lurching beat and life returned to his frozen muscles.

Kole turned and ran.

CHAPTER
18

"HALT!" THE KNIGHT SHOUTED, his voice ringing through his beaked helmet. His mount snorted.

Kole darted away into a dark, muddy alley, heading away from the square. Smoke from the burning townmaster's residence swirled about him. The mud sucked at the boots he'd borrowed from Darvin.

Behind him, the knight shouted a command to his horse. Hooves squelched in the mud. Kole didn't look back. Emerging from the alley, he jumped up onto the boardwalk and ran for another road on the other side.

From along the boardwalk, near the water, Kole heard more shouting as a knot of armed villagers spotted him. He jumped down into the mud and ran on just as he heard hooves pound against the boardwalk behind him. A horse whinnied, then the hooves galloped off in another direction.

He didn't know where he was going. There was nowhere to run to. Hale's Crossing was his home. All he knew was this town and the villages that surrounded it. Now those surrounding villages had turned on Hale's Crossing, spurred to madness by fear and the knights of the Hallowed Order. His home was overrun and ablaze. Where could he go?

He didn't know. He felt lost, untethered. But he had to get out of town. He had to get back to Darvin and Mugsy. He couldn't abandon them here—if they found Darvin, he would face the same fate as the rest of the town.

On he ran, through the mud and the black smoke that blotted out the stars above. His lantern swung in his hand, the hood half lowered so that he could barely see where he was going. He jumped a fence and startled a coop of chickens as he sprinted past.

And then he was out, past the last outbuildings, beyond the outskirts of Hale's Crossing. The crackle of fire and the shouting of villagers grew distant, smothered by the smoke. Kole took off through the long grass, heading for the copse of trees on the edge of the swamp where he'd hitched Mugsy. He would get the horse, get Darvin, and...and...

He didn't know. He would figure it out on the way.

Hoofbeats thudded against the ground behind him. The sound sent cold fingers reaching up Kole's spine. As he ran, he glanced back.

The scales of the knight's armor glinted in the moonlight. A lantern dangled from the horse's saddle, though it cast little light. Neither the knight nor the horse seemed concerned by the prospect of galloping along the uneven ground in the dark.

Through the dark eye holes in the knight's helmet, Kole could feel the man's stare. For a moment he almost froze, like a field mouse frozen before a swooping owl. Some wild part of his brain told him to throw himself to the ground, to try to hide in the long grass, to go still and quiet and pray that the rider passed on.

But he knew that was suicide. There was no hiding, not here in the field. His only hope was to get to the trees, and then into the swamp. The knight wouldn't pursue him into the swamp. Would he?

Kole forced his burning legs to pump harder, to fight against the tangling grass and the soft earth. The smoke in his lungs made him hack and cough as he ran. He focused his attention on the cover of the wood ahead of him.

He wasn't going to make it. He realized that as the pounding hoofbeats grew louder behind him. He was too slow, the horse too fast. He ran anyway, propelled by fear, waiting to feel the fiery pain of a sword slashing at his back.

The hoofbeats grew deafeningly loud. Kole cringed in anticipation.

With a rush of wind, the knight went galloping past him, cutting off his escape less than twenty yards from the trees. The knight yanked on the reins and the horse reared as it came to a stop.

The knight jumped from the horse, landing on his feet with a clank of his armor. He marched toward Kole, hands at his sides.

Kole turned to run, but his foot slipped in the mud. He stumbled, and by the time he'd found his feet the knight was nearly on top of him.

"Don't run, boy," the knight said. It was a voice used to being obeyed.

"If you are untainted, you have nothing to fear."

Kole spun back toward the looming knight. In the faint light from his lantern, he thought he could make out the glint of the man's eye inside his beaked helmet.

He grabbed the hilt of Catgut's sword and jerked it free of its sheath. Trembling, he held the sword up, point aimed toward the knight. The armored man stopped.

"Stay back," Kole said.

The knight regarded the sword. "A fine blade. Where did you get it?"

Ignoring the question, Kole took a step back. The knight followed.

"Stay back!" Kole yelled.

"This is foolish, boy. Put down the sword before I put it down for you."

Kole swallowed. He didn't move.

Quicker than he could follow, the knight's hand went to his own sword and drew it from its scabbard. In the same motion, he sliced at Kole. The knight's larger sword struck Catgut's short blade hard enough to send a shock wave up Kole's arm. The sword flew from his aching hand, landing in the grass a few feet away.

Kole turned to run again. The knight reached him easily, grabbing him by the cloak and nearly hauling him off his feet. Kole dropped his lantern and tried to shout, but his smoke-filled lungs spasmed and he fell into another coughing fit.

"I think the Knight-Captain will want a word with you, boy," the knight said as he started dragging him back toward his horse.

Though Kole was only a couple of inches shorter than the knight, he felt powerless to resist the man's pull. Gods, he was tired. His lungs burned with the smoke he'd inhaled. His muscles seemed sapped of all life. At least now it would be over, perhaps. At least now he could rest.

And yet he twisted in the knight's grip anyway, driven to fight by some primal instinct. The sight of that arrow striking his father flashed through his mind. He looked at the fire rising from Hale's Crossing. Distant screams still punctuated the night. Anger and grief swirled inside him.

He reached out—reached *in*. Reached deep inside himself to that new part of his mind—or perhaps the part that had always been there. And as he reached toward it, it reached toward him, lovers once parted, now reunited.

A veil fell over Kole's eyes and he could see the world around him as it truly was. He felt the knight's blood pulsing through him, hot and liquid.

Before he could doubt himself, he began to speak. The language of reality poured out of him, as warm and smooth as honey.

With a hiss, the knight shoved Kole back, releasing him. As Kole fell into the long grass, still speaking his incantation, the knight snapped a thin chain from around his neck. A black crystal, no larger than Kole's thumb, dangled from the end of the chain. It spun in wild circles, seeming to cast a shadow all about itself. Kole stared at it, trying to read the crystal as he could read the knight's flesh beneath his armor. But the crystal seemed to swallow all knowledge, all color. It hurt to look at.

Kole spoke faster. He wanted to crush the knight's heart within his chest. He wanted to kill him for what he'd done to Da.

As if sensing the sorcery in the air, the knight's horse suddenly bolted. The knight clutched at his chest. But his flesh was resisting the sorcery. It wasn't as easy as Kole had thought to kill a man with sorcery. He needed to get closer. He crawled toward the knight, his incantation reaching a crescendo.

The knight closed his gauntleted hand around the black crystal and crushed it. Black dust trickled from his closed fist and swirled up around him, carried by some unnatural wind.

Kole felt his voice catch in his throat. His lips still moved, but the words were stolen away as soon as he spoke them. The red veil that had passed across his eyes faded and lifted, giving way to a faint black nothingness that spiraled around the two of them.

The knight inhaled deeply. As the spell was sucked away, the knight straightened, his pain gone. The light from Kole's lantern, still lying in the grass a few feet away, flickered and dimmed. Even the stars above seemed colder for a moment, more distant.

"Sorcerer," the knight said softly, turning his beaked helmet toward Kole.

Raising his sword, the man advanced on him.

A figure appeared from the darkness behind the knight, roaring. Startled, the knight began to turn.

The head of a war hammer slammed into the side of the knight's head. His beaked helmet crumpled and a few drops of blood sprayed from the eye holes. The force of the blow knocked him off his feet.

As he fell into the grass, the other figure stepped into the pool of lantern light.

Mara no longer looked like some holy avenger bathed in divine light. There was mud in her hair and the left side of her face was swollen and bruised. She had abandoned her chain mail somewhere along the way. As she stepped up to the fallen knight, Kole could see that she was favoring her left leg.

But the fire in the freebooter's eyes blazed brighter than Kole had ever seen it before. She spared him a glance, then stared down at the knight.

Wheezing breaths came from inside the knight's crumpled helmet. Kole caught a glimpse of a wide eye staring out of one eye hole. His sword had fallen from his reach, but he groped at his belt for a dagger.

Mara slammed her hammer down square into the center of the knight's helmet. Metal buckled. The knight made no sound. His hand jerked once and then he went still.

Panting, Mara wrenched her hammer free of the twisted metal of the helmet. Blood glistened on the hammer's head. She turned toward him.

Kole stared at the dead knight for a moment, breathing heavily. Then his gaze shifted to Mara. The distant fire burning through Hale's Crossing lit half her face, concealing the other half in shadow.

"You're alive," Kole rasped. It was the only thing he could think to say.

She didn't answer right away. Holding out her hand, she said, "Water."

"Oh. Yes." He scrambled to his feet, then fumbled for the waterskin at his belt and tossed it to her. She uncapped it and drank greedily, gulping down all that was left in the half-filled skin. Gasping, she wiped her mouth and tossed the skin back to him.

"You saved me," Kole said.

Mara didn't answer. Without turning away, she stepped past the dead knight and snatched up Catgut's fallen sword. Kole suddenly became aware that the screams in the distance seemed to be fading.

He licked his lips. "How...how did you get out of the temple?"

Her eyes flashed to meet his. The fire in them had not dimmed.

"I'm going to ask you a series of questions." Her voice was flat. "You will answer them without hesitation. Do you understand?"

"What? Mara, we have to...we have to do something. Hale's Crossing—"

"You will answer my questions," she said, taking a step closer. Kole's eyes darted from the hammer she held in one hand to the sword she held in the other. He took an involuntary step back.

"Mara, what are you doing? We can't stay here There are more knights in town. When this one doesn't come back..."

"It is a risk we will take. Now, you will answer my questions. Do you understand?"

He swallowed. "I...I guess. What—"

She straightened, and her voice took on a dictatorial tone. "Suppose you are walking along a lonely road. It is summer, midday, hot. You are growing hungry. Coming the other way you see an old woman traveling alone. She is carrying a basket. What do you do?"

"What do I...?" Kole shook his head. "What is this?"

"Answer the question," Mara snapped. Kole thought he could see her hand tightening around the hilt of the sword. "What do you do?"

Kole dragged his hand through his hair. Had Mara lost her senses in the temple, like Wolfun had? He considered trying to make a run for it, but another glance at the weapons in her hands convinced him to stay put.

"I...I greet her, I guess," he said. "What does this have to do with anything?"

Some of the intensity left Mara's gaze, but she did not take her eyes off him. Gods, it was hard to meet her eyes.

"Look at me," she said. "Not at the town. Not at him." Without taking her eyes off him, she jabbed the sword toward the dead knight. "Me." She took a breath. "The old woman greets you back. She shows you what is in her basket. It is full of red, ripe apples, the biggest you've ever seen. She tells you to take one. What do you do?"

This was nonsense. When he didn't answer right away, she pointed the sword at him.

"What do you do?" she snapped.

"I...I take an apple," he said.

"Then what?"

"I thank her. And I take a bite. Gods, Mara, what is wrong with you?"

"As you bite into the apple, you taste something sour. You look down and see that the apple is brown and rotten. Worms wriggle about inside. You have bitten into one. What do you do?"

Kole grimaced. "I spit it out. Mara, please—"

"The woman cackles. She is mocking you. What do you do?"

He threw up his hands in frustration. "I drop the apple. I keep walking."

Mara studied him closely. Her mouth formed a tight line.

"The afternoon wears on. Your feet are growing tired. As you pass through a wood, several men and women burst out from behind the trees, surrounding you. They are armed. They have a hound with them. It bares its teeth. How do you feel?"

"Scared. Like I do now."

"The dog barks. One of the men demands you give up your coin purse. He says he will kill you if you do not. What do you do?"

"I give him my purse."

"And then what?" She took a step closer, staring deep into his eyes.

"And then...and then I hope they leave me alone."

Mara fell silent. Kole shifted in place. His town was burning in the distance. His family was probably dead by now, or worse.

Just as he was thinking of a way to distract Mara and escape, the strength seemed to go out of her. She slumped with exhaustion, planting the head of her hammer in the mud and leaning on it heavily. She exhaled and looked at him.

"You're not mad," she said. "You're infected. But you're not mad."

"That's what that was about? You were...you were testing me?"

She nodded slowly.

He paused. "How is it possible? Why am I not mad?"

She just frowned. "Come on. We need to get out of here."

"Wait," he said. "Angok. Did he make it out?"

Mara just lowered her eyes and shook her head.

"Quintus?"

"It's just us." She glanced toward the burning town. "And if we don't leave right now, we'll be dead too. Or worse."

He looked to the flames rising from Hale's Crossing. "My home—"

"It's gone."

"My family is still there. I saw my da. He was alive."

Is he still alive, though, with that arrow in him?

He pushed the thought aside. Mara was staring at him as if she could read his mind. For a second, he thought maybe she could.

"We can't stay," she said simply. "I'm sorry."

"Sorry?" The word was a spark, and his grief was the tinder. A sudden anger flared to life. "What good is sorry? Listen to me. My family are there. They're still alive. We can save them."

"You know we can't. We'll die if we try."

"You killed one knight!" He stabbed a finger toward the knight's body. "You can kill more."

Her face hardened. "You put great stock in my skill." She spoke as if the words left a bad taste in her mouth. "Catching a lone knight off-guard is one thing. Interrupting a raid in progress is something else entirely. How many knights did you see in there? How many armsmen? How many peasants with pitchforks and axes? You think me immune to such weapons? Do you think you are? By the Gambler, you were lucky to escape with your life."

"We can sneak in. Some of the townsfolk are holding out in the guildhall. If we can get them out—"

"The guildhall is a trap. There is no way out of there."

"How would you know?"

"Because what you call the guildhall is actually a granary. A granary from the late Imperial period. I have seen dozens like them across the Remnant. They were all designed with a single entrance and narrow windows to deter theft. The townsfolk inside have trapped themselves. If they have any sense, they will surrender before the knights grow impatient and decide to burn them out." She shot a look toward the town. "Kole, listen to me. It will not be long until the Order begins scouring the fields for any who escaped Hale's Crossing. The resistance at the guildhall may be the only reason they haven't done so already. We must take the opportunity those townsfolk have given us. We have to put as much distance between ourselves and the town as we can before dawn breaks."

He pressed his palm to his temple. It felt like his head was splitting in two. "I can't just leave. I can't just do nothing."

"Survival is not nothing. Your death will not save your family. Neither will mine." She paused, her voice softening. "Believe me when I say I know the pain you feel right now. I have felt it keenly and often. Sometimes it is harder to retreat than to charge. I am not saying that your family cannot be saved. I am saying that we cannot save them tonight."

He stared at the town. Mara's words had been like cold river water quenching the fires of his anger. Gods, he felt so helpless.

Mara looked to the horizon. "We can't go east. The Hallowed Order has more knights stationed in Baybury. We'll have to skirt the swamp and head south. We go to Locket. We can find a ship there to take us to Godsmouth."

A ship? Godsmouth? A couple of hours ago he'd thought he was coming home at last. Now Mara was talking about traveling to Godsmouth, capital city of the Golden Remnant. It seemed crazy.

There was a distant shout from the direction of the town. Silhouetted against the flames was a figure on horseback. They seemed to be scanning the dark fields surrounding Hale's Crossing.

"Down," Mara hissed, crouching in the grass. She reversed Catgut's sword and held the hilt to him. "We go. Now."

He took the sword and sheathed it with shaking hands. Mara gestured to him and started off through the grass. He stared after her.

"Wait," he said. "Darvin."

She paused. "What about him?"

"He's hurt bad. Unconscious. He's in the trees over there, with the packhorse."

"Mugsy? She's still alive?"

Kole nodded.

Mara chewed her lip. "She always was tough. But she'll be too conspicuous. We need to be discrete. The villagers around here will be suspicious of us. A packhorse and an unconscious boy bring too much attention."

"We can't carry Darvin ourselves," Kole protested.

She didn't speak, but the look in her eyes made her thoughts clear. Kole shook his head.

"No. I'm not leaving him."

"Boy, listen—"

"No," he snapped. "You listen. I carried him out of that temple. I got him out of that swamp. I fought off snakes and swamp cats to get him here. His whole family is there." He pointed toward the burning town. "Dead by now, probably. I'm all he has left. I'm not leaving him to die."

"Then what do you propose we do?"

Kole hesitated. He looked back at Hale's Crossing one more time. His heart was being torn in two. If he left, he was abandoning his family. If he stayed, he would die.

He glanced down at the dead knight lying in the grass nearby.

"I have an idea."

PART III
FLIGHT

CHAPTER
19

ARA GRUMBLED SOFTLY as they hurried through the long grass toward the copse of trees where Kole had hitched Mugsy. A soft clanging accompanied every step.

"It chafes," she complained.

"Do you have a better idea?"

She frowned but said nothing. After a moment's silence, she went back to adjusting the armor they'd stripped off the knight's corpse.

The knight had been taller than Mara, bulkier, so his armor ran large on her. At least in the dark the poor fit wasn't too noticeable.

Mugsy whinnied softly as they approached. Hearing the packhorse, Mara hurried ahead.

"There, girl," Mara whispered, touching her hand to the horse's nose. She'd decided to forgo the gauntlets since the poor fit made them nearly unusable. The packhorse nuzzled her palm.

Darvin still sat tied to Mugsy's back. He was so quiet that for a moment Kole thought he was dead, but when he brought his ear close to the boy's mouth he could hear the faint rasp of his breath.

"He hasn't woken fully since the temple," Kole told Mara. "He talks in his sleep sometimes."

"Let me look at him." She took the lantern from him and lifted Darvin's head. He didn't make a sound. She peered close, taking his pulse and then examining his head. She was quiet a few seconds.

"He has suffered a head injury," she said. "But that may not be all that afflicts him. He may be suffering from flash sickness."

"What?"

"A reaction to the raw Ember sorcery Quintus unleashed."

Kole swallowed and glanced at Darvin. "He's infected?"

Mara shook her head. "Quintus used a pure vessel. But that was Ember source. The most destructive of sorceries. When released in an uncontrolled manner it can have effects beyond the physical." As she spoke, she opened her pack and retrieved a small green vial. Holding open Darvin's eyelids, she spilled a drop of the vial's contents into each eye.

"What kind of effects? Will he die?"

Chewing her lip, she turned back to him. "I don't know. I'll do my best to keep him alive. Quintus was always better versed in matters of the arcane." With a sigh, she returned the vial to her bag. "I know a physik in Locket who may be able to help. If we can get there."

Mara looked as exhausted as he felt. The prospect of fleeing into the night without rest made his feet ache. He stifled a cough as his smoke-filled lungs demanded a chance to recover.

But as much as it hurt to admit it, Mara was right. They couldn't stay.

She unhitched the horse and started leading them through the trees away from Hale's Crossing. "If we encounter any locals on the road, I'm a knight of the Hallowed Order and you are a local guide aiding me in my quest to root out the source of corruption in the region. We suspect Darvin is infected and we are taking him to receive judgment. That should be enough to encourage the locals to keep their distance."

"What if we encounter more knights?"

"Then we run. This armor won't fool them." She paused. "I need you to understand that if that happens, we may be forced to abandon Mugsy and Darvin."

Kole said nothing. It wouldn't come to that. He wouldn't let it.

He looked over his shoulder. The burning town was already hidden from Kole's sight. There was a hard lump in his chest.

It wasn't too late. He could still go back. He could do...*something*.

"I'm sorry this happened," Mara said softly, glancing back at him. "I'm sorry it's still happening."

Kole swallowed, blinking back tears. Then he turned his back on Hale's Crossing and followed her into the dark.

"Why did you come back for me?" he said after a moment. "Why did you save me back there?"

She was quiet for so long that Kole was beginning to think she hadn't heard the question. Finally, she spoke.

"I heard you in the temple. After Quintus…after he destroyed that fell creature, I heard you. I heard you using sorcery. I was barely conscious. I thought I was dreaming." She paused. "You were gone by the time I came to."

He swallowed. "Did you follow me back just to kill me?"

She shook her head. "I heard you speaking as well. After you cast your spell, I heard you speaking. Yours were not the words of a madman."

"I don't understand why I'm still sane."

"Neither do I. Not fully. I have heard rumors about people like you. Those who have been infected but do not succumb to the madness, at least not immediately. Some innate resistance, perhaps. A familial trait, just as certain Sundarin clans have a remarkable resistance to consumption. Or perhaps it is random. I don't know."

"You've never met anyone like that? Like me?"

"No." She stopped, then turned back to face him. "But there is something you must understand. You may be unaffected by the madness for now, but that does not mean you are not infected. When you use sorcery, you will still release the infectious miasma. Others who are exposed to that miasma can become infected. And they will not be as lucky as you. The sorcerer's plague will destroy their minds. It will drive them to madness and destruction."

Mara's eyes flashed as she stared at him. He withered beneath her gaze.

"In many ways, you are more dangerous than an ordinary sorcerer," she said. "Usually, the mind of an infected person is torn apart so rapidly that their condition quickly becomes apparent. Often they can be dealt with before serious harm is done. But you are different. You could go from place to place, spreading your infection and leaving a trail of madness and death behind you."

A cold chill swept through Kole's bones. "Aren't you afraid I'll infect you?"

"No. I am immune to the plague."

"Immune? How?"

"That isn't important right now. What is important is that you understand what you are. What you can do. You must not use your sorcery again. The risk is too great. I cannot be infected, but you could still infect Darvin or some passerby. You could cause an epidemic, like that which claimed Vale City some thirteen years ago. No matter what, you must resist the urge to use your power. Do you understand?"

Swallowing, Kole nodded.

Eyes hard, Mara turned away and continued leading Mugsy on through the wood.

They soon emerged to find another muddy field. They paused at the edge of the wood for a few moments, scanning the darkness for Hallowed Order armsmen or roaming villagers that had been whipped up into a murderous frenzy. But there were no lights moving through the tall grass, no shadows watching. With a nod from Mara, they continued on.

Kole guessed it was after midnight by the time they found a road, if it could even be called that. There were muddy ruts that suggested the road saw occasional cart traffic—farmers and fishmongers moving their stock among the villages that dotted the area.

The land got wilder the further south they went. From off to their right Kole could smell the faint stink of the swamp wafting over the fields and through the tangled woods. They were entering more sparsely populated territory, where the great shadow of Notte's Mire drove away all but the hardiest settlers.

Kole was dead on his feet. He was struggling to remember what it was like to not be walking, always walking. His stomach was tight with hunger pains. Mara only had a single meal's worth of rations left, which they split between them as they walked.

In truth, Kole was thankful for the exhaustion and the aches and the hunger. They created a thick fog over his mind, drowning out thoughts and memories. It was a relief to let Mara take the lead while he followed along in silence.

A few hours before dawn, Kole asked Mara, "How far until we know we're clear of the Hallowed Order?"

She looked at him. "I killed one of their number and you are a sorcerer. They will follow us from one corner of the world to another."

"They don't know I'm a sorcerer," Kole said.

"They will when they find the dead knight. You remember the crystal he used to defend against your sorcery? It leaves a residue. When they find that, they will know what it means."

Kole glanced at the empty road behind them, half expecting to see a troupe of riders charging toward them. Would this nightmare never end?

He felt a hand on his shoulder, gentle yet firm. He looked back to meet Mara's eyes.

"It's just the two of us now," she said. "You understand? Darvin hovers near death, and Mugsy, as strong as she is, can only follow our lead. It comes down to us. I need you to watch my back. Just as I will watch yours. Our fates are intertwined."

Kole nodded his understanding. "Like the bird and the hippopotamus."

The ghost of a smile touched Mara's lips. "Angok loved that story. I don't think he even knew what a hippopotamus looks like."

Kole looked north once more. He imagined he could see the faintest whisper of smoke rising from beyond the horizon, where Hale's Crossing stood.

"The others," he said. "Angok. Catgut. Quintus. Does it hurt, knowing they're gone?"

"Like a sword through my heart."

Kole nodded, turning back to her. "Then what do we do?"

"We go on," she said simply.

CHAPTER
20

HE TRADING POST had been abandoned for years. It sat at the corner of an old crossroads, once well-traveled and now fallen into disuse. The wilderness pressed in close around the muddy, rutted roads, the trees casting long shadows in the pre-dawn light.

The trading post itself was a tall building of whitewashed timber with a slanting roof and small windows fitted with leaded glass. The roof and one wall had partially collapsed from the damp and the weight of leaves. An elm tree had muscled its way into the space left behind.

A thick tangle of weeds and grass surrounded the abandoned trading post and its neighboring stables. But through the overgrowth, behind the half-collapsed building, Kole could just make out a timber roof atop a stone well.

Kole and Mara crouched in the trees just out of sight of the road, studying the trading post. Mugsy was hitched to a tree nearby, Darvin murmuring softly atop her.

Kole's eyes burned. He could still feel the smoke irritating them, even though they were hours now from Hale's Crossing. They'd walked all through the night, the burning town at their backs.

Twice, mobs of villagers roving the countryside had appeared out of the darkness around them, torches and lanterns burning bright. Both times there had been just enough time to get off the road before they were spotted.

Kole had lain in the damp dirt and watched them pass—men and women and even children, all clustered together as if they were no longer individuals but some dangerous, fearful whole. They had reminded him of Mertyn Walter's family, except it was panic, not sorcery, that had fused them together.

He shuddered and licked his dry lips. Mara had drunk the last of their water hours ago, when she'd first reappeared and killed that knight. Most of the creeks this close to the swamp were too muddy and fetid to drink from. The well behind the trading post could be the only unguarded source of water for miles.

But Mara forced him to wait. They'd been watching the trading post for ten minutes now. There were no signs of movement.

"We have to risk it," Kole whispered. "We can't get to Locket without water."

Mara didn't move.

"Neither can Mugsy," Kole added.

That did it. Mara's lips tightened and she shot a look at the packhorse. The horse had already fallen asleep standing up.

With a grunt, Mara took hold of her hammer. "All right. Wait here."

She crept forward through the trees, paused at the edge of the small clearing, then strode out into the open, her armor clinking.

Nothing moved.

Kole watched as she hurried to the collapsed wall of the trading post. She peered in through the opening, then moved around the side of the building and disappeared from his sight.

Kole waited in the shadow of the trees. There was a sick knot in his stomach, one that had not come untied since leaving Hale's Crossing. The sight of that arrow striking Da kept flashing before his eyes. He kept seeing the sword slip from Da's grip, the twitch of his muscles as he'd fallen.

And here Kole was again, hiding and scared, as helpless as a newborn lamb. It filled him with a sick, directionless, all-encompassing anger. The feelings came at him in waves: rage and fear, nausea and exhaustion. He couldn't hold them all at once. They threatened to break out, leaving him curled up in the dirt, weeping.

After what seemed like an hour, Mara emerged again. She hurried back to the tree line.

"It's clear," she said. "Let's do this quickly and get out of here."

It was a mercy to have something to do, a goal to distract him from his own grief. Leaving Mugsy asleep and tethered to the tree, he followed Mara into the clearing. He glanced through the ruined wall of the trading post as they hurried past. Inside, he could see close-packed shelves, many of them rotten and collapsed. The place had been picked nearly clean. Only a few items remained—he caught a glimpse of a badly rusted iron trap and some strips of what might have once been rabbit skins hanging up on one wall.

They fought their way through the weeds to the well. Between the two of them, they were able to shift the wooden cover that had been left over the well's opening. There was a winch to lower a bucket, but the rope was rotted and the bucket had so many holes it had become a sieve.

"I think I saw a bucket inside the trading post," Mara said. "Go get our rope."

Kole nodded and hurried back to Mugsy. The horse didn't wake even when he searched through her saddlebags to find the coil of rope. Darvin groaned in his sleep.

The sun was beginning to rise when Kole returned to the well. Mara joined him a few moments later with a small wooden bucket. She cast a wary eye down the well.

"Do you think it's drinkable?" he asked.

"We can only hope."

Kole tied the rope to the bucket and lowered it into the well. He felt it begin to take on water.

Together, they hauled the bucket back up. The water was clear, and when Kole dipped his cupped hands into the bucket and took a sip, it tasted cool and clean. He drank greedily.

"I take it it's good, then?" Mara said, eying him.

He murmured agreement, still drinking. The water soothed his raw, smoke-burned throat and went partway to filling the hole in his stomach.

"All right," she said, pushing him out of the way with her hip and scooping up some water for herself. "Save some for the rest of us."

Once their thirst was sated, they filled another bucket and returned to Mugsy to replenish all the waterskins they had.

Mugsy woke with a start while Kole was halfway through filling the third waterskin. Snorting, the horse danced away and tensed her back legs for a kick.

"Easy," Mara said, taking Mugsy's bridle and stroking her nose. "You're all right, girl. Here." Mara gestured and Kole handed her the half-full bucket. The horse shot Kole one more glare, then deigned to drink.

Darvin groaned at the horse's movement. The ropes that tied Darvin to Mugsy's harness were starting to chafe him, raising red welts anywhere they crossed exposed skin. Kole tried to adjust the ropes, but he knew they would only chafe somewhere else.

There was no other choice. They couldn't carry Darvin themselves. And they couldn't leave him. Mara had said there was a physik that could help in the city of Locket, but right now Locket seemed a long way away.

Birds sang in the trees around him, as if mocking his despair. He tried to block out the sound and focus on what needed doing.

But as Kole was dribbling water into Darvin's mouth, he became aware of a distant rumbling. It had crept up on him, no more than a vibration in the earth at first. Then, just on the edge of hearing, came the sound. He lowered the waterskin and glanced at Mara.

"Do you hear that?" he asked.

She stopped stroking Mugsy's nose and cocked her head to the side. Her eyes grew wide.

"Riders!" she hissed, quickly untethering Mugsy and pulling down into the undergrowth. "Get down."

He could hear the sound more clearly now: it wasn't rumbling, it was the sound of several sets of hooves pounding along the road from the north. He suddenly remembered the sound of the knight charging at him across the field as he tried to flee back into the swamp. His heart grew suddenly cold.

It's just villagers out on a ride, he told himself. *Or a merchant caravan.*

But few villagers had riding horses of their own, and large merchant caravans didn't come down these rural roads. Not with that many horses. Not at speed.

Mara grabbed him by the tunic and pulled him down next to Mugsy as the riders appeared. From where they were hiding, Kole could only catch glimpses of them between the leaves. It was enough. The riders were not villagers or merchants.

They were Hallowed Order.

At the sight of the beaked helmet worn by the leader of the column, an involuntary moan tried to worm its way out of Kole's throat. He clapped a hand over his mouth to stifle it. For a moment it seemed as if he could see the fires of a burning Hale's Crossing reflected in the knight's helmet. Spots danced in front of his eyes. He suddenly wanted to be sick.

He felt Mara's hand grip his shoulder. She brought her lips to his ear.

"Breathe," she whispered softly. "Breathe. Nice and slow. In. Out."

It was the same tone she used when whispering to Mugsy. He supposed that should make him angry. It didn't. It made him want to cry.

"Breathe," she said again.

He realized he'd been holding his breath. As he allowed himself to breathe, he suddenly wanted to suck in the air, to get as much of it into his lungs as he could. Instead, he focused on Mara's breathing, tried to match his to hers. Slowly, the panic subsided.

He blinked away the spots that had formed in his vision. Out on the road he caught glimpses of other riders. Five, maybe six of them. They didn't wear the knights' beaked helmets, but their shaved heads and blue surcoats flapping in the morning light marked them as armsmen of the Hallowed Order.

The riders were slowing. The gallop became a canter and then the knight called a halt. As the pounding hoofbeats ceased, Kole could hear the snorting and panting of the horses. They were all large, strong beasts, none of them less than two hands taller than Mugsy.

Mugsy whickered softly at the scent of the foreign horses. Mara took hold of the packhorse's nose, turning her calming whisper on Mugsy now instead of Kole.

As Mara's hand left his shoulder, he shifted slightly so that he could see the knight through the trees once more. It was a man, he thought, taller than the armsmen that sat behind him. Or perhaps it was just the size of his destrier that made it seem that way.

The knight sat up straight, helmeted head turning from the dirt cross-roads to the ruined trading post. Dark eyeholes passed over the place where Kole and Mara hid. Another moan threatened to escape Kole's throat.

"What is this place, good man?" the knight's voice rang from his beaked helmet.

A reedy response came from among the other riders. "An old trading post, if it pleases you, Knight-Protector. Not been in use since I was just a boy, I should think."

One of the armsmen leaned forward to pat his horse's flank, giving Kole a glimpse at the man who'd spoken. It wasn't an armsman, though he was sitting on the back of one of their horses, clinging nervously to the rider.

He was a middle-aged man with a receding hairline and ears that seemed too big for the rest of him. He was bundled in a woolen cloak of a similar style to the one Kole had brought with him. His accent, too, was local. He must have been from one of the nearby villages, though Kole couldn't put a name to him.

A local guide, he realized. Someone who could help the Hallowed

Order navigate the countryside and hunt down those who had escaped Hale's Crossing.

Kole's fear suddenly gave way to a rush of anger. Was it not enough for these villagers to burn Hale's Crossing? Did they have to become the knights' toadies as well? What did the man hope to gain? A few pieces of silver? Divine favor?

"Search it," the knight commanded.

The armsmen dismounted. One remained with the horses and the local guide, while the others fanned out and headed toward the trading post.

Kole shrank back into the undergrowth as the armsmen swept past. Right now, the shadows around them were deep, but as the morning wore on even the thick woods might not be enough to hide them. Mugsy and Darvin especially were at risk of being seen.

But they couldn't move. There was no way to head deeper into the woods without making noise.

From where they were hiding, Kole watched as two of the armsmen ducked inside the ruined trading post. Two more headed to investigate the stables.

From the road came a heavy clank of armor. Kole turned back to see that the knight had dismounted and was striding through the weeds toward the stone well.

Kole's chest suddenly tightened. *The well cover.* It would be obvious that it had been moved recently. Would the knight see it? Would he understand its significance?

The knight kicked his way through the overgrowth and shoved aside a pile of rotted crates stacked behind the trading post. They tumbled into the grass and, seemingly satisfied, he moved on. He cracked open the door of the outhouse that backed onto the main building. Some small furry animal burst out and scurried away into the grass. The knight watched it go.

Then he turned toward the well. He stared at it for several seconds, unmoving. Then, slowly, he made his way over to it.

Kole realized he was holding his breath again. *Breathe,* he told himself. *Just breathe.* He tried, but he couldn't quite remember how. His lungs seemed too tight.

The knight stopped beside the well cover that Kole and Mara had shoved into the grass. He stared at it for a second, then turned to examine the rotted rope and hole-filled bucket that sat alongside. Reaching out a gauntlet-clad hand, he ran a finger along the stone of the well. Was there a mark there? Some scratch they'd made hauling water out?

Lifting his head, the knight turned and scanned the surrounding woods. For the second time Kole felt the dark, eyeless gaze touch him. This time, though, it did not pass straight over. This time, it paused.

Kole felt Mara's hand on his shoulder again. She squeezed so tight it nearly hurt.

Don't move, the hand said. *Not an inch.*

For an hour-long second they stayed like that, crouched motionless in the undergrowth. His muscles were cramping up. The pounding in his ears drowned out the birdsong above them.

The knight turned away.

The tension flooded from Kole's muscles. He wanted to collapse into the undergrowth.

"Ma," Darvin cried in his sleep.

The knight froze. Kole clamped a hand over Darvin's mouth, stifling another groan. Slowly, the knight turned back toward the woods.

Mara met Kole's eyes and adjusted her grip on her hammer.

"Knight-Protector!" an armsman called. "Locals approaching!"

The knight turned back toward the road as the other armsmen emerged from the trading post and stables.

"Anything?" the knight asked them.

"All clear."

He nodded. "Very well. With me."

As they marched back toward the crossroads, Kole heard a commotion growing louder. There was a rabble of voices and a muffled shouting. Exchanging a glance with Mara, he quietly shifted so he could see what was happening through the leaves.

A half-dozen villagers were approaching from the eastern branch of the crossroads, dragging something between them. As they got closer, Kole saw that it was an old man. His round face was swollen and bloodied. A rag had been tied into his mouth to gag him, though he was still trying to shout through it.

"My lord!" one of the villagers called out as the knight came to meet them.

"I am no lord, good woman," the knight said. Though his face was concealed by his helmet, he seemed to be smiling as he spoke. "Just a man. What have you brought? Is this a fugitive from Hale's Crossing?"

"No, my lo… No, sir. This here's old man Potts. Lives outside our village. Whitefield that is, down eastaways. Bit of a hermit, he is."

"Being a hermit is not a crime, good woman."

"No. But harboring fugitives is. Three of them he was hiding in his cellar, those Paleth boys from Hale's Crossing. I saw them running through the fields, I did. Potts took them in."

"Is that so?" The knight's black gaze turned toward the beaten man. "And where are these fugitives now?"

"We got 'em tied up in Whitefield. I can show you."

The knight looked back toward the trading post. Kole could feel him considering it.

So at least a few others had got out of Hale's Crossing. The Paleth brothers were decent enough. They'd never been unduly cruel to Kole and his family. His stomach knotted at the thought of what awaited them now.

Maybe others had got out as well. Not Da, perhaps, but what about Ma? Arabeth? Could they have escaped the mob?

"Very well," the knight said after a moment. "Brothers, poison the well and fire the trading post. Let us ensure that any fugitives who come this way find no shelter here."

"Yes, Knight-Protector," one of the armsmen responded. He began barking orders to the others.

Kole was amazed by how fast the armsmen were able to set the rotting building on fire. They were well-practiced, he supposed. In minutes the trading post and stables were both ablaze. Kole could feel the heat from their hiding spot in the woods. Mugsy shifted nervously, but the crackle of the fire drowned out any sounds she made.

One armsman put on gloves and covered his mouth and nose with a cloth mask, then poured the contents of a glass bottle into the well. He tossed the bottle in after.

Then, less than fifteen minutes after the mob of villagers had arrived, the Hallowed Order troops were mounted once more. The knight cast one last look toward the woods where Kole and Mara were hiding. Then he spoke a command and the column of riders began to follow the villagers back toward Whitefield, leaving the trading post burning behind them.

Kole and Mara hid in the woods until the Hallowed Order had long passed out of sight. When they were sure they were alone, they carefully rejoined the road.

"That was too close," Mara said. "We cannot stay on the roads, even rural ones. We have to head into the wild." She looked at him. "You know this region better than me. Where can we go?"

Kole chewed his lip, trying to clear his head so he could think. "We could cut through the Renegade Hills. It'll be rough going, especially for Mugsy. They say there's bandits up there, but not much else."

She nodded, looking south toward the rugged hills rising up ahead of them. "The hills it is."

CHAPTER
21

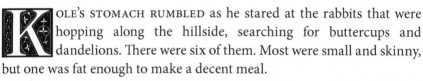OLE'S STOMACH RUMBLED as he stared at the rabbits that were hopping along the hillside, searching for buttercups and dandelions. There were six of them. Most were small and skinny, but one was fat enough to make a decent meal.

He was so hungry he could eat it raw.

Mara crept back to the hillside where he hid, carrying the braided hemp sling she'd dug out of Mugsy's saddlebag. "Have they moved?" she whispered.

He shook his head. His eyes ached. He needed sleep. "Still there."

"Good." She reached into her pocket and pulled out one of the smooth stones they'd gathered from a dry creek bed a few hours ago, just before they'd left the lowlands and made their way puffing and grunting up into the hills.

The Renegade Hills rose from the landscape like shards of broken glass pushed up from the hells below. The country was rugged, pitted with hidden rabbit holes and littered with scree. He was sure it was only a matter of time until one of them turned an ankle, especially considering how exhausted they all were—Mugsy included.

Mara was struggling to get a stone seated in the sling's pouch. Kole watched dubiously as the bullet slipped free and fell into the grass just as she was about to start swinging it.

"Are you sure you know how to use that?" he whispered.

She shot him a tired glare and picked up the stone. This time, at least, she managed to seat the stone and start spinning the sling. Kole backed off to give her space.

The fat rabbit sensed movement and stood up straight, a leaf in its mouth. Its ears twitched.

Mara let the stone fly. It sailed far over the rabbit's head. The family of rabbits scattered a few feet, then went back to their foraging.

Mara muttered a curse under her breath. "The Champion can cast all slings into the second hell. Give me a bow any day."

Kole remembered Catgut's bow. It was somewhere back in the swamp, the waxed string probably rotted through by now. Nothing lasted long in the mire. Nothing except that cursed temple, anyway.

Memories of the temple tumbled through his head—the scraping sound of snakes slithering against stone, the fetid stink of that feeding room. His stomach turned.

Forcing the memories back to the deepest recesses of his mind, he held out a hand to Mara. "Let me try."

"You know how to use it?"

"Sometimes Ma sent me or Arabeth out hunting whenever the townsfolk decided our money wasn't good enough to buy their fish."

She shook her head. "Only out here would a merchant let local superstition get in the way of profit."

She handed him the sling and another stone bullet. He slipped the stone into the sling pouch and crept forward.

Rubbing his tired eyes, he tried to bring the rabbits into focus. He didn't know how much longer he could go on without sleep.

Food first, he told himself. *Then sleep.*

He waited until the fat rabbit went still once again. Then he spun the sling quickly and released one end.

But his exhausted muscles betrayed him. The bullet flew a couple of inches wide, slamming into the ground next to the rabbit in a puff of dust. The rabbits scurried for their holes.

Kole cursed. Mara approached and he held out the sling for her to take.

"No," she said. "You were closer than me. Try again."

"I think I'm too tired. There's some blackberry bushes up on the hill over there. That'd be something, at least."

"Try once more. I'm in a mood for rabbit."

He supposed rabbit did sound better than berries. Nodding, he slipped another stone into the sling and waited for the rabbits to emerge again.

"I want you to try something," Mara whispered. "Something I remember Quintus telling me. Something Flesh sorcerers from the border regions of the Empire used to be able to do."

He glanced at her, his heart growing still. "You told me not to use sorcery."

"And I meant it. But this isn't a spell. It's just…using your senses. Look, now's your chance."

She pointed. She was right—the rabbits were as hungry as he was. They'd emerged from their holes, and the fat rabbit was once again munching on a thistle. It was a little further away now. He started to creep forward.

"No," Mara said. "Try from here."

"It's too far. I'm too tired to make the shot."

"Just try. Listen. Quintus said that Flesh sorcerers made good hunters. They could train themselves to reach out with their minds, sensing breathing, heartbeats. It helped them find game."

"I can see the damned rabbit already."

"It's not just about seeing it. It's about…connecting with it." She shrugged her armored shoulders. "I think. Something like that, anyway."

He turned back to the rabbit. It was true that in the temple, before he'd remade his leg, he'd sensed something. It was almost like he'd been able to hear Darvin's heartbeat, and the heartbeat of the snake that had attacked him. It had been like hearing a song sung in another language.

He wasn't sure how he'd done it. It wasn't like speaking an incantation. It was more like listening, or reading. Understanding the life around him, rather than changing it.

Exhaling, he looked at the fat rabbit. He could sense nothing except what his eyes showed him. Carefully, he reached out with his mind.

The world grew quiet. He could no longer hear the wind, and the afternoon sun didn't seem so bright. But then he felt something. Something inside him—his own heartbeat, smooth and steady. He could feel his lungs expanding; he could taste the sweet air entering him.

And he could sense Mara too. Her heartbeat was strong. Hot blood rushed through her arteries. For a moment it seemed he could see every drop of it pulsing through her body.

He reached out further. And he found the rabbit. Its heart was beating fast. Its muscles were filled with explosive power, ready to send it darting away at the first sign of danger.

This time, he knew, it wouldn't get the chance. He brushed his senses against its life flame, feeling the warmth there.

He could use his sorcery. He could hold its muscles still while he walked right up to it and wrung its neck.

But he didn't need to. The rabbit's life glowed bright in his head. How could he miss?

He spun the sling and let the bullet fly. The rabbit glanced up, its heart skipping a beat.

The stone crashed into its breast. The heart beat once more and went still. The life flame was snuffed out.

Kole came gasping back to the real world, his senses retreating. A bitter taste filled his mouth. He blinked at the brightness of the sky.

Mara steadied him. "Are you all right?"

Swallowing, he nodded.

"You really did it, didn't you?" she asked.

He hesitated, then nodded again.

Mara exhaled. "I thought maybe..." She shook her head. "I don't know."

"You thought maybe I wasn't a sorcerer after all?"

"It seems stupid when you put it like that."

She studied him a second longer, her face unreadable. Then she gave him a strained smile.

"Let's go get our dinner," she said.

They made camp in a natural hollow among the hills, where a rocky overhang would provide some degree of cover from the elements. Kole put Darvin in the best bit of shelter and dribbled a little water into his mouth before he went searching for firewood. He could only find an armful of dry sticks, but they could only risk a small fire in any case.

As Kole prepared the rabbit, Mara set down her pack and tended to Mugsy. Her slim backpack was overstuffed—Kole could see the sharp corners of two books straining against the fabric.

For the first time since he'd left the temple, he thought about the book that Quintus had found in the arcanum, the book he'd thrown to Mara before he sacrificed himself to destroy the abomination. It was clear to Kole now that it had been that book—not the promise of treasure—that had drawn the freebooters to the idol of Gnothea. He'd seen the truth in Quintus's eyes there at the end.

He stared at the backpack a little longer, hardly paying attention to the rabbit he was skinning. Then he looked at Mara—at her bruised face and her hard lines. She had finished brushing down Mugsy, and was now stripping out of the ill-fitting armor. The light of the setting sun caught in her hair and illuminated the strange runes tattooed across her scalp.

"Who are you, really?" he asked softly.

She paused midway through unstrapping her greaves.

"What do you mean?" she asked without glancing at him.

"You're no ordinary treasure seeker. None of you were."

She laid her greaves down and sat back in the dirt. "Treasure comes in many forms."

"Most freebooters like the shiny forms."

"Know many freebooters, do you?"

He had nothing to say to that. She shot him a small smile.

"Consider yourself lucky," she said. "Most of the ones I've known were sour bastards. I met a man once that had tried to plunder one of the dead cities of the Slave Kings. In the process he disturbed a pride of desert lions living there. They ripped his jaw clean off before he and his companions managed to kill two of the beasts and drive the rest away. He replaced his jaw with one from a dead lioness."

"Really?"

"That's what he told me." She shook her head. "At least I think that's what he was trying to say. He was a little hard to understand."

"And did he go into that dead city in search of old books?"

"No. He preferred rubies." She pulled her bag over to her and carefully removed the book that Quintus had found in the temple.

It was a smaller tome than the other book in Mara's bag, the one he'd often seen her puzzling over. It was thick, though, almost as thick as it was wide. Its cover was not leather—instead it seemed to be crafted from a plate of brass. The impression of an eagle in flight was etched into the metal. There was an inscription beneath the eagle, written in a language Kole didn't recognize. Heavy hinges clung to the spine, worked with fili-gree and ancient runes. As Mara turned it over in her hands, he saw that there was a latch stretching from the front cover to the back, preventing the book from being opened. There was no lock that Kole could see, but a pale gem—a pearl, perhaps—was set into the center of the latch, sur-rounded by a circle of runes.

"What is it?" Kole asked, the rabbit dangling from his hand.

"I don't know," she said.

Kole gave a disbelieving grunt. "You went into the temple searching for that book. You must know what it is."

"Quintus did," she said. "Or thought he did, at least. He just called it the Thesis."

"Didn't you ask him what was in it?"

"Quintus never gave a straight answer to anything. His only joy in life came from speaking in riddles. It helped him feel like the smartest man in the room."

"But you risked your life. All of our lives." Something simmered inside him. "Based on what? Quintus's riddles?"

"You didn't know Quintus like I did. He said the book is important, so it is."

"Important?" Kole snapped. He suddenly realized he was looming over Mara, the rabbit in one hand and a knife in the other. He couldn't remember getting to his feet. "Important? How many people died for that *important* book?"

As if in response to his raised voice, Darvin gave a soft groan. Mara didn't look at him. "Sit down, boy."

"Don't call me boy!" All his grief and anger and exhaustion was bubbling out of him at once. He jabbed the knife toward the book. "You said there was treasure down there. If we hadn't been too busy looking at ancient books, we could have filled our packs with gold and been out of there before those snakes ever found us."

"You don't understand—"

"No! No, I don't. I don't understand. And neither do you, apparently. You can't even tell me what they died for!"

Mugsy whinnied nervously. Standing, Mara patted the creature's nose and then reached into her pack. She pulled out a drawstring sack and tossed it into the dirt at Kole's feet. It clinked as it landed. Something golden peeked out the top.

Kole stared at the bag for a moment, then nudged it with his foot. He could see the shape of rods moving about inside. No, not rods. Scepters. The scepters Wolfun had looted before everything went wrong.

"There," Mara said. "Your treasure. It'll be worth a few coins if we can find a fence. It's something, at least."

Kole exhaled, trying to rid himself of the turmoil of emotions that swirled inside him. What use was the treasure now that his family was... was...

He slumped. He wanted to lash out. He wanted someone to blame for everything that had happened.

Exhausted, he sat back down, leaving the bag of scepters lying in the dirt between them. After a moment, Mara returned the book to her bag and came over to start the fire.

"We call ourselves the Wayfarers," she said.

She scraped flint against steel and sparks flashed in her eyes. The tinder caught.

"We are an organization dedicated to the acquisition of knowledge and artifacts from before the world was riven," she continued. "We hunt not treasure, but the lost lore of our ancestors."

She stared into the growing fire, feeding twigs into the flame.

"Why?" he asked.

"We… The Wayfarers believe that the only way to stave off destruction is to sift through the ruins of our past and find where our ancestors went wrong. They hope that a solution can be found on some ancient tablet or in a long-forgotten tome."

"What destruction? What solution?"

Mara sat back on her haunches. "We're dying, Kole. All of us. The world is diseased. If a treatment cannot be found, all will be lost."

"I don't understand. You're talking about the plague?"

She nodded. "The plague, yes. And more. The world was dealt a mortal blow when the plague struck. The fires of the Outbreak no longer burn like they once did, true. But the embers still glow, scattered about the world, ready to flare once more. Here in the Golden Remnant the infection still spreads, no matter how many towns and villages the Hallowed Order puts to the torch. Only thirteen years ago Vale City became corrupted and was destroyed, along with tens of thousands of its proud citizens. With the Vale Road under tight control, the western Remnant has been slowly choking to death ever since. In Godsmouth, the Ratcatcher Guild wages an endless war against the plague rats in the undercity, and yet entire neighborhoods still succumb on a yearly basis. There are sections of the city that have been under permanent quarantine for more than a century.

"Other lands fare no better. Only a handful of the Nizaan islands still stand, while the rest are now nesting grounds for chimera and tribes of corrupted subhumans. The Silken Fleets grow smaller every year. In the north, the Caravan Lords are becoming ever more fractured, while even the savage Gor tribes are losing territory to the desert wyrms. In the east, the Choir of the Undying raids frontier settlements as it gathers its strength for an overwhelming assault on our lands. Sundar wars with itself for the few resources that remain in the south. And over everything hangs the shadow of the plague, threatening to snuff out what little light remains. It will be a long, slow death. One that may not come for a century or more. But if nothing is done, the last fragments of civilization will fall."

Kole swallowed. "You've seen these things yourself?"

"Some."

"But...you could be wrong."

"Perhaps," she said. "I hope so."

Kole wanted to believe she was mistaken. But after watching fire and madness claim his town, the prospect of civilization's total destruction no longer seemed far-fetched. He shivered, though the evening had not yet grown cool.

"You said you think there's an answer to be found. Is it in that book?" He jerked his head toward Mara's pack, where she'd stowed the locked tome.

"Part of an answer, maybe. That's what Quintus thought. He thought this book could help save us all. It could change the world, Kole. That is why it is imperative that we get it to those who know what to do with it."

"Should we try to open it?"

"That is not our role. I have neither the skill nor the inclination to bypass the lock. And judging by the cover, it is written in some variant of High Yuleen. Perhaps Quintus could have deciphered some of it, but it is beyond my ability to read."

Kole frowned. "There must be other people who can read High whatever."

"Yuleen," she said. "And yes. Quintus had made contact with a scholar by the name of Sygil Fairider in Godsmouth. He thought she would be sympathetic to our cause. We may be able to convince her to help us." She grimaced. "Though it's a risk I'm not sure I want to take."

"Because of the Hallowed Order?"

She nodded. "Blackspire, their stronghold, lies within Godsmouth's walls. They are strong there. Even the Moonlit Tyrant does not act against them lightly. They have agents all over the city. The Wayfarers slip through the city frequently, but to make contact with a famous scholar like Fairider invites death down on our heads. The Hallowed Order is suspicious of scholars at the best of times. They may already be keeping an eye on her."

Kole realized he still hadn't finished skinning the rabbit in his hand. As Mara fed the fire, he went back to preparing their meager meal.

"Preacher Gameson back home used to say the plague was a curse from the old gods," Kole said. "He said that humans became greedy for knowledge they had no right to, so the gods turned the gift of sorcery into a blight to punish us for our arrogance."

Mara nodded. "The Hallowed Order holds that same belief. They think that what the Wayfarers are doing could invite more divine wrath upon us all."

"You don't believe that?"

"I believe humans too often look for meaning where there is none. The Gambler knows how much rests on the roll of a dice."

Kole hesitated. "You said the Wayfarers believe we can save ourselves. That we can find a solution."

"That's right."

"But you don't believe that, do you?"

She didn't say anything for a long time. Kole began to wonder if he'd somehow offended her. He finished skinning and gutting the rabbit, then set a pot above the fire. It would be a thin stew with little to season it, but his stomach growled at the prospect just the same.

"I'm not sure what I believe anymore," Mara said quietly.

Kole looked at her. As the evening deepened, shadows passed across Mara's face.

"Then why are you here?" he asked. "Why go to the temple in the first place?"

"Duty. Atonement, maybe." She sighed. "I'll let you know when I figure it out myself. But what I believe doesn't matter right now. I just know I need to get Quintus's book to the Citadel. That's what he would want. That's what matters."

"What is this Citadel? Your home?"

"As close as I have to one."

"And it's in Godsmouth?"

"Close by," she said. "It's hidden. If the Hallowed Order were to find us, everything we have worked for would be destroyed."

"And there are people there who can help me? People who can help me understand what I am?"

"Yes." She smiled. "You will like it there, I think. I do."

"Maybe," he said.

But he was doubtful. Maybe the Citadel was Mara's home, but it wasn't his.

His home was lost.

CHAPTER
22

HERE WERE ONLY a few signs of civilization up in the Renegade Hills. A goatherd's shack here, a lonely hovel there. Whenever they came across one, Mara insisted they steer clear. Sometimes Kole wondered if her paranoia was unwarranted. Surely they were safe enough here, where the goats outnumbered the people several times over.

But it wasn't worth the argument. At least they were having no trouble finding food. There were enough rabbits up here to make anyone sick, and Kole was getting better and better at hunting them.

On their third day in the hills they made camp an hour earlier than usual. Mara said the spot they'd found would be the best campsite they were likely to some across that day. It could conceal them well, and there was a creek nearby as well as a small wooded valley that would provide plenty of firewood.

All that was true, but Kole also noticed the sheen of sweat on Mara's forehead, and how gingerly she sat down on the hillside when they stopped. The pain in her hip was getting worse. They couldn't keep pushing on at the pace they were going, not in country like this.

"I'll fetch some firewood," he told her after he'd laid Darvin down alongside her and unloaded Mugsy's burdens.

Mara scanned the surrounding hilltops. "Don't go too far."

He nodded and left her to make camp.

He filled his waterskin at the creek and then made his way into the valley, heading for the thin woods that lay nestled amid them. The trees looked dry and stunted—he didn't like his chances of finding decent game, but at least there'd be plenty of firewood. He'd brought the sling and a few stones in case he spotted anything worth trying to bring down.

He held the scabbard of Catgut's sword to keep it from rattling as he began to pick his way through the woods. No use scaring off whatever game there might be.

The sword had become a comforting weight at Kole's side. Mara had insisted he not take it off except when he was sleeping, and even then he should keep it beside him.

Mara was never further than an arm's reach from her hammer. Sometimes she seemed to cradle it as closely as a lover.

For some reason that made him think of Kateen Miller, the girl from Hale's Crossing he'd once had a crush on—a crush that maybe, he admitted, he'd never fully gotten over. She was a pretty girl, red-cheeked and dark-haired.

Of course it had only ever been an idle fantasy—she had never shown any interest in getting tangled up with a corpse dragger. Likely she would've ended up married to some wholesome young man from one of the nearby villages.

He wondered what had happened to her. Was she lying dead among the charred ruin of Hale's Crossing? Had she escaped? She had family in Fairhill. Maybe she'd been visiting there when the Hallowed Order put Hale's Crossing to the torch.

He hoped she was still alive. Kateen was never cruel like Darvin and his friends. She was a kind person. She didn't deserve to suffer.

A sudden ache filled Kole's heart. The pain was almost great enough to make him drop the dry sticks he'd gathered and curl up in the grass, weeping.

He thrust all thoughts of Kateen Miller and Hale's Crossing from his head. Those memories filled his head enough while he slept—he didn't need to entertain them during the day as well. The thoughts were too sharp. He could feel them cutting into his mind every time he allowed them to become unsheathed.

As he caught his breath, he got a whiff of a familiar smell. Woodsmoke and meat. A cooking fire.

He froze and stared up through the thin canopy. Between the branches of the barren trees he caught sight of a thin column of smoke drifting up from beyond the nearest ridge.

That wasn't Mara's doing. Their camp was behind him. Someone else was in the hills.

Indecision flooded him for a moment. Some of Mara's paranoia had rubbed off on him. Was this just the home of another lonely hermit? Or had the Hallowed Order finally caught up with them?

He forced himself to breathe. He couldn't afford to panic. They hadn't seen any sign of the Hallowed Order since they began traveling through the hills—there was no reason to assume this was them now. But he had to be sure.

He put the pile of firewood down and crept up the ridge, his heart hammering in his chest. Leaves crunched deafeningly loud beneath his feet.

The woods thinned as he neared the top of the ridge. On the wind he caught the faint sound of voices. He got down on his belly and crawled the rest of the way until the floor of the shallow valley came into view.

It wasn't the Hallowed Order. But it wasn't another goatherd's cottage either.

Kole counted eleven men and women in the camp. There were children as well, three of them. One was only a toddler. The others looked around nine or ten.

A skinny goat was roasting above a fire in the center of the camp. The smell made Kole's mouth water. Around the cooking fire were several tents and two large wagons with wheels designed to contend with the rough country. Five skinny horses were tied to makeshift hitching posts on the edge of the camp. A large, black hound slept nearby.

All three of the children—even the toddler—seemed to be preparing the evening's meal, along with two of the adults. The others were scattered around the camp, some dicing and drinking, others mending clothes and tents. One was fletching arrows while another sat at a table counting a small pile of silver coins. There were sentries as well, three of them, each sitting a few yards out from the camp's perimeter. They were all armed with bows.

Hunters? Up in these hills, it wasn't likely. The goat on the spit had almost certainly been poached.

Kole looked again at the man counting coins, and then studied the eclectic mixture of clothes the gang wore. Some of their tunics and cloaks were little more than rags, but Kole spotted finer items among them—one wore a silk cape and another had a silver necklace that glinted with jewels.

No, these weren't hunters. They were bandits.

Kole scrambled back below the skyline and hurried down into the woods. They had to get out of here. Up here, bandits were as much a danger as the Hallowed Order.

Even if the bandits didn't kill them, they would be happy to take Mugsy and their weapons and everything else of value they had. Without a horse and supplies Kole and Mara would never make it to Locket before the Hallowed Order caught them.

There was still a chance. The bandits didn't know they were here. Mara hadn't started a fire. They'd been quiet. If they left now and pressed on through the night, they would be safe.

He crunched through the leaves, his hand on his sword. The afternoon was growing late. He just needed to—

A twig snapped off to Kole's right. He spun as he heard a pile of dried branches tumbling into the undergrowth.

A woman was staring at him, a pile of fallen firewood at her feet. She was dressed in a green wool-spun tunic, well-worn riding breeches, and a pair of boots that were far too fine for the rest of her outfit. Her ragged hair was cut short and there was a cruel twist to her lips.

As Kole turned to run, the woman swung her bow from her shoulder and tugged an arrow from the quiver at her hip.

"Run and I drop you, little rabbit," she said as she nocked the arrow.

He froze, eyes darting about wildly. The trees around him were too thin and widely spaced to offer much in the way of cover. And she was close, too close. If she was any sort of shot, she could put an arrow in him before he could scramble out of sight.

She moved slowly closer, each footstep careful and deliberate. "Hand off the sword, little rabbit."

He realized he had drawn two inches of steel. He could charge her. It might scare her enough to send the first arrow wide. He'd be on her before she could nock the second.

But he looked into her eyes and saw no fear there. Wariness, perhaps. And hunger, and a cold ruthlessness. But no fear.

Kole was scared, though. Even after all he'd seen since entering Notte's Mire, he was still scared. Maybe it was *because* of all he'd seen that he was so scared.

He slammed the sword back into its scabbard and lifted his hand away from it. He was ashamed to see how much his fingers were trembling.

"There," the woman said. "Ain't that better? Now we can talk, civil-like."

"I don't have any money."

"You got a sword, though. What's a farmboy like you doing with a sword?"

He swallowed. "I found it."

"Did ya?" She laughed. It was a harsh laugh. "Just lying about, was it?"

He said nothing. He had to get away. He had to warn Mara.

The woman stepped closer. As if reading his thoughts, she said, "Where's your camp, little rabbit?"

"I don't have one."

"No?"

"No," he said.

"You're just out here all by your lonesome, with no horse and no pack. Nothing but a sword and the clothes on your back. That right?"

He shut his mouth before he could get caught in another lie. The woman grinned a predatory grin. She scanned the woods around them.

"Where you from, little rabbit?" she asked him.

"Near Baybury."

"Yeah? What village?"

He picked the only one he could think of. "Maybrook."

"No kidding? I got an uncle in Maybrook. Don't sound much like you, though. I got an ear for accents, you know. If I were a betting woman—and I am—I'd say you come from somewhere a little west of Maybrook."

As he listened to her words, Kole became aware of her heartbeat. He could sense it across the space between them, hot and wet and steady. His own heart was galloping like a racehorse.

Without meaning to reach out with his senses, he became aware of other heartbeats around him as well. Small, quick hearts—the hearts of nearby animals. Though the thin woods seemed sparsely populated, he could sense the life hidden all around him—a family of badgers in their burrow, a lone owl sleeping the day away. He could feel the rapid beat of a mouse on the edge of his perception. And closer, concealed in a nearby bush, he could sense the life flame of a grouse or pheasant.

"You know," the bandit said, "one of our boys went into town for supplies the other day. He got talking to some folks. Apparently there was some kind of hubbub up in Hale's Crossing a few days ago."

Kole's breath caught. He didn't trust himself to speak.

The woman nodded, her piercing eyes never leaving his face. "That's right. Maybe you heard. Got the Hallowed Order involved, even. Those shiny knights and their bald little armsmen have been all over the place these last few days. Stopping traffic, asking questions. Been bad for business. I'm wasting away over here. You know what they've been looking for?"

Kole said nothing.

"Runaways," she said. "They say a few folk got out of Hale's Crossing before the place burned to the ground. Tainted folk, maybe. Infected, even. Those glorious knights are offering rewards for information. And bounties on any captured runaways. What do you think of that, little rabbit, all alone in the hills with soot on your bootstraps?"

He had to get away from her. If she took him back to her camp there would be no chance of escape. They would take him to the Hallowed Order. And it would all be over.

Why doesn't she call to her friends? If she shouted at the top of her lungs they might hear. Then there would be no chance of him slipping away. Was she worried the shout would spook him?

No, he realized. She was worried the shout would spook whoever else was back at Kole's camp. She must have suspected they were camped nearby. Better not to put them on alert. Better to wait until she could gather her friends quietly and maybe capture a few more bounties.

"You did well to make it all this way," she said. "But it's time to stop running now, little rabbit. I'm going to introduce you to some friends of mine. They'll make sure you're nice and comfy until we can get you where you belong. Come on, now." She jerked her head back toward the ridge.

"Wait," he said quickly, still formulating his plan. "I have gold."

"Do ya?" She smirked like she didn't believe him. "And here you was telling me you didn't have any money."

"I lied."

"Where'd a boy like you find gold?"

"I got it off an Order armsman. Same as this sword. Some townsfolk managed to kill him during the raid."

"And you robbed him?" She tsked. "What would your mother say?"

"The gold is in my pocket. You can have it if you let me go." He tried to sound panicked. It wasn't hard.

"I can have it either way," she said. But she glanced at his pocket. Her lips twitched. He could see her doing sums inside her head.

He had no gold. He knew any bounty on his head would be worth more than a few coins anyway. And he knew that she knew that. There was no way she would let him go.

He was counting on her greed. On that cunning he could see in her eyes. She could take him back to her camp right now and there would be nothing he could do about it.

But then she'd have to share his gold with her friends. If she took his gold here, though, where there was no one about, she could keep it all to herself and still get her share of the bounty.

That was what he was counting on. That her greed would outweigh her caution. That it would outweigh her loyalty to the other bandits in the camp.

He could feel her heart beat a little faster in excitement as she worked through the same thoughts. The feeling was almost pleasurable.

"Show me, then." She tapped the string of her bow. "And keep your hand away from that sword."

He nodded quickly, letting his hand shake as he slipped it into his pocket. He dug deep, pretending to be fumbling for his coin purse.

"Quit messing about," she snapped. "Show me."

"Here." He pulled his hand from his pocket and took a step toward her. As he did, he kicked a loose rock toward a nearby bush where he could sense another heart beating.

A large grouse burst from the bush and took flight, swooping past the bandit's head. She cursed and flinched, her arrow slipping from the string.

Before she could recover, Kole dropped a round stone into the sling he'd pulled from his pocket. He began to spin it just as the bandit saw what he was doing and nocked her arrow once more.

He released one end of the string and let the stone fly. Even with his heart pounding, the practice he'd had hunting rabbits served him well. Even before it hit he knew the shot was true.

The bullet struck the woman's hand just before she loosed her arrow. He heard bone crack and the bandit cried out. Her arrow sailed harmlessly past Kole's shoulder.

He charged. Fear pushed him forward, fear and desperation. The pounding of the woman's heart filled his ears. Her eyes went wide.

He pulled Catgut's sword from its scabbard. The bandit began to draw another arrow, saw she wouldn't have time to loose it, then dropped her bow and reached for her belt knife.

Without slowing to bring the sword's blade to bear, Kole hammered the pommel into the woman's face. Her nose cracked. Before she could cry out again, Kole threw his weight into her and brought her down with him on top.

His knee slammed into her stomach and he watched her gasp for breath. Her heartbeat was as fast as his now. He could almost taste her blood in his mouth. She raised her hand.

He brought the sword's pommel down again. It slammed into her forehead. She groaned and went still.

Kole knelt panting atop her, raising the sword above his head. She was still alive. He could still sense her heartbeat, though he was beginning to lose his grasp on it. The strange feeling of connectedness that had come over him earlier was fading away, replaced with a bitter taste in his mouth and a sick churning in his stomach.

He looked down at her, sword still raised. Blood trickled from her broken nose and the side of her head. The cruel sneer that had twisted her lips was gone.

His hands trembled around the sword grip. For a moment it seemed like he was back at the headstone outside Hale's Crossing, sword raised to bring down on Mertyn Walter's neck. He saw the sword falling, the blade cutting into the sorcerer's neck. He could still feel the blade getting stuck. He could hear the noises Mertyn had made—

He rolled off the bandit and vomited into the undergrowth. It was mostly acid—he'd barely eaten all day. He retched again, even less coming out this time.

Have to go. Get up.

Shakily, he spat the taste from his mouth and picked himself up. He looked toward the ridge.

Had the other bandits heard? Were they coming? He couldn't hear anything over the pounding of blood in his own ears.

He looked down at the woman's unconscious form once more. And then he turned and staggered back toward Mara as fast as he could.

Mara was brushing Mugsy when he came running back to their camp. She took one look at him, dropped the brush, and reached for her hammer.

"What is it?"

"Bandit camp. Over the ridge." He pointed, only then realizing he still hadn't sheathed his sword.

"Did any of them spot you?" she demanded.

"One found me in the woods. A woman. She said there were bounties on our heads."

She glanced at his sword. "Is she dead?"

"Unconscious. I—"

"Get Mugsy ready to go." She rushed past him, her face hard. "We leave in ten minutes and we do not stop until dawn."

"Where are you going?"

"Just get ready to leave!" she called over her shoulder.

She charged toward the woods and was lost from his sight.

He stared after her for a moment, then shook himself out of his trance. He felt cold all of a sudden. He couldn't stop shaking.

She was right. They couldn't stay.

With trembling hands he quickly loaded the saddlebags and other supplies back onto Mugsy. The horse snorted and glared.

"Sorry, girl. No choice."

He kept muttering to her as he filled a nosebag with oats and secured it to her nose. Talking to the horse calmed Kole more than it did her. He quickly lifted Darvin onto her back and tied him in place, ignoring the boy's groans.

He was pulling on his pack when Mara returned. There was a touch of pink in her cheeks, as though she'd run the whole way there and back. Her stolen armor clinked as she approached. He couldn't read her face.

"What happened?" Kole said.

She ignored the question. Pulling on her own pack, she said, "It's time to go."

She grabbed hold of Mugsy's reins and tugged on them a little more forcefully than was necessary.

"There's blood on your armor," he said.

She glanced down and wiped the smear away with her hand.

"What did you do?" he asked, hurrying to catch up with her. "Did... did you kill her?"

Her head snapped around, hard eyes fixing on him. The gaze was so cold he could feel it.

Her jaw worked, then she lowered her eyes and faced forward again. "Right now the world is against us. You must remember that." She looked at him again, her earlier coldness gone. "Are you all right? Are you injured?"

"No. No, I don't think so."

They were silent for several seconds. Then she said, "You did well. We were unlucky. A little careless, maybe. That's my fault, not yours."

His stomach lurched again. He forced down the urge to vomit. Part of him wanted to tell her how scared he'd been, how he'd vomited after. How it was somehow both better and worse facing another human being than it had been in the temple with the snakes.

He wanted to tell her about the hunger he'd seen in the woman's eyes, and he wanted to tell her that there were children in the camp, and that they didn't look so different from the children around Hale's Crossing.

But he didn't tell her. He didn't say anything. As the sky darkened, they traveled on in silence.

An hour after sunset, the howl of a dog echoed across the hills behind them. Without speaking, they both began walking a little faster.

CHAPTER
23

THE STORM CAME out of a clear sky, announcing its arrival with a thunderclap that echoed across the hills. The afternoon light soon failed as black, roiling clouds swept in, bringing a torrent of rain with them.

Mugsy danced nervously as the downpour swept over them. Lightning flashed above the hills in the distance. Darvin's increasingly weak moans were drowned out entirely by the roar of the sudden rain.

They were miles from the remains of the last burned-out hamlet they'd passed through. For three more days after fleeing the bandit camp they'd made their way south through the hills along barely used trails, hardly seeing a soul.

"We have to find shelter!" Kole shouted, teeth chattering as the rain quickly soaked through his worn tunic. The wind had an icy chill to it. "The cold will be the death of Darvin."

Mara threw their only spare cloak over Darvin and pointed to a nearby hill. "High ground," she said. "We might be able to find something from there."

They hurried up the slope, boots slipping in the mud. Mara grunted as she went down, gripping her hip. The limp she'd had ever since she emerged from the swamp had been growing worse by the day.

Kole stopped to help her back to her feet, but she waved him off. "Go. Before we lose visibility entirely. Quick!"

He nodded and hurried on up the hill.

The world around him was gray by the time he reached the summit. Wind howled, piercing flesh and bone. His reforged leg twinged in the cold, burning like a bad toothache. Shivering, he brought his arm up to shield his face as he scanned the surroundings.

Lightning flashed in the distance. It wasn't here yet, but it was getting closer.

Mist rose in the valleys around him. He couldn't see more than half a mile in any direction. Scattered woods lurked in the distance, but the trees there were thin and dead, with little to offer in the way of protection. Rocky outcrops might keep off the wind but offered no shelter from the rain. A dried riverbed cut through the landscape. It was quickly returning to life as the rain rolled off the hills.

In one of the valleys, Kole spotted a trio of foxes—or maybe wild dogs—running for cover at the base of a cliff. Just before the gray haze swallowed them, they passed through a gap in a long rocky outcrop.

No. Not an outcrop. Kole strained his eyes against the haze. There was something there. A ruined wall of pale stone. Beyond, in the shadow of the cliff, a tall structure leaned precariously to one side.

He hurried back down the hill to where Mara was limping along, pulling Mugsy behind her.

"Anything?" she shouted over the rain.

"A ruin." He pointed. "At the base of a cliff."

"Does it have a roof?"

He shrugged. "Only one way to find out."

The ruined tower had once been surrounded by a thick stone wall that looked better suited to defending a castle. Some sections of the wall still remained, though time and some ancient devastation had torn holes in it, and the earth had partially buried what was left.

The damage to the wall was at its worst where it approached the bottom of the cliff. The stone there was blackened. No moss or lichen grew on it. The ground too was different there, the earth seared red. Only a few patches of thorny weeds grew.

As they neared the ruin, Kole looked up at the cliff that loomed over them. The cliff face seemed unusually smooth, as if the stone had been polished by a giant's hand. At the top of the cliff, balanced precariously on the edge, was more of the same blackened stone that formed the wall, although it had been worn down by wind and rain. It was as if the land below the ruin had been cleanly severed, thrusting half of it up into the air, or perhaps collapsing the other half into the valley below.

Kole had serious doubts about the structural integrity of the ruin, but by then his teeth were chattering so loudly he could barely hear the roar of the rain. The temperature was dropping fast and the storm showed no sign of abating. They needed to get somewhere warm, and soon.

They formed a single file and Kole scrambled up crumbling, ancient stone through one of the collapsed sections of the wall. Mugsy's hooves slid and clattered on the stone behind him, but at last they made their way through.

A jungle flourished inside the wall. Wildflowers almost as tall as Kole reached up around him. An old stone outbuilding was almost entirely swallowed by ivy dotted with tiny white flowers. He caught glimpses of broken flagstones beneath the grass, but life had overtaken the cold stone.

The remains of other outbuildings stood open to the elements to their left and right. Though their roofs had long since collapsed, Kole spotted the three foxes curled up in one of the buildings, shining eyes staring at them as they passed.

The outbuildings would offer little shelter from the rain. But across the courtyard, leaning away from the cliff face, stood the tower itself. It was three times the height of the inn at Hale's Crossing. Maybe it had once been even taller—he wasn't sure how much of the tower lay buried.

Ivy crawled halfway up toward the damaged roof, covering many of the windows. Something that might have been the main door was almost entirely buried beneath the dirt and foliage, but a partially collapsed balcony looked like it might provide a ramp up to a door on the next floor.

Kole's attention was drawn to a huge object lying half-buried in the dirt next to the tower. It looked like a collection of giant brass rings. The rings were arranged inside one another so that together they formed a great sphere choked with vines and weeds. Kole realized the object must have once been attached to the top of the tower.

"What is it?" he said over the sound of the rain.

"An Aetherlight beacon," Mara said. "To allow messages to be passed over great distances. This must have been a frontier vox station." She looked up at the cliff face looming over them, then grunted. "Be on your guard. We may not be the only ones seeking shelter from the storm."

Kole quickly circled the tower, looking for any other entrances, but other than the collapsed balcony their only option seemed to be to try to climb the ivy to one of the upper windows. Since neither of them fancied the idea of hauling an unconscious Darvin up two stories—or leaving poor Mugsy out in the rain to fend for herself—they decided the balcony was their best bet.

The stone of the half-collapsed balcony was slick with moss and strewn with loose stones. Kole helped Mara clamber up first. After ten minutes of grunting and swearing they finally managed to haul the packhorse up the slope after her. Despite the physical effort, Kole was almost numb with cold by the time he climbed up the balcony after them and passed through the arched doorway into the shelter of the tower.

Kole muttered a prayer of thanks to whatever gods were listening. Wind howled through the tower, but compared to the gale outside it was nothing but a pleasant breeze. With trembling hands he finally got his lantern lit and raised it high to inspect the the place they'd found themselves.

It was a single, round room that took up the entire width of the tower. On the far wall Kole could make out a set of stairs curling upward toward the next floor. Another set, closer to the balcony, led down to what Kole presumed used to be the ground floor.

The center of the room was raised up on a large platform. Atop the platform were rows of desks—many broken. Around the base of the platform were shelves separated into individual pigeonholes. A few empty brass lanterns still hung from the walls, and Kole could see other points where more lanterns had once stood.

Scraps of ancient paper crunched under Mugsy's hooves as they moved away from the doorway to a spot where the rain didn't reach. Kole tried to read whatever writing had been inscribed on the paper, but it had faded so badly it was indecipherable.

On the cliff side of the tower they found evidence of an old campfire with a couple of the ancient chairs pulled up near it. Clearly the tower had served as shelter for other travelers in the past.

They gathered together some scraps of paper and pieces of old, broken furniture to start a fire in the existing fire pit. The old wood resisted burning at first, but at last it caught and the fire's warmth began to cut through the freezing cold.

They laid a shivering, moaning Darvin beside the fire, and Mara retrieved her green vial from her bag. She dripped a little more of its contents into Darvin's eyes, then fed him a little of the thin porridge they'd been giving him whenever they stopped to rest. The unconscious boy sucked the porridge from the spoon and murmured something incomprehensible.

Kole stood by the fire for several minutes, the cold in his bones slowly receding. It was his turn to wash Darvin and change the rags they'd tied around his hips and groin, but Kole was in no hurry to perform that particular task. Mara pulled up an ancient chair and tested her weight on it. It groaned, but held. Rubbing her leg, she settled down on the chair.

"Is it bad?" Kole nodded at her leg.

"Burns like the fourth hell whenever I go uphill," she said. "I'll be all right in a few minutes. I'd kill for a few sips of Angok's sugar ale, though."

Kole opened Mugsy's saddlebags and brought out the catch they'd made the night before. "How about rabbit instead?" he asked, holding the two dead animals up by their legs. He was starting to get sick of the taste. Rabbit was the only game they'd managed to catch since leaving Hale's Crossing.

Mara eyed the rabbits with distaste. "Perhaps if we leave them out long enough they'll ferment into something alcoholic." She looked out the window at the rain slicing down. "All right, I suppose we might as well cook them. I don't think we'll be traveling again today."

Kole nodded and glanced around. As much as he wanted to stay by the fire, there was a nagging sense in the back of his head that he should not get too comfortable yet.

"I should have a look around," he said. "Make sure we're alone."

She looked for a moment like she might argue. As she began to stand, though, she cringed suddenly and gripped her sore hip. Sitting down again, she nodded. "All right. Just be careful." She glared down at the rabbits. "I suppose I'll deal with this."

"Why the frown?"

"I hate cooking," she said. "We always made Angok do it. That man could burn a boiled egg, but he never quit."

Her words brought to mind Da's enthusiastic cooking attempts. He would always jump at the chance to cook the family's dinner. Too often, though, he would get overexcited and make some catastrophic mistake that rendered the meal inedible. The memory brought a smile to Kole's face, quickly followed by a sharp pang in his chest.

Mara's gaze roamed across his face, and he thought she could tell what he was thinking. She nodded slightly, then glanced around them. "Be wary while you're looking around. Touch nothing. This place was once filled with Aetherlight sorcery. Sometimes that kind of sorcery...lingers."

Nodding, Kole picked up his lantern and moved to the stairs.

He descended the stairs carefully, wary of any loose steps. Large cracks ran across the wall beside him, and a few of the steps were so obviously damaged he avoided them entirely. The lean of the tower meant that the stairs sloped beneath his feet.

He got halfway down the stairs before his feet met soil. Whatever the ground floor had once been, it was now buried. An earthy musk filled the air. Clusters of mushrooms thrived in the dark dampness. He didn't recognize them, so he decided against picking some for their dinner.

Lifting his lantern, he peered into the far corners. The only creatures he could see dwelling down here were the insects that scattered in the light.

He went back up and took the other set of stairs that curled up to the next floor. That floor was much like the one Mara and Mugsy were occupying, filled with desks and shelves and scattered paper.

The only difference was that there was a skeleton sitting at one of the desks.

The skeleton was slumped over the desk, clad in faded rags. Kole swallowed as he approached. The ancient remains gave off a faint musty scent. Whatever had killed the poor unfortunate had left no trace.

If the body had once held any valuables, they were long gone. Judging by the many open drawers and the papers scattered across the room, the tower had been picked over by treasure hunters long ago. Even most of the inkwells had been taken.

Muttering a quiet prayer for the soul of the long-dead person sitting at the desk, Kole returned to the stairs and continued to the uppermost floor.

The whistling of the wind through the tower took on a ghostly wail as he emerged on the top floor. Cracks and holes dotted the domed ceiling, through which rainwater trickled. There were no windows. Neither were there any desks or shelves or skeletons.

There was, however, a mirror. It was so grimy Kole didn't realize what it was when he first entered the room. When he came closer, though, he could make out the dim shape of his own reflection staring back at him through the filth that covered the mirror's surface.

It filled nearly the whole room, a great circle rimmed by a ring of brass. It stood upright, held in place by a brass pole that stretched from the floor to the ceiling. It occurred to him that that pole might have once reached through the ceiling to attach to the huge ringed sphere that lay next to the tower outside.

A pair of intersecting cracks stretched across the surface of the glass mirror, splitting his reflection into pieces. He'd never seen a single piece of glass this big before, let alone one so smooth.

As he approached the mirror, the sight of his own reflection shocked him. For a moment he thought it was Da staring back at him. It had been more than a week since he'd had a good look at himself in anything clearer than a muddy pool of water. He couldn't believe how much he'd changed in so short a time.

He was leaner, that much was obvious. His eyes looked sunken, though maybe that was a trick of the light. Filth was matted in his hair and a thin layer of dark fuzz covered his cheeks and chin. New lines pulled at the corners of his eyes. It seemed to him as if he'd aged several years in the space of a week.

But it was more than that. The look in his eyes had changed. It was more sorrowful—though Kole decided no one could blame him for that. And there was fear there too—a haunted look that he wasn't sure would ever fully disappear.

Kole stepped closer, until he was almost nose-to-nose with his own reflection. There was something else he could see through the grime that coated the mirror's surface. Something that he could almost dismiss as another trick of the light. The faintest tinge of red ringing his irises.

Swallowing, he stepped back from the mirror. Perhaps it wasn't a good idea to look too deeply. He turned his attention to the mirror itself.

If the mirror was silver-backed it had to be worth something, though clearly no treasure hunters had managed to steal it yet. Kole had no idea how anyone would get it out in one piece, even if they had enough man-power to carry it and a strong enough saw to cut through the pole that held it in place.

He went around to the other side of the mirror expecting to see the back of it, but there was a mirror on that side of the disk as well, cracked in the same way. He frowned, confused. What was the point in one mirror of this size, let alone two set back to back?

It didn't matter—what mattered was that they were alone in the tower. No monsters nested at the top of the tower, no bandits were camped in the basement. They would be safe enough here until the storm abated.

He started to make his way back to the stairs, but as he passed the mirror something in the reflection caught his eye. He froze for a second, then backed up and peered through the filth coating the mirror's surface.

He glanced behind him, seeing only the wall of the tower and a couple of cracks where rainwater dripped through. Then he looked at the reflection in the mirror again. There, behind a layer of grime, were the stairs down. The stairs that were on the other side of the mirror.

He wasn't seeing a reflection. He was looking *through* the mirror.
Because it wasn't a mirror at all. It was more like a lens.
He stared into his reflection's eyes. His reflection stared back.
And then it began to move on its own.

CHAPTER
24

OLE'S REFLECTION TURNED AWAY, disappearing behind the crack in the glass. Kole staggered back from the mirror.

Sorcery.

With his heart in his throat, Kole edged slowly to the side, so that his reflection came back into view. The boy in the mirror stared back at him with wide, scared eyes.

There was a sword in the reflection's hands. A headsman's sword. Its rounded point was set against the stone floor. Another figure came into view from behind the crack. A thin, bruised man, dressed in filthy rags. He was bound and gagged and slumped over a flat-topped rock.

"Mertyn Walter," Kole breathed.

His reflection stared out at him. Its hands twitched nervously around the hilt of the headsman's sword. Then, silently, the reflection raised the sword high.

Mertyn Walter lifted his head. The gag had come loose. Without a sound, his lips began to move. Red smoke issued from his mouth. It swirled through air, dancing unnaturally. Kole's reflection hardly seemed to notice as he inhaled the sorcerous miasma.

The reflection brought the sword arcing toward Mertyn's neck. With a groan, Kole flinched away, bile spilling into his throat. He didn't want to look upon his failure. Not again. He couldn't bear to watch Mertyn twitching, gurgling, suffering, the sword jammed in his neck.

Lightning flashed through the holes in the ceiling, followed a second later by the crack of thunder. When the light faded, the image in the mirror had changed.

He saw a figure draped in heavy purple robes. The person's face was hidden entirely in shadow. A pair of pale, gnarled hands grasped a great ring of keys, hundreds of them. As the figure silently picked through the keys, Kole caught a glimpse of a strangely designed key. It was long and thin, with no teeth and only a strange white gem at the tip. At the base of the key was a carving of an eagle in flight.

The image of the figure faded and was gone. A moment later, something else appeared. He saw a gleaming city perched on a cliff top at the end of a great peninsula. Waves crashed against the cliff, sending salt spray up toward the walled city. There was a keep at the highest point—a palace, really—with gold-rimmed windows and soaring arches. Gulls flocked around the highest tower where a great blue banner waved. The image of a tree was worked in gold upon the fluttering banner.

Kole stared, rapt, as the image changed once again. He found himself looking into a great hall worked with colorful mosaics and golden banners. Guards with plumed helmets and long spears stood at attention at each of the pillars that held the vaulted ceiling aloft. Sunlight poured through two dozen windows. Out one window, beneath a blue sky streaked with white cloud, he could see a five-sailed ship on the sparkling water.

At the far end of the hall was a great wooden throne that seemed as if it had been grown, not carved. Leaves sprouted from young shoots all along the throne's great back. There was a man sitting in the throne, regal and smiling. He extended a hand toward Kole...

...and the image shifted. The light became gray. The mosaic floor was suddenly streaked with filth, the colors dimmed by the ravages of time. The banners were torn or destroyed entirely. Corpses wearing tarnished armor lay scattered about the hall.

The man still sat in the throne, slumped over. For a moment, Kole thought he was dead. But then, slowly, the man lifted his head.

His flesh seemed to crack and splinter as he moved. The skin that had once been a light brown was now dark and thick, almost like tree bark. A thin crown of gold sat amid hair that stretched out like dead twigs. Ancient eyes stared out of that unnatural face.

Kole suddenly realized that the man was no longer sitting in the wooden throne. His body was sunken into it, fused with it. He was the throne, and the throne was him.

The man's bark-like lips moved. And though there was no sound, Kole could somehow hear the words on the wind that howled through the tower.

Deathbringer, the wind begged. *Please.*

Something slammed into Kole's middle, knocking the wind from him. He hit the floor.

The image in the mirror flickered once and then disappeared. In the reflection that remained, Kole saw himself lying on the floor with Mara on top of him.

Only then was he able to tear his gaze from the mirror. His voice died in his throat and he realized he'd been speaking. He couldn't recall what he'd been saying.

Naked fury painted Mara's face. Her fists were balled in the front of his tunic.

"Who?" she said through gritted teeth.

Kole just stared back at her, confused.

She pulled on his tunic. "Who were you communicating with?"

"I...I don't..."

With a grunt of annoyance, she released him and sat back on her haunches. "You gods-damned fool. Talk to the Sage next time and see if he'll put some sense in that hollow skull of yours." She shot a suspicious glare toward the mirror. "What did you tell them?"

"I didn't...I didn't tell anyone anything."

"You might as well have announced our position to the world!"

Kole shook his head, trying to gather his thoughts. He pushed himself up until he was sitting. His ribs ached where Mara had tackled him.

"I saw a man," he said slowly. "Or what used to be a man. I think he wanted my help."

Mara stabbed a finger into his chest. "I don't care if he told you he has the secret to eternal life. Forget what he said. Forget everything you saw."

"But—"

"That thing is dangerous." She pointed at her own reflection in the mirror. "Anyone could be on the other end. And you invited them into your head, by the gods! I told you to be wary of Aetherlight sorcery, not to dabble in it!"

"I wasn't dabbling. I wasn't doing anything." He looked at the mirror. "It just...started showing me things."

She stared at him. "You don't even realize what you were doing, do you?"

"I wasn't doing anything," he said again, less sure of himself this time.

"Do you know why I came up here? I saw light out the window. It was coming from the beacon in the weeds outside. It was glowing with the light of a thousand stars. I thought you must be in trouble. So I came up to find you. And there you were, speaking an incantation."

Swallowing, Kole shook his head. "No."

"Artifacts like this don't just turn on by themselves," she said. "They require a sorcerer's power. An Aetherlight sorcerer can open a connection between vox stations, but only so long as another sorcerer—even a Flesh sorcerer—accepts the connection. That's what you did. You accepted that connection, Kole."

A Flesh sorcerer. Is that really what I am? His stomach churned. He suddenly felt almost as exhausted as he had when he reforged his own leg.

At the thought, a sharp pain shot up the leg, then disappeared as quickly as it had come.

"He called me Deathbringer," Kole said quietly, more to himself than to Mara.

"Who did? The man you were communicating with?"

Kole nodded slowly.

"That's because you told him what you are," Mara said. "What you were raised as."

He pictured himself bringing the sword down on Mertyn Walter's neck. "I didn't tell him."

"You allowed him to see," she said. "The result is the same."

Kole went quiet and Mara exhaled. She stood, bracing her bad hip, then held out her hand to him. After a moment's hesitation, he allowed her to help him to his feet. He felt dizzy for a second before he was able to find his strength.

"Don't come back up here," she said, leading him back toward the stairs. She narrowed her eyes at the mirror as she passed. "We leave as soon as the storm abates. Before dawn, if we can."

Kole nodded. His legs trembled as they started down the stairs. Rain sliced in through the broken windows that lined the stairway.

"You have to learn control, Kole," she said.

"I know," he mumbled.

"We'll be in Locket soon. There are thousands of people packed into the city. I am immune to the plague, but the people of Locket are not. If you use your sorcery there—"

"I know!" he snapped. "I know what I am, Mara. I've seen what people like me are capable of. I've seen…I've seen…" He swallowed and shook his head. "I put a sword through the neck of the only sorcerer I ever met. How do I learn control if every other sorcerer in the world is a madman? Who's going to teach me? You?"

Her mouth formed a line. She looked away.

"I'm trying, all right?" he said. "I'm trying."

"I know you are." Mara stopped and looked at him. She didn't seem to notice the rain blowing through the window behind her. "I can't help you. By the Sage, I wish I knew how to, but I don't. This is your burden, and yours alone." She paused. "I am sorry for that. Truly."

Kole's throat closed up. Silently, he just nodded his thanks.

"There is strength in you, Kole Felmen. Without it, you would still be in the swamp. Cling to that strength. Once we get to the Citadel we may be able to find you some help. There are many wise people among the Wayfarers. There are tomes and scrolls there that may be able to shed some—"

"Light," Kole said suddenly.

"Exactly."

"No." Kole pointed out the window behind Mara. "Light."

She spun as Kole lowered the hood of his lantern. Outside, the shape of the damaged wall that surrounded the tower was barely visible in the gray haze. Black clouds blanketed the sky, looming over the valley. But just beyond the wall, coming closer, was the flickering light of a lantern guttering in the rain and gale.

A bolt of lightning struck a hilltop half a mile away, filling the valley with sudden light. Kole caught sight of two figures staggering through the rain toward the hole in the wall—one limping, the other supporting them. Then darkness returned and the two figures disappeared behind the wall.

Mara twisted back to face him, eyes hard. "Keep Darvin quiet and stay out of sight. I'll handle this."

CHAPTER

25

HAMMER IN HAND, Mara moved to the doorway that led out onto the collapsed balcony. Kole crouched in the dark a few feet away, ready to clamp a hand over Darvin's mouth the instant he started moaning in his sleep. Their small fire had been doused, and only a sliver of light came from beneath the hood of Kole's lantern. Mugsy snorted nervously nearby.

The possibilities chased each other through Kole's head. Was it the bandits? Had they tracked Kole and Mara down for killing their friend? Or was it worse than that? Had the Hallowed Order finally caught up with them?

Mara was a shadow beside the doorway. She didn't move. Wind howled through the doorway, making Kole shiver.

For several long minutes he couldn't hear anything except the roaring rain. From where he was crouched he couldn't see the courtyard outside.

Perhaps they would move on, whoever they were. Or perhaps they'd seek some meager shelter in one of the half-collapsed outbuildings. Kole and Mara could simply wait until the strangers had departed before leaving the tower. No one would need to know they were here.

Then Kole saw light from a lantern below dancing across the top of the doorway, and he heard a man speaking quickly in a language he didn't understand. It sounded northern—some Ashashi dialect, maybe. There was a grunt of pain, and the sound of boots scraping against wet stone.

"I'm afraid this tower is taken, gentlemen," Mara called without moving into the doorway. "You'll have to find somewhere else to stay."

The sounds of exertion went quiet. Kole imagined he could hear some hissed whispering, though it could have been the wind. A moment passed.

"Good day to you, ma'am," a voice called back. "And what a day it is! Bracing! Although my companion might disagree. We saw a light—"

"Move on," Mara said, harder.

"We mean you no harm. Truly. Our horses were startled by the lightning. They threw us and bolted. Spry as I am, I landed well enough, but my companion wasn't so lucky. He says his ankle is broken. I think it's just twisted. He can be a babe about these things. Either way, we cannot travel further today. And I'm afraid we'll succumb to the elements if we're out here after nightfall."

Even in the dark, Kole could see Mara's frown deepening. "You may stay in one of the outbuildings."

"There isn't a roof between them, and I could drive a cart through some of those holes. Please, ma'am."

"We can't just leave them out there," Kole whispered.

Mara hissed at him to be silent, then she turned back toward the doorway. "It is not safe. I am a knight of the Hallowed Order, transporting a poor wretch who may be infected with the taint."

"Ah! Well, you needn't worry on our behalf. My companion and I are sheltered by the arms of the Dreaming Empress. No infection will touch us."

The Dreaming what? Kole wondered.

"Then let your desert goddess shelter you from the rain," Mara called. "You cannot enter the tower."

Slowly, Kole rose and crept past Darvin toward the window. Mara hissed at him again, but he ignored her. Keeping back from the window, he carefully lifted his head and peered out.

Both men were cloaked, so it was hard to make out details. The one in front—the one who'd been speaking, Kole assumed—had his lantern raised as he peered into the doorway. Kole could just make out a damp, forked beard peeking out from the hood of his cloak. The other man was leaning heavily against the collapsed balcony. He was clearly favoring his right leg. As the wind caught the injured man's cloak, Kole glimpsed the hilt of a sword at his belt.

As if sensing Kole watching him, the man lifted his head and turned toward the window. Kole ducked out of sight, but not before he glimpsed a pale face marked with a strange pattern of thin, vertical stripes.

"Please, ma'am," the man with the lantern called again. "I have some honey-roasted ham that we could share. A gift from a kind local. And… let's see…ah, I have some wine as well! I can't speak to the vintage, but the bottle survived my little tumble off the horse. A good sign, wouldn't you say?" When Mara said nothing, he tried once more. "Please. You'll be killing us if you send us away."

Mara glanced back at Kole, her lips tight. There was a question in her eyes.

"Ask them if they have any weapons," he whispered.

"Are you armed?" she called.

After a moment: "Yes. My companion is."

"Tell him to throw his weapons in. There are bandits in these hills. I won't take any chances."

"Are you armed?" he called back.

"Yes."

"That doesn't seem fair."

"Then take your chances in the storm," she said.

A laugh rose up, light and airy. "I thought I was rid of hard bargainers when I left the north. It seems I was mistaken."

He spoke quickly to his companion in that foreign tongue. The other man said something back. His voice was deep—croaking, almost. As the seconds stretched on, Kole saw Mara tightening her grip on her hammer.

A curved sword still in its scabbard was tossed through the doorway, clattering to the stone at Mara's feet. A moment later came a second weapon—a coil of chain with a hooked blade at the end.

"Is that all?" Mara asked. "Because if I find so much as a knitting needle on either of you I will kill you both where you stand."

There was another pause. Then came a curved dagger with a bone pommel and a small belt knife.

"Do you require our bootlaces as well?" the man asked.

Mara stepped into the doorway and stared down at them for a moment. Then, without a word, she jerked her head and stepped back, collecting their weapons as she went.

The man who'd done the speaking was the first to come. He tossed his lantern up and scrambled up the collapsed balcony, apparently being given a boost by his friend. At last he pulled himself all the way up, exhaled, and gave Mara and Kole a broad smile.

For a moment, Kole thought the man had suffered some head wound that had left his face streaked with blood. But he quickly realized that the deep red stain across his face was actually a birthmark.

"Ah!" The man pointed at Kole and addressed Mara. "Is this the wretch you mentioned?"

"No."

"I thought he didn't look very wretched." He offered a bow. "Redwyn of Ironmast. Your hospitality is much appreciated."

Given the forked beard and the language he'd been speaking, Kole had been expecting a northman—an Ashashi, maybe. But though this Redwyn had styled his beard in a northern fashion and he seemed to be wearing one of their white robes beneath his cloak, his olive skin and familiar features indicated his ancestors at least had not come from so far afield. He was a short, thin, middle-aged man. Kole felt sure there was little muscle beneath the cloak.

When Mara didn't reply, Kole said, "I'm Kole. And this is Mara."

She shot him a look but said nothing.

"A pleasure," Redwyn said.

He opened his mouth to speak again, but the sound of grumbling rose up from down below. The language was incomprehensible to Kole, but he felt certain that at least half the words spoken were curse words.

"Excuse me," Redwyn said. "My friend is getting cold."

He crouched down and replied to his companion in the same language, stretching an arm down to help the other man up the slick stone of the balcony ruin. The small man nearly toppled forward as he tried to haul his friend up. More grunting rose up from down below.

"Shouldn't we help?" Kole said to Mara.

She leaned against the doorway, folded her arms, and said nothing.

Kole shook his head. "You're impossible." Sighing, he pushed past her and stepped out into the rain.

Crouching beside Redwyn, he reached out to the man struggling up the balcony.

"Take my hand," he said.

The man's hood fell back as he turned to Kole. Kole nearly jerked back in surprise. The man's eyes were completely black. There were no whites, not even any differentiation between pupil and iris. Kole couldn't even be sure the man was looking at him.

But he is. I can feel it.

Those impossibly black eyes were set into a strangely colorless face. It was not the pale skin of a Sundarin. Despite the exertion and the pain and the wind whipping at him, there was no pink in his cheeks. He was bone white, almost stony in his complexion.

Kole saw now that the thin stripes running down the man's face were scars. They'd clearly been put there intentionally—no animal or enemy could place the scars so perfectly. He had no beard, no hair. And—Kole realized suddenly—no eyebrows.

Kole didn't know if the man had understood his words, but he'd grasped their meaning. After staring at Kole for a second, he reached out and wrapped one large hand around Kole's.

Together, Kole and Redwyn hauled the man up the slope. As he reached the top and found purchase, Kole and Redwyn toppled back.

"Heavier than he looks, isn't he?" Redwyn said, panting. "Thank you… Kole, was it?"

Kole nodded silently, still staring at the strange, hairless man. The man had pulled his hood back up and was slowly getting to his feet, grimacing at the pain in his leg.

"Come," Redwyn said, picking up his lantern. "Let's get out of this rain, shall we?"

He started for the doorway, but Mara stood in the way, unmoving. "You didn't tell me your friend was a Gor."

Gor. Kole looked at the white-skinned man. He'd heard stories of the savage northern tribesfolk that dwelt in the furthest deserts, making their homes among the sand-covered ruins of lost cities. He'd always thought them myths.

"Don't mind Juragar," Redwyn said. "He looks fearsome, but he's a pussy cat."

Mara's lips tightened, but she backed away from the doorway and allowed them to enter. While Redwyn helped Juragar limp inside, Kole went and got the fire started again. Darvin moaned as Kole stepped over him.

Redwyn threw back his hood and shrugged out of his rain-soaked cloak. The man's hair was sun-bleached and his face was weathered, though it made him appear ruggedly good-looking despite the birthmark. He glanced around the ruined tower and then turned his attention to Darvin. "Ah. Your tainted wretch. Is he a friend of yours?"

"A soul in need of aid," Mara said. "Don't approach him. In fact, it's probably better if you make your camp upstairs. You'll find paper and wood you can use to build a fire."

Redwyn grinned. "You Hallowed Order types are always so prickly. Come, can't we at least share your fire while we warm up? Juragar and I will sleep upstairs come nightfall if you insist, but after such a harrowing experience I feel in need of a little company."

Mara sighed deeply. "Where's that wine you promised?"

CHAPTER
26

WHILE THEY ATE and drank around the fire, Redwyn examined his friend's injured foot. The ankle was swollen, though the Gor's bone white skin showed no discoloration. Redwyn poked and prodded the leg, wiggling toes and speaking to Juragar in his strange tongue. As near as Kole could tell, Redwyn seemed entirely fluent in it.

The two had a small argument—or maybe it was just banter—then Redwyn waved his hand and helped the Gor prop the leg up on an old chair.

"Just a twisted ankle, as I said," Redwyn told Mara and Kole. "Although you'd never guess it by the way he's carrying on."

He gestured to the Gor, who was sitting perfectly still and silent.

Redwyn fished in his sodden pack and pulled out a drenched white robe that was the twin of the one he was wearing. He wrapped it tightly around Juragar's injured ankle, slapping the Gor's hand away when he moved to take it off.

"He's young," Redwyn said. "Doesn't know what's good for him. Didn't even want me helping him walk after the horses bucked us. Thought he could hop all the way to shelter himself." He shook his head. "He's not dying in a ditch that easily. That's twice I've saved his life now, and I want the chance to make it an even three."

He turned and spoke to Juragar, then barked a laugh and gestured to the Gor's ankle. Juragar was stony faced, staring back with those impossibly black eyes.

"He hates when I save him," Redwyn said. "Proud people, the Gor. Even this one. Doesn't matter that he once carried me for three days with no water across the burning sands after I was stung by a daggertail. A blood debt only works one way, apparently."

"How did you meet him?" Kole asked around a mouthful of honey-roasted ham. The meat that Redwyn had brought out of his pack had been soaked with rain, but it was the best thing Kole had eaten in weeks.

"Poor boy was cast out of his tribe on his thirteenth nameday. Corrupted, they called him. With nothing but a waterskin and a dagger he was sent out to wander the wastes."

Redwyn glanced over at Juragar, all his earlier mirth gone. The Gor turned to meet the other man's eyes, though he remained silent. Though Juragar's strange features made it difficult to determine his age, Kole suddenly wondered if the Gor wasn't much older than him.

"The vultures were eying him up for a meal when I found him," Redwyn said. "I was traveling with a caravan of pilgrims when I spotted the carrion birds circling. It wasn't the first time I'd seen vultures flying like that, nor the last. But that time…that time the Empress must have whispered in my ear. So I went, and I looked, and I found him. Just a boy, clawed by some desert beast, half-dead."

He looked over at Darvin then, who had gone quiet again. For several long seconds Redwyn said nothing. Then, like a fire sparked to life, his easy grin returned. "His tribe were wrong. Juragar wasn't corrupted. He was blessed. Blessed by the touch of the Dreaming Empress."

"Who?" Kole asked.

Redwyn's eyes lit up. He took a deep breath and opened his mouth.

"No," Mara said. "The boy doesn't need a sermon. Neither do I."

The man bowed his head. "For a moment I forgot the company I was in. I've spent too long spreading the Word out here. But I suppose after all the horrible business in Hale's Crossing none of you are in the mood for my blessings."

The ham stuck in Kole's throat at the mention of his home. The smell of the burning town came back to him suddenly. His appetite vanished.

"I must admit I'm surprised to find a member of your order this far south," Redwyn said to Mara. "I'd heard the townsfolk who survived Hale's Crossing were being escorted to Baybury so they could be assessed for corruption." As he spoke, his eyes drifted again to Darvin.

Survivors? Kole tried to inhale with the ham still stuck in his throat. He choked for a second, coughing and spluttering. Mara handed him a waterskin.

"We don't discuss Order business with outsiders," she said.

Redwyn raised his hands. "Of course, of course. I meant no offense."

With the help of some water, Kole finally managed to dislodge the ham in his throat. Still coughing, he wiped the water dribbling from his chin.

If there were survivors at Hale's Crossing, his family might be among them. At this very moment they could be on their way to Baybury. And all this time Kole had been traveling in the other direction, getting further and further from them.

Gods, how much would Arabeth be suffering? At best, the prisoners would be taken to Baybury by cart—at worst, they'd be walking there in chains. Either way they'd be traveling by day, beneath the heat of the sun. Arabeth would be in agony.

The thought of her pain was a burning coal in his chest. He had to do something. He had to help her.

He opened his mouth to ask Redwyn what else he'd heard, but Mara's knee nudged him before he could speak. He glanced over to find her staring at him. Though she didn't move, he could read the look in her eyes.

Say nothing, she was telling him.

He was tired of feeling helpless. He should never have left Hale's Crossing. He could have hidden in the swamp until the knights stopped searching for him. Then, when they were gathering up their prisoners, he could have followed them, or rescued them, or…something.

Exhaling, he picked up the bottle of wine Redwyn had brought and filled his tin cup. He drank the whole lot in a single gulp.

Redwyn eyed him as he drank, then offered them both a smile. "Well, our business is no secret. We were planning to take the Vale of Twelve back to Godsmouth, but given the loss of our horses, I think it'll be wiser for us to head to Locket and find passage by sea. A few sailors of my faith often make port in Locket and wet their throats at the Diving Kraken. They will aid us, I'm sure. The Empress' faithful take care of each other." He looked toward the window as lightning flashed once more outside. "Juragar and I owe you a debt for allowing us to share your shelter. Perhaps we could travel together to Locket. That is where you're headed, isn't it?"

When Mara said nothing, he continued.

"Our purses are light, but perhaps we can offer assistance on your journey. It may go some small way to repaying your kindness."

"There is nothing to repay," Mara said.

"Try telling that to him." He gestured toward Juragar. "If he hadn't already pledged himself to my service he'd be prostrating himself at your feet."

The Gor chewed his ham as he stared at them all with his black eyes. If he understood anything that they were saying, he gave no sign of it.

"Forgive me for saying," Redwyn said to Mara after a moment, "but you are unlike any Hallowed Order knight I have ever met."

Mara didn't move, but Kole became suddenly aware of the hammer that rested next to her. He swallowed and tried to catch her eye. If Redwyn figured out that they weren't who they said they were, what would Mara do? Would she kill them like she killed that bandit?

Neither Redwyn nor Juragar seemed to notice the tension that had filled the room. Mara reached out, her hand stretching past the handle of her hammer to pick up the pot of rabbit stew.

"You know many of my Order?" she asked.

"Of course," he said. "My family is House Ironmast of Godsmouth. Our history with the Blackspire goes back two hundred years. Although things haven't been so rosy since we were embraced by the Dreaming Empress. I'm sure you know all about that."

"House politics never interested me," Mara said.

"Me neither, if I'm honest. That's why I went on my pilgrimage." He studied Mara, considering her. "Perhaps it's the accent."

"Excuse me?"

"Most of the Order are raised from the streets of Godsmouth. There's a touch of that in your voice. But there's more. You've spent some time in the far north. Beyond the Cracked Wastes. Yes?"

Mara paused with a spoonful of stew in her hand. "Some."

"The Domed Cities." Redwyn leaned forward. "The City of Salt?"

She shook her head. "City of Crowns." She brought the stew to her lips and drank.

"Ah. You were…?" At a nod from Mara, Redwyn lowered his head slightly. "I'm sorry."

Kole looked from Redwyn to Mara. "What is it? What's the City of Crowns?"

When Mara didn't answer, Redwyn said, "It is where the slave dealers of the Domed Cities ply their trade."

Kole blinked, then looked at Mara. "You were a slave?"

"Not for long," she said simply.

They all fell silent. The fire crackled and popped as the storm outside continued unabated.

A moan from Darvin split the silence. Kole poured some broth from the rabbit stew into his tin cup. Crouching down next to Darvin, he spooned the broth into the boy's mouth.

Mara continued to eat, ignoring the look that Redwyn was giving her.

"A strange journey," Redwyn said to her, "to take you from a slave to a knight. Then again, the Dreaming Empress herself was born a slave."

"Strange, as well," Mara said, "for a Godsmouth noble to become the apostle of a desert goddess."

Redwyn smiled at that, stroking his forked beard and looking down at his white robe. "I suppose all our journeys are strange when we look back at them, though they seem to make sense at the time." He took one last drink of his wine, then stood and helped Juragar to his feet. "The day grows late, and my eyes grow heavy now that my belly is full. My friend and I will retire upstairs and leave you in peace. Our deepest thanks for your kind hospitality."

Mara nodded. "*Badi haa*, Redwyn of Ironmast."

The man smiled broadly, touching a fingertip to the center of his forehead. "*Badi haa*, my friends."

Juragar inclined his head as well, then the two of them shuffled slowly up the stairs.

Kole continued feeding Darvin until he was sure the two strangers were gone, then he put down the spoon and cup and returned to Mara's side. She sipped at her wine as she looked toward the stairs.

"They know, don't they?" he whispered. "They know you're not Hallowed Order."

"Maybe."

"What do we do?"

She didn't answer right away. Kole glanced again at the hammer resting next to her. He pictured the head of that hammer crushing the skull of the knight whose armor Mara now wore.

"I won't let you kill them," he said.

He regretted the words as soon as they left his mouth. Her eyes snapped to meet his. Emotions flashed across her face: fury, then pain, then something that might have been grief.

Her fingers twitched toward the handle of the hammer and Kole instinctively shied back. But her hand just tightened into a fist and she jerked to her feet, downing the last of her wine and tossing the cup to the floor.

"We leave before they wake. They'll be slowed by the Gor's injury. We can make it to Locket ahead of them. We push hard until we get there. With luck the rain will have hampered the Hallowed Order's search for us. We may yet get away even if the Order talk to these two and find they're on the right trail."

"We could ask Redwyn to keep our secret."

"No. It will only confirm his suspicions. He may go running right to the Hallowed Order in search of a reward." She spread her bedroll out beside her hammer. "You take first watch. If either of them come down those stairs, wake me and draw your sword."

Without taking off her armor, she lay down and faced away from the fire. She didn't speak another word.

Sighing, Kole looked over at Mugsy. The horse eyed him back. He got up, stroked the horse's nose, and then sat down in a chair by the window with his sketchbook in hand.

With one eye on the dark hills outside and the other on the stairs, he began to sketch one of the images he'd seen in the mirror upstairs: a gleaming city perched on a peninsula, standing tall above the waves below.

CHAPTER
27

MARA CRIED OUT in her sleep.

Kole had been slumped down in his chair, lulled almost to sleep by the sound of the rain. Now he jerked to his feet, reaching for the sword he'd propped beside the chair.

"Run!" she murmured, her armor clinking as she tensed. "Quintus, run!"

Exhaling, Kole released the death grip he had on the hilt of Catgut's sword. He listened for a moment. There was no movement from Redwyn and Juragar upstairs.

"No," Mara called out. "No, don't. Wait, just wait!"

Kole stared at her. The fire had burned low. Shadows danced in the corners of the tower.

Was she dreaming about the temple? The gods knew that that horrible place had haunted Kole's dreams nightly since he'd left. But Mara had always seemed to sleep so soundly.

She gave an anguished moan, as if the sound was being pulled from her throat. She curled up on herself, shivering. No, not shivering. Shaking. She was sobbing.

Kole stood shocked for a moment. Mara, sobbing? It didn't seem possible.

Shaking off his surprise, he crouched down beside her. Tears streaked down her face.

After a moment's hesitation, he reached out and took hold of her hand.

Her muscles tensed.

"Should have been there," she murmured. "I'm sorry. I'm sorry."

He squeezed her hand. "It's just a dream, Mara."

Her eyelids fluttered and her hand tightened around his.

"Gili?" she breathed.

He didn't recognize the name. "No. It's Kole."

She opened her eyes and stared up at him. "Kole." Swallowing, she released his hand.

"You were having a nightmare."

She sat up, still trembling slightly, and wiped the tears away with the back of her hand. She looked embarrassed. "Sorry. Did I wake you?"

He shook his head. "I was on watch."

"Of course." She looked toward the stairs, then at the rain out the window. She lowered her voice so it wouldn't carry upstairs. "What time is it?"

"I'm not sure. Midnight, maybe."

"Then you should get some rest. It may be hard to come by until we're in Locket." She stood and picked up her hammer.

"Who is Gili?" he asked.

She paused. "An old friend. One I haven't seen for many years."

"Is he dead?"

"Get some rest, Kole."

She put another chair leg on the fire and made her way to the window.

"It's just the two of us now," Kole said. "You told me that the other day. We need to watch each other's backs. That's what you said."

She looked back at him, silent.

"I'm trying to watch your back," he said.

"I know." She lowered her eyes. "I know. I think it's just…it's this place. This tower is full of ghosts. Or maybe I am." She smiled sadly at him. "This is what I get for drinking before bed."

The ancient chair creaked as she lowered herself into it, the hammer across her knees. She laid a hand on the hammer's head.

Kole sat down on his bedroll, but despite the hour he wasn't tired. He stared into the flames.

"You called out to Quintus as well," he said quietly. "Were you dreaming of the temple?"

"Yes," she said after a moment.

He pulled his knees up to his chest. "Did he have family?"

"He used to have a daughter."

"Really?"

She nodded. "Only the Cripple knows how that came about. Perhaps he was once a more charming man. Or a less abrasive one, at least." She shook her head. "I never heard him talk about her, or the girl's mother. He was a scholar of some sort in Godsmouth before joining the Wayfarers. Apparently he was away translating some ancient texts when his daughter caught the plague. She was executed before he returned."

"Gods. Was that why he became a Wayfarer?"

"I never asked."

"What about the others? Angok? Catgut?"

"Angok has two boys. Well, they're not really boys any more. The youngest is about your age."

Kole frowned. "I didn't think he was old enough to have children my age."

"They're not his by birth," she said. "But they are his kin. They were his older brother's children. But his brother died somehow, and his wife took badly ill. Angok helped her and the boys make it out of Sundar. Adopted them as his own family."

"Where are they now?"

"The Citadel, probably, unless they're out on an expedition of their own. You may meet them one day, gods willing."

Kole swallowed. He didn't know how he felt about that. Would they want to know how Angok died? Could he bring himself to tell them?

"And Catgut?" he asked.

"Catgut? Family?" She shrugged. "Not even the Sage knows for sure. Everything about her was a closely guarded secret. All I know is she drank like a fish and tried to sleep with anything that had a pulse. She even tried to bed me once. I think she made a pass at Quintus as well, just for the sport."

She smiled at that, a smile that lingered for a moment and then was gone.

"And you?" he asked.

"Me?"

"Do you have family?"

There was a look in her eyes he couldn't read. It was as if she was trying to grasp a memory that was eluding her. "No. A long time ago, maybe. But no. Not anymore. I just have the Wayfarers now. I suppose they are a family of sorts." She looked at him. "What do you dream of? The temple?"

Swallowing, he nodded. "And Hale's Crossing. And my family. Not bad dreams, not all of them. Some are more like memories. Fishing for tadpoles with my sister. Working with my da. Sitting by the fire with Ma while she taught me my letters."

"Those dreams are worse, sometimes," Mara said. "When you wake and remember all you've lost."

"They might not be lost. You heard what Redwyn said. The knights were taking folk to Baybury. My family could still be alive."

"They could be," she agreed. "But if so, they are beyond our reach." She touched her bag, where she kept the tome they'd taken from the temple. "Our goal now is to get to Godsmouth, and from there to the Citadel to deliver the Thesis. That is what matters most."

"That's your goal. Not mine."

"You're right. Your goal is to learn control. Control you can only learn at the Citadel. You will only endanger your family if you return to them now."

"Then when? When am I supposed to save them?"

"Keep your voice down," she whispered.

He ignored her. "My family could be out there suffering. Every day we're getting further and further away from them."

"And what would you have us do?" she hissed. "Ambush a prisoner transport caravan? Launch an assault on whatever dungeon the knights are planning to lock them in?"

"No, but—"

"The Order's influence stretches to every corner of the Golden Remnant and beyond. They have the ear of every baron, lord, and tyrant in the land. Their coffers are fat and their reputation is impeccable. That is the enemy we face, and we face it alone. It's just us, Kole. Just us." For a moment she seemed to be weighed down by some enormous burden. Then she exhaled slowly and she looked at him again. "Do you think Hale's Crossing was the first town to be set ablaze by the torches of the Hallowed Order? Do you think it will be the last? In the years since the Outbreak how many people have felt the same pain you feel now? How many have witnessed their families torn apart?"

Kole didn't answer. Right then, he didn't want to care about the grief of others. He had enough of his own to deal with.

"It will get worse, before the end," Mara said. "Unless we stop it."

He frowned. "Stop what? The Hallowed Order?"

"The Hallowed Order is a fever. It is the disease itself we must cure."

Kole stared at her for several seconds, then glanced toward the bag that held the Thesis. "You're talking about the plague."

She hesitated as if fearing she'd said too much. Glancing toward the stairway, she whispered, "Yes."

"You're trying to cure the plague."

"Lower your voice," she said, shuffling closer to him. "Yes, that is one of the primary goals of the Wayfarers. A cure. An inoculation. Something that could halt the spread."

"And you think the Thesis holds that cure."

"I don't know, Kole. When I said Quintus never told me what it contained I was telling you the truth. All I know is that he was excited. More excited than I've ever seen him before. These last few days I've been thinking on it, and…" She sighed. "I want to believe it. There have been so many false leads over the years. So many expeditions that came to nothing. So many deaths. I want to believe in this. But I'm not sure I do."

"Then why go to all this effort?"

"Because I have been wrong before. You must understand what a cure would mean. You can see what's at stake here. Not just for us, but for your family. For a thousand thousand families."

He put his head in his hands. He was just the son of a corpse dragger. All he wanted was his family back. That was burden enough. All this—the plague, the Thesis, it was all too much.

"I know how badly you want to turn around and head for Baybury," Mara said softly. "No doubt the Hallowed Order is hoping you will do just that. But I need you, Kole. Help me get the Thesis to the Wayfarers. Do that for me, and I will do whatever is in my power to help you get your family back. I swear it to you, by all gods dead or alive. Help me, Kole. And I will help you."

He looked up to see her staring at him intently.

"Why me?" he asked. "Why not just do this yourself?"

"Because one person is vulnerable where two are not. Because you know too much to risk leaving you behind. Because you are a sorcerer, and that means you have as much to lose as I do. Because I'm afraid to go alone." She offered him a small smile. "Because you carried Darvin out of that swamp, even though you hold no love for him. Maybe that's it. Maybe I hope you will do the same for me, should it prove necessary."

Kole stared into the fire. *Da, what do I do?*

If he were a different kind of sorcerer, perhaps he'd be able to use the mirror upstairs to reach out to his family. He could see if they were still alive. He could ask them what to do.

But he was what he was. And this was a decision he had to make for himself.

"All right," he said softly, feeling like a traitor to his own family. "We continue to Locket."

Mara nodded and exhaled as if she'd been holding her breath.

"Thank you," she said.

He just nodded.

"Get some sleep," she told him. "And dream better dreams than I did."

With a sigh, he lay down on his bedroll. The muscles in his reforged leg twitched uncontrollably until at last he drifted off to the sound of the rain hammering at the tower outside.

Mara woke Kole an hour before dawn. The storm was nothing but a memory now, swept away to some distant land.

Kole was silently packing in the darkness when he felt a prickling at the back of his neck. He turned around to see Redwyn sitting on the steps, watching him.

"Good sleep?" the priest asked.

At the sound of his voice, Mara stopped loading Mugsy and turned, her face hard.

"You're up early," she said flatly.

Redwyn grinned. "One might say the same to you. Need help packing?"

"We're fine. Thank you." Mara continued tightening straps, not turning her back on Redwyn.

The priest shrugged as if he hadn't noticed her tone. "Do you mind if I get past you? I need to go outside. Nature calls."

Mara gestured toward the fallen balcony. Redwyn rose, rubbed the sleep from his eyes, and made his way down the stairs. He glanced over at Darvin's unconscious form, then his eyes met Kole's.

As he passed Kole on his way to the balcony, he paused and whispered, "Are you in danger, friend?"

Kole started. Redwyn was studying him intently, as if trying to read his reaction.

Was it a threat? Did Redwyn know what they were running from?

"What do you mean?" Kole said at last.

Redwyn glanced toward Mara. "That one, she—"

"Hey." Mara stomped over to them, her armor rattling. "I thought you said you needed to piss."

Redwyn held Kole's eyes a half-second longer, then turned to Mara, smiling broadly. "It is fortunate, then, that the Dreaming Empress blessed me with excellent bladder control. Excuse me."

He strode toward the balcony. As he reached it he glanced back and smiled at Kole and Mara. His gaze lifted toward the stairs and he gave a shake of his head so small that Kole wasn't entirely sure he hadn't imagined it.

As the priest went outside, Kole looked back. Juragar stood at the top of the stairs to the upper floor, staring down with his black eyes. He raised a fist in some gesture Kole didn't understand, then turned and limped back up the stairs.

Mara leaned close to Kole. "What did the priest say to you?" she whispered.

"He asked me if I was in danger."

She grunted. "Come on. It's time we get out of here."

Mara left behind the weapons Redwyn and Juragar had surrendered, along with the two fingers of wine still at the bottom of the bottle. After some consideration, they kept the remainder of the ham for themselves.

They loaded Darvin onto Mugsy and carefully led her down the ruined balcony. Redwyn stood outside, hands folded together within the sleeves of his white robe.

"Safe travels, friends," he said. "Perhaps one day we might repay your hospitality."

Mara tugged on Mugsy's reins. "That will not be necessary. We will not meet again."

"Perhaps."

His enigmatic smile sent a shiver down Kole's spine. He turned away from the priest as they made their way through the hole in the outer wall. But he could feel Redwyn's eyes on him long after they'd passed out of sight.

CHAPTER
28

KOLE HIT THE GROUND and Mara pressed the tip of the branch to Kole's chest, keeping him pinned in the dirt.

"Good," she said, lifting the branch and stepping back. "You're getting better."

Kole nursed his wrist where the branch-sword had struck a moment before, disarming him. A nasty welt was already starting to form.

"I don't feel like I'm getting better."

"You lasted longer that time."

"Going down in three strikes instead of two, you mean?"

"Three strikes is good. Most fights don't last even that long. Forget what the stories tell you of duels that take hours. If you haven't won the fight in the first ten seconds, you've lost it."

He picked himself up, stifling a groan. "Yeah, but I *did* lose it."

She ignored him. "Your footwork is improving too. But you're still too defensive. Technique is important, but so is aggression. A technically superior fighter can easily be overwhelmed by a bold warrior willing to risk injury or death. You're a strong young man with good reach. Use that. Don't let me out-finesse you. You need to come at me hard and kill me first. No hesitation."

He nodded, not meeting her eyes. He just kept thinking about Mertyn Walter, and that bandit who had ambushed him in the woods. Both times someone else had had to finish what he had been unable to do himself. He was no stranger to death, but the further he got from home the more he found he wanted no part in it.

Mara lowered her branch, her face softening as she studied him. "Maybe that's enough practice for today."

"No." He gingerly picked up his own branch and returned to the ready position. "Let's go again."

As much as he wanted to take the chance she was giving him, he knew he had to keep practicing. Mara couldn't be beside him every moment of the day. He needed to be able to protect himself. And Darvin as well.

Darvin lay in the corner of their small campsite, pale and motionless beneath the blanket Kole had placed over him. He rarely even groaned anymore, and Kole hadn't seen him open his eyes since they made their way down from the Renegade Hills three days ago and joined the Southern Way, the main trade route linking Locket in the south to Baybury in the north. Mara said they were only a day's travel from Locket now. One day until they could find Darvin a physik.

He hoped they weren't already too late.

Mara studied him a moment longer, then nodded. "All right. One more session. Then we rest." She lifted her branch. "Begin."

Their branches cracked together as Kole desperately tried to parry a strike aimed for his throat. Even as he was turning the strike, her branch-sword slipped to the side and came stabbing toward his flank.

He stepped back quickly, bringing his sword down to defend again. He couldn't block the blow entirely. The branch scraped past his ribs, leaving him gasping for breath.

"Stop defending!" Mara barked. "Kill me!"

With a shout, he ducked below her next strike and slashed at her face. For the first time in the fight Mara was forced to take a step back. Kole's slash whipped past her face.

Then she took a step forward and her branch was buried in Kole's gut.

Kole went to his knees, struggling for breath. His eyes watered.

Mara dropped her branch and took him under the arm. "Sit down. Lean forward. Your breath will return soon."

He sat down on the ground and clutched his bruised stomach. "I think," he gasped, "that's enough practice for tonight after all."

Mara laughed softly and brought him his waterskin. When he could breathe a little more easily, he took a long drink.

Sitting down beside him, Mara leaned back and looked up at the late afternoon sky. They were camped just back from the trade road, in a well-sheltered spot that looked like it had seen frequent use by travelers over the years. There were many inns and villages along the Southern Way, but renting rooms around here was expensive. The poor and thrifty preferred to camp out.

Mara no longer wore the stolen Hallowed Order armor. They'd buried it in a field before joining the Southern Way. It would have attracted too much attention on the busy road.

Better to style themselves as village folk instead, travelers heading to Locket in search of a physik. The story was close enough to the truth that Kole hoped it would hold up to scrutiny.

After so long in the wild, Kole was nervous this close to civilization. Gods, some parts of the Way were even paved, the remnants of some ancient road.

There were even soldiers on the road at times—not Hallowed Order, but militia from Locket. Luckily, they seemed more interested in warding off bandits and highwaymen than searching for fugitives from up north.

After a few minutes, Kole was able to stand again. He lifted his tunic and saw a purple bruise already spreading across his stomach. "This is going to hurt for a week."

Mara rubbed the fuzz on her scalp. She had the decency to look a little sheepish. "You overcommitted."

"You told me to be more aggressive!"

"I didn't tell you to throw yourself on my sword."

He shot her a glare, lowered his tunic, and went to feed Darvin.

Soon after joining the Southern Way they'd risked entering a village to purchase some supplies for the last leg of their journey to Locket. After days of grass and berries, Mugsy had been excited to have oats again. The horse had practically danced with joy.

They'd bought a small pot of honey as well. Kole added a little of it to some thin porridge and crouched at Darvin's side, spooning a little at a time into his mouth. The boy's cracked lips barely moved, but he did eventually swallow the porridge.

After a few minutes, Kole realized Mara was watching him. He looked up.

"What?"

"Nothing. I was just thinking…" She frowned as if trying to gather her thoughts. "I've been doing this a long time. I've seen a lot of people die. Seen a lot of people hurt so bad they couldn't go on anymore. Sometimes physically, sometimes mentally. Some I liked. A lot I didn't. Some of the ones I liked abandoned me when I needed them most. And some of the ones I hated fought alongside me to the bitter end." She shrugged. "It's just…it's funny how things turn out."

He nodded and looked down at Darvin. "I think I know what you mean."

The night drew close. When Kole had finished feeding Darvin, Mara took over, giving the boy some of her tinctures. Kole started building a fire. When it was burning, Mara joined him and they ate a little of the salted beef they'd bought along with the honey and oats. She opened her huge tome across her lap and puzzled over it by firelight.

As Kole ate, he massaged his reforged leg. It always ached after a day's travel. Not just a muscle ache, but something deeper, a pain that never really went away.

"What was sorcery like?" he asked suddenly. "Before the Outbreak."

She stopped chewing and glanced up from her book. "Quintus would be able to tell you more than me."

"Quintus isn't here."

"No," she agreed. Lowering her head, she sighed. "There were five great branches of sorcery. Five lores. Each sorcerer was bound to one of those lores."

"Could they choose which one they learned?"

"No. It was something within them—some spark they were born with. Until the advent of the plague, of course."

She fell silent for a moment, staring into the crackling flames. Somewhere, an owl hooted.

"As far as we can tell," she said, "the five lores were not all corrupted at the same moment, though all succumbed in the end." She held up a fist and extended her thumb. "The Lore of Silver was the first to be tainted. Silvers were craftsmen, builders—their sorcery gave them the power to reshape stone, metal, earth. All the greatest structures and artifacts from before the Outbreak were created by those gifted in the Lore of Silver.

"The Lore of Aetherlight was corrupted next." She extended another finger. "It was also known as the Lore of Starlight, or the Lore of Eyes."

"The vox tower," Kole said. "That was Aetherlight sorcery, wasn't it?"

She nodded. "Aetherlight was the most uncommon of the lores. Its sorcerers were concerned with thoughts, dreams, emotion. With the aid of their beacons, Aetherlight sorcerers could send thoughts and images over great distances. Some could treat diseases of the mind. A few, it is said, could even read and interpret the threads of reality to divine some hints of the future."

"Did any of these Aetherlight diviners predict the coming of the plague?"

"Apparently not." Another finger went up. "The third lore to be tainted was that of Embers. Ember sorcery is destruction in its purest form. As wood and air can be converted to fire, so an Ember sorcerer converts matter to energy."

"Like what Quintus did to that abomination in the temple," Kole said.

"Yes. The vessel he threw contained raw Ember source. Most Ember sorcerers used their magic in similar ways, either as soldiers or miners. The more skilled of them could control the release of energy more carefully, using it to propel vehicles or projectiles.

"The Lore of Shadow was corrupted soon after. Shadow sorcery concerns itself with light and the absence thereof. The lamps that lined the roads of the Lamplight Empire were tended by Shadow sorcerers." She pointed back toward the Southern Way. "Some of the lamp posts still stand. You may have seen them. Shadow sorcerers could also rip light from the air to plunge an enemy into darkness, or fill the night with a blinding glow. A powerful tool, Shadow sorcery. The most skilled practitioners could even reshape light and color to form images that others could see. The light shows of the Ribbon Theater in Godsmouth were said to draw audiences from across the Empire and beyond."

She raised her little finger so that she now held up an open palm. "And at last, the final lore fell. The Lore of Flesh. What some cultures called the Lore of Life. The lore with which you are currently infected."

Kole nodded, glancing down at his reforged leg.

"Flesh sorcerers can manipulate and reshape life itself," Mara continued. "They were highly valued as healers. But in the twilight days of the Empire, some delved into darker applications of their sorcery. They became fleshcrafters, creating new forms of life. Some tried to create perfect warriors and fearsome beasts of war. One particular cabal attempted to create a race of subhumans that drew pleasure only from service."

"A slave race," Kole said.

"Yes. Although they tried to paint it as a more palatable alternative to slavery. They claimed that if they could create a species with no higher aspirations, a species that *enjoyed* being slaves, there was no moral concern in using them as such."

Kole felt suddenly unclean. "Did they succeed?"

"Not as they'd hoped."

He nodded, glad of that, at least. "When I tried to use my sorcery against the knight outside Hale's Crossing, he had something. A crystal. When he crushed it, it seemed to suck the sorcery from me. What was that?"

"Void," she said. "In the last days of the Empire, when the authorities were desperate for some solution to the Outbreak, they began to grow crystals that could nullify active sorcery in the vicinity. The Empire attempted to use the crystals to halt the spread of the plague, but by then it was too late. The Hallowed Order has hoarded most of the Void crystals that still remain."

Kole chewed over her words. "In the temple, when I first used sorcery, I spoke some sort of incantation. It was like I was rewriting reality with it."

Mara nodded. "The language is a precise thing. Pure. Almost mathematical in its basis. By speaking an incantation—or inscribing that incantation upon an object and applying a measure of Source—a sorcerer can instruct the world how they wish it to be. But a single syllable wrong, a lone error in grammar, and the meaning of the incantation can be drastically altered, with terrible results."

Kole swallowed. "How do I know this language?"

"The plague. Despite being called the sorcerer's plague, is not just a plague of sorcery. It is a plague of language. When the miasma infects someone, it grants them knowledge of the language. Incomplete knowledge, perhaps, but enough for them to alter reality around them. Enough to wreak terrible havoc."

"And the…the madness?"

She stared into the fire. "In my time I have encountered many with afflictions of the mind. By the Cripple's grace, I have suffered a few such afflictions myself. Afflictions that bring despondence and hatred of the self so great those affected wish for death. Afflictions that set a man's heart pounding and steal his breath away. Afflictions that force a soldier to relive the deaths of her friends long years after they have passed." She shook her head. "The plague madness is unlike any of those. It is a rot upon the mind. It is the slow destruction of the self. Whether that rot comes from the language itself, or whether it is tied to the vector by which the language is transmitted, I do not know. All I know is that it is incurable and inevitable." She glanced at him. "Almost inevitable."

Why me? he wanted to ask. *Why did Mertyn Walter succumb while I did not?*

But he knew there was no answer there. Was it fate? Or was it as Mara had once said: a roll of the Gambler's dice? Simple luck, or some accident of birth, like that which had made Arabeth so intolerant of sunlight.

They lapsed back into silence for several minutes. He knew what he wanted to say next, but he had to choose his words carefully.

"In the vox tower," he said slowly, "I was shown things."

She looked at him sharply. "I told you to put that place out of your head."

"I saw a city on a cliff. And a man. A king, maybe. He was—"

"Kole," she snapped. "Forget what you saw. It can bring you nothing good. You should never have used that thing in the first place."

"Just listen! You said that Aetherlight sorcerers could use those beacons to communicate over huge distances. Well, something communicated with me. Some*one*. Another sorcerer."

She turned away and tore a bite out of her jerky. "What of it?"

He stared at her. "Isn't it obvious? If there's another sorcerer out there, then maybe he can teach me to—"

"No!" Mara shouted loud enough to make Mugsy whinny nervously. She didn't seem to notice. "Listen to me, Kole, and listen close. This sorcerer who tried to talk to you is dangerous."

"Not to me. I'm already infected."

"To you most of all! That sorcerer is mad. He already got inside your head from however many hundreds of miles away. What could he do if he found you? What could he do if you let him in again? Could he overwhelm your mind with his own madness? Could he strip away the sanity that— through some miracle—you have been left with? Have you even thought about that?"

His jaw tightened. He turned away. Gods, he was tired of her speaking to him like this. Like a child.

"I need to learn somehow," he said.

"You don't need to learn how to use your sorcery. Not from someone like that. You must learn how *not* to use it. Why do you think I've been teaching you how to use that sword? So that if you are threatened, you will put your faith in steel, not sorcery!"

"This?" He scoffed and picked up the sheathed sword he'd taken from Catgut's corpse. "If the Hallowed Order finds us, I'm supposed to defend myself with this? Against trained warriors in full armor?"

She leaned forward, eyes flashing. "If the Hallowed Order finds us, you run. You run, and you don't look back."

He gritted his teeth and dropped the sword beside him. *Run*. It was all he ever seemed to do.

"You're scared of me," he said. "Aren't you?"

"Of course I am! I'm terrified. We're about to enter the largest city in the region. There are more people there than you've ever seen in your life. And you're a sorcerer. A plague-bearer." She held up a finger. "One slip, Kole. That's all it will take. One slip, and hundreds of people will die. Thousands, maybe."

"Then why take me at all?"

She stood, throwing her jerky to the ground. "Because you're my—"

A choked gargle interrupted her. They both spun toward the sound.

Darvin was convulsing. His eyelids were open and his eyes had rolled back in his head. His limbs jerked unnaturally, like a puppet having its strings pulled.

"Get my bag!" Mara shouted as she ran to Darvin's side.

Kole darted to their pile of supplies and grabbed Mara's pack. She was attempting to roll Darvin onto his side when he arrived. Darvin vomited the small amount of porridge Kole had managed to get into him.

"What's happening to him?" Kole said.

Ignoring him, Mara upended her bag on the ground and grabbed a medicinal vial. "Hold his head."

Kole did as she said. Darvin's skin was burning to the touch. His face had gone bright red and he was slick with sweat. He thrashed, muscles straining against Kole's grip.

Mara put her hand on Darvin's chin, forcing his jaw open half an inch. She spilled a few drops from the vial into his mouth and then released him. Darvin's jaw snapped shut with a click.

"All right." Mara stepped back, waving Kole away. "Give him space."

Kole's arms were already aching by the time he released Darvin and backed away. His thigh hurt too—one of Darvin's flailing limbs must have struck him.

Long seconds passed. Then, slowly, Darvin's convulsions subsided. As he grew still, Mara returned to his side, checking his breathing and looking inside his mouth.

"What was that?" Kole was whispering, though he didn't know why.

"A seizure." Mara opened another of her vials and measured a little liquid into a thimble-sized cup.

"I know that. But he's...he's getting worse, isn't he?"

Mara hesitated, then sighed. "I think so."

Kole stared at Darvin. Maybe if he died it would be a mercy. He would never know about Wolfun's death or the burning of Hale's Crossing. He would never have to bear that weight.

"Don't lose hope," Mara said. "Not yet. The physik I know in Locket is one of the best. If we can get Darvin to her, he still has a chance."

"Why do you care?" The words came out sullen, petulant. He hated himself for it.

Maybe Mara was right to treat him like a child.

In the firelight, he saw her jaw tighten. For a moment it looked like she might be about to say something. But she just went back to treating Darvin.

"Get some rest," she said. "If we leave early tomorrow and push hard, we may shave a couple of hours off our journey."

He stood staring at her, feeling angry and guilty and scared. Like a child.

He tried to think of something to say, but all the words sounded wrong in his head. So he sat down next to the fire and took his sketchbook out of his bag. His mind was whirling too much to allow him to sleep.

He thought for a moment, trying to clear his thoughts. He looked over at Darvin, remembering one of their last interactions before they'd gone into the temple—when Darvin had asked for the picture Kole had drawn of Tilda.

He brought his charcoal to the paper and drew Angok, then Quintus, then Catgut and Wolfun and Tilda.

The fire was burning low by the time he finished. When it was done, at last he could sleep.

PART IV
REFUGE

CHAPTER
29

CCORDING TO MARA, Locket was a small city. To Kole, who until now had never traveled more than a few days from Hale's Crossing, it was overwhelming.

The city curled protectively around a bay at the narrowest point of the Neck, jealously guarding its ports on the Sea of Reavers. The sails of tall-masted ships were scattered across the green sea like the folded paper boats Kole used to make with Arabeth.

Spires and chimneys reached up above the walls of weathered and patched black stone. But the city had spilled beyond the confines of the walls, sprawling out across the surrounding grassland. The ramshackle buildings grew taller the closer to the city they got, all packed in close as if clamoring to get inside the walls. Smoke hung like a smudge of ink above it all.

Even before they reached its outskirts, Kole was astounded by the bustle in the outer city. It was like watching ants swarming around their nest. Locals leaned out of windows, hanging washing from the lines that crisscrossed between the crooked buildings. Hawkers dragging hand-drawn carts stopped wherever they could find a free spot on the hard-packed dirt streets and began shouting the virtues of their wares at those coming into the city. Gangs of children wearing little but rags roamed the streets, no doubt hoping to part travelers from the contents of their pockets.

Just as Kole's eyes were adjusting to the scale of the city, the smell hit him. He'd grown up trapped between the stink of fish and the reek of the swamp, but this smell was enough to make his eyes water. It was suffocating—the smell of thousands of unwashed bodies pressed in tight, punctuated by occasional wafts of sewage and stale ale and sweet incense.

Mara jerked her head at Kole, leading him down the main dirt thoroughfare of the outer city. The ramshackle buildings closed in tight around him. The thick air seemed hard to breathe.

Kole shrank back as a gang of children swarmed around them, pawing at Mugsy's saddlebags. At a shout from Mara they all scattered, disappearing down winding alleys.

Mara seemed to have no trouble leading Mugsy through the growing throng of locals and visitors. Kole didn't know where to step. He kept nearly bumping into people, earning himself dark glares.

"Watch where you're stepping, farmboy," a one-legged local snapped as he hobbled past on a crutch, headed for the tavern across the street.

Kole murmured an apology. The weathered man glared at him a moment longer, then his gaze dropped to the sword at Kole's hip. His eyes narrowed and he limped away, grumbling to himself.

"Be careful," Mara said quietly, watching the man go. "The Free Lady's law is loose here in the Warrens. Violence and vice are close comfort to those who have little else."

As the one-legged man shoved open the tavern door and staggered inside, Mara's eyes drifted toward a middle aged woman sitting on the steps of a small wooden temple dedicated to Ur, the god of the Sea of Reavers. The woman was drawing deeply from a pipe as long as Kole's forearm. Faint blue smoke spilled from her nose as she exhaled, and Kole caught the scent of something sickly sweet.

Mara jerked her head at Kole. "Come."

"We can find a good physik here?" Kole asked doubtfully as they continued along the narrow street.

Mara shook her head. "Inside the walls. I know someone, though I have not seen her for many years. I may be able to convince her to help us. If she is still there. And still alive."

"I wish you sounded more confident."

"As do I."

"And what about a ship?" Kole asked.

"The ports are accessible through the inner city. Once Darvin is dealt with, we will see about finding passage to Godsmouth. We may even be able to charter a ship. I do not wish to linger here waiting on some merchant captain's whims."

"Chartering a ship will be expensive, won't it?" he said. "Do you have the coin? Because I don't."

"There are many wealthy people within the walls. Not as wealthy as some in Godsmouth, but wealthy enough. A handful are collectors of ancient artifacts. Others deal in such things. If we can fence some of the scepters we took from the temple, we'll have enough to get us to Godsmouth."

"Won't that draw attention to us?"

"The kinds of dealers who trade in old world artifacts know how to be discreet. They don't want their collections seized by authorities fearing the taint of sorcery."

Her words were sure, but Kole had gotten good enough at reading Mara to see the tension in her face. She was worried.

They continued further along the main thoroughfare, waving away hawkers and passing roadside taverns filled with music and raucous laughter. The walls of Locket loomed closer. He could see now that some sections of the ancient walls had crumbled and been later patched with dark bricks. The patched sections looked no less imposing than the rest.

Ahead, the street became clogged with travelers and merchant caravans. Some were craning their necks to look over the crowd, while others sat atop their wagons and carts, muttering impatiently. The line filled the street and seemed to stretch all the way to the city walls. Peering between a pair of mounted travelers, Kole caught sight of a large gatehouse set into the city walls. A green banner hung limply atop the gatehouse.

A few minutes passed and they'd only shuffled forward a few steps. More travelers joined the queue behind them.

"Excuse me, gentlemen," Mara said to one of the riders ahead of them. "Do you know what's causing the delay? Are the gates closed?"

"One of the Free Lady's militia captains searching for contraband, no doubt," said the rider, a plump man with a curled mustache. "Doesn't look good when half the court is stupefied from smoking too much of that Half-man's Oil." He spat in the dirt. "Damned merchant-nobles and their gutter fashions."

Kole and Mara exchanged a look. Despite the afternoon sun and press of bodies around them, Kole felt something cold slowly closing around his chest.

"Want me to have a look?" he muttered to Mara.

She nodded. "Don't go too far."

He squeezed out of the crowd and made his way along the side of the street, dodging the travelers who had given up on the queue to search for a tavern. He hurried past a money-changer's shop that was built like a miniature fortress, with an iron-banded door made to withstand a battering ram. A tall, bearded guard glared at him until he'd passed on.

When the street straightened and the gatehouse loomed ahead of him, he climbed a set of rickety stairs to the second-story veranda of an alehouse. Leaning over the railing, he finally saw what was causing the delay.

The cold feeling that had been closing around his chest suddenly squeezed tight. He stared for a moment longer, then hurried back down the alehouse stairs. He shoved his way back through the crowd. The insults hurled his way no longer bothered him.

Something must have shown on his face when he finally found Mara again. She took one look at him and her own face darkened.

"What is it?" she asked.

Kole swallowed and leaned close. "They're here. The Hallowed Order is here."

CHAPTER

30

KOLE SAT ON the steps of the temple to Ur, attacking the food they'd bought from a street vendor: a few strips of shredded chicken and gravy stuffed into a flatbread pocket. It was the best thing he'd tasted in weeks—mostly because it wasn't rabbit. He just couldn't figure out how to eat it without getting gravy all over his hands and tunic.

Mara was pacing back and forth in front of him, her own uneaten chicken pocket leaking gravy on her boots. Mugsy stood sullenly in place next to Kole, still bearing Darvin. The boy had been silent since his seizure the previous night. He was pallid and would barely swallow the water and porridge Kole fed him. He was dying—Kole was sure of that.

The first hints of orange were creeping across the sky. They'd spent the last of the afternoon confirming that all three gates into Locket were manned not only by the local militia, but also by members of the Hallowed Order. There was at least one knight at each gate, accompanied by three or four armsmen with the shaved heads and blue surcoats of the Hallowed Order.

Each man, woman, and child entering the city was interrogated by the knights while the armsmen searched carts and poked spears into sacks of foodstuffs. The local militia looked on sourly, muttering among themselves. It was clear that the militia were upset to have their authority superseded by the Hallowed Order, though they were apparently unable to do anything about it.

"We need to get inside those walls," Mara said as she paced. "Or we'll be walking all the way to Godsmouth. I don't fancy a week spent trudging through the Ratwood. And the Vale of Twelve is out of the question. It will bring us too close to the Order garrison at Vale City."

They'd been through this three times already, but Kole humored her once more. "Maybe we can bluff our way through the gates. They may not have a good idea what we look like."

"They know what we look like," Mara said firmly. "The townsfolk they captured at Hale's Crossing will have told them all they need to know. If it was just a few militia on the gates I'd risk it. We could always bribe our way through if talking failed. But the Hallowed Order won't be so easily bypassed."

"There must be other ways into the city."

"Well, we won't be climbing." She frowned at the great black walls. "The ports are protected by the walls. If we wait until night we might be able to steal a fishing boat from down the coast and get in by sea."

"Mugsy can't ride in a fishing boat."

"Maybe we leave Mugsy behind. Or sell her." She glanced at the horse, who stared sadly back at her.

"And carry Darvin through the city ourselves?" Kole said.

"If we must." She growled to herself and dragged a hand across her face. "Except going by water will be almost as dangerous as trying to sneak through the gates. If they have any sense they'll be watching the bay."

"What about sewers? Cities have sewers, right?"

"Does it smell like the Warrens have a sewer system?" Mara said. "All the sewers beneath the inner city lead to the sea. Not to the outer sprawl."

Kole finished his meal and licked his fingers. "Someone in this place must know how to get in there." He eyed a tavern down the street, where a group of young men and women were passing around one of the long pipes he'd seen people smoking ever since he'd arrived in the city. "That man before said people were smuggling Half-man's Oil into the inner city. The smugglers might have ways of getting in other than the gate."

"I don't know any smugglers. Do you?"

He shook his head. "We could ask around."

"We'd be dead in an alley before morning. The gangs that run the Warrens don't take kindly to curious outsiders. And that's if the militia don't catch wind of us first." She sighed and looked up at the darkening sky. "We need to find somewhere to stay. I don't want to be on the street after nightfall. Not in the sprawl."

Kole looked up and down the main thoroughfare. There were many inns and taverns along the street, though with the holdup at the gates the inns were filling quickly with travelers looking for a place to spend the night. There were a number of temples as well, not just to Ur and Un and the Watcher of Souls, but also smaller shrines for the ancestor gods of several Sundarin clans. Kole had seen many Sundarins among the locals here—most of them gathered into small communities of their own, apparently claiming entire streets for themselves.

"Aside from the pickpockets it doesn't seem so bad out here," Kole said.

There was a comforting anonymity here in the sprawl, at least. All his life Kole had lived among townsfolk who knew exactly what he was, what his family were. Here, though, he wasn't a Felmen. He wasn't a corpse dragger. He was just another traveler. People only glared at him for not knowing the ways of the city, not because of his family. No one veered away from him in disgust or made warding signs against his impurity.

It felt...liberating. For the first time in his life he dared to think that someday he could be something other than a corpse man.

"It's not bad here on Gate Street," Mara agreed. "Not during the day. But beyond the main thoroughfares is the real sprawl. There, the gangs rule. When night arrives they'll come skulking out of the back alleys. The only people the gangers won't touch after sunset are the priests and the ratcatchers. Even the gangs understand their survival hinges on keeping the Warrens rat-free."

Kole cast his eye toward the deep shadows growing in the dark alleys. His earlier unease came creeping back.

"They'll come after us even if we're armed?"

"If we're armed, we must be guarding something valuable." She shrugged. "In any case, we should avoid unnecessary trouble. We don't need the attention, and I don't want you to..." She glanced at him and trailed off.

"What?" he asked.

She hesitated. "I just don't want you to be tempted to use...extreme methods to defend yourself."

Sorcery. That was what she meant. She worried he couldn't control himself.

He bristled at her words. He was tired of being treated like a child holding a lit match and a flask full of oil.

Mara finally seemed to notice the gravy dripping down her sleeve. She frowned and stuffed the chicken pocket into her mouth.

"I'll go see if I can find us an inn that still has vacancies," she said with her mouth full. "You wait here."

He suppressed his annoyance. "Maybe we should stick together."

She shook her head, swallowing. "We won't get lodging anywhere if they see Darvin. They'll worry he's contagious. Better we sneak him in once we've already got a room. I won't be long. You'll be safe enough here at the temple."

He gestured to her mud-stained clothing.

"Try and find a place that does baths," he said. "I think we both need one."

With a nod, she hurried off down the street.

"What do you think, Mugsy?" Kole asked the horse. "Any bright ideas for getting past the gate?"

Mugsy snorted. Kole looked up at the darkening sky. The last few gulls were flying back to the coast, their scavenging done for the day. Already their squawks were fading.

"It's a pity you can't fly," he said to Mugsy. "We'd be over the walls in no time."

He looked down at his hands, and for a moment in his mind's eye he could see every bone, every muscle, every tendon and ligament and blood vessel. A picture formed in his head, as it did sometimes when he was staring at a blank sheet of paper, preparing to draw some scene or figure. It was a hazy image, half-formed, no more than a sketch.

But for a moment, he thought he saw how he could do it. How he could rearrange his bones, twist his own flesh, until his arms were not arms anymore, but wings—wings to carry him over the walls and into the inner city.

He thought of the abomination they'd encountered below the idol of Gnothea. A creature that might once have been a man before it was turned into a monster, or perhaps some avatar of a primitive snake god. If sorcerers could do that, could he not transform himself in the same way?

His reforged leg gave a sudden twinge of pain, dragging him out of his thoughts. The pain and muscle spasms had been growing more frequent in the last couple of days.

Gods, if he couldn't even fix his leg properly, how was he supposed to give himself wings? He pulled up the cuff of his trousers to watch the muscles in his upper calf twitching erratically. The skin around his knee was a sickly purple. When he touched his hand to his leg it felt unusually cool.

He took a few deep breaths, rubbing the twitching muscles until the leg finally relaxed.

What had he done wrong when he'd reforged the leg? Mara had said that a sorcerer's incantation was a precise thing. Had he said the wrong word, transposed some syllables?

He supposed he should be thankful that he hadn't put the leg on backwards. Or lost it entirely. He thought of the one-legged man he'd seen earlier, limping into the tavern. Kole never would have made it out of the swamp in that state.

The sound of footsteps came from behind him. Kole hurriedly pulled his trouser leg down and glanced over his shoulder toward the temple entrance.

The temple was a small, simple thing made of whitewashed timber. It had a peaked roof, and atop the the iron spire jutting from the center was a large wind vane shaped like a sea serpent. The vane groaned with every slight change in the wind.

The doors were wooden too, but the timbers were gray and aged and spotted with long-dead barnacles, as if they'd been dredged up from a sunken ship.

One of the doors creaked open to allow an elderly couple to emerge. The wife dabbed at her eyes with a handkerchief while the husband shuffled along beside her, staring at something far away.

Kole stood, but the couple barely seemed to notice him as they descended the stairs and started off down the street. He stared after them.

"How many times do I have to tell you oilers," came a hoarse voice from the temple doors, "that you can't smoke here. Get moving."

Kole turned to see a weathered old man with a stooped back standing in the doorway, glaring down at him with gray eyes. The man's hair and beard were both wild and shockingly white. Yellowed toenails curled from his bare feet. His left arm ended in a stump where his hand should have been. The only item of clothing he wore was a heavy canvas robe that looked like it had been made from a strip of a ship's sail.

It was Kole's second time meeting a priest of Ur, the brash, violent god of the Sea of Reavers. The first had been an itinerant cleric who was quickly evicted from Hale's Crossing after a run-in with the local preacher.

That man had been younger than the priest who now stood before Kole. Both had the same wildness in their eyes—a wildness that made Kole shrink before the intensity of the man's gaze.

"I'm not an oiler," Kole said. "I just—"

"Hmmph." The priest frowned at Darvin's limp body sitting astride Mugsy. "What's wrong with him? Doesn't look much like a seaman to me."

"He's not. We're not. We're from out of town. My friend is sick. We're looking for—"

"Does this look like a temple of healing?" the priest barked. "Ur doesn't care about sick boys. Try your luck with the herbalists down Spice Alley. Or talk to the barbers on Scissor Row, if there's something needs taken out of him. Now go on. I can't have a horse shitting all over my steps."

There was a niggle in the back of Kole's head. Some half-formed thought. He looked after the elderly couple, where they'd disappeared down some side street.

"Why were they so upset?" he asked.

"You'd be upset too if your daughter was lost at sea." Wrinkled eyes narrowed. "Sometimes folk think they can bribe Ur into spitting out their loved ones. They hope one day they'll find their daughter washed up on shore, if only they can offer something in return. But it doesn't work that way. Ur claims his due." He lifted his stump of an arm. "Always."

For a moment, Kole found himself preparing an incantation to restore the priest's hand. The sorcerous words sprang to mind unbidden, so rich and sweet he almost couldn't keep himself from speaking them aloud.

He caught himself in time, swallowing the words and banishing them from his mind. A cold sweat prickled at his forehead. Control. He had to learn control.

The priest was staring at him strangely. Panic suddenly gripped him.

Gods. Was I speaking aloud?

He prepared to run. But with a crooked scowl, the priest simply lowered his stump and waved his good hand at him.

"Off with you, then. You and your friend." Shaking his head, he turned and began to shuffle back through the door of the temple. "Country bumpkins," he muttered loudly.

The thought that had been smoldering in the back of Kole's head suddenly flared to life. Just as the priest was pushing the door closed, Kole jumped up the stairs. He pressed his palm against the door, holding it open.

"The dead," he said. "Where do they go?"

The priest's white eyebrows lowered. "What? Don't you know your theology, boy?"

"Not their souls," Kole said. "The bodies."

"Giving up on your friend already, I see." The priest shook his head. "I don't deal with bodies. Ur rarely surrenders them."

"I'm not talking about folk lost at sea. I'm talking about people who die in there." He pointed down the street, toward the walls of Locket. "In the inner city. Where do their bodies go? They don't burn them in the city, do they?"

"Of course not," the priest snapped. "That's what the Great Crematorium is for." He pointed south. "Down the coast."

"And how do the bodies get there? Are they taken through the streets?"

The priest gave a look of disgust. "You can't cart a body through the whole salt-blasted city! It's unclean."

"Then how?" He leaned close enough to smell the hint of rum on the priest's breath. "How are the bodies moved?"

CHAPTER
31

HEN THEY ARRIVED outside the inn Mara had found for them, Kole's heart sank. He didn't think they'd be getting a bath tonight after all.

It was four stories tall, a narrow, creaking monstrosity crammed against a tenement building on one side and a stinking alley on the other. The bottom floor was a tavern. An indistinct drunken roar poured out through the windows. Even before they stepped inside, the stink of stale ale was almost overwhelming.

"I've got us a room on the top floor," Mara said. "It was the last inn I could find that still had vacancies."

Kole looked up at the fourth floor windows. "I think I preferred camping on the side of the road."

"You haven't even seen inside yet."

"No, but I've smelled it."

They made their way toward the tavern doors, dragging Darvin between them. Kole hoped it looked like they were dragging their drunk friend back to bed. The inn had no stables of its own—they'd had to leave Mugsy a block away at a merchants' stables.

"Wait here a second. We have to go through the tavern to get to the stairs, and I neglected to tell the innkeeper about our sick friend." Mara let him take Darvin's weight and opened the door a crack. She paused a few seconds, then gestured. "All right. I think we're clear."

She took Darvin's other arm once again and they shouldered open the tavern door.

The tavern was full to bursting. Patrons sat hip-to-hip on benches set in front of a dozen long tables. The evening was growing dark, but the staff had only bothered to light a handful of candles. A haze of smoke hung in the air, and Kole smelled the now-familiar scent of Half-Man's oil burning in a dozen pipes throughout the room.

"That's the innkeeper over there," Mara said over the noise, gesturing with her chin toward a plump man trying to intervene in an argument near the back of the tavern. "Let's get upstairs before he sees us with Darvin. If we get kicked out we might be camping after all."

She led him through the crowd of stumbling drunks toward a narrow staircase off to one side of the tavern. As they passed the long bar—still unattended as the innkeeper tried to prevent an argument from becoming a brawl—Mara paused and glanced around.

"Get Darvin to the stairs," she said, slipping out from under Darvin's arm again.

Kole nearly dropped Darvin as he struggled to take his weight. "Where are you going?"

But she didn't answer. She weaved through the crowd toward the bar and Kole lost sight of her.

"I wish she wouldn't do that," Kole muttered to Darvin. The boy didn't respond. His face was gray and his skin clammy. He hadn't made a sound the whole way here.

Dragging Darvin with him, Kole staggered toward the stairs. Something prickled at the back of his neck. He could feel eyes watching him.

He glanced around to see a man and a woman curled up together on a couch against the wall. The man had his arm around the woman's bare shoulders as she puffed on a long pipe. They were both staring at him.

Without taking her eyes off him, the woman turned and whispered something in the man's ear. His lips curled into a cruel grin, revealing a gold-plated tooth.

Mara suddenly reappeared at Kole's side, taking Darvin's weight again. "Let's not linger," she said.

They hurried from the tavern and dragged Darvin's limp body up three flights of narrow, creaking stairs. A humid heat filled the stairway, and Kole was sweating by the time they finally reached the top floor. He wished again that they'd been able to find somewhere with a bathhouse.

They emerged in a narrow hallway, all bare timber and no decorations.

A single lantern burned halfway down the hall. Mara consulted the numbers crudely painted on each of the dozen doors, pulled a key from her pocket, and fumbled it into a lock. They stumbled inside.

The room was tiny. There were two small cots that each stretched from one wall to the other. In between them was a strip of bare floor just wide enough for someone to sidle down. Opposite the door was an open window. There was no glass in it and the shutters were broken. At least that might help relieve some of the stuffy heat that filled the inn.

They lowered Darvin onto a cot and Kole lit a candle. Fleas from the cot bounded around Darvin, hungry for a meal.

They dumped their packs and Mugsy's saddlebags by Darvin's feet, then Mara closed the door and checked it was locked. They sat down facing each other on the unoccupied cot, each with their back to a wall. The cot was so short that their knees touched in the middle.

"All right," Mara said. "Tell me about this plan of yours."

He kept his voice low. The walls here were thin. "There's a tunnel."

Mara eyed him warily. "What kind of tunnel?"

"A tunnel for the dead," he said. "The priest of Ur back at that temple told me about it. The people here are just as nervous around the dead as those back home. They think the dead are impure. They think that handling a body—even being in the presence of one—is a risk to the purity of the soul."

Mara nodded. Kole supposed none of this was news to her. He wondered if people believed the same thing all over the world.

"Back home," Kole continued, "when someone died, we'd build a pyre outside town and burn the body there. But you can't go burning bodies within the city walls. So the bodies go to the Grand Crematorium, a couple of miles east of the city.

"But first the body has to be brought there. You can't just carry a corpse all the way out of the city. The streets and the gates are for the living. They can't be used to ferry the dead. So the bodies are taken to mortuaries throughout the city. And those mortuaries have tunnels running beneath them. They all connect up to form a passage that travels below the city, beneath the walls, and all the way to the Grand Crematorium." He leaned forward. "That's how we get into the city."

Mara looked dubious. "I hope you're not suggesting we fake our own deaths."

Kole shook his head. "Wouldn't work. The ashers—that's what they call corpse draggers around here, apparently—the ashers only take bodies from Locket to the Crematorium. We need to go the other way."

"And how do we do that?"

"We ask."

"We...ask?"

Kole nodded. "There's no other way. We can't sneak all three of us and Mugsy through the Crematorium and into the tunnel. We'll be caught for sure. The priest of Ur said the Dead Road is in use day and night. So we'll have to ask permission from whoever runs the Crematorium. Bribe them, maybe."

Mara was already shaking her head before he'd finished speaking. "No. It's too dangerous. We'll have to involve too many people. People we can't trust. What's to stop these ashers turning us in the instant we arrive?"

"I don't think they will."

"And what exactly gives you such confidence?"

"Because I'm one of them."

She stared. "You've never met them before."

"No," he agreed. "But if I tell them I'm a corpse dragger—"

"No," she snapped. "Absolutely not. You'll only be giving them more information to identify you with. Sage grant me sight, the Hallowed Order may have already been in contact with them to ensure none but the dead travel that tunnel."

"We have to try." Frustration tinged Kole's voice. "It's the best plan we've come up with so far."

Mara shook her head. "We wait. We bide our time and look for another opening. Maybe we can cause a distraction and slip through one of the gates that way. Or we find a way in by boat."

Kole gestured to Darvin curled up on the flea-infested cot. "And what happens to Darvin while we *bide our time*. We lost too much time just getting to Locket. We don't have any left to spare."

"Listen to me. You don't seem to realize what's at stake here. Darvin's life means nothing. Our lives mean nothing. Do you understand? Quintus knew that, when he sacrificed himself. You don't matter. I don't matter. All that matters is this." She patted her pack. "The Thesis must get to the Citadel. And if I have to choose between that and saving Darvin's life—"

Outside the room, a stair creaked. Mara jerked her head toward the door, raising a hand to silence him. She didn't need to. He'd heard it too.

For a moment, he heard nothing else. Then came a whisper, and another creak.

Kole's breath caught. In this place there was no shortage of noise.

Drunken footsteps on the stairs. Bawdy singing echoing up from the tavern below. The sound of lovemaking from nearby rooms.

But it was the quiet that made him reach for the hilt of his sword. The whispering. The inn's patrons didn't care about waking sleeping guests. The only reason for quiet was if they wanted to sneak up on someone.

Kole's hand trembled as he began to draw his sword. Steel hissed against leather.

Mara glanced at him. "No," she whispered. "Put out the light."

She shifted silently on the cot, bringing her eye to the door's keyhole.

Kole blew out the candle just as another floorboard groaned in the hallway outside their room. He still clutched his sword, two inches of steel glinting in a shaft of moonlight through the open window.

Why wasn't Mara standing? If Hallowed Order soldiers were coming, they couldn't face them sitting down.

As if sensing his thoughts, she put out her hand without taking her eye from the keyhole. Her shape was still in the darkness. *Don't move*, she seemed to be saying.

A second stretched out for what felt like an hour. A light shone beneath the crack in the door. A voice hissed.

There was a crash and the groan of splintering wood. Kole stifled a cry.

But the door to their room didn't move. Footsteps stomped. The light beyond the door flickered, shadows passing in front of it.

"Nine hells!" came a man's growl. "Empty! That fat bastard lied to us."

Another voice spoke, low and deadly. "Was more than just the innkeep that saw them."

There was a thud like a cot being thrown against a wall. A door creaked open.

"Oi!" a woman yelled from down the hallway. "Keep it down. Some of us have clients to entertain."

"What clients?" Boots stomped down the hallway. "Who do you have in that room?"

"Hey, what do you think you're doing? Get out!"

Mara rose silently and turned to Kole. Her eyes glinted in the moonlight.

"Get Darvin," she whispered. "We're going out the window."

"The window," he repeated. He looked out at the towering shack of a building that sat across the alley from their room. "We're on the fourth floor!"

She slung her pack and Mugsy's saddlebags over her shoulders, then slipped her hammer into her belt. "Yes. The top floor. We'll go over the rooftops."

"Search the floor!" one of the men outside growled. "You, guard the stairs."

"Quickly," Mara hissed.

Kole swallowed his arguments. His chest felt tight. As quietly as possible, he pulled on his own pack and hauled Darvin over his shoulders. The boy didn't weigh as much as he once had. Kole was thankful Darvin no longer moaned even when he was moved.

Mara grabbed hold of either side of the window frame and hauled herself up onto the sill. Kole heard her stifle a groan—her bad hip wouldn't make this easy, and neither would Kole's aching leg.

She crouched there, looking down and then up. Then she reached up, tugged on something, and swung herself out into the dark.

Her legs dangled for a moment as wood groaned. Slowly, she hauled herself up and out of sight.

Kole moved to the window. The footsteps outside were growing closer once more. Another door was kicked open and a yelp of surprise came from inside.

With Darvin a dead weight on his shoulders, Kole poked his head out the window and looked down. His head swam as he stared at the dark alley below. It seemed even higher now than it had when they'd first arrived in the room.

In the dim light of a lantern, Kole spotted two figures loitering at the alley mouth. They weren't Hallowed Order. Didn't look like militia soldiers either. In the gloom Kole got the impression of rough men dressed in clothes too fine for their demeanor. Each wore a hat with a thin brim and a rounded crown.

"Kole," Mara hissed from above him. He looked up to find her lying on the edge of the slanted roof, staring down at him.

She stretched out a hand. "Give me Darvin."

He hesitated. In his head he saw Mara slip off the roof as she tried to take Darvin's weight, sending both of them falling to their deaths in the alley below.

But at the crash of another broken door somewhere down the hall, he put his fears aside. Bracing himself against the window frame, he lifted Darvin up as high as he could.

Mara got her hand around the boy's upper arm and pulled. He heard a hiss of air escaping her lips. She slipped an inch closer to the edge.

But then she was still again. She must have anchored herself somehow with her other hand. With Kole supporting Darvin's weight as best he could, Mara slowly hauled him up.

At last Mara managed to pull Darvin's upper body onto the roof. Kole helped her boost his legs up the last couple of feet, then he heard Mara drag the rest of him up and out of sight. Roof tiles clinked.

Kole shot a glance back down to the men at the mouth of the alley. They hadn't moved. Kole prayed the noise from the ground-floor tavern continued a little while longer.

Swallowing, Kole turned away from the dizzying drop below him and looked up toward the roof. There was a support beam just below the overhanging lip of the roof—that must have been what Mara used to pull herself up. The beam protruded from the wall just far enough that someone might be able to hook their fingers over it.

Mara had made it look so easy.

There was a light in the window of the room alongside theirs. As Kole crouched on the windowsill, trying not to look down, he heard a crash from the neighboring room. A woman screamed. Someone cursed, then the stomping bootsteps approached the next door.

Their door.

With his heart in his throat, Kole leaned out, reached up, and grabbed the support beam. He felt a splinter dig into his finger. Shoulders groaning, he began to pull himself up. His boots scrambled for purchase on the window frame. He felt his hand slipping and shifted his grip.

His fingers sank into wood that was too soft. Before he could shift his hand again, the chunk of rotten timber came away in his hand. His stomach lurched as he swung, all his weight on the fingers of his left hand.

Mara's arm darted out from the darkness above and grabbed his right wrist. The wrenching in his shoulder ripped a gasp from his throat.

"I've got you." Mara's whisper was strained. "Come on."

With Mara's grip on his wrist, he was able to lift himself toward the roof. The muscles in his chest and abdomen burned at the effort. He gave silent thanks for all the hours Da had forced him to spend swinging the headsman's sword at tree stumps.

He'd just pulled his upper body onto the slanted rooftop when he heard someone kick in the door to their room. Light spilled out the window.

Kole pulled his legs up as high as he could. A moment later, he heard the floorboards in the room creaking as someone navigated the narrow space between the two cots.

There was nowhere to rest his legs, and he couldn't scramble up onto the roof without making a sound. Mara lay silently beside him, one hand still on his arm. She barely breathed.

From inside the room came a creak and a swish of cloth.

Go, Kole willed the man. *Search another room.*

But the footsteps came closer. A gloved hand appeared on the windowsill, the leather shining in the light of a lantern.

A man stuck his head out the window and stared down at the alley below. Kole's breath caught in his throat. All he could see of the man were his shoulders and the top of his hat. If Kole let his legs drop, he'd be able the kick the man's hat right off his head.

The man leaned out further, lifting his lantern so its light reached the alley below. Kole was lit up. Exposed. If the man looked up—or if the two in the alley mouth did—he'd be seen for sure.

"Anything?" came a growl from the hallway.

The man in the window withdrew his lantern and turned back toward the door. "No."

"They ain't on this floor."

"Then search the next. And bring the innkeeper to me. I want another word with him."

The footsteps retreated, and so did the lantern light. Kole waited ten more seconds, then hauled his legs up onto the roof. He met Mara's eyes. Darvin lay slumped on the roof slates next to her, unmoving.

"Who are they?" Kole whispered.

"Gangers hoping for a bounty," Mara said. "Someone must have recognized us. Champion protect us. I'd hoped our presence here would go unnoticed another day or two." She rose to a crouch, careful not to slip on the roof tiles. "Come on."

Kole picked himself up. Smoke billowed from a chimney near them. From up here, Kole could look over the cramped streets of the Warrens and see lights burning behind shuttered windows. It was still early—many in the outer city would be awake. The noise from the tavern below hadn't abated. If any of the neighbors looked out their windows and saw Kole and Mara on the rooftops...

It didn't pay to think about. With aching muscles, Kole pulled Darvin back over his shoulders.

"If those gangers were looking for us," he whispered, "why did they go to the wrong room?"

"I switched our rooms," Mara said. "When we were coming in I went behind the bar and swapped our key with another."

Thank the gods for Mara's paranoia. He hurried across the rooftop behind her, his back aching with Darvin's weight.

"Where do we go?" he asked.

"Across the rooftops. Then down to the street."

"We need to get Mugsy. I can't carry Darvin the whole way."

Mara nodded. "Once we're clear of the inn, we circle around and get Mugsy from the merchants' stables. Then we leave."

"Leave where? We still need to get inside the city."

"I know. I know. We'll figure it out. But if we don't get off this roof we won't be going anywhere."

They hurried quietly across the rooftop, trying to stay low so the roof's slant would hide them from side at least. Kole cringed at the rattle and clink of the roof tiles underfoot. He could feel sections of the roof bowing beneath him as he moved, groaning under the combined weight of him and Darvin.

On one side the inn faced the street, and another met the alley. But on the other two sides it backed up against neighboring buildings. One of the buildings—some sort of tenement—had small balconies with flimsy railings jutting from some of the floors. One was close enough for them to reach.

"Here," Mara said. She climbed the railing and dropped onto the tenement balcony. She gestured. "Pass Darvin to me."

Together they got the boy onto the balcony, then Kole climbed down after. The balcony creaked beneath them.

The door leading off the balcony was closed, and the windows alongside were shuttered and dark. Mara tried the door. It was locked.

She slipped her hammer from her belt. Kole glanced around. There were candles burning in several nearby rooms, but he could see no one looking out. Across the street, through an open set of shutters, he glimpsed a middle-aged man with his back to the window and a mug in his hand making grand gestures as he joked with someone else in the room.

"Are we clear?" Mara whispered.

"Wait."

Taking a deep breath to try to calm his pounding heart, Kole reached out with his other senses. A hundred heartbeats suddenly pressed in against him, so close they were almost suffocating. The great mass of human life surrounded him, making it impossible to single out any one heartbeat.

Shut it all out, he told himself. He tried to withdraw his senses, focusing on just the life that was closest to him. Even that left more than a dozen beating hearts, some slow, others fast and excited.

For a moment, hidden beneath the others, Kole thought he sensed another heartbeat, weak and fluttering. A second later it was lost from his sight. It was like trying to spot a candle flame beside a bonfire.

It was no use. He closed his mind to the life around him. He'd have to rely on more mundane senses. The man in the window opposite laughed at something, then strode out of sight. Kole glanced around at the other windows and saw nothing moving.

"Now," he said.

Mara brought her hammer down on the lock. It made a hollow *thunk*. Wood splintered.

She shouldered open the door as Kole picked up Darvin once again. A cry of surprise came from somewhere below them, but they were inside before Kole could see who had made the sound.

The apartment was dark. The only light that penetrated the gloom came through the door they'd just broken open. Kole got an impression of a small room, not much bigger than the room they'd shared at the inn. An insect the size of a small rat skittered away along the wall. A foul smell sat thick in the air, decay and waste and despair.

Mara was already across the room, trying to force open the door on the other side. Kole stumbled through the darkness after her, accidentally kicking a bowl that had been abandoned on the floor. A swarm of disturbed flies buzzed about angrily.

There was a cracking of wood as Mara forced the thin door. Just beneath that sound, though, Kole suddenly became aware of another noise. A soft, rattling breath.

Kole spun toward the sound, straining to see what had made it. In the dark corner of the room, he suddenly became aware of the silhouette of a person lying on a mattress.

The person's shape was small and bent. Not a child, but an adult withered away almost to nothing. He took a step forward as the soft breath came again.

Get out, said a voice in his head. *Just go.*

But without meaning to, he reached out once more with his senses.

And he sensed it again—that heartbeat so weak he could barely distinguish it over all the other life flames burning in the building around him.

It belonged to a woman. She was old. And she was dying.

He didn't need to strain his senses to see what was killing her. It almost seemed to glow within her. It was life. Life unrestrained, life out of control. It had begun in her lungs—he could sense the tumor there, growing even as the rest of her withered. From there it had spread, like weeds overtaking a garden.

He took another step toward her. He could see the cancer now. He *knew* it, he could see its name repeated over and over in that language of life that sang in his head.

Distantly, he became aware that someone was talking to him. He blinked, still seeing the cancer dotted like glowworms through the woman's body. Darvin's limp form weighed heavy on his shoulders.

"Kole," Mara was saying. "We have to go."

He realized she had the door open. There was a dark hallway outside. She stared at him, then looked past him to the dark corner where the woman lay.

He looked back at the dying woman. "I…I can…"

Mara's voice softened. "No. You can't."

He growled with frustration. Even if this woman could find a physik— even if she could afford one—she was beyond help. But Kole could do something. He could try, at least. He could try to bring the cancer under control. He could give her a second chance at life.

Only to damn her. Only to leave her infected, like you.

He shut himself off from her, withdrawing his senses and blinding himself to her pain. He turned away. And he left her there in that stinking room to die.

CHAPTER
32

OLE IGNORED THE LOOK Mara gave him as he carried Darvin out into the hallway. She led him quickly down the tenement stairs to a back door that opened onto a side street.

Pulling up the hood of her cloak, Mara cracked open the door and peered out. Gesturing for him to follow, she slipped outside.

They hurried down the dark, empty backstreet, slinking through the shadows like thieves. No one bothered to light the Warrens' streets. Maybe the gangers preferred it this way.

The stables where they'd lodged Mugsy appeared out of the gloom. The building was brick, unusual when most of those around it were simple timber. It mostly served merchants coming and going from the city, especially those who didn't want to pay the higher prices to stable their cart-horses in the inner city.

Mara bypassed the closed double doors at the front of the building and hurried to the side door. She hammered on it until at last it opened. A boy, maybe fourteen years old, squinted out, a lantern in hand.

"Help you?" he said, stifling a yawn.

"We've come for our horse."

"Now?"

"Yes. The dappled Helisian mare. End stall." She pushed a handful of silver coins into the boy's hand. "As quick as you can."

He peered down at the coins, straightening. "Yes, ma'am. Right this way." With a glance at Kole and at Darvin slumped over his shoulders, the boy ushered them inside and shut the door behind them.

The smells of horse and clean hay tickled Kole's nose as they followed the stable boy through the building. There was space for sixteen horses, and by the look of things they were nearly at full capacity. Most of the horses were sleeping, but one or two poked their heads over the stall doors to investigate the commotion.

Mara hurried past the stable boy and opened the door to Mugsy's stall. The horse woke with a snort and staggered to her feet.

"Where's her tack and harness?" Mara asked the stable boy as she led Mugsy out of the stall.

"Harness room." The boy gestured to a door. "It'll take me a few minutes to—"

"We're in a rush. Show me." She hurried the boy toward the door.

"I'll get Mugsy ready," Kole said, lowering Darvin onto a bale of hay.

Mara nodded and she disappeared into the harness room with the stable boy.

Kole pulled off Mugsy's blanket and found a brush. The horse looked grumpy to have been woken, but she remained still as he quickly brushed her down and checked her hooves. He didn't know how far they'd be traveling tonight or on what sort of roads. The last thing they needed was for Mugsy to throw a shoe.

"Sorry, girl," Kole muttered as he worked. "One of these days we'll all get a proper night's sleep."

A door creaked somewhere behind Kole. He assumed at first it was just a horse pushing against its stall door. But then he heard a footstep on the stone floor of the stables.

The door. The stable boy didn't lock the door.

Kole turned just as a man appeared. He wore a faded crimson waistcoat and a round-topped hat. A sword was sheathed at his hip. His hands were thrust into his pockets.

As he stepped into the light of a lantern, Kole suddenly realized he recognized him. It was the man from the tavern, the man with the gold tooth who'd been entwined with that woman on the couch.

He was thin and half a head shorter than Kole, but there was an easy confidence in the way he moved. He cast his gaze around the stables, not really looking at Kole.

"Stable boy," he said, "you see anyone come in here the last hour? A tough-looking woman and a boy carrying some half-dead…"

He trailed off as his gaze settled on Darvin's unconscious form lying atop the hay bale. His eyes snapped to meet Kole's. Kole just stared back, frozen. He sensed the man's heartbeat, felt it quicken.

The man reached for his sword. Kole snapped out of his trance and grabbed the hilt of his own blade.

He swept Catgut's sword from its scabbard and brought the blade to guard just as the ganger's sword came slicing toward him. More out of instinct than conscious thought, Kole shifted his feet and turned the attack aside. Steel rang as their blades clashed. Mugsy squealed and danced back into a corner.

The man's lips peeled back, revealing his gold tooth. His nostrils flared as he hacked at Kole again.

Kole took another step back and fell into the stance he'd practiced a hundred times with Mara on their way to Locket. Kole parried the man's strike, sending the blade slicing past his face. He felt a hot cut open up on his cheek.

The ganger didn't slow. He pressed his advantage, forcing Kole back another step.

Stop defending! Mara's voice rang in his head. *Attack!*

Gritting his teeth, Kole dodged a strike aimed for his neck, pressed forward, and sent a thrust toward the man's gut.

The man tried to twist aside. Kole's sword bit into his flank. He sensed the ganger's heartbeat lurch with pain.

With a clumsy swing, the ganger slammed his crossguard into the side of Kole's head. It was enough to daze him for a second—enough to allow the ganger to stagger back, clutching at his wounded side. Blood dripped between his fingers. All around, horses squealed in panic.

The ganger turned and ran for the door, opening his mouth to shout. "They're—"

Mara appeared out of the darkness near the entrance to the harness room and drove her hammer into the ganger's chest. Kole heard ribs break—he *felt* them break. The ganger's mouth hung open as he stared wide-eyed at Mara.

He was dead before he hit the ground.

A black, bitter taste filled Kole's mouth before he could shut off his senses. He planted a hand on a wall to keep himself from falling.

Mara kicked the ganger's fallen sword away into a corner and then looked to the door with hard eyes. Kole heard no one else coming.

Leaving the dead ganger where he lay, Mara strode quickly over to Kole. "Are you hurt?"

Kole touched a shaking hand to his cheek. The cut burned, but it didn't seem deep. "No. I don't think so."

A soft moan came from the entrance to the harness room. Kole raised his sword in panic before he realized it was only the stable boy. He was standing in the doorway with his hands over his mouth, staring at the dead ganger.

"It's all right," Mara began, slipping her hammer into her belt and raising an empty hand toward him.

The boy darted back into the harness room, nearly tripping over the tack and harness he and Mara had left lying in the doorway. Mara let him go and went to calm Mugsy.

Kole suddenly realized there was blood on his sword. Still trembling, he wiped the blood on the blanket he'd taken off Mugsy and returned the sword to its scabbard.

"There will be more," he said.

Mara nodded without taking her eyes off Mugsy. She was approaching the horse slowly, one hand raised. "Get the harness. We have to get out of here."

He forced his heavy legs to move. As he moved toward the doorway to the harness room, he couldn't keep himself from staring at the dead ganger's caved-in chest.

When he got close, he noticed a crumpled piece of paper sticking out of the ganger's pocket. Edging closer, he gingerly reached down and plucked it out. He smoothed the paper and held it up to the light.

It was a pamphlet issued by the Hallowed Order. Eight simple portraits had been inked on the paper, crude but recognizable. One was a picture of Kole himself, with his name below it. There was a picture of Darvin too, alongside sketches of Wolfun and Tilde. Above those were less distinct pictures of all four of the freebooters, including Mara. The pamphlet offered a sizable bounty for their capture.

"Mara," Kole whispered.

She turned and he silently handed her the pamphlet. Her face darkened.

"We have to get out of the Warrens," Kole said. "We can't stay here."

She stuffed the pamphlet into her pocket.

"Tell me again about this tunnel."

CHAPTER
33

ROM A DISTANCE, in the dark, the Grand Crematorium was a thing of majesty. The tallest of its eight peaked roofs reached nearly as high as Locket's walls. Arched windows looked out from every surface of the red brick building. In front of the grand entranceway was a long courtyard lined with statues, their heads bowed in mourning. And behind the Crematorium, glistening in the moonlight, was the Sea of Reavers. Waves crashed against the rocks below the Crematorium's cliff-top perch, threatening to erode the earth from beneath it.

But as they got closer, Kole began to notice the layer of soot that coated the windows and blackened the Crematorium's peaks. Two great chimneys reached higher than even the tallest roofs, endlessly belching black smoke into the air. A cloud of the stuff hung above the Crematorium and stretched out over the surrounding landscape like a dark god reaching out a shadowy arm.

Kole could taste the soot as they made their way across the lamp-lit courtyard toward the Crematorium. It was a taste he knew all too well. Tiny black flakes danced in the air around them. Mugsy snorted her displeasure as her hooves clacked on the broken cobblestones.

Lamps dotted the courtyard, casting a pale glow. The statues that flanked the courtyard each wore a shroud of soot over their heads and shoulders. There was a cleansing fountain in the center of the courtyard. It looked no less filthy than the paving stones around it.

They led Mugsy up the shallow steps to the dark oak doors of the

Crematorium's entrance. The doors were shut fast. There was no knocker, but Kole spied a small bell alongside the doorway. With a glance at Mara, he rang the bell.

There was a wait of several minutes before he heard shuffling steps from the other side of the door. A cold wind blew in off the Sea of Reavers, making the cut on his cheek sting.

Finally, the door creaked open. A short, balding man in brown robes appeared, holding an ornate lantern. He bowed his head.

"My apologies," he said in a thin voice. "But there are no more services tonight. To whom do you wish to pay your respects? If they have not yet been cremated I can provide a time for you to return in the morning."

The man didn't look at them. He was licking his lips nervously.

Gods, does he already know who we are? Kole glanced around, half-expecting to see Hallowed Order armsmen emerging from behind the soot-covered statues in the courtyard. But nothing moved in the night.

He turned back. The bald man seemed to cringe as he waited for them to respond. Slowly, something dawned on Kole. This man was like him. A corpse dragger. An asher. He was used to being treated with contempt and disgust.

Had Kole been like that too? Cringing and downcast?

"We are not here to pay respects," Mara said.

The man lifted his eyes in surprise. For the first time he glanced past Mara and Kole and spotted Darvin tied astride Mugsy. A panicked look crossed his face.

"Deepest apologies," he stammered, "but you cannot bring the deceased through the main doors. There is a side entrance—"

"He's not dead," Mara interrupted. "We're not here about him. We want to talk to whoever is in charge here."

He lifted his eyes once again, even looking at their faces for a moment before returning his attention to their feet. "The Nametaker doesn't receive visitors without prior arrangement. And never at this hour. Please return in the morning and I will see if arrangements can be made. My apologies."

Before they could respond, the asher shut the heavy door in their faces. Kole and Mara exchanged a glance.

"There goes that idea," Mara muttered.

Kole glanced up at the smoke billowing from the chimneys, then turned back to Mara. "Let me try."

Mara studied him. She chewed her lip.

"What are you going to do?"

"I'm going to tell him what I am."

"No. Kole, it's too dangerous."

"I won't give him my name."

"How many other corpse draggers escaped Hale's Crossing? You saw that pamphlet. The Hallowed Order already knows all they need to know about you."

Kole gestured back toward the city. "We can't go back to the Warrens. We need to get inside the walls. We need to get somewhere safe. This is a risk, I know. But so is doing nothing."

Mara glanced at the empty road behind them. With a sigh, she nodded. "No names."

"No names," he agreed.

He stepped up to the door and rang the bell again.

After a few moments, the door creaked open a few inches and the bald asher peeked out again.

"Apologies," the man said. "I really cannot help you tonight. Please—"

"No apologies are needed, friend," Kole said, stepping forward.

The asher shied back as far as he could while still keeping a hand on the door. Kole stopped, raising a hand to placate the man. The motion caused the asher to flinch.

"It's all right," Kole said. "I'm one of you."

The man hesitated, raising his head.

"I'm a corpse man as well," Kole said.

The words felt strange on his tongue. He'd been a Felmen his whole life, but the last few weeks seemed to have scrubbed that part of him away, leaving little more than a residue. He felt like he was putting on a disguise, pretending to be someone he no longer was.

"You…you are?" The bald man looked doubtful.

"My whole life."

"Who are you? Where are you from?"

"I can't tell you that."

The asher frowned. His scraping deference gave way to suspicion. "Why not?"

"I just can't," Kole said. "For your safety as much as ours. We need help. We need to talk to the Nametaker. Help me, please. As one corpse dragger to another."

The old asher gave them one last suspicious glower. "Wait here. I'll see what I can do."

With a swish of his brown robes, he closed the door in their faces once more.

A minute passed, then two. Mara shifted restlessly, clenching and unclenching her right fist.

At last, the Crematorium door swung open once more. A tall, rail-thin woman stared out at them from behind a pair of spectacles. She was older than the asher who had first opened the door. Her gray hair was cropped short without care for how it looked. She wore the same brown robes as the other asher, except hers were more frayed, with ink stains across the sleeves.

Without glancing at Mara, she fixed Kole with a hawkish look.

Nodding to herself, the woman stepped through the door and closed it behind her. "Let us walk the courtyard while you tell me why you're here."

Without waiting for a reply she started down the stairs, clutching her hands together behind her back. Mara and Kole exchanged a look, then they both followed the woman, bringing Mugsy with them.

"I'm a—" Kole began.

"Yes, yes. Pyke told me. And I am the Nametaker. I enter the names of all who enter our furnaces into the Book of the Lost. You have a similar custom where you are from?"

Kole nodded. He thought of the burning townmaster's residence, and realized the records of Hale's Crossing's dead were probably all ash by now.

"Do you have a name?" Mara asked.

"No. And neither do you, so I'm told." She grinned, showing the points of her teeth. "When I die, then I will have my name back. For now, I am the Nametaker."

They reached the bottom of the stairs and began to stroll between the looming statues that lined the courtyard. The lamplight that filled the courtyard was dulled by the thin haze of smoke that filled the air. Kole resisted the urge to cough.

"Ask me what you came to ask, then," the Nametaker said. "My work for the night is not yet finished."

Kole glanced at Mara, but she just looked at him expectantly and said nothing. He swallowed.

"We need access to the passage beneath the Crematorium," he said.

"That passage is for the dead and those who bear them." She glanced back at Darvin's limp form. "You told Pyke your friend was still alive."

"He is. But he's dying. He's beyond the help of herbalists and wise men. He needs a proper physik."

"So take him to one."

"We're trying to. He's beyond the help of any physiks working in the Warrens. We need to get him to the inner city."

The Nametaker paused before the dirty fountain in the center of the courtyard. Ash swirled on the surface of the water.

"You wish to bypass the checkpoints that the Hallowed Order has established at the gates." She looked at him over her spectacles. "Why?"

For a moment he felt frozen beneath her gaze. He swallowed. Had she already seen a pamphlet with their faces on it? Did she already know who they really were?

Mara spoke. "We need to get the boy into the city. His life depends on it. But the Hallowed Order will not let him through. They fear he is contagious."

"Is he?" the Nametaker asked.

"No. He has suffered a head injury. He needs a physik's attention, or he will die." She removed a golden scepter topped with a ruby from a drawstring sack tied to Mugsy's harness. "Perhaps a donation to your Crematorium will make the decision easier for you."

She held the scepter out to the Nametaker. The other woman pursed her lips, keeping her hands behind her back.

"You are not the first to want to use the tunnel. For most, taking the Dead Road is inconceivable, but every now and then along comes a smuggler who thinks he has the stomach to walk it. Some of them wanted to make donations as well. Why should I help you when I turned them away?"

"Because I'm no smuggler," Kole said. "I'm like you. I'm a corpse man. I don't fear the Dead Road."

"So you claim."

The Nametaker removed one hand from behind her back, but she didn't reach for the scepter. Instead, she leaned over and dipped her fingers into the ash-filled water of the fountain.

"Let us drink to the dead," she said, looking up toward the plume of pyre smoke belching from the Crematorium's chimneys. Then, cupping her hand, she scooped the blackened water from the fountain and brought it to her lips. She swallowed. Water dripped down her chin. She lowered her hand and grinned, revealing ash-stained teeth.

A test. It was one thing to walk a road reserved for the dead. It was another to imbibe their ashes.

Mara looked disgusted. Kole couldn't blame her. Where was this woman's respect for the dead? Ashers were supposed to tend to the deceased, to set their souls free and dispose of their empty bodies.

"Will you drink with me, boy?" the Nametaker asked.

Kole hesitated. Not because of her disrespect for the dead. Not really. And not because he was afraid to be tainted. He was already tainted. Deep down, he knew that no matter what he did, no matter where he went, he always would be.

But if he swallowed these ashes—here, in front of Mara—he wouldn't be able to pretend anymore. Not to Mara, and not to himself.

He glanced at Mara. She said nothing, but the revulsion was plain on her face.

He'd spent so much of his life seeing that expression on the faces of those who looked at him. Mara had never looked at him like that, though. She'd looked at him with concern, with frustration, with kindness. Even, once or twice, with fear.

But disgust? He wasn't sure he could face that.

This isn't about your feelings. Darvin needs a physik. And if Mara is right—if the Thesis really does hold the key to a cure for the plague—then it has to get to people who know how to use that information.

Even if that means Mara never looks at you the same way again.

Rolling up his sleeve, he dipped his hand into the fountain water.

"To the dead." He brought a scoop of the dirty water to his mouth and drank.

It tasted like woodsmoke—a taste he'd never really gotten rid of since Hale's Crossing had burned around him. He dried his hand on his cloak, leaving a sooty smear behind. He couldn't bring himself to look at Mara.

"Have I proved myself, Nametaker?" he asked.

The old woman licked the ash off her teeth, then held out her hand to Mara.

Kole forced himself to meet Mara's eyes. It was what he'd feared. Her face was fixed in a look of revulsion. Kole's cheeks burned with shame. He looked away again.

At last, Mara handed the scepter to the old woman. The Nametaker weighed the object in her hand, examining it closely in the lamplight.

"Here in Locket, trade of such items is restricted. I trust you have the necessary paperwork to accompany such an artifact?"

"Misplaced, I'm afraid," Mara said flatly.

The Nametaker tutted. "Careless. I hope you are not as careless when leaving the Dead Road. It would be a shame if I had to enter your names into the Book of the Lost." She slipped the scepter beneath her robes. "Come, then, but tread softly. Ashers are an easily startled breed."

CHAPTER
34

OLE AVOIDED MARA'S EYES as they passed through the doors of the Grand Crematorium. He didn't want to see that look again— that look like she was going to be sick.

They stepped into a giant hall with a floor of grimy tiles and walls studded with soot-stained windows. The aroma of incense was almost suffocating, the pungent smoke drifting from dozens of bronze censers hanging from the towering ceiling.

Stone plinths dotted the hall, each surrounded by eight empty chairs— all of them with peeling paint and tattered cushions. If the rituals here were anything like the ones back home, families would come and place some prized possession or well-used tool of the deceased on the plinths to represent the dead before speaking their farewells. The bodies of the deceased wouldn't enter this hall—Kole guessed they'd be stored below ground until it was time to cremate them.

The balding asher who'd answered the door—Pyke, the Nametaker had called him—was half-heartedly pushing around a broom, making little progress against the accumulated filth traipsed in by mourners. His eyes widened as he saw them enter.

"Nametaker!" he squawked. "I must protest—"

She waved her fingers at him, brushing him off as if he were a speck of dust. "This is none of your concern, Pyke. Be about your duties."

He scowled as they passed, hands tight around his broom.

When they were out of Pyke's earshot, the Nametaker spoke. "I have heard that the Free Lady's militia is conducting occasional sweeps of the inner city, under instructions from the Hallowed Order. You will be conspicuous on the street late at night. Where do you hope to find your physik? Galith's Ward?"

Mara hesitated, then sighed and said, "Bondtown."

The Nametaker pursed her lips as if in thought. "The Omen House is in Bondtown. A mortuary that has not seen use in some time. There were some accusations that the staff there were stealing organs from the deceased. I had to disavow them." She shrugged. "If you come out of the Dead Road there you should only have a short journey to your physik. You'll find signs in the tunnels to direct you. Once you come out, try not to get caught. The keeper of the Omen House no longer answers to me. If he catches you, he will surely turn you in to the militia."

Kole was more worried about the Hallowed Order than the local militia. A trip to the city dungeons followed by ritual purification sounded preferable to whatever the Order knights had planned for a sorcerer.

The Nametaker led them across the main hall to a large set of curtains that concealed a wide staircase leading down to the lower level.

The air grew hotter as they descended. Sweat prickled at Kole's forehead. Despite her heavy robes, the Nametaker didn't seem to notice the temperature.

Kole stopped and gaped as he reached the bottom of the stairs. They were in a huge brick room filled with six great furnaces—giant bulbs of brass with metal chimneys reaching up to the ceiling. Each furnace was being worked by a pair of robed ashers, mostly young men and women, all sweating in the terrible heat. Kole hoped the robes weren't as flammable as they looked.

A short queue of corpses wrapped in white linen lay next to each furnace. Kole watched as one pair of ashers picked up a corpse and heaved it onto a metal slab set on rails in front of a furnace. There was a scroll tucked beneath one of the ropes that held the shroud closed. One asher removed it and unrolled the paper.

After reading its contents, the asher began the funerary rites, beseeching the Watcher of Souls to guide the deceased's soul to the Beyond. The asher spoke woodenly, reciting the words from rote.

On the other side of the room, another pair of ashers were just finishing the rites for another corpse. They returned the scroll to the shroud, then one asher hauled open the heavy metal door set into the front of the furnace. Kole could feel the heat of the fire from across the room.

The ashers rolled the metal slab to the opening and tilted it up so that the body slid into the furnace. There was a *whoosh* and a flare from within the furnace as the fire ignited whatever accelerants the body had been treated with. The ashers closed the door and went to retrieve the next body in line.

There was a bad taste in Kole's mouth that had nothing to do with the smoke or the chemical smell of embalming fluid. This...this just didn't seem right. It wasn't how the dead should be treated.

These ashers didn't know the deceased. The bodies could have been logs being fed into a smith's furnace for all the care they were shown. It was all so mechanical. So impersonal.

As another pair of ashers opened a furnace door nearby, Mugsy whinnied nervously, drawing stares from the ashers at the nearest furnaces. The Nametaker raised a hand to them, gesturing for them to return to their work.

"Is there no other way to the Dead Road?" Mara nearly had to shout to make herself heard over the roaring furnaces. "We are trying to be discreet."

"This is unavoidable, I'm afraid. Do not fear. The furnace workers rarely come into contact with those outside our order. And they know better than to gossip." She glared at the ashers as she spoke. They all turned back to their work, but they kept glancing furtively at Kole and Mara.

The Nametaker led them through the furnace room, ignoring the glances of the ashers. Kole felt exposed. With every step he was growing more and more uneasy about this whole plan.

Too late to back out now. He glanced over at Mara, then looked away again before she could meet his eyes. He could still taste ash beneath his tongue.

The next chamber wasn't quite as hot as the furnace room. Dozens of stone tables filled the room. Shelves fixed to the walls were stocked with large glass bottles and vials. Gutters had been carved into the stone floor, leading from beneath each table to a pair of central canals that flowed toward a drainage grate in one wall. Fluids of red and black flowed slowly along each of the gutters.

A sharp chemical stink mingled with the more familiar scents of death. Mugsy snorted at the smell and Mara brought her sleeve to her mouth.

There were more ashers here, each tending to a body set atop one of the tables. The bodies were all naked or in the process of being disrobed to be washed and treated with oils and embalming fluids.

"Do not let us disturb you," the Nametaker said as the ashers stopped their work to stare at the intruders. "We are merely passing through."

Her words did nothing to stop the staring. Kole kept his head down, trying not to let them get a good look at his face.

Without slowing, the Nametaker led them through the preparation room toward a large door made of black wood set into the back wall. Mara muttered under her breath as she stepped over the fluid-filled gutters running through the room.

Kole spotted a loose tooth sitting in one of the gutters, abandoned. How long had it been there, separated from whoever it had once belonged to? Was the rest of the body already ash, perhaps floating in that fountain in the courtyard?

Just before they reached the door, the Nametaker stopped at an unoccupied table. The stone surface was stained brown. Oblivious, she thrust her hands into the voluminous pockets of her robe and pulled out a jar of ink, a pen, and a scrap of paper. She set the items down on the table.

"If you are challenged on the Dead Road," she said as she scribbled a symbol on the paper, "show them this. Those of our order will know its meaning. Please have the courtesy of destroying it once you are through."

Kole took the paper. On it was drawn a symbol that resembled seven double-headed arrows emerging from a circular center. He didn't know what it meant—perhaps it was the Nametaker's personal mark, or some sort of asher code. Maybe she expected him to know what it was, since he was a corpse dragger. But he was beginning to realize that being an asher and being a corpse dragger were very different things.

They moved to the black door. As they approached, the Nametaker glanced back at Kole.

"I would speak with you, before you enter." She glanced at Mara. "Alone."

Mara tensed but said nothing. She shot him a look.

"What about?" he asked the Nametaker.

The old woman just grinned at him, ash still caught in her teeth. Kole swallowed, tasting soot in his own mouth.

Gesturing, she led him to a quiet corner of the preparation room. Knives and saws and clamps were arranged with precision on a stone bench, all gleaming in the candlelight that burned from chandeliers overhead.

Turning, she leaned in close to him. Even over the chemical stink of the room he could smell the mustiness of her robes. He wondered how long it had been since she'd washed them—or herself.

"You play a dangerous game, corpse man." Her grin widened. "Corpse boy, perhaps."

He stiffened. "What game?"

"This." She gestured at him, at the sword at his hip, and then at Mara and Mugsy and Darvin. "Them. You are a corpse dragger. I believe that. But them?" She pointed again at Mara, the gesture obvious enough that the freebooter couldn't have missed it. "They are not. You do not belong with them."

"They don't care who I am." He tried to believe it, but he could still picture the disgust on Mara's face when he'd drunk the ash.

Her eyebrows knitted like he'd just said something incredibly stupid. "Who cares what they think? It is you I am concerned with. You defile yourself by associating with them."

He frowned. "I don't understand."

"You think we separate ourselves from them for their benefit? To keep them pure?" She shook her head. "It is we who are pure. We are the instruments of the gods. All those priests in the city, they scrape and beg and bribe, always in fear of the gods. Not us. All who die come to us, so that we may deliver them to their final resting place. We are chosen. We are blessed to have such a sacred duty bestowed upon us."

Kole opened his mouth to speak, but the Nametaker spoke faster, her eyes wide and zealous. Specks of spittle struck Kole's cheek.

"To shirk that duty is to turn your back on the greatest of gods. That is a foolish thing to do. All die in the end, corpse boy. The Worm King claims all eventually." The fire in her eyes dimmed as she composed herself. "It is not too late to turn back. I can find you a place here, among your own kind."

He looked over at the ashers working nearby. The thought of spending the rest of his life in this place, feeding one body after another into a blazing furnace, made him shudder.

"I understand your reluctance," the Nametaker said. "I know what it is like to look out at the world and yearn for a different life."

She leaned in close, close enough that a stray white hair tickled his cheek. "But remember, boy: Life is fleeting. Death is eternal."

She stared intently into his eyes, as if waiting for an answer.

He said nothing. Seconds stretched out. At last, her face tight, the Nametaker straightened and swept around him, striding back toward the great black door where Mara waited. Kole stood in place for a moment, unnerved. Swallowing, he hurried after her.

"This is the entrance to the Dead Road," the old woman said cooly. "You will find candles and lanterns in the antechamber just through the door. It is a long journey to Locket, made all the longer by the darkness. Ensure you have enough light to see you there safely."

She turned as if to leave, then paused.

"Oh," she added. "Stay on the main road and do not approach any unmarked passages, even if they appear gated or locked. Do not stop to rest. And do not answer any calls."

"Calls?" Mara frowned.

"The Dead Road is an extension of a tunnel network that was present long before the Grand Crematorium was constructed. Some remnant of the city that once stood here. I have heard rumors that some of the tunnels stretch miles below the ground. Some say that it even connects with the undercity of Godsmouth." She laughed at that. "I do not pay heed to rumors. Nonetheless, over the years many ashers walking the Road have reported hearing distant calls. Cries for help, some say. Others report sounds that resemble those of beasts. Likely they are hearing little more than distant echoes distorted by the tunnels."

"Has anyone tried to investigate the sounds?" Kole asked.

"Over the years several young and foolish ashers have strayed from the Dead Road. They do not often return. Fallen down some dark shaft, most likely. Or else they get lost and wander until their light fails and the darkness swallows them." She gave them a ghoulish grin.

"We appreciate the warning," Mara said. "We have no interest in dallying down there."

"Good." The Nametaker gestured to the door. "Fine travels. I hope your friend finds the help he needs."

She glanced at Darvin's limp body, then gave Kole one last pointed stare. With a nod, she turned and strode away, leaving her musty scent lingering behind her.

Mara seemed for a moment like she was going to say something. Kole quickly turned to the black door before she could speak. Taking a deep breath, he pulled on the iron door lever and pushed the door open. It didn't make a whisper as it swung into the darkness beyond.

Mugsy snorted uneasily. *You're an idiot for bringing us here*, she seemed to be saying.

He had to agree.

CHAPTER
35

THE ANTECHAMBER AT the beginning of the Dead Road was a small, unlit brick room. Though the furnaces were not far away, the antechamber was strangely cool and damp. The only other exit was a gaping archway on the opposite side of the room. A breeze blew from the tunnels beyond, carrying a sour scent.

Kole decided he'd rather not know what caused the breeze.

As the Nametaker had said, there were stores of fat white candles in the antechamber. They gathered a few for their pockets, then lit the two lanterns they had with them. As soon as they had light of their own, an asher closed the door behind them. The lever made a cold *thunk* as it shut.

A cold sweat broke out across Kole's forehead. The walls suddenly felt too close, the air too thick. The flickering lights of their lanterns made their shadows stretch up behind them, tall and misshapen.

"Kole?" Mara's voice seemed to come from far away. "Are you all right?"

You're not in the temple. There are no snakes here. No monsters. Just the dead. The dead can't hurt you.

"Kole!" Mara laid a hand on his shoulder.

He jerked away from her touch. "I'm fine." The words came out harsher than he'd meant them. He turned away, but he could feel her studying him.

"Let's take a minute," she said.

He took a deep breath, trying to slow his racing heart. "No. We should get moving." He turned away from the looming shadows and took a step toward the archway ahead of them. "Let's just get through this."

"She shouldn't have done that to you," Mara said.

Kole stopped, still staring into the dark archway. "Who?"

"The Nametaker. She shouldn't have made you drink the water. That was cruel." She paused. "I shouldn't have let it happen. I'm sorry."

Slowly, Kole turned to face Mara. There was no disgust in her eyes. Just...regret.

"I could see how much it hurt you to do it," she said. "I could see you didn't want to. But I let it happen anyway. Because we needed to get inside." She sighed. "I know I've been somewhat single-minded since we left the temple. And long before that as well. This Thesis, it's a...a terrible weight, and I want to be rid of it. I've pushed you hard. I've pushed all of us hard. Made us do things both of us would rather have avoided."

She brushed the head of her hammer with her fingers. A hint of shame passed across her face in the candlelight.

Kole opened his mouth to speak but didn't know what to say.

She looked at him. "When we first met outside the inn at Hale's Crossing, I thought you would be just like all the other hirelings that have come and gone. Just another lantern bearer who ran the instant things went sour. But you weren't. You still aren't, though you have changed. I don't know if you see it, but you have. You've become...you. If that makes any sense. Maybe it doesn't. I don't know."

Mara shook her head. She seemed frustrated, like she was struggling to express herself.

"I was once a lot like you, I think," she said. "But sometimes it feels like I've been whittled down, beaten and sharpened over and over until all I am is a tool in service of the mission. It gets so that the mission is all I can think about. That any sacrifice is worth it if it advances the mission. But that's not right. Not always. I...I need you to remind me of that. I need you to remind me that there is more than just the Thesis at stake."

She glanced over at Mugsy and Darvin. The horse was still, but she whinnied nervously, her eyes swiveling all around. Darvin could've been mistaken for one of the corpses in the preparation room.

"Can you do that for me?" Mara asked.

Swallowing, Kole nodded. "I think so."

"Thank you." She paused. "I'm glad you're with me, Kole."

Kole didn't trust himself to speak, so he just nodded again.

Mara hung her lantern from Mugsy's harness and took the horse by the reins. Lifting his own lantern, Kole took a deep breath and stepped through the wide archway leading off the antechamber. Mara and Mugsy followed.

At first, the tunnel was the same brick as that of the antechamber. The lantern light revealed no other passages, nothing but the tunnel stretching away before them.

After a couple of hundred feet there was a change, as if whoever had dug the tunnel had broken through the wall of a much older passageway. This new passage was wider and taller, with a smooth stone floor and slender pillars supporting an arched ceiling.

As Kole entered the older passage, he noticed shining gemstones scattered across the ceiling, glinting in the light from their lanterns to resemble a star-filled sky. There were flakes of paint on the pillars. He tried to make out the ancient artwork, but it was too badly faded. Gilded torch sconces sat empty along the walls and pillars.

The brick tunnel met the older passage at an angle. Once, the ancient passage had extended in both directions, but a crude cage of iron bars had been constructed to block off the eastern passage. Kole brought his lantern up to the bars and peered down the blocked-off passage. There was little to see, but the sour smell grew stronger.

They continued on in the only direction available to them. After a few minutes they began to encounter other passages. Closed doors covered some of them, painted with warnings not to enter. Others were blocked with iron bars.

But most of the passages they passed were open and unbarred. If they wanted to, they could wander off in any direction they chose. Wide staircases descended even deeper into the dark. Kole felt the cool breeze rising up from below. Arrows and words of warning were painted on the walls next to any open passage, directing them back to the correct path.

They passed wide alcoves, each big enough to be rooms all of their own. Debris had collected in the corners. Perhaps the alcoves had once been shops or market stalls for whoever had traversed these tunnels in days gone by. Surely this place had not always been a cold, dark ruin made for ferrying the dead.

"Is it possible, what the Nametaker said?" Kole whispered. "That there's a whole network of tunnels below us? That some of them stretch all the way to Godsmouth?"

"I don't know," Mara said. "Perhaps. I would guess these tunnels are comparatively new, maybe a thousand years old. The ones below, though?" She shrugged. "The world is old. Far older than the Golden Remnant, or the Lamplight Empire before it. Thousands of years. Tens of thousands. Whole civilizations have risen and fallen in that time, civilizations we now cannot even put a name to. A thousand thousand generations of people, all gone, utterly forgotten even to the most ancient histories we still have. I suspect not even the gods know who they were. Most would not care, in any case."

Kole glanced into an archway as they passed. A steep stairway led down into the dark. There was something carved into the stone above the archway, but he couldn't read the strange letters.

He suppressed a shudder and turned away from the darkness. "I didn't think you believed in the gods. Not the new ones, anyway."

"You mean Ur and Un and the Worm King and all the others? They aren't new. Not most of them. But yes. I believe they exist."

"But you don't worship them."

"There is nothing to worship," she said. "Any more than one would worship a wild beast. Or that thunderstorm that caught us a few days ago. If you are threatened by a wild animal you may be able to distract it with a cut of fresh meat. If you watch the skies carefully enough you may be able to predict the coming storm and find shelter until it passes. But worship?" She shook her head. "This is not humanity's world, and those gods are not humanity's gods. They are wild. They are fickle and dangerous. They can be navigated, like a raging river can be navigated if one has the necessary experience. But they are not on our side. They are not benevolent. They just *are*."

"Even your dead gods?"

Mara shook her head. "The five were different. They were not always gods. They were mortal once."

He frowned. "How can a mortal become a god?"

"I don't know. I know that they were heroes long ago, when the gods were even more ruthless than they are now. Sorcery was a wild, untamed thing then. The borders between our world and the hells below were thin. Demons born of raw primordial energy raided us relentlessly, crippling every burgeoning civilization. Humanity could not thrive—it could only survive. Until the five rose up. Five heroes from across the known world. They took the fight to the hells themselves. They took the wild sorcery and bound it into the five lores, splitting it into its component pieces like sunlight split into a rainbow. By breaking the sorcery down, taming it, humanity could harness it for themselves." She smiled at Kole. There was a light in her eyes that only appeared when she started evangelizing. "So the legends go, anyway."

"Could these tunnels have been built during those days?"

"No. The five are older than these tunnels. Much older." She brushed her hand along a pillar as they passed. "Still, there is something familiar about the architecture here. I just can't quite place—"

She was cut off by the sound of something hissing from the dark passageway ahead.

Snakes. Kole's panic came flooding back.

With a frightened neigh, Mugsy reared, yanking the reins from Mara's grasp. Darvin's limbs flailed limply atop the horse.

"Mugsy," Mara said. "Be calm."

She reached for the reins. With a scream of terror, Mugsy spun. Her rump slammed into Mara and sent her crashing against the passage wall, gasping for breath.

The hissing in the dark was suddenly drowned out by another sound—a tortured wail that echoed down the tunnel. It rang in Kole's ears so loud it hurt.

Mugsy danced in place, her eyes wide with fear. As Mara tried to catch her breath, Mugsy's tail swished over her. The horse squealed, its muscles tensing.

Kole's legs suddenly unfroze as he saw what was about to happen. He threw himself at Mara, tackling her to the ground.

Mugsy kicked, her hooves slamming into the passage wall where Mara's head had been a moment before. The horse's shoes rang on the stone.

Then, with one last squeal, Mugsy bolted.

CHAPTER
36

"WAIT!" KOLE SHOUTED. He could hardly hear himself over the wailing that filled the tunnel.

In the light from the lantern attached to Mugsy's harness, Darvin's flailing limbs cast dancing shadows on the ceiling. A moment later, the horse galloped down a side passage and disappeared from sight.

Kole disentangled himself from Mara and clambered to his feet. Mara said something to him. He couldn't make it out over the wailing.

He ran to the passage Mugsy had disappeared down. Just as he reached it, the wailing ceased. So did the hissing. Kole's ears rang in the sudden quiet.

He lifted his lantern and stared down the side passage. It sloped down into the earth. At the edge of the lantern light, he thought he could see the passage branching. Mugsy's hoofbeats echoed in the distance, but he could see no sign of her.

Footsteps approached him. He spun and reached for his sword.

Mara raised her hands. "It's me." Her face looked drawn in the light from the lantern.

"She's down there somewhere." He pointed. "And Darvin with her."

"I know. Let's just...let's think for a second. The Nametaker said we shouldn't—"

"I know what she said."

Mara stared down the dark passage. "It's not like Mugsy to react like that. I've taken her to some bad places, and I've never seen her that panicked."

"We have to go after her. We can't abandon Darvin."

"Or the treasure. We won't be getting a ship to Godsmouth without gold. But if we get lost down there searching for her..." She let the words hang in the air. "Sometimes Catgut used to mark our route with chalk so we'd be able to find our way back."

"Do you have any chalk?" he asked.

Mara shook her head.

"I could try my charcoal," Kole suggested. He fished the charcoal stick out of his bag and tried to draw an arrow on the passage wall. But the mark was barely visible against the dark stone, even when he knew exactly where it was.

He grunted in frustration. Putting down his lantern, he quickly rummaged through his bag. There had to be something they could use.

Finding nothing, he put his hands into his pockets and touched the candles he'd taken from the antechamber at the beginning of the Dead Road.

"Candles," he said. "We can break up our candles and leave them burning on the floor as we go. We can use their light to help guide us back."

After a moment's hesitation, Mara nodded. "All right. It'll have to do, Champion protect us. But we stick together and go carefully. We don't know what these passages hold."

They took out all their candles. They'd taken eight from the antechamber, not counting the one in Kole's lantern and the one Mugsy had galloped away with.

"We'll need some for the rest of the journey through the Dead Road." She set three candles aside, leaving five behind.

"We can break each of these into three," Kole said. "As long as Mugsy hasn't gone too far they should stay lit until we get back. And if they burn out at least we can look for the puddles of wax."

"Fifteen markers." Mara glanced down the dark passage. "If we use them all and we still haven't found Mugsy, we have to go back. Understand?"

Kole nodded. There was a knot in his stomach. "All right."

They quickly cut up the candles and freed a wick on each. Lighting the first from Kole's lantern, they dripped some wax on the floor just inside the entrance to the passage and sank the stunted candle into the puddle. The light danced uncertainly. Above, the gemstones embedded in the ceiling glittered in response.

"Quiet and careful," Mara reminded Kole. "Let's go."

They crept down the sloping corridor. The floor here was so smooth Kole worried he'd lose his footing. Alcoves dotted the wide passage, holding only shadows.

The air smelled damp. In the distance Kole could hear something dripping, and a faint rushing sound, like water. The sound echoed strangely through the tunnels.

The passage ahead branched. With a glance back to check that he could still see the candle burning at the top of the passage, Kole crept forward to the intersection and shone his light left and right.

"Did you see which way she went?" Mara whispered.

"I think I heard her galloping that way." He gestured to the right.

Mara frowned. "Sound can be deceptive in tunnels like this. How sure are you?"

"Not very."

Mara crouched and peered at the floor, as if hoping to see hoofprints on the stone.

"I wish Catgut were here," she said after a minute. "She could track an ant across a desert."

Kole shifted impatiently. The longer they lingered, the further away Mugsy might get. It had been minutes now since he'd last heard her hooves. Was that because she'd stopped? Had she fallen into a hole or injured herself? Or was she just too far away? Was she still galloping into the dark, even now?

There was one way he might be able to find her. "Give me a second," he said.

Taking a deep breath, he reached out with his senses.

The tunnels were cold. Dead. Black. No rodents nested in the walls. There were no spiders spinning webs in the corners. He couldn't sense any bats, any glowworms.

In the terrible darkness, Mara's life flame burned blindingly bright. It was almost too much. He could feel its heat—he could feel her heart beating as if it were his own.

He turned his senses away from her, stretching out further. Reaching deeper into the tunnels. Something about this place seemed to smother the senses.

And then at last he found something. It was distant. He couldn't make out a heartbeat, not this far away. But it was there—a single point of warmth amid the cold.

"I think I've found them," Kole said. He wasn't willing to withdraw his senses in case he couldn't find the spot of warmth again.

"How...? Oh." He felt Mara rise beside him. He didn't look at her. If he did, he'd be blinded by her life flame all over again.

"This way." Kole started down the right-hand passage.

"Wait."

Mara took his lantern from him and lit another candle to mark their way. Kole waited impatiently. The life he'd detected was at the very edge of his senses. He had to strain just to keep it from slipping away from him. Mugsy—if it was Mugsy—seemed still now, but if she started moving again, he might lose her entirely.

"All right," Mara said as she planted the lit candle at the junction. "Let's go."

Kole nodded. His head was already starting to ache with the strain. "I can't watch where I'm going. I need to focus."

She looped his arm through his. "I'll make sure you don't fall down any stairs. You just tell me where we need to go."

They made their way forward. After a minute, more passages appeared, more doorways, more stairs. Some led up, some descended sharply into the darkness.

Kole could only guess at the route Mugsy had taken. He knew where the life was, but getting to it was another story. His senses were entirely blind to the cold stone that surrounded them.

Mara made him halt every time they turned a corner or took another passageway so that she could mark their trail. Time was running out—the candle they'd left at the entrance to the Dead Road had to be half burned out by now.

They emerged from one passage into a large, octagonal room with a circle of pillars holding the ceiling aloft. One pillar had fallen, smashing the top half of some ancient idol to dust. If Mugsy had come through here, she hadn't stopped—he could still sense her further on, not moving.

They were getting closer, though. He didn't have to strain as much to keep her light in his mind. A minute later the light began to resolve into two separate life flames, each pulsing with their own rhythm. One was strong and quick, the other so weak it was almost undetectable.

Mugsy and Darvin. It had to be.

He tried to pick up the pace, but Mara kept a tight grip on his arm, keeping him from rushing ahead.

The sound of running water was growing louder. Was that where

Mugsy had stopped? Why? It didn't seem likely that she'd stopped there just to have a drink.

They were so close. He could feel Mugsy's heartbeat clearly now, and Darvin's as well. He could sense Mugsy's fear and the life slowly leeching from Darvin's body, little by little.

They came to another intersection and Kole started down it. But Mara stopped, holding him tight.

"This is the last candle," she said. "We can't go any further."

He blinked, letting his senses recede. His whole head ached like his arms used to after an hour practicing with the headsman's sword. They were in a tight web of passages. There was a pale yellow residue on the walls here, like salt left behind after the tide had gone out. The air felt thick and humid. It had gotten warmer, somehow.

"No," Kole said. "They're just down here. I can feel it."

"I believe you, but—"

"No," he said again, more firmly. "We can reach them. We just have to remember how to get back to here. It'll be one more turn. Maybe two."

She looked doubtful. "I can't hear her."

"That's just because of the sound of the water. She's close."

Mara rubbed her eyes. "You're sure?"

"Yes."

She looked into his eyes, nodded to herself, then lit the last candle and planted it on the floor.

"Do not lose your bearings," she said.

They crept along the tunnel, passing doorways that opened into darkness. Kole paused beside a larger archway on their left, where the sound of the water was loudest.

"This way," he said.

The corridor was short and sloping. The yellowish residue grew thicker on the walls and floor. It crunched underfoot. Kole thought he could make out the shape of a hoofprint where some of the residue had been scraped away.

The sound of rushing water echoed ahead of them. With Mara leading the way, they stepped cautiously out through another archway.

The chamber was so vast their light couldn't illuminate all of it. Fallen pillars lay scattered in chunks across the cracked, residue-streaked floor. There had to be a ceiling above them, but Kole couldn't see it. He couldn't even make out any of the glittering gemstones that studded the ceilings in the passages they'd passed through.

A ravine split the chamber in two. It had to be at least fifteen feet across. His lantern light barely reached the other side, but he got the impression the chamber stretched out far into the darkness.

The sound of rushing water was coming from the ravine. Kole could see spray glinting in the light from the lantern.

Mugsy stood on the cracked, crumbling stone at the edge of the ravine. Her tail swished nervously as she stared down into the darkness. The rest of her was completely rigid.

Darvin was slumped over her neck, limp and still. He didn't make a sound.

But something did. A sound was coming from inside the ravine. It was almost drowned out by the rushing of the water, but it was there.

It sounded almost like coughing. A dry, persistent, never-ending cough. The sound made every muscle in Kole's body tense. He realized he was grinding his teeth.

He didn't want to look into the ravine. He didn't want to see what was down there. Mara had grown still beside him, her eyes wide.

"Mugsy," she hissed. "Come."

The horse's tail twitched again. She didn't move.

"Mugsy." Mara whistled softly. When Mugsy still didn't move, Mara began to edge slowly forward.

Reluctantly, Kole followed.

They approached cautiously. Mugsy was standing right at the edge of the ravine. The stone was badly cracked beneath her front hooves. If they startled her, she might slip into the ravine, taking Darvin with her.

Mara muttered to Mugsy in a low voice as they crept closer. Mugsy's ears twitched, but still she didn't turn.

As they got closer, Kole could see that Mugsy's eye was fixed on whatever was in the ravine. That horrible coughing continued from below. Whoever was making the noise didn't even stop to take a breath.

Kole resisted the urge to reach out with his senses again. He already knew what he'd find. He'd only felt two heartbeats in this room—Mugsy's and Darvin's. There was nothing down in the ravine.

Nothing alive, at least.

Still muttering, Mara reached Mugsy's side and carefully reached out to take hold of the horse's lead. "It's all right, girl. Let's go. Come away, now."

Kole came around Mugsy's other side, laying a hand on the horse's shoulder to let her know he was there. Her muscles rippled with fear.

The coughing grew louder. It became a horrible hacking, the sound of someone trying to cough their own lungs out.

Kole didn't want to look. He knew he shouldn't. But something was pulling at his mind, tempting him toward the ravine. He couldn't help himself.

He turned. And he looked.

CHAPTER
37

HE RAVINE WAS as deep as it was wide. White water rushed along the bottom, flowing from some unknown source and disappearing out into the darkness.

Directly below, the water churned around a small island of stone in the middle of the river. The island was no more than a couple of feet across. A circle had been carved into the stone, encompassing most of the island.

In the middle of the circle, squatting down and facing away from them, was a creature. In the lantern light it seemed like a smear of ink across reality. Its edges were ill-defined.

Kole got the impression of a slender body with two legs, two arms, a head. It moved, and yet it didn't. It seemed to blink from position to position, with nothing to connect one moment and the next.

The thing was doubled over and coughing violently, black arms clutching its abdomen.

Kole felt Mugsy being pulled away from the edge by Mara, but he couldn't bring himself to follow. He just stared at the creature, horrified and enraptured. Something about the thing was intoxicating in its ugliness.

He wanted to go to it—he wanted to throw himself into the ravine and offer himself up. And yet at the same time he wanted to run, he wanted to put out his eyes so he wouldn't have to look at this thing that his mind couldn't comprehend.

Suddenly, the creature gave one last retching cough. Something splashed onto the stone at its feet. The dark liquid shimmered with color, like lamp oil.

Almost as soon as the fluid hit the stone, it began to evaporate. Thin clouds of yellowish steam rose into the air above the ravine, spreading beyond the bounds of the circle that seemed to hold the creature trapped.

A jumble of sounds washed over Kole, carried by the thick yellow steam. Hissing, and wailing, and a manic laughter, and the crackle of a blazing fire. Smells, too: an acid stink, roasted meat, freshly-spilled blood. The sensations bombarded him, sucking the breath from his lungs.

And then, just as suddenly, they were gone. Blinking, Kole looked down into the ravine again.

The creature was looking up at him. Or it seemed to be, though it had no eyes that Kole could see. The only thing it did have was an opening set into the middle of its head.

Inside was a blackness even deeper than the rest of its body. He would have called the opening a mouth, except that implied lips, teeth, jaws. There was none of that. There was a tongue, though—a black, bulbous tongue that writhed inside.

Kole suddenly felt dizzy. He was distantly aware of Mara calling his name. It took all of his will to tear his eyes from the horrible creature.

Mara was dragging a resisting Mugsy away from the ravine. The horse seemed to be having trouble lifting her legs. She was as rigid as a statue.

Kole could feel himself being pulled toward the ravine as well. He resisted the urge to gaze at the creature. If he looked at the thing again, he might never be able to look away.

The creature was coughing again. He didn't understand what the thing was, or what it was doing down here. His head ached just thinking about it. Instead, he focused on taking one step and then another, following Mara and Mugsy toward the archway.

As he put distance between himself and the ravine, each step became easier. He caught up with Mara and added his strength to hers as they pulled Mugsy away from the ravine and the coughing.

"What is that thing?" He was ashamed how much his voice shook. "It's not alive. I can't sense it. So what is it?"

Mara just shook her head. "Something that doesn't belong here."

"But—"

"Don't," she said. "Don't try to make sense of it. There's no sense to be made. It is evil, and it is not of this world. It will destroy you if it can, just for the sport. That is all you need to know."

Kole swallowed. From the depths of his memory came half-forgotten sermons spouted by the preacher of Hale's Crossing—sermons filled with ancient myths and threats of hellfire.

"A demon?" he whispered.

Mara didn't look at him. "Come on."

They dragged Mugsy through the archway and into the dark passages beyond. His head felt thick, but he tried to remember the way back to the last candle they'd left. There was a right, then a left. From there, they should be able to see the candle's light.

Some of the tension finally started to leave Mugsy's muscles as they passed out of sight of the ravine. The coughing followed them a while longer, then that too faded.

Mara stroked Mugsy's flank as the horse began to calm down. "You're all right, girl. It's over now."

Kole spotted a familiar passage opening. The last candle would be just around the corner. Relief filled him. The creature—whatever it was— wasn't following them. It seemed to be trapped down there in the ravine. Thank the gods.

As Mara led Mugsy on, Kole took back his lantern and stepped around the corner.

The passage was dark. There was no candle. No puddle of wax. Nothing.

"It was here," he said.

Mara came around the corner behind him. She stopped and looked up and down the passage. "Did we take a wrong turn?"

"No. This is the passage we came down. The candle should be right there." He pointed to the floor, trying to suppress a rising panic.

They needed to get out of these tunnels. They needed to get away from that creature in the ravine. He turned back toward Mara and Mugsy.

Darvin was staring at him.

Kole stared back. Darvin's lips moved as if he was trying to speak.

"Darvin?" Kole whispered.

"Ma," Darvin said. "Ma's crying again."

Kole swallowed. Where was Darvin's ma now? Dead? A charred corpse? Taken away in chains by the Hallowed Order?

"It's all right," he lied, trying to keep his own panic from infecting his voice. "Your ma's safe."

Darvin blinked, and for a moment Kole thought he saw some lucidity in the boy's eyes. Darvin stared into the light of the lantern, then looked at the darkness surrounding them.

"No," Darvin rasped. "Gods, no. Don't leave me down here, Felmen. Don't leave me alone in the dark."

Before Kole could respond, Darvin's eyes rolled back and he went limp again. He continued to mumble wordlessly for a few more seconds before he fell back into silence.

Kole lowered his lantern. Once their last few candles burned out, they would all be alone in the dark.

"Maybe…maybe we should try to find the next candle," Kole said. "Maybe that one is still there."

Mara peered into the darkness around them. "Do you remember the way?"

"I think so." *I hope so.*

Mara just nodded.

Taking a deep breath, Kole set off in the direction he was sure they'd come from. He couldn't see the light from the candle yet. But maybe it had just burned out. Please, let it just have burned out.

But as he got closer to the spot he thought the candle should have been, he saw nothing. No flame. Not a drop of wax on the stone floor.

He stopped. Sweat prickled at his forehead.

The tunnels are changing. They shift when you aren't looking.

He squashed the thought. That was nonsense. It would take powerful sorcery to shift thousands of tons of stone like that. He'd hear it. He'd feel it.

There had to be another explanation. Maybe something else had taken away the candles. Some other creature.

You would have sensed its heartbeat. Unless it's another demon.

He forced himself to breathe. It didn't matter. They'd just have to find their own way back. Where to from here? Which way had they come? The passage to their left, surely. Or was it? All these tunnels looked the same.

"We must have gotten turned around," Mara said. "We head back toward the room with the river and try another path."

They were on the right path, he was sure of it. The longer he stared down at the empty floor, though, the more that certainty slipped away.

As he turned back toward Mara, the candle in his lantern burned out. Once he replaced it, they'd only have two more candles left to take them to the end of the Dead Road. If they ever escaped this maze of passages and got back on the right route.

He opened the door of his lantern. But as he was reaching into his pocket for their second-to-last candle, he glanced up at the ceiling overhead.

The gemstone-encrusted ceiling glittered faintly, as if catching the light of a candle flame. But Mugsy was several feet back, her lantern illuminating a patch of the ceiling above her.

Kole turned back. The gemstones shone above an intersection a couple of feet away. He made his way over to the spot. There was no candle on the floor. He passed his hand over where he thought the candle had been. He couldn't feel the heat of a flame. But his hand seemed to cast shadows on the gemstones when it passed over the seemingly invisible source of the light.

"It's…it's here," he said. "The candle is here. We just can't see it or feel it." He turned back. "How is that possible?"

Mara hurried over, leading Mugsy behind her. As she approached, Kole thought he caught a glimmer of light shining in her eyes.

She looked up at the ceiling, then down at the floor. "I don't think the creature back there can leave the ravine. But it seemed to be responsible for the sounds we heard—the hissing and the crying. Maybe it can have other effects as well. Maybe it can conceal things."

Kole turned his attention back to the ceiling. "We don't need the candles themselves. We just find the spots where the ceiling is illuminated."

"If the candles haven't already burned out," Mara said.

"I was trying not to think about that."

They hurried down the passage, all caution gone now. They couldn't afford to take their time.

Another patch of faintly glimmering gemstones appeared on the ceiling ahead of them, as if a hole in the stone was revealing the star-filled sky above. They hurried on to another intersection marked with shining starlight, and then another.

Kole counted them off as he went. They were close now. Just another couple of turns and they'd be back on the Dead Road. They passed another patch of reflected light.

And then there were no more shining gems.

Kole stopped again, staring at the dark ceilings stretching away from them.

No. Not when we're so close.

He glanced back to see the gemstones behind them flicker and grow dark. The candles were burning out. They were too late.

Mara stopped beside him and laid a hand on his shoulder.

"We're nearly there," he said quietly. "We're nearly back to the Dead

Road. I know it."

"Do you know which way it is?"

Kole swallowed and shook his head. "You?"

"I could make a guess. But that's all it would be."

He sighed. "That's all we've got. We…" He paused. "Do you hear that?"

She cocked her head to the side and went quiet. A moment later, the sound came again. A scraping of leather against stone.

"Footsteps," she said. "Could be another trick."

"Or it could be someone walking the Dead Road. What choice do we have?"

Mara hesitated. "None that I can see."

More footsteps echoed down the passageway. They were getting closer. Kole set off toward the sound, his hand tight around the hilt of Catgut's sword. Mara and Mugsy followed.

Up a sloping passage, Kole caught sight of a lantern's glow approaching. Kole raced up the slope toward it. He was terrified it would vanish, and they'd be alone in the dark once more.

He burst from the passage and someone cried out in alarm. The footsteps stopped.

The lantern's bearer staggered back a step. She was draped in heavy robes with the hood pulled up. Behind her came two more robed men carrying a thin, prone figure on a stretcher between them.

Kole let out a strangled cry of his own, prying his fingers from the grip of Catgut's sword.

"Who goes there?" the lantern bearer called. She sounded young, though with her hood up he couldn't make out her features. "You shouldn't be down here!"

Mara and Mugsy appeared from the passage a moment later. The robed figures all turned to stare at the horse.

"This is the Dead Road?" Kole said.

"Y…yes," the lantern-bearing asher said. "What are you doing down here? Where did you come from?"

"We have permission," Kole said quickly. "The Nametaker has granted us leave to walk the Dead Road." Suddenly remembering the paper the Nametaker had given them, he fumbled in his pocket for it. He approached the ashers and presented the symbol the Nametaker had drawn for them.

Warily, the asher took the paper and studied it carefully in the lantern light. Now that Kole was closer, he could tell he was right: she was young—maybe even younger than him. He wondered if she knew what was trapped in the tunnels below the Dead Road. Would she still walk it, if she knew what was down there?

Looking unsure, the girl showed the symbol to the stretcher-bearing ashers behind her. One of them grunted and frowned deeply, the corners of his lips so downturned Kole wondered if the man was even capable of smiling. But at last he jerked a nod and the girl handed the paper back to Kole.

"This is very unusual," the girl said.

"So I'm told."

Kole glanced at the corpse lying atop the stretcher. It was a shriveled old man dressed in fine but well-worn clothes. His eyes were partly open, staring blankly up at the ceiling.

Another log for the furnaces.

He suppressed a shudder at the thought of the dead being brought so close to the creature that lived in that ravine. The people of Locket worried about the dead tainting the living, but maybe they should have been more concerned about their deceased loved ones being exposed to that demonic corruption.

He pushed the thoughts aside. They needed to keep moving, especially with so few candles left. "We'll leave you to your work."

The girl nodded and the ashers continued on, giving Mara and Mugsy as wide a berth as they could manage. The asher with the downturned mouth frowned darkly at Kole until they'd passed.

When the ashers' light had faded, Kole met Mara's eyes.

"Are you all right?" Mara asked.

"I'm not sure," Kole answered honestly.

She nodded her understanding. "We'll be out of here soon."

Kole looked in the direction the ashers had gone. "Should we tell them, do you think? Should we tell them what's down there?"

"Do you feel better now you know?"

"Not at all."

"Then I think you have your answer."

CHAPTER
38

AFTER ANOTHER HOUR on the Dead Road they came to a narrow side passage with the words *Omen House* painted over the archway in neat letters. The passage was so tight they had to travel it single file. Kole took the lead, lighting the way while Mara brought Mugsy along behind.

The air began to grow warmer. The passage was sloping upward.

From out of the gloom came a broken section of the passage wall. Kole shone his light through, revealing another small antechamber like the one at the beginning of the Dead Road. There were candles and a couple of lanterns hanging from hooks on the stone wall. A thick layer of dust suggested they hadn't been used in some time.

"Here," Kole said.

They crept into the antechamber. The door leading out of the chamber was smaller than the one at the start of the Dead Road, but it was made of the same black wood. Mara handed Mugsy's reins to Kole and moved to the door, pressing her ear against it.

"Anything?" Kole whispered.

She shook her head. Taking hold of the door lever, she slowly eased it back. The lever's stiff metal joints squealed, making Kole cringe.

With a glance at Kole, she pulled the door open a few inches.

Kole held up his light and looked into a stone room with a low ceiling and no windows. The only pieces of furniture were two large wooden tables set side by side. A censer hung above each table, unused.

Kole breathed a sigh of relief as they stepped into the room and he shut the door behind them. If he ever set foot on the Dead Road again, it would be too soon.

They moved slowly across the room so that Mugsy's hooves wouldn't ring too loudly on the stone floor. Kole tensed at every sound. They couldn't afford to be caught. Whoever operated the Omen House could be asleep upstairs.

Mara moved to the doorway opposite as Kole led Mugsy carefully between the two wooden tables. Just as they were reaching the other side, Mugsy's rump bumped a shelf. Jars rattled. Something fell.

Kole dived, catching the object before it could hit the floor. It was a half-full bottle of pale green fluid—some sort of preservative. He exchanged a nervous glance with Mara and gingerly returned the bottle to the shelf.

Mara cracked the door open and held up her hand. They both listened. Even at night, the city wasn't totally silent. He could hear the distant sounds of hooves on cobble. A bell rang somewhere out in the night.

But the Omen House remained silent. Mara gestured and they made their way through the door and up a gently sloping ramp.

It came out in another room, this one decorated in somber blacks. There was a long desk here, along with some large cabinets and a few scattered pieces of paper. The flowers in the vase atop the desk were shriveled almost to dust. Frosted windows were set about the room, letting in faint moonlight.

Some sort of reception, Kole supposed, where bodies could be received and their details recorded. Or it once was, at least. It had clearly not been used in some time. Was it true, what the Nametaker had said? Had the staff here been stealing organs from the deceased? Who would buy such things?

They doused their lights and Kole crept to the mortuary's entrance. The doors were fitted with small square windows, giving Kole a glimpse of the street outside. Lampposts were dotted along the narrow, cobbled lane, chasing away the shadows. The windows of the tall brick-and-timber buildings across the street were dark, their shutters pulled. The only sign of life was a tomcat prowling along the top of a stone wall, tail twitching.

"Any militia?" Mara whispered.

"Looks clear. Do you know how to get to your physik?"

Mara peered out the window beside him. "I hope so. It's been a long time since I was here."

Kole tried the door. It was locked. He glanced at Mara.

"Do we break it?"

She cast a nervous glance at the ceiling. If there was anyone else in the Omen House, they'd be upstairs. The sound of a lock breaking would almost certainly alert them.

"There must be a key around here somewhere," she whispered.

They spread out, silently searching the reception. After a few minutes, Kole lifted up a pile of papers tucked into the bottom drawer of a desk and found an iron key.

He gestured to Mara and they hurried back to the door. A floorboard creaked upstairs.

Kole slid the key into the lock. It turned.

Kole returned the key to the drawer he'd found it and then they slipped outside as quickly as they dared. As soon as Mugsy was through the door, Kole carefully closed it behind them. Hopefully the keeper of the Omen House would simply assume he'd left the door unlocked himself.

Now that they were outside, Kole could see that the mortuary they'd just left was smaller than most of its neighbors, a converted house with a strip of weed-filled garden running all around it. The windows upstairs were shuttered and dark.

Kole breathed deep as they hurried away from the Omen House. The taste of salt hung in the air. They weren't out of danger yet, but it was a relief to have the stars above him—the real stars, not the pale imitations glittering on the Dead Road's ceiling.

The city was quiet. In the distance he could hear the faint sound of a fiddle in a tavern, and the occasional shout from men working late on the docks. Here, though, the neighborhood was asleep. It was well after midnight.

Mara led him quickly along the lamp-lit streets, pausing at every intersection to try to gain her bearings. The houses around them were often three stories tall and packed tight, peaked roofs stretching toward the stars.

Though the houses here were more ostentatious than the ramshackle buildings of the outer sprawl, they were nothing compared to the towering mansions Kole glimpsed over rooftops in the westernmost quarter of the city. Those buildings had circular towers and glittering spires that reached high enough to peek over the walls. He'd thought extravagance like that was reserved for the Domed Cities far to the north.

As they were approaching a tree-lined avenue, they heard heavy boots on the cobbles ahead. Mara jerked her head and they retreated into the dark of an alley. Kole's breathing seemed too loud in the close confines.

A few seconds later a pair of militia strolled past the mouth of the alley. It was a man and a woman, both dressed in faded green gambesons and ill-fitting helmets. Cudgels slapped at their thighs as they walked.

They were murmuring to each other too quietly for Kole to make out. If they'd heard Mugsy's hooves on the cobbles a minute ago, the sound didn't seem to interest them. The militia continued on, their bootsteps slowly fading. Kole allowed himself to breathe.

"Not far now, I think," Mara whispered as they exited the other end of the alley. "Yes, just down here."

They hurried down an avenue with a line of rose bushes running along the center. The houses here were larger, many with their own gardens out front. Lights were burning in the windows of one house, the sounds of a party coming from inside.

"Here," Mara said as they came to a house halfway down the avenue. It was smaller than those on either side of it, but still had room for gardens and a large orange tree. There was a paved approach to allow carts to drive right up to the front door, and what looked like a small stable off to the side.

"Your physik sees patients here?" Kole asked. The place seemed too fancy to act as a hospital.

"The ones who can afford it," Mara replied. "Come."

Glancing at the empty avenue behind them, Kole followed Mara up to the house. The dark windows stared down at them.

There was an iron knocker shaped like a disembodied hand clutching a ball in the center of the front door. Mara banged it hard, waited a few seconds, then banged it again. Kole glanced back at the street, watching for any more militia patrols.

A faint light appeared in the crack beneath the door. There was a fumbling of a key in a lock. The door swung open.

The woman was among the smallest Kole had ever met. Not just short, but impossibly slender as well. In her nightclothes she reminded Kole of a doll brought to life.

Her short dark hair was tightly curled. There was a streak of gray in it. She looked up at them with large, expressive eyes, a candlestick in her hand.

"Good gods," she said. "Were you trying to wake me up or bash the door down?"

Mara smiled. "It's good to see you, Medicus Gery."

The woman peered up and down at Mara. "You look all right for once. Unless the arrow is in your back this time." She craned her neck to see.

"I'm fine, Gery."

"Hmm. Tell that to the leg you're favoring." She turned her owl-like eyes on Kole. "This one's new."

"This is Kole," Mara said. "And before you ask, he's fine too. We're here for him." She gestured toward Mugsy.

"I don't do horses," the physik said. "Sedating them is a nightmare."

"Not the horse." Mara tugged on Mugsy's reins, walking the packhorse forward into the pool of light. She pointed at Darvin. "Him."

"Ah. Are you collecting farmboys now?"

She came forward and lifted Darvin's head. The boy didn't react as Medicus Gery took his pulse and touched two fingers to his throat.

"Hm," the physik said, though Kole wasn't sure whether the grunt was encouraging or not.

Finally, she sighed. "All right. Better bring him in then, I suppose. Oh. Mara?"

"Yes?"

"It's good to see you too."

CHAPTER
39

KOLE'S STRENGTH LEFT HIM as soon as he saw the canopied featherbed in the guest room on the second story of Medicus Gery's home. There was a thick woolen blanket of cool blue, a set of linen sheets, and a stack of pillows so high he didn't understand how anyone could possibly use them all at once.

"You're in luck," Gery said as she led him into the room and lit the candles at the bedside. "I have no other patients in residence at the moment, so you can have a room to yourself. I'll have my apprentice bring up a basin for you in the morning."

"Maybe I should stay awake," he said weakly, his eyes never leaving the bed. "Darvin—"

"You'll only be in my way. I'll see to your friend. Mara, you're down the hall."

The physik strode away. Mara paused at the doorway to Kole's room and offered him a smile. There were dark rings beneath her eyes. Kole wondered if he looked as tired as she did.

"Gery knows what she's doing," Mara told him.

"Of course I do!" came the physik's voice from down the hall. "I didn't spent six years at the August College of Medical Sciences for the parties." She paused, then added, "Though they were excellent parties."

Mara ignored the physik. Kole nodded and returned her smile. The two of them had carefully brought Darvin into the house and laid him out on the bed in Gery's examination room on the bottom floor. Before Gery shooed them out of the room, Darvin had looked as close to death as Kole had ever seen a live man come.

But Mara was right. Darvin was in the physik's hands now. They'd got him here. They'd done all they could. Mugsy was stabled. Mara was off to bed. It was time Kole got some sleep as well.

"Thank you," he said to Mara.

For a moment Mara's smile seemed to falter. Maybe it was just weariness.

"We'll talk about our next steps tomorrow," she said. "Get some sleep."

She pulled the door closed and left him. He realized suddenly that this would be the first time in weeks he would sleep alone, with no one nearby keeping watch. As he unbuckled his sword and sat on the bed to take off his boots—no, they were still Darvin's boots, even if he'd been wearing them for days—he wondered if he'd even be able to sleep, or if worry and fear would keep him awake until the dawn.

He barely managed to get under the blankets before he was out.

There was someone in the room with him when he woke.

He sat up with a start, his head still filled with dreams of an alien creature coughing and retching in the darkness, corrupting all around it.

His hand found Catgut's sword resting beside him. Fingers tightening around the hilt, he tugged the blade free of the scabbard and swung it toward the intruder.

The person beside his bed let out a short, sharp scream. Crockery hit the floor and shattered.

Blinking away his nightmare, Kole cast his eyes about the sun-filled room. It took him several seconds to remember where he was. Fine linen sheets were tangled around him. The guest room's curtains were open and sun was streaming in through the open windows.

A red-headed Sundarin girl was backed against the wall and staring at him with wide eyes. She was around his age, plump and pretty and utterly terrified. A broken bowl of what smelled like pumpkin soup formed a thick puddle at her feet.

Kole realized he was still gripping the sword tight, pointing it at the girl like a madman. Horrified, he fumbled the blade back into its sheath.

"I'm sorry," he stammered. "I…I was having a nightmare."

The girl squeaked an apology of her own. Still trembling, she crouched and started to pick the pieces of the broken bowl out of the spilled soup.

"Let me help," Kole said, clambering out of bed.

The girl flinched away from him like a nervous bird about to take flight. He stopped, not wanting to scare her any further.

Soft, quick footsteps came from the hallway and Medicus Gery appeared in the doorway. She cast her eyes over the scene.

"Anybody hurt?" she asked. "No? Khahra, please go fetch the mop from downstairs. There's a good girl. I'll help our guest."

The Sundarin girl darted from the room in a flash of skirts.

Kole's heart had slowed its hammering now, leaving behind a wrenching shame. What if he'd hurt the girl? What if he'd killed her?

"I'm sorry," he said to the physik. "I just…"

"You've had a hard journey, haven't you?"

Kole just nodded, his throat tight.

"Khahra is new. Lovely girl. A little skittish. Clever, though. She'll make a good physik one day." She glanced at the sheathed sword sitting on the bed next to Kole. "Perhaps you should put that by the vanity while you sleep. The dreaming mind can be a fearful mind. And a fearful mind is not always rational, especially when old ghosts come to haunt us."

"Yes, yes, of course," Kole said. "I'm sorry."

She crouched down and began picking up the rest of the broken crockery. Kole bent to help her.

"You have a lot of ghosts for someone your age," she said, glancing at him. "Like Mara. I would not approach that woman while she was having nightmares. Not if she had a weapon handy."

"Where is Mara?" He was surprised she hadn't come running when the Sundarin girl screamed.

"She went out a couple of hours before noon. Said something about finding a ship."

The Sundarin girl returned with a mop and bucket. She began cleaning up the mess without looking at Kole.

"And Darvin?" Kole asked Gery.

"First, get yourself cleaned up."

She gestured to a steaming basin of water that sat on the floor by the vanity, accompanied by a thick towel and some folded clothes. He must have been deep in his dream if he hadn't heard the Sundarin girl bringing them in.

"We'll get you another bowl of soup," Gery said. "It's good soup. I have a good cook."

"I'm not that hungry."

"You're skin and bones, boy. Eat. Bathe. Then I'll let you see your friend."

Gery was right. It was good soup.

The food did wonders for his nerves, as did a wash and a change of clothing. When he came downstairs, Medicus Gery took Kole aside and talked to him about Darvin.

"Mara told me what happened to him," she said. "Flash sickness. It is a dangerous thing left untreated. You were lucky Mara has some skill in that area. He would not have made it here alive without her. As it was, it was a near thing."

He swallowed. "Will he live?"

"I don't like making promises. I've had to break too many. Raw sorcery of the kind your friend experienced is dangerous to both body and spirit." She paused. "I'm doing all I can. He requires a very specific cocktail of medicines to break the grip of the flash sickness. If that can be done, though, he may live, though it will take time for his full strength to return."

"What are his chances?"

"I put it to the flip of a coin. No more."

Kole nodded. He felt...empty. He'd brought Darvin all this way. Someone he didn't even like, someone who'd tormented him every chance he'd got.

Yet the two of them might be all that remained of Hale's Crossing. The only ones still free, at least.

And now it all came down to chance. A roll of the Gambler's dice, as Mara would say. It was a strange thing.

"Can I see him?" he asked.

The physik took him to the examination room. Now that it was light and he wasn't so exhausted, he got a better look at the place. It seemed to have been converted from a sitting room. The floors were smooth tile and two full walls were filled with shelves and cabinets displaying a dizzying array of bottles and vials. A third wall was taken up by bookshelves that were so full of tomes that several piles of books had to be stacked on the floor alongside. Two standing mirrors had been fitted with wheels so they could be moved about the room to direct sunlight where the physik needed it. An alcoholic smell hung in the air.

There were two narrow beds in the room. One was empty. Darvin lay in the other, covered with a clean white sheet.

A rubber tube snaked down from a bottle secured to the bedpost, pouring some dark fluid through a needle into Darvin's elbow.

Khahra was attending to Darvin. Her red hair was tied back with a white headscarf. She sat on a stool next to the bed, spooning some concoction into Darvin's mouth. His eyes were closed and his lips barely moved, but he seemed to be swallowing.

"How do you know what to give him?" Kole asked Gery. He was whispering, though he didn't know why.

"Training and experience."

"They teach you how to treat flash sickness at the…where did you say you trained?"

"The August College of Medical Sciences." Gery smiled and shook her head. "No. They did not teach me that. But over the years Mara and her friends have brought me a number of ancient texts from pre-Outbreak libraries. Some of those books contained ancient remedies used by the physiks and healers of the old empire. Sorcery was much more common then, of course, so they needed to know how to treat its side effects. Interpreting the text has been an ongoing challenge, but I daresay you would not find a physik more learned about such things this side of the Windless Peaks." It was not a boast, just a statement of fact.

"Darvin is lucky," Kole said. "I think Mara was afraid you might have retired."

"Retired?" she barked as she ushered him out of the room. "Phwaah! What am I supposed to do with retirement? Put on a frilly dress and get drunk with the merchant-nobles? Take up knitting? Good gods! I'd down a whole bottle of poppy milk just to end the boredom."

Mara returned to Medicus Gery's house late in the afternoon.

She pulled him aside just as they were heading to dinner in Gery's dining room.

"I've found us a ship," she whispered.

"What kind of ship?" Kole asked.

"A Nizaani junk called the *Feathered Arrow*. It probably spends half its time as a corsair ship. I wouldn't be surprised if they've already got a hold full of contraband they're planning to smuggle out of port. But it looks fast, and the captain isn't afraid of dodging any patrol ships we might run into on our way out of the bay. They depart for Godsmouth in two days, and we've got passage if we can stump up a down payment by tomorrow."

He thought of their near-empty purses. "How much will it cost?"

"More than we have on hand," she said as they sat down at the table.

Gery's cook had laid on an impressive meal for them: freshly baked bread with butter and cheese, roasted lamb, potatoes, carrots, fried oranges from the physik's own orange tree, cherry tarts, and spiced wine. There were even small pieces of something Gery called chocolate, which was apparently imported to Locket at great expense.

Kole felt ashamed to see all the food laid out before him. It was extravagant. He hadn't paid for it, and he hadn't even helped prepare it. He felt like he was tainting the meal just with his presence.

The cook was a fat, jovial man named Sloan, who had laid out the feast and then left without even sampling it. From what Kole could gather, he and the other servants he'd encountered here—a gardener, a housekeeper, and a groom—didn't actually live in the house. Instead, they had their own homes with their families somewhere else in the city.

Gery and Khahra had joined Kole and Mara for dinner. As Kole carefully filled his plate—ensuring he wasn't taking any more than anyone else—Mara looked at Gery.

"I need to talk to you about...antiquities," Mara said. She glanced toward Khahra, who was sitting there quiet as a mouse.

Gery followed Mara's gaze, then smiled. "You can speak freely. Khahra knows how to keep a secret."

Mara frowned as if unsure, then nodded slowly. "We have some old world treasures we need to fence. Scepters. Gold and silver, mostly, with some gemstones inlaid. It's been a long time since I was here. Who are the local players?"

Gery leaned back in her chair and swirled the wine in her cup. "Romino the Gray is the most obvious choice. Had a touch of consumption two winters back, but he's still kicking. I know a few others among the merchant-nobles that might be interested. Want me to introduce you?"

"I'd rather avoid any meetings if at all possible. We're trying to keep a low profile."

Gery eyed Mara. "There have been an awful lot of militia on the streets the last few days. They aren't looking for you, are they?"

Mara stabbed a roast potato with her fork and said nothing.

"Of course," Gery said. "Why ask when I already know the answer?" She sighed and drummed her fingers on the table. "I suppose I could take this treasure of yours off your hands and sell it myself once you're gone. Though you might not get as much as you'd hoped."

"That's all right. We just need to cover our fare and leave us some for the rest of our journey. "Eight hundred silvers, maybe. That should leave you plenty of room to weasel a profit out of your buyer."

"Seven hundred," Gery countered. "To cover the boy's medical costs."

"You haven't even seen the scepters yet."

"What does that have to do with anything?"

Mara frowned. "Seven sixty."

Gery slapped the table hard enough to make the plates rattle. Kole jumped.

"Deal!" the physik said. "But only because you're my friend."

"Are you sure you don't want to see the scepters first?"

The physik waved the question away. "I'm sure they're quite fine. I know you wouldn't try to shortchange me. You don't have it in you. That's why you'd have a terrible time living in this city."

Mara inclined her head in agreement, the two women sharing a private smile. Mara turned back to Kole. "Do you need anything before we leave? Supplies for the journey?"

"Boots," Kole said.

"Did you wear yours out?"

"They're not mine. They're Darvin's. I lost mine at the temple, so I borrowed Darvin's. But he might need them back soon."

Mara looked for a moment as if she was going to say something, then seemed to change her mind. "All right. Boots. Maybe some new clothes for both of us."

"All of us," Kole corrected.

"Yes. All of us." She sighed and glanced out the window that looked toward the stable. "We'll have to leave Mugsy behind, I'm afraid."

The thought pained Kole more than he expected it to. The horse would be happy enough here. Happier than trudging through swamps, anyway.

But she'd been with them so long. She'd borne Darvin's weight. Kole never would've gotten the other boy out of the swamp without the packhorse's strong back and steady heart. They'd walked the Dead Road together. To leave her behind felt...wrong.

"Do you have need of a horse?" Mara asked Gery.

"No. But I'll look after it anyway. For another twenty silvers."

"That's not how it works. You don't get paid to buy a horse."

"I'm not buying it. I'm stabling it. You'll be back for it, I'm sure."

"This time I doubt it," Mara said.

Kole glanced at Gery. "How long before Darvin is ready to travel?"

"It is hard to say."

"Two days?" Kole asked.

She frowned. "In a hurry, are you?"

Kole just nodded.

"Your friend has been unwell for some time," Gery said. "I think it's unlikely he'll be going anywhere in two days."

Kole's heart sank. "Is it possible, though?"

"Possible? Yes. But in my experience it's better to plan for what is likely, not what is possible."

Kole and Mara looked at each other. He knew what she wanted to say. And he knew what he would say back. But neither of them spoke.

They ate the rest of their dinner in silence.

Darvin woke the next day.

Khahra came to fetch Kole from the garden when it happened. He'd found a spot at the back of the property where he was concealed from the road but could still drink in the afternoon sun. His reforged leg seemed to ache less in the warmth. He'd been out there since noon, drawing in his sketchbook to try to clear his head. The book was so full now he'd had to start sketching in the margins.

"Medicus Gery says he may not be conscious for long," Khahra told him in a small voice as he slapped his sketchbook closed and quickly followed her back inside. "The flash sickness has taken a great toll on him."

Darvin's eyes were open as Kole stepped into the examination room. He was in bed, his hands limp at his sides. Gery was there too, spooning something steaming and foul-smelling into his mouth.

There was little color in his face. His cheeks looked hollow, made worse by the patchy, dirty stubble that covered his jawline. He swallowed the physik's concoction, grimaced, then turned sunken, bloodshot eyes toward Kole.

"That you, Felmen?" he rasped.

Kole nodded and approached the bed. "It's me."

Darvin gave a slight nod, heavy eyes sliding closed for several seconds. Kole thought he'd fallen asleep again, but then Darvin's eyelids lifted once more.

"I didn't believe him," he whispered.

"Believe who?"

"Angok. About...about ratmen. About monsters."

"Me neither."

Darvin raised a trembling hand and rubbed his throat. "Snakes. I remember snakes. Was I dreaming?"

"No."

"No. I didn't think so. The last thing I remember...a flash. Is everyone...?"

"You, me, and Mara. And the horse. We're all that made it."

He nodded and stared up at the ceiling. "How...how did I get out?"

"I carried you."

He nodded again. Then he began to weep softly.

He dozed for a few minutes after that. Just as Kole was about to leave, Darvin woke again.

"Where are we? Baybury?"

"Locket," Kole said.

"Locket," Darvin echoed, frowning. He seemed lucid enough to recognize that that was strange, but not enough to tell why. "Don't know anyone in Locket."

"Me neither."

"Is Ma here?"

Kole swallowed. "No."

Darvin frowned again. "Thought she'd be here. Thought I heard her." He blinked up at Kole. "When are we heading home?"

Kole hesitated. He wasn't sure he had the heart to tell Darvin what had happened to Hale's Crossing. Not when he'd only just awakened. Not when his survival was still far from certain.

He was spared the need to lie. By the time Kole opened his mouth, Darvin was out again.

"That's enough for today," Medicus Gery said softly, putting a hand on Kole's shoulder and steering him out of the room. "He needs more rest."

Nodding, Kole said, "This is good, right? If he's waking up, he must be doing better."

He took a look at Gery's face and his faith wavered.

"We'll see," she said. "We'll see."

CHAPTER
40

FOR THE FIRST TIME since leaving Hale's Crossing with the freebooters, Kole was beginning to feel safe again.

It was an illusion, he knew. There was a reason he hadn't left Medicus Gery's home since arriving. From his bedroom window he could see militia patrolling the streets day and night. They seemed to circle the house like sharks around a raft.

But when he closed the shutters, he could almost pretend they were free and clear. All they had to do was get to the ports and board their ship when the time came. Then, perhaps, the Hallowed Order would finally lose their trail.

He sat down to dinner on the evening before they were due to leave, another feast laid out in front of him. He still felt stuffed from lunch. When he smelled the meat pie and the potatoes roasted in duck fat, though, he couldn't stop himself from loading up his plate.

"I'm afraid," Gery said when they were nearly finished, "that Darvin isn't safe to travel yet."

Kole froze, fork halfway to his mouth.

"The signs are encouraging," Gery continued. "He is responding well to the treatment. Perhaps a seventy percent chance of survival. But only if he remains in our care a little longer."

Mara didn't speak, so Kole did. "How much longer?"

"Two more days, perhaps, if all goes well."

Kole glanced at Mara, then back at Gery. "And if he leaves tomorrow morning? What are his chances then?"

Gery spread her hands. "Slim."

"You could tell us what to do. What medicines to give him."

"Not that simple, I'm afraid. We are giving him a complex cocktail of medicines that need to be constantly refined. You can't just slap some ointment on his elbow morning and night."

Mara set her fork on her plate with a *clink*. Dabbing her mouth with a napkin, she stood. "Gery, Khahra, please excuse us. Kole and I need to discuss our plans."

"Of course," Gery said. "We'll have dessert when you return. Sloan makes an excellent apple pie."

Mara met Kole's eyes. With a knot in his stomach, he stood and followed her into the sitting room.

She sat down on the edge of a couch and pressed her hands together.

"We have to leave him, Kole," she said.

"No."

"Gery will take good care of him. She'll get him back on his feet."

"And then what? Where does he go from here? His house is ash. His family is dead or captured. Gods, he doesn't even know how much he's lost."

"I'm sure Gery could find work for him."

"Work? In Locket? What about the Hallowed Order? If they know who we are, then they know who he is. They're all over the city. They'll find him."

"Gery can shelter him for a time." Even she sounded doubtful about that.

"So he just sits in this house, hoping the Order doesn't find him? How long will it be until the knights give up the pursuit? Years?"

"His life will be no better with us," she said. "We still have a long way to go. Do you think he really wants to follow us all the way to Godsmouth with the Hallowed Order hot on our heels?"

Kole thought about it. "I don't know. I don't know what he'd want. I don't think he's the same person he was when he first left Hale's Crossing. I think he'd want to do *something*, though. Not nothing."

Mara sighed. "This is moot. You heard what Gery said. He's not fit to travel."

"He will be in a couple of days."

"The *Feathered Arrow* won't wait a couple of days."

"So we get another ship. There are ships coming and going all the time.

I've seen them from the balcony. You found one. You can find another."

"I already gave them a down payment."

Kole sank into an armchair opposite Mara. He tried a different argument. "Darvin isn't going to sit inside like a caged bird for months on end. I'm sure of that, at least. When he finds out what happened to Hale's Crossing, he'll try to leave. He'll try to return north. Gery won't be able to stop him. He'll try to leave, and he'll be caught before he gets out of the city. He stands out too much. He's not local."

Mara pursed her lips and said nothing.

Kole pressed harder. "When the knights catch him—and you know they will—what will they do to him?"

She hesitated. "The same thing they'd do if they caught us."

"Torture?"

"Maybe."

"Darvin is a stubborn asshole, but he'll talk in the end."

"He's been unconscious," she said. "He doesn't know what we're planning."

"He knows enough. Enough that they might piece it together, if they haven't already."

She massaged her forehead. "Maybe we should have left him at Hale's Crossing after all."

"You didn't, though. And you won't leave him now. Quintus would have left him. So would Catgut. Maybe even Angok. But not you. You're not cruel enough to abandon him to that fate."

"Champion lend me strength," she muttered. "One day you're going to get us all killed, boy. Or maybe I will."

They fell into silence for several seconds. Mara sat with her head in her hands, thinking deeply.

Kole knew what she was thinking about. Even now, she kept the Thesis within arm's reach. It sat in her backpack at her feet, just as it had done during dinner. She took the pack with her when she went out. She probably slept with it in her bed. She was charged with taking it back to her Citadel, and she worried over it as much as Kole worried over Darvin.

Something struck him then, something that hadn't occurred to him before. For Kole, Darvin was the last remaining connection he had to a home that no longer existed. To Mara, the Thesis—and her mission—were her last connections to Angok and Catgut and Quintus.

This mission was more than simple duty to her. It was the final promise she'd made to her friends before they were taken from her.

He felt ashamed he hadn't seen it before. He'd been too worried about Darvin, worried about his family, worried about the Hallowed Order.

"Mara," he said softly.

She lifted her head out of her hands and offered him a small, sad smile. "You're right. Quintus would abandon him. But Quintus isn't here. All right. We wait two more days. But if Darvin isn't ready to travel by then, we have to leave without him. Understand?"

Kole nodded. "Thank you."

She stood, picking up her pack. "I'd better go talk to the captain of the *Feathered Arrow* about getting a refund on our down payment."

"What about dessert?" he asked.

She paused. "All right. Pie first, and then I try to convince a corsair to willingly hand over gold he's probably already spent." She sighed. "Grant me the Gambler's luck."

Exhaling, Kole reached out with his senses.

His sight dimmed. The world grew quiet. But in his mind's eye, other things became clear. He sensed a cat outside the bedroom window, prowling along the garden wall on the hunt for prey. He felt Khahra's strong heartbeat in the examination room downstairs, alongside Darvin's flickering life flame.

He became aware of himself. He could see his own life written across reality in crimson light. He could hear his own blood rushing through his arteries.

And he sensed the wrongness in his reforged leg. He could see the way his own flesh tried to reject what had been remade. He could see withered muscles and weakened bones.

Without closing himself off from the life inside him he opened up the heavy textbook he'd smuggled out of Gery's examination room and turned to the page he'd marked—a detailed illustration of a human knee with the skin peeled back and the muscle groups exposed. Splitting his attention between the book and his leg, he tried to make sense of what he could see in his mind's eye.

An ache grew behind his eyes. It was draining to split his attention like this. But he pushed on anyway. He might not have another chance to consult a book like this—not until he got to the Citadel at least.

Da had taught him a little about anatomy, enough for a headsman's needs. And Ma had taught him some basic herbcraft. On Gery's bookshelves, though, was a wealth of knowledge—more than he knew existed outside what he'd seen in the ancient temple of Gnothea. Tomes like this one filled with detailed illustrations of bone structures and blood vessel networks and muscle groups. Another book he'd flipped through expounded on the means by which the body was controlled by the mind. There were whole shelves of dense texts filled with descriptions of diseases and their treatments.

There was no way for Kole to absorb even a sliver of the information contained within Gery's books—not in the few days they had here. But he had found himself trying anyway, picking books off the shelves and sneaking back to his room to pore over them.

He sat at the desk in his bedroom, head pounding as he glanced between the book and his leg. After half an hour of study, he was growing more confident that he could match the things he saw in his mind's eye to the textbook's illustrations. Here was where the sartorius muscle inserted, and there was the meniscus that helped cushion the knee joint. Everything was where it should be.

But still, something was wrong. It wasn't like the cancer he'd sensed inside the old woman's body in that stinking tenement room. There, the tumors had blazed with life even as they killed her, like weeds choking a garden.

There was nothing like that here. His leg just seemed weak. Faded. The light of its life seemed dim and sickly compared to his other leg.

He'd considered showing his leg to Gery. But what if she realized what had happened to it? What if she figured out what he was? He couldn't take the risk.

He shut the anatomy textbook in frustration and turned his attention away from his reforged leg. He sensed that cat again—it had found a mouse and was toying with it. He could sense the cat's hungry excitement and the mouse's desperate fear.

Another heart was beating in the hallway behind him, coming closer. He recognized it now: Gery's heartbeat. She was approaching his room.

Kole shut himself off from his sorcerer's sense and blinked as the world came back into focus. As sound returned, he heard Gery's quick, light footsteps in the hallway. Kole snatched up the textbook, hurried to the bed, and shoved the book beneath the mattress. Gery had already scolded him once for sneaking off with one of her textbooks. She was fiercely protective of the tomes. If she caught him again, he wouldn't put it past her to start locking the examination room. Then he'd never find the information he needed.

Gery threw the door open without knocking. Kole straightened. He kept his face smooth, hoping his guilt didn't show.

She peered up at him with her large, expressive eyes, then glanced suspiciously around the room.

"Just standing around doing your stretches, were you?" she said dryly.

Kole cleared his throat. "Something like that."

"Hmm." She cast another glare around the room. "You haven't seen my copy of Nilsin's Illustrated Anatomy, then?"

He shook his head quickly. "Maybe Khahra has it."

"She's got enough to study without taking on more." She frowned at him. "You'll let me know if you find it, won't you?"

"Of course."

"Of course." She narrowed her eyes. "Are you sure you can remember everything I told you about your friend's treatment? Do you need me to go over it again?"

"I think I've got it."

It had taken a full day of cajoling before Gery had finally relented and taught him what he needed to know about managing Darvin's treatment. Even once he was safe to travel, Darvin would need regular doses of different tinctures and potions until his full strength returned. It didn't feel right to put that burden entirely on Mara. She had enough to worry about.

Gery's expression softened as she studied him. She folded her arms. "I've been thinking. I don't know what you and Mara are mixed up in. And I don't want to know. But it seems to me like you're on a fool's errand. Anything that draws the attention of the Hallowed Order has to be."

Kole shifted in place and said nothing.

She pursed her lips. "Now I've got nothing against freebooters. It's just that you don't seem much like one to me. Just because Mara likes to dive headfirst into trouble doesn't mean you have to follow her."

"I'm not following her," he said. "We're in this together."

"Well, if you have to be in trouble, better to have a friend beside you, I suppose." Her face hardened and she pointed a finger at him. "I'd better not catch your grubby hands pawing at my bookshelves again, though, boy. Those books aren't for bully boys who like strutting around with swords on their hips. You want to spend your life hunting treasure and running from the Order, be my guest. But you leave those books for those with higher aspirations."

She turned and strode toward the door, then paused and glanced back. "Of course, Khahra will be off to Godsmouth in a few months to take her entrance exams for the August College, and I'll be in need of someone to mix medicines and change bedpans. Not many monsters to fight around here. Just a lot of textbooks to study—enough that an apprentice might drown in them."

She gave him one last hard stare. Then she left, closing the door behind her.

Kole stared after her. Was she offering what he thought she was offering? A place here? A chance to train as her apprentice?

The Nametaker, too, had offered him a job. The idea of working in the Grand Crematorium had made his stomach turn. He couldn't face a life spent working in that place of mechanized death.

But Gery was offering something different. She was offering an escape from corpse handling. He could become something else. He could help people. He could be respected. He could learn.

With the sorcery inside him, think what he could do. He wouldn't need to actually use his sorcery. But with the senses the sorcery had granted him, he'd be able to open his mind and see a patient's afflictions written clear across reality.

He thought of the dying woman they'd found in that tenement in the Warrens. If he had a physik's skills, maybe he could have helped her.

But even before the dream had a chance to take root, the cold touch of reality caused it to wither. He couldn't stay here. None of them could. The Hallowed Order was sniffing at their heels. They had to leave, and soon.

Besides, he'd made a promise to Mara. He'd promised to help her get the Thesis to her Citadel. If the book really was as important as she said it was, he couldn't abandon their quest. He couldn't abandon Mara.

And what of his family? Would he just let them suffer in the hands of the Hallowed Order while he sat around playing physik?

He strode to the window and stared out, enjoying the warmth of the sun on his face. Maybe one day, when his family was safe and this was all over, he could return and ask Gery if she would still be willing to take him as an apprentice. Maybe one day, after he'd freed his family, he would even learn how to cure Arabeth's aversion to the sun—not with sorcery but through a physik's skill.

He enjoyed the fantasy for a few minutes. Then he glanced down at the street and saw a pair of militiamen patrolling outside. The fantasy came crumbling down.

He was a sorcerer wanted by the Hallowed Order. He would be hunted the rest of his life. In his heart, he knew there would be no quiet careers for him, no servants, no house on a tree-lined avenue.

There would only be running. Running and hiding, until one day he found himself on a headstone just like Mertyn Walter, the headsman raising a sword above him.

Kole pushed open the door to Gery's stables and breathed in the smell of clean hay. The groom had finished for the afternoon, so Kole had the place to himself.

At the moment there were two horses stabled here. One belonged to Gery—a brown carthorse that pulled Gery's carriage if she had to transport a patient. The other, of course, was Mugsy.

Mugsy put her head over the door as he approached the end stall. She was looking much better than she had when they'd first arrived in Locket. The groom had spent the better part of a day getting her cleaned up after the long journey. He'd reshoed her and treated the scrapes and cuts and insect bites. A change of diet had even helped her regain some of the weight she'd lost.

"Got a treat for you, girl." Kole unwrapped the bundle he'd brought. Mugsy's nostrils flared as she sniffed the handful of strawberries he'd smuggled out of Gery's pantry when the cook wasn't looking.

With what he thought was a happy snort, Mugsy gulped down the strawberries. He stroked her nose while she ate.

Mara's two day deadline was nearly up. If she could find them another ship, they could be leaving as early as tomorrow. Kole had wanted to check on Mugsy one last time before they left, though looking at her now he felt a bit foolish. She'd be much happier here, in Gery's care. No more wading through swamps or trudging along steep hillsides in the thundering rain.

"I wish I could stay too," Kole told her. "But you deserve a rest. You did good. Thank you."

The horse turned her eye on him and sniffed at his pockets.

"That's all the strawberries I have," he said. "But I'll tell Gery you like them. She'll make sure you get plenty. How about that?"

Mugsy snorted.

The stable door creaked open. Kole turned to see Mara entering, wearing a loose-fitting shirt of pale green in the fashion of many of the locals. She took off the headscarf she wore whenever she ventured into town and approached Kole and Mugsy.

"Thought I might find you here." She had her pack slung across her back as usual, and Kole could make out the shape of her hammer partially hidden by the billow of her tunic.

"Just saying goodbye," Kole said. "She likes strawberries."

"Who doesn't like strawberries?" Mara rubbed Mugsy's shoulder. The horse nuzzled her happily.

"Any luck?" Kole asked.

Mara shook her head. "Not yet. I'll head back to the docks this evening and try again. I'll take anything at this point. We can't afford to linger here much longer."

Kole nodded. Mara hadn't fully relaxed since they'd arrived at Gery's house. Kole always found her staring out windows or poring over her strange unreadable book with ever more intensity. Once they were on a ship, maybe she'd be able to stop looking over her shoulder.

Mara took her pack off her shoulder and crouched down to open it. It was more full than usual.

"I stopped by the market on the way home," she said. "Thought I'd pick up a few last minute supplies, since I managed to talk half our deposit back from the captain of the *Feathered Arrow*. I found these for you. I think they should be about your size."

She pulled out a slightly crushed pair of oiled leather boots and handed them to Kole. There was a pattern of vines embossed on the dark leather, making them seem fancier than anything he'd worn before. The soles were thick, though, made for traveling, not dancing.

"I know they look a little…" She gestured at them. "But I'm told they're popular among artisans and workmen in the city. They seem sturdy enough."

He didn't know what to say. He settled on, "Thank you."

He kicked off Darvin's well-worn boots and slipped his feet into the new boots. He'd never had new boots before.

"How do they fit?" Mara asked.

"Good. Really good." He stood and walked back and forth a few steps. Darvin's boots had been giving him blisters—these ones felt like they were padded somehow. He'd never worn anything this comfortable before. He was going to feel guilty giving Darvin back his boots while he strutted around in these.

Mara nodded approvingly, then reached into her bag once more. "I found you something else as well. I wasn't sure exactly what you use, but… here."

It was a sketchbook. After a moment's hesitation, he took it. The paper was thick—almost luxurious. She handed him another smaller package as well, containing several new charcoal sticks of different sizes.

"I saw your book was nearly full," she said. "Is this—?"

He hugged her.

He wasn't sure why he did it. He'd never hugged anyone who wasn't family before. Maybe that was it. After all they'd been through together, it almost seemed like she was family.

She was as rigid as a board at first. Then, slowly, she put her arms around him and hugged him back.

"You smell like horse," she said.

"I think that might be Mugsy."

"No, it's definitely you."

He pulled away, grinning, and looked down at the sketchbook. "Thank you. Really."

Mara shook her head like it was nothing. "I thought you could use the book for your studies as well."

"What studies?"

"Gery tells me you've been loitering in her examination room, pestering her with questions and stealing her textbooks."

"Not stealing. Borrowing." He thought again about the offer Gery had made to him. His heart felt heavy.

Mara seemed to sense his change in mood. "When you see the Citadel's archives," she said with a smile, "Gery's bookshelves will seem quaint by comparison."

"You have medical books there?"

"Among many others." She nodded. "And yet it never seems to be enough. Still, I'm sure you'll find plenty there to quench your thirst."

The thought was comforting. He knew the journey wasn't over yet, but he felt like he could see the end. Once he got to the Citadel, once he learned how to deal with what he was, then he could plan for his next move. Then he could think about getting his family back.

Will you want to, though? he wondered. *When you're safe at last, with archives full of books to distract you, will you really be willing to venture out into danger again?*

He would. Of course he would. His family was depending on him. He wouldn't let himself forget.

Mara gave Mugsy one last rub on the shoulder. "I'm going to miss you, girl," she told the horse.

Mugsy blinked back at her.

With a sigh, Mara glanced out the window. "There's still a couple hours of sunlight left. Let's get some training in."

Kole hesitated. He'd been intending to spend a couple more hours studying the anatomy book he'd hidden in his room.

Some of his reticence must have shown on his face. Mara raised an eyebrow. "A few days here and you're already going soft on me?"

"No," he said, pushing all thoughts of books aside. A textbook wouldn't help him survive. Neither would dreams of becoming a physik.

If he was going to carry a sword, he needed to know how to use it. They weren't out of danger yet.

CHAPTER
41

HAT EVENING, DARVIN joined them for dinner. He ate little and barely spoke, but the fact that he was able to sit there at all seemed somehow miraculous.

"The worst of the danger is past for you," Medicus Gery told Darvin as she peeled a grape for herself. "You are lucky you are young. Young minds are resilient. They bend and flex where an old mind like mine would break."

Darvin tried to spoon some peas into his mouth. His hand trembled and most of the peas ended up in his lap. As he chewed the ones that he'd got into his mouth, he looked down at those he'd dropped, his face dark.

His voice was a slow rasp. "I still feel…"

"Foggy?" Gery suggested.

Darvin nodded.

"It will pass," she said. "Your friends will help you with your medicines. If I had my way I'd keep you under observation another couple of days. But I think you will be fine to travel."

"Travel," he echoed. Darvin's eyes lifted from his plate to look at Kole and Mara. He frowned. "Are we going home?"

Kole swallowed. He was hoping Mara might answer for him, but she kept her mouth shut.

"No," Kole said. "We're going…somewhere else."

He glanced at Gery and Khahra. The physik had insisted that she wanted to know as little as possible about their journey. Mara said it was for the best.

Darvin's frown deepened. "Don't know if I can do much walking."

"You won't need to. We're taking a ship." That much, at least, they hadn't been able to hide from Gery.

"A ship." Darvin's eyes glazed. He stared into the middle distance for a moment, then his fork slid from his hand and clattered on the floor. He slumped, but Gery—who was sitting nearest him—caught him before his head hit the plate.

"He lasted longer than I expected," she said. "At least there will be more dessert for us. Kole, help me get Darvin to his bed, will you?"

Darvin muttered a little more as they helped him shuffle back to his bed, though Kole couldn't make out the words.

It had been another lucky escape for Kole. One day, Darvin would be lucid enough that Kole couldn't wriggle out of telling him the truth. He didn't want to know how Darvin would react when he found out.

Mara was pulling on her pack when Kole returned from helping Darvin to his bed.

"I'm heading back to the port," she said.

"Want me to come with you?"

She shook her head. "Safer if I go alone. Go through our supplies and make sure we've got everything we need. Gambler grant us luck, we might be leaving tomorrow."

"Good luck, then."

She waved and slipped out into the night. Kole closed the door behind her.

After checking their supplies, Kole went in search of the anatomy textbook he'd hidden in his room. It was gone. In its place was a book of Ashashi fairy tales he'd seen on one of the physik's bookshelves.

He cursed. Gery must have come looking for her missing textbook. The book of fairy tales, he assumed, was her idea of a joke, or maybe some sort of punishment for sneaking off with her books when she'd already scolded him about it.

He nearly left the book sitting on the vanity and went to bed, but for the first time in days he wasn't bone-tired. Besides, he needed to be awake when Mara came back in case she'd found a ship. So he pulled up a chair and opened the red leather cover.

The tome was thick and the text small. He soon realized the legends assumed the reader was steeped in Ashashi cultural traditions. Kole had no idea why, for example, an Ashashi bride had to pour a bucket of water over her groom's head before she was wed, or why pouring it over herself instead was such a grave insult that the feud could only be ended with a knife fight between the mothers of the bride and groom.

There was a certain rhythmic style that came through even in the translation, which made the stories pleasant to read. He began to let the stories wash over him, not worrying if he didn't understand a phrase or Ashashi ritual.

He was deep in the adventures of a wandering sandwyrm rider when the sudden yowl of a cat outside brought him back to the present. There was a clatter of something being knocked onto the cobble street, then the skittering of retreating paws.

He looked up. The candles were burned down—he'd been reading for more than an hour.

He wasn't sure exactly why the cat's cry set him on edge. The city was thick with stray cats—they were allowed the run of the place as long as they kept the rat population down. They hissed and fought outside his window most nights.

But tonight…tonight something was different.

He got up. In the distance there was music—there was usually music in the evenings. A carriage wheel squeaked somewhere down the avenue, accompanied by the slow hoofbeats of the carriage horse. From just outside the window came a soft metallic rattle. It sounded like the rattle Angok's chain mail had made as they crept through the corrupted temple of Gnothea.

Kole's breath caught in his throat. Quietly, he picked up his sword. Pressing himself against the wall alongside the leaded glass window, he peeked out across the gardens at the street below.

Five armsmen wearing the mail and blue surcoats of the Hallowed Order were streaming quietly down the garden path toward the front door of the physik's house. Two bore crossbows with bolts nocked. Two more had swords drawn and round shields raised, and the last man bore a large hammer. The light from the nearby street lamps glinted off their shaved heads.

They didn't speak. The only sounds were the scrape of their boots on the path and the rattle of their mail.

Behind them, almost sauntering, came a knight.

The knight had no weapons drawn. A greatsword was slung over the knight's back, with a second smaller blade at the hip. Dark eyeholes stared out of the beaked helmet.

The armsmen disappeared below the lip of the window. Kole could hear their soft footsteps as they approached the front door. Panic froze him in place.

Run! a voice in his head screamed. It sounded like his da.

But where could he run? Where was there left to go?

Movement caught his eye. Across the street, in the dark of an alley, Kole saw a shape. Eyes glinted in the reflected lamplight.

Mara.

She was crouched in the alley's shadow, hammer in hand, watching the Hallowed Order about to storm the house. They didn't seem to have noticed her.

Kole wanted to shout out to her, though he didn't know what he would say. Would he ask her to rescue him? Or would he tell her to run?

She must have spotted the Hallowed Order as she was returning from the docks. If she'd been a few seconds later she might have been caught in the street.

She couldn't possibly see him from where she was. Kole was almost entirely out of sight. But for a moment, across the garden and the street, he thought their eyes met.

Mara put a hand to the strap of her backpack, as if she were feeling the weight of the tomes it contained. Then she glanced up at Kole's bedroom window one last time.

From downstairs came a loud thud and the crack of breaking wood. He heard the front door slamming open and armsmen charging inside.

Mara turned and disappeared into the dark of the alley.

Downstairs he heard Khahra scream. Boots stomped on the stairs.

Outside, the Hallowed Order knight had stopped on the path a few feet from the front door. Slowly, the knight looked up, staring through black eye holes at Kole's bedroom window.

He was suddenly certain that he'd seen this knight before. It was her—the knight who'd been giving orders at Hale's Crossing.

There was shouting from somewhere else in the house. Medicus Gery was berating someone. There were boots in the hallway, then the door to his room crashed open.

"Drop your sword and surrender!" a man barked.

Kole turned. The armsman in the doorway was a young man, not much older than Kole. There was a sheen of sweat on his shaved head. The tip of his sword was pointed at Kole.

Kole looked down at his own sword. He hadn't drawn it, but one hand was wrapped around the hilt and the other around the scabbard.

A strange, hopeless calm settled over him. He could feel each beat of his heart. He could feel the air rushing into his lungs.

He weighed his options. There was no going out the window. It was too small to squeeze through. Not to mention the fall. The only way out of the bedroom was the doorway the armsman was standing in. To escape, Kole would have to go through him.

Could he do it? Maybe. The armsman wasn't a knight. He was young. Kole could sense his heart hammering. He could taste the man's excitement, his nervousness.

Sorcery. It's your only chance.

But he'd promised Mara he wouldn't use sorcery in Locket.

Mara's gone, the voice in his head reminded him. *You saw her go. The Thesis is all she cares about.*

It was too dangerous. If he infected someone else, the plague would spread rapidly in the close confines of the city. Besides, there was still a chance the Hallowed Order didn't know what he was.

You have no choice.

From downstairs came a slap of skin against skin, then Khahra cried out again. And just like that, Kole made his decision.

He released his grip on the hilt of his sword and threw the sheathed weapon to the floor at the armsman's feet. The armsman kicked it into the hallway, then backed up a step and jerked his sword at Kole.

You fool. You just doomed yourself.

All Kole's false calm was suddenly swept away by a wave of despair. He felt like a rat pinned beneath a cat's paw. He was caught at last.

"Move!" the armsman barked.

With his heart in his throat, Kole followed.

CHAPTER
42

HE ARMSMAN LED HIM at swordpoint along the hallway. Another armsman was kicking open doors one by one, searching the upstairs rooms. He wouldn't find Mara, at least. That was something.

Things had gone quiet downstairs. As he was forced down the stairs, he could hear an angry, muffled voice coming from the dining room, and the scrape of a chair against the floor. With sharp steel at his back, Kole moved woodenly toward the dining room.

Gery and Khahra were sitting at the dining table, hands and ankles tied, cloth stuffed in their mouths. An armsman stood behind each of them. Through another door came the fifth armsman, dragging a barely conscious Darvin. The boy was muttering slurred curses, though he didn't seem to be fully aware of what was going on. The armsman dumped Darvin in a chair next to Gery and then stomped out again. Darvin slumped forward, hitting his head on the table.

The knight was seated at the head of the table, one elbow resting casually against the hardwood. She'd taken the greatsword off her back and now it rested—still sheathed—against her chair.

"This one was upstairs," the armsman behind Kole said.

"Good," came a woman's voice from within the bird-skull helmet. "Resume your search."

The armsman retreated. Though Kole couldn't see the knight's eyes, he could feel her looking at him.

"Do I need to gag you?" she asked. "Are you going to wake up all the neighbors with your shouting?"

"No," Kole said.

"Good. It wouldn't help anyway. We are here with the full support of the Free Lady." She kicked out the chair next to her, then gestured to it with a gauntleted hand.

Swallowing, Kole moved around the table. He couldn't feel his legs. The two armsmen still in the room gave him suspicious glares.

He glanced at Khahra and Gery. Khahra's cheek was red and blotchy as if she'd been struck. Her eyes were wide and wet. Gery seemed to be pouring all her energy into giving the knight a death glare.

Kole lowered himself into the chair. He could smell whatever oil the knight used to polish her armor.

"Is there anyone else in the house?" she asked him.

"No."

"No other patients? Servants?"

"No patients." Kole tried to keep his voice even. "The servants have gone home."

The knight nodded. "Good. And the other one?"

"What other one?"

"The freebooter. Our sources say you were traveling with a woman."

Kole swallowed. *They know.* "She left."

The knight was silent for several seconds. Then she unfastened some hidden strap and removed her helmet.

She was his ma's age, maybe a little older. Round-faced and brown-skinned. Perhaps she had some Ashashi blood in her. The left side of her cheek was pockmarked with tiny scars. They could have been acne scars, but somehow Kole doubted it.

A dark fuzz of short hair clung to her scalp. She rubbed her head as if to smooth out the hair, then pushed back her chair and stood.

Even in armor, she had an easy saunter. She moved to the side of the room where a side cabinet held a collection of half-filled liquor bottles.

"Do you drink?" she asked without looking at him.

"Not tonight," he said.

She nodded, turned over a glass, and pulled the stopper out of one bottle. After giving it a sniff, she poured herself two fingers of the dark liquid and returned to her seat. She lifted the glass as if toasting something. No one else moved.

She took a slow sip. With a satisfied nod, she put the glass down in front of her.

"You are Kole Felmen of Hale's Crossing," she said.

It was not a question—just a statement. Kole didn't think it possible, but his chest suddenly felt even tighter. He struggled to breathe.

"I am Knight-Captain Pruska of the Hallowed Order," she continued. "I command the Eighth Wheel. It is a pleasure to finally meet you."

"You should let them go." He managed to keep his voice from shaking as he nodded toward Gery and Khahra. "They have nothing to do with this."

"They will not be harmed."

"Someone hit her," he said, gesturing to the bruise forming on Khahra's face.

"She tried to run. She will not try it again." She glanced at Khahra, and the girl shrunk beneath her gaze. Tears rolled down her cheeks.

Knight-Captain Pruska considered the girl for a moment, then gestured to one of the armsmen. "Take the women to the sitting room. I want to speak to this one alone."

The armsman grabbed Gery by the collar and hauled her to her feet. The physik snarled something incomprehensible through her gag.

Khahra was still crying as the armsman forced the two of them out of the dining room. Darvin groaned at the sound. He tried to lift his head, but failed.

Knight-Captain Pruska took another sip of her drink, then set the glass down and rotated it between her fingers.

"That's better," she said. "A little peace. Now we can talk frankly. Where to start?" She considered for a moment, then turned her cold eyes back on him. "Did you kill my man outside Hale's Crossing? Or was it the freebooter?"

Kole said nothing.

Pruska studied him, then shook her head. "Not you, I think. He was killed by a blunt instrument. Your freebooter friend carries a hammer, I'm told. Where is she?"

"I told you. She left."

"So you say. When did she go?"

"Days ago," he lied.

"Where did she go?"

"I don't know."

"How did she leave? On foot? Did she have a horse?"

"A ship," he said, thinking quickly. "She found a ship."

"What kind of ship?"

"Nizaani, I think."

"Does this ship have a name?" she asked.

"I don't remember. Something arrow, I think."

She nodded, then looked over at Darvin. The boy's eyes moved about slowly below half-closed eyelids, uncomprehending. He murmured something that Kole couldn't make out.

"What is wrong with him?" she asked.

"He hit his head."

Sighing, Pruska reached out and touched a finger to the sword resting against her chair. "If I drew this blade and held it over his head," she said, "would you start telling the truth, I wonder?"

Kole's breath caught. "You said you wouldn't harm him."

"I said I wouldn't harm them." Without taking her eyes off Kole, she stabbed two fingers toward the door that Gery and Khahra had disappeared through. "I am not in the business of hurting physiks and their apprentices. But the boy is a fugitive from Hale's Crossing, like you. His life is mine to do with as I see fit." She returned her hand to her sword and tapped a finger against the hilt. "Now. Let us talk about truth. You entered the city through the Dead Road."

He tried to keep his face smooth, but something must have shown.

"You thought I wouldn't know that?" she asked. "Did you really expect the ashers to keep their mouths shut? Why? Because you paid them off? Because you think you're one of them?"

You fool. Mara had been right. She'd warned him not to trust the ashers, not to give them his name. He'd known it was a risk, but he'd thought...

He didn't know. He supposed it was the same thing he'd thought when he demanded that they stay here another couple of days. He'd thought the risk was worth it. Maybe, in the depths of his heart, he'd thought they were safe. Already free and clear.

Gods, after all he'd been through, he was still so naive.

"It was one of the underlings, if you're wondering," Pruska said conversationally. "You paid off the Nametaker, but the put-upon little bald man who answers the door got nothing out of the deal. He fretted over it for a day or two before his conscience finally got the better of him. He was so worried about the corruption you had brought to the Dead Road, the corruption you might bring to the city. After that it was a simple matter of uncovering where in the city you had exited the Dead Road and finding out where the nearby physiks lived."

At least Mara had got away. At least his stupidity hadn't got her caught too.

"The people of Hale's Crossing," he said. "My family. Are they still alive?"

"Last I heard. They were to be assessed for corruption."

"What does that entail?"

"Questioning. Spiritual assessments. We have people who are very good at these things."

"And what happens to them then?" he asked.

"That depends on the results of the assessments."

She went silent as footsteps approached. The armsman who'd first confronted Kole reappeared in the doorway with Kole's bag in hand.

"The house is clear, Knight-Captain. The freebooter isn't here. But I found something that might interest you among the boy's things."

She gestured and he approached, handing her Kole's old sketchbook.

Kole fought down the urge to run as she began to flip through the pages. It would do him no good. The growing panic in his heart tried to argue otherwise.

From another room, Kole heard Gery's muffled shout. Darvin shifted, rubbing his head drowsily. "What time is it?" he slurred.

The knight was silent as she flipped through the pages. She paused, lingering on the sketch he'd drawn of Mertyn Walter's family merged together in a heap of flesh and screaming faces.

"How long have you been infected?" Pruska asked without looking up from the sketchbook. "Since the execution of Mr. Walter? Or before?"

The urge to bolt became almost overpowering. He became acutely aware that the armsman who'd found the sketchbook was now directly behind him, sword still drawn.

"I'm...I'm not..." Kole began.

"What did we say about lies?" Pruska warned him.

He swallowed. "I'm not mad," he whispered.

She shrugged. "What of it?"

He blinked at that. Her drink was in her hand again. She swirled it as she flicked through his sketches.

"What? Did you think you were special?" she asked. "We come across three or four people like you a year. Infected and capable of infecting others, but still sane enough themselves, at least in the short term. It is uncommon, certainly. But you are not unique."

Somehow, that both relieved and disquieted him. There were others out there—others like him. He didn't want to be unique, he wanted guidance.

But the knight's words only raised more questions.

"If that's true," he asked, "then why don't more people know about it?"

She answered his question with one of her own. "Do you know why humankind endures, Mr. Felmen? Why all life endures, despite the dangers that hound us at every turn?" She leaned back in her chair. "Fear. Fear is what keeps us safe. A horrible, gut-churning emotion, is it not? Worse than pain, I think. You have felt fear before, haven't you? True fear? Fear for your life? Fear for those you love?"

"Yes," he said, his voice a whisper.

"Yes. I see it in you. It is nothing to be ashamed of. I have felt it often. It is why I still live. It is why you still live as well. Fear is healthy. It is necessary. It keeps us from oblivion."

"What's your point?"

"What do you think would happen if everyone knew about people like you? What would they do if they became infected? If their loved ones became infected? Would they still report the infection? By the gods, it is hard enough to get people to make such a report now. But they do it. Often enough, at least. They do it because they know what will happen if they don't. They do it because they fear for themselves. For their families. Because they know that the execution of one child is better than the entire family succumbing to the plague.

"But what if they knew about people like you? Would they still offer up their sons and daughters to the headsman? Or would they hope? Would they hope that their child, their special little baby, was the one in a thousand who wouldn't go mad? How many villages would be corrupted by that hope? How many cities? How many would die?"

"There are other ways. Quarantine them, or—"

"I am not here to debate this with you, Mr. Felmen. I am simply answering your question. You do not know about others like yourself because we do not let it be known. Because we *cannot* let it be known."

Kole nodded and looked down at his hands. He supposed it made a certain sick kind of sense. The Hallowed Order knew plenty about fear. It was how they'd whipped up the villages around Hale's Crossing into a frenzy, after all.

There was another question, one he didn't want to ask. He took a deep breath and asked it anyway.

"What do you do with them? With people like me?" He looked up. "Do you kill them?"

"You are still infectious. If you cast a spell now—and if the man behind you did not put a sword through your throat in time—you could infect us all. Your friend here as well. Maybe even the physik and the pretty little Sundarin girl. And then they would all have to be killed. Would I kill you to save them? Absolutely. Without hesitation."

He believed her.

She stared at him and leaned forward, her chair creaking beneath her. "You think me cruel?"

"No."

"No?"

He thought about Mertyn Walter. "I've done the same."

She nodded. "Did you put a sword through Mertyn Walter's neck because you hated him?"

"No. Of course not."

"Then why did you do it?"

"Because someone had to. To protect others. To protect Hale's Crossing."

"Exactly," she said. "I love humanity. I love it dearly. I love them." She gestured to the door Gery and Khahra had gone through. "I want them to have a future. It is not your fault that you must die. Just as it was not Mertyn Walter's fault. But it must be done nonetheless."

"So what are you waiting for?"

Instead of answering, she changed the topic.

"Can I ask you something, Mr. Felmen?"

"I suppose." He glanced around at the scowling armsmen. Refusing didn't seem to be an option.

"What does it feel like?" she said.

"Sorcery, you mean?"

She nodded. "I've heard scholars describe it in mathematical terms. Or linguistic terms. They talk about sorcery as if it is an extremely precise language. But I have heard the incantations of many sorcerers. They did not sound like they were spouting dry mathematical formulae. They sounded like they were singing. It sounded like music." She leaned forward. "Is that what it's like?"

Kole swallowed. "There is a rhythm to the incantation. A melody. I think that melody might be as important to the incantation as the words themselves."

"I was at Vale City thirteen years ago." Pruska gestured to the pockmarks on her cheek. "That's where I got these. You know what happened to Vale City?"

"The plague."

"That's right. It started from the top. That's unusual. Normally the lower classes are infected first. Either through contact with plague rats, or else some mad traveler comes wandering into the city outskirts and starts casting his sorcery before anyone can stop him. This time it began with the Vale Lord's family. His wife was first, we think, though we still don't know for sure."

She looked at her drink, then picked it up and quickly downed the rest in one gulp. Pushing back her chair, she went to refill her glass.

"The plague madness manifests differently depending on the kind of sorcery." She poured herself another drink, nearly filling the glass this time. "Did you know that? Flesh sorcerers—I assume that's what you are— tend to become overly curious and ambitious. They think they can cure every disease. They think they can improve upon the natural order. Some simply see flesh as a putty to be molded as they see fit. Ember sorcerers are different. That's what the Vale Lord and his court became. The madness that accompanies Ember sorcery makes a man short-tempered. Paranoid. Prone to bursts of extreme violence. They divide everyone around them into strict groups. Loyal or disloyal. Ally or enemy."

As she returned to her seat, she frowned into her drink.

"By the time my Wheel reached the city gates, Vale City was burning. The outskirts were a smoldering ruin. The Vale Lord had decided the poor commoners who lived there were planning a revolution. We found their bodies. Pieces of them, scattered across the streets. Blackened husks blasted from second-story windows, every bone broken. Some had tried to escape the city. They were piled up near the gates, charred, torn limb from limb. Animals, too: cats, dogs. There were babies—"

She stopped herself, brought the drink to her lips, and then put it down again without taking a sip. After a moment, she folded her hands in front of her as if she didn't trust herself with them. She looked at Kole.

"We waded through all that. Dismounted and made our way up the hill to the fortified center of the city, using the ruins as cover. We were nearly at the walls when the madmen spotted us. There were few left at that stage. Most had destroyed themselves or each other. But those who survived were devastating enough. They were positioned atop the walls, overlooking the killing ground that the Vale Lord had fastidiously maintained between the citadel and the rest of the city. To get into the citadel we needed to mount an assault on a blasted section of the wall. And to do that, we had no choice but to charge two hundred yards across open ground.

"I can still hear those Ember sorcerers singing, even now. They brought fiery death upon us with the most beautiful melodies I've ever heard. And the Vale Lord himself, on the balcony of his keep, was the greatest of them all. He sang right up until I put an arrow in his throat. He was dead by the time we took the walls and made our way up into the keep. I cut his head off anyway, just to be sure.

"It *was* beautiful though. That singing. Beautiful and terrifying. Like a storm at sea." She looked up at him and offered an apologetic grimace. "Forgive me. It helps sometimes to tell old war stories. And I think, perhaps, you understand me a little. You are young, but you have seen much. Felt much."

She looked as if she expected him to say something, though he didn't know what. Nodding to herself, she glanced at Darvin, then looked back at Kole.

"Let me ask you one more time. Where is the freebooter?"

"I don't know. I honestly don't. She didn't want to stay. But I couldn't leave until Darvin was better."

Knight-Captain Pruska studied Darvin for a moment, then looked back at Kole. "Did she find what she was looking for?"

"Who?"

"The freebooter. Did she find what she was looking for in whatever ruin she led you into? You were with her, weren't you?"

"She didn't tell me what she was looking for," he said. "I was just the lantern bearer."

Pruska gave him a crooked smile that told him she didn't believe him. She gestured to the armsman standing behind Darvin.

The man snapped into action, grabbing Darvin's wrist and jerking him forward so roughly his head slammed into the table again. The boy gave a slurred curse, unfocused eyes rolling about in his head.

Kole shouted and began to rise. The armsman behind him shoved him back down in his seat and pressed his sword to Kole's throat.

As the other armsman pinned Darvin's arm to the table, Knight-Captain Pruska got to her feet. She left her greatsword where it rested, instead drawing a dagger from her side.

"The boy is a hunter, is he not? A bowman." Pruska turned to the armsman. "Let's start with his bow fingers."

The armsman unfolded Darvin's fist, stretching out the boy's index and middle fingers. Pruska stepped forward, touching the dagger's point to the exposed index finger, just below the first knuckle.

"Stop!" Kole yelled. "Leave him alone!"

"I warned you where lying would get you, Mr. Felmen." She began to press down on the dagger. A bead of blood welled up from Darvin's finger. He groaned and tried to pull away, but the armsman was holding him tight.

A sick panic flooded Kole's stomach. "It was a book!"

Pruska paused but did not remove the dagger. "What did you say?"

He stared at the knife, feeling the touch of steel at his own throat as well.

"In the ruin. She found a book."

"Is that so? And what was in this book of hers?"

"I don't know. Really!" He said as Pruska's knife hand tensed once more. "It was locked! The book was locked."

She pursed her lips and fixed him with a stare. "Describe this book."

"Small, but very thick. It was bound with some sort of metal. Brass, maybe."

"Did it have any designs on it?"

He hesitated, then nodded slowly. "A bird in flight."

Pruska exchanged a look with one of her armsmen but said nothing. "Where is this book now?"

"The freebooter took it when she left."

It was the truth. He prayed it would be enough to convince her.

She stared at him for a minute, then two. It was a struggle not to squirm in his seat. It felt like she could see into his soul.

Darvin continued to struggle weakly against the armsman that held him, murmuring dazed curses as blood welled around the point of the knife.

At last, Knight-Captain Pruska lifted her knife and nodded to the armsman that held Darvin. He released the boy, and Darvin curled his arm against his chest, murmuring something too quiet to hear.

Pruska wiped her knife clean on a napkin and returned it to its sheath. From outside Kole heard a cart or carriage come to a stop. Someone whistled sharply.

Pruska handed Kole's sketchbook to the armsman holding Kole's bag. "Bring his things with us. I'll want to examine them more closely later." She turned back to Kole. "Time to go now, Mr. Felmen. I apologize for the indignity, but I'll have to bind and gag you for the journey. Purely a precaution. Fear not. The journey will not be a long one."

She stood and nodded at the armsman standing behind him. There was a scrape as the man sheathed his sword, then he pulled out a knot of cloth from his belt pouch.

Kole's heart hammered. This was his last chance. He had to use his sorcery before it was too late.

But he couldn't. Not without infecting everyone in the room.

The armsman brought the gag to his mouth. A thought struck him.

"I have a question," he said, twisting away from the armsman.

Pruska paused and held up a hand to forestall the armsman. "Speak."

"Why did you do it? Why did you burn Hale's Crossing?"

"There was an infection," she said.

"Mertyn Walter was infected," he agreed. "Were there others?"

"Other than you, you mean?" She shrugged, her armor clinking. "Is one sorcerer not enough?"

"Mertyn was already dead when you arrived. Dead and burned." He frowned, giving voice to thoughts that had been niggling at him ever since he found Hale's Crossing in flames. "How did you learn of his infection so quickly? Baybury is two days' hard ride from Hale's Crossing. You had to receive the news, travel west, round up a mob from the local villages, and put Hale's Crossing to the torch, all within a few days. Did you even have time to confirm the infection?"

Pruska looked at him and said nothing.

"You pursued us all this way," he said. "You came yourself, a knight-captain. To catch me?"

"You think highly of yourself, Mr. Felmen. I already told you. You are not special."

"Were you chasing the freebooters?" he breathed. "Or what they found in the swamp?"

Pruska gestured to the armsman. "Gag him. Let's go."

"Did you burn the town just to flush them out?" Kole shouted as the armsman approached. "Did you send the plague rat that infected—?"

The armsman stuffed the rag in his mouth and tied it in place. His shouts became muffled. He took a step forward and felt the steel of the armsman's sword pressed against him.

Glaring at Pruska, he went still as the armsman bound his wrists behind his back.

"Bring the other boy as well," Pruska said, gesturing to Darvin. "He'll need to be assessed. Who knows what he's been exposed to."

"And the women?" an armsman asked.

The knight pursed her lips. "Tell Brother Ilin to stay with them for now. They'll need an assessment, but it can wait until morning. I suspect they are untainted. Tell Ilin to ensure they are comfortable and unharmed."

"Yes, Knight-Captain."

With a nod from Pruska, the rest of the armsmen began to troop out of the physik's dining room, escorting Kole and dragging a groaning Darvin along behind them.

He was led through the doorway, out into the entrance hall, and through the broken front door. The streetlamp directly across the street had gone out, leaving a patch of darkness ahead of him.

Out in the street was a wagon hitched to a pair of draft horses. It held a large cage made from thick iron bars. The driver held aloft a lantern as he watched them approach. He was unarmored, but his shaved head and blue surcoat marked him as Hallowed Order.

Kole had wondered if his courage might come to him once he was outside. He'd pictured himself breaking free of the knot of armsmen, making a run for the alley across the avenue. It would be nearly impossible to get away without taking a crossbow bolt in the back, of course. A near suicidal gesture. But since he was going to his death anyway, wasn't it better to take any chance he could, no matter how slim? Better to run now, before he was locked in an iron cage with even less chance of escape.

He didn't run, though. The anger he felt did not cause his heart to swell with courage. He just walked, rope chafing his wrists. He walked right up to the cage on the back of the wagon and watched as an armsman pulled open the small barred door. The hinges squealed, sending a shiver down his spine.

Faces peeked out from neighboring windows, watching the spectacle with wide eyes. A small child was shouting something with excitement.

No one lingered on the street, though. The Hallowed Order didn't arrest thieves or murderers—they arrested sorcerers. And none of Locket's good and honest citizens wanted to get mixed up in something like that.

None of the armsmen were willing to touch him with anything other than the points of their swords, so with his hands bound behind his back he awkwardly climbed the iron step and nearly fell into the cage.

There were two thin planks of wood that served as benches, one on each side of the cage. Crouching to keep his head from hitting the bars above him, he carefully sat down.

Darvin was thrown in after him without reverence. The boy cried out in pain, the shock bringing him out of his stupor for a moment.

"Who did that?" he slurred, eyes sliding open. "I'll kill you!" He struggled against his bonds. Unfocused eyes swiveled toward Kole. "Felmen? What...what are they...they...?"

The rest of his sentence faded into incoherent murmuring.

Kole tried to shout at the armsmen through the gag. They just slammed the cage door shut with a clang. The heavy lock crunched closed, sending a shiver down Kole's spine.

That was it, then. This was how it ended. Would Knight-Captain Pruska do it herself? Would she swing the sword that took his head? Or did she have people for that?

Would he die tonight? Surely she wouldn't leave a sorcerer alive for long.

Pruska had her helmet back on. She stood at the end of the path, watching as the armsmen secured the cage. He glowered at her.

Was he right? Mertyn Walter's infection, the burning of Hale's Crossing—had it all been a cover? It would have been easy enough to slip a plague rat into a merchant's wagon or set it loose on the outskirts of the town. Then, once it infected someone, the Hallowed Order would have any justification they needed to burn the town and capture its citizens. They could find out what the townsfolk knew about the freebooters and their expedition to the idol of Gnothea. Maybe they even hoped to capture the freebooters before they departed, or once they'd returned with the spoils of the temple.

Perhaps the Hallowed Order had caught wind of the Wayfarers' quest for the Thesis. Perhaps they wanted to ensure that such ancient knowledge remained buried forever, lest the gods be driven to vengeance once more.

Even to Kole the whole thing seemed a paranoid fantasy. And yet he couldn't shake the look he'd seen in Pruska's eyes when he'd voiced his suspicions.

Four armsmen formed up around the wagon—two in front, two behind. The driver hung his lantern from a hook beside his seat and took up the reins. With a satisfied nod, Pruska marched slowly past the wagon, her greatsword slung over her shoulder. She turned the dark, eyeless holes of her beaked helmet toward Kole as she passed. He forced himself to stare back.

She continued to the front of the wagon and addressed the driver. "We'll take them to the Bottle Ward cells."

"The militia aren't much going to like that, Knight-Captain," the driver said, glancing back through the bars at Kole and Darvin. "They didn't even want us requisitioning this wagon."

"The militia can bring it up with the Knight-Commander." She moved to join the two armsmen waiting at the front of the column. "Forward."

The driver cracked the reins and the wagon jerked forward. Darvin gave another groan. The column began to advance.

A voice rang out down the street. "Wait, please! Just a moment."

A white-robed figure appeared out of the darkness ahead of them, one hand raised. The thin white hood of his robe drooped low over his face. Something about the man's voice seemed familiar.

"Move aside," Pruska replied as she raised a hand to order the wagon to stop. The armsmen beside her reached for their swords.

The robed man stopped and raised a second hand, but he remained in the path of the wagon. "Deepest apologies, Hallowed Knight. I was merely in the neighborhood and saw you transporting these wretches. Tainted, are they? A tragedy. I wish to offer them the benediction of the Dreaming Empress. May I approach?"

"You may not, priest. Move aside."

The robed man began to walk slowly toward the column. "All men deserve the Empress's blessing, even those who are damned. If you'll just let me—"

Pruska's beaked helmet jerked toward the armsman next to her. "Get him out of here."

"Gladly." The armsman drew his sword and advanced on the robed figure. "All right, goddess-lover. Are you going to move yourself or—"

Something whistled faintly. An arrow suddenly sprouted from the side of the armsman's neck.

The soldier's surprised gasp immediately became a gurgle. He turned slowly back toward the wagon. Eyes wide, he clutched at the arrow that had passed through his neck. Blood poured from between his fingers. He tried to take a step and sank to his knees instead.

Pruska spun toward the wagon and pointed at the driver. "Get them out of here!" she barked.

The driver cracked the reins and the wagon lurched forward, nearly throwing Kole from his seat.

A moment later he caught a flash of movement from the alley on the other side of the avenue. By the time Kole registered the sound of a twanging bowstring, an arrow was buried in the side of the driver's chest. He dropped the reins and screamed.

Panicked, the horses picked up speed. Pruska grabbed the uninjured armsman next to her and hauled him out of the way of the galloping horses. The armsman with the arrow in his neck didn't move as the horses trampled him.

The wagon wheel rolled over the body and Kole's head slammed against the bars overhead. Pruska was coldly barking orders at her men. One armsman with a crossbow had already taken cover behind a tree in the center of the avenue and was lining up a shot on whoever was loosing arrows from the dark of the alley.

With his head throbbing, Kole blinked away stars. The driver was no longer screaming. He was no longer moving at all. The wagon was out of control. The panicked horses galloped down the cobbled avenue directly toward the white robed man.

The priest remained in the street, making no move to get out of the way of the horses. He simply threw back his hood and raised his hands.

The man was smiling, unconcerned. His face was marred with a deep red birthmark. A birthmark Kole recognized.

It was Redwyn, one of the men they'd shared the vox tower with while waiting out the storm.

Questions tumbled through Kole's head, the panic giving him no time to ponder answers. How was Redwyn here? What was he doing? And why was he letting himself be trampled?

Kole tried to shout a warning through the gag. He doubted he could be heard over the pounding hoofbeats and the shouts of the armsmen.

Still Redwyn didn't move. The man simply stood, hands raised above his head, and closed his eyes. Kole twisted away. He didn't want to watch the man get run down.

But the wagon was slowing. The horses' panicked gallop became a canter, then a trot.

Just as they were about to collide with Redwyn, the horses both pulled suddenly to the right. They whipped past close enough to make the priest's white robes billow.

The horses halted as the wagon came alongside Redwyn. They whickered and then went still.

Redwyn lowered his hands, opened his eyes, and smiled up at Kole.

"So I understand your friend isn't Hallowed Order after all," he said.

CHAPTER
43

KOLE STARED AT REDWYN.

A shout rose up from back down the avenue. The tallest of the armsmen was hurrying toward them, sword drawn. Further back, Brother Ilin—the armsman who'd been left to guard Medicus Gery and Khahra—was charging out of the physik's house.

Two other armsmen wielding crossbows were using the avenue's trees for cover as they fired into the alley across the street. Pruska crouched beside them and stared toward the alley, sword in hand. From her belt she drew a small silver horn. Lifting her helmet, she blew the horn three times. The sound rang through the night.

"Get away from the wagon!" shouted the tall armsman charging toward Kole and Redwyn. Behind him, Brother Ilin rushed to catch up.

Redwyn ignored them both. He drew a small belt knife. "Give me your wrists."

Kole sat with his back to Redwyn and presented his bound wrists. Seemingly unaware of the armsmen racing toward them, Redwyn started sawing through the rope. Kole tried to shout a warning through the gag.

"Halt!" the tall armsman roared, stepping forward to strike.

From behind the armsman came the rattle of a chain and a scream of pain. The tall armsman paused in his attack and glanced back down the avenue.

Brother Ilin stood clutching his arm, his sword lying in the street beside him. Blood streamed from a huge gash in the soldier's arm, staining his blue surcoat.

Another figure was emerging from between the hedges of a nearby garden. The man's white, hairless head and strange features made him instantly recognizable. Juragar, Redwyn's Gor friend.

The Gor held a long, thin chain in both hands. He was swinging one end of it in circles, and in the lamplight Kole could see the flash of a cruel hooked blade cutting through the night.

Brother Ilin tried to pick up his sword with his left hand. Without a trace of emotion on his scarred face, Juragar shifted his feet and released one end of the swinging chain.

The blade whipped through the air and plunged into Ilin's left arm, just below the sleeve of his mail shirt. With a yank, Juragar ripped the hooked blade free, eliciting a second scream from the armsman.

Juragar advanced menacingly, swinging the chain again. The wounded armsman didn't stay to find out where the blade would strike next. Trailing blood from both arms, Ilin ran off down the street.

As the taller armsman turned to face Juragar, Kole finally felt his bonds loosening. Redwyn sliced through the last few strands, and then he was free. Blood rushed back into his hands, making the skin prickle. He ripped the gag from his mouth.

"What—" he began.

"Get your friend loose," Redwyn interrupted, handing him the knife handle-first. "I'll see what I can do about this lock."

Redwyn moved to the back of the wagon and peered at the heavy lock. With a grunt, he inserted the point of a cloak pin into the lock and began to wiggle it.

Kole crouched at Darvin's side and started to cut through the ropes that bound him. The boy's confused eyes swiveled to meet Kole's in the dark.

"I hear screaming," Darvin murmured. "Am I dreaming?"

"No. It's real. We're getting out of here." He glanced at Redwyn. "I think."

Redwyn paid no attention to the sounds of fighting. Behind him, the tall armsman was moving to engage Juragar. Another horn sounded a few streets away, a reply to Knight-Captain Pruska's call.

The whistling of arrows seemed to have ceased. Kole looked up and saw the dark eyeholes of Pruska's helmet facing him. He felt her cold gaze on him as she weighed up the situation.

It's not enough, he realized. Juragar couldn't fight Pruska and the two other armsmen alone. He opened his mouth to tell Redwyn to leave him, to run.

But Pruska's helmet turned back toward the alley. Something moved in the alley mouth. It was too far away for Kole to make out in the darkness.

Pruska saw it, though. And whatever she saw made her turn away from the wagon and lift her greatsword in both hands.

"With me!" she shouted to the two armsmen beside her. She charged toward the alley. Drawing their swords, the armsmen followed her.

Kole stared, stunned. Pruska was risking their escape. Why?

"Why are you helping us?" Kole asked Redwyn. "How did you know where we were?"

Redwyn didn't glance up from the lock. "Your friend found us celebrating our good fortune with some fellow faithful in the Diving Kraken. The Empress has been smiling on us. Juragar's leg is almost healed, the last stretch of our journey was blessed with good weather, and we even found ourselves passage back to Godsmouth." He worked the cloak pin deeper into the lock. "As for your first question? It is simple. If not for your hospitality, Juragar and I might've died that night in the storm." The lock popped. With a grin, Redwyn lifted the bolt and pulled open the cage door. "A debt must be paid."

Kole finished cutting through Darvin's bonds. He handed the knife back to Redwyn and pulled Darvin out of the wagon.

A short way down the avenue Juragar's foe lay on the ground, screaming and wiping at the blood spilling across his face. "I'm blind! I'm blind!" the man yelled.

From the alley across the street came the clash of weapons and the grunts of people fighting. With the streetlamp nearest the alley extinguished, Kole could see little more than shadows dancing and blades flashing. Pruska was among them, her armored form moving with speed and grace.

The stomping of boots on cobble was growing closer. More Hallowed Order, maybe, or militia reinforcements. They would be here in a minute.

Juragar approached quickly, black eyes studying Redwyn as if worried he might have been injured. There was a splash of red across the Gor's cheek, though he didn't appear to be wounded.

"Where's Mara now?" Kole asked as he pulled Darvin's arm over his shoulder.

Redwyn pointed his chin toward the figures fighting in the dark of the alley.

Kole's chest tightened. "She's alone? We have to help her."

"We help her by getting out of here before the whole city descends on us. Come. We must reach the ports. Your friend said she'd meet us there."

Kole hesitated, then swallowed and turned away from the alley. *Mara's tough. She knows what she's doing.*

He took a few steps, pulling Darvin along with him. His reforged leg spasmed under the extra weight and he had to bite his tongue to keep from crying out. Darvin tried to take his own weight, but he stumbled over his own feet, dazed and exhausted.

Darvin's medicines, he suddenly remembered. They were in his bag.

"Take him," he said to Redwyn, pushing Darvin toward the priest. "Start moving. I'll catch up."

"Where are you—?" Redwyn began, but Kole was already running.

He limped as fast as he could toward the blind, screaming armsman. Hanging from his shoulder was a bag—Kole's bag. The armsman groped for him as he approached, hearing his footsteps, but Kole forced himself to ignore the man's pleas as he jerked the pack from his shoulder.

"Help me!" the man begged. "I'm blind!"

Kole picked up the armsman's fallen sword. The grip was sticky with blood. Swallowing, Kole tore his eyes from the soldier's bloodied face, tucked the naked sword into his belt, and sprinted on.

Just as the first squad of militia soldiers emerged from a side street, he turned and hurried back toward Redwyn and Juragar.

The fighting across the street seemed to have moved deeper into the alley. One of the armsmen was limping out of the alley dragging a broken leg behind him. The clash of weapons seemed more distant now.

Kole looked at the sword in his hand and nearly went after Mara. He stopped himself. His foolishness had gotten them into this situation in the first place. She was fighting now to distract Pruska and give him and Darvin a chance to get away. He had no choice but to trust that she could handle herself.

How much longer can she keep fighting, though? You remember what she said. If you haven't won a fight in the first ten seconds, you've lost.

He shook his head. Mara knew what she was doing. He had to believe that.

For a panicked moment he thought he'd lost Redwyn and the others, but as he ran past the abandoned wagon he spotted Juragar standing at the corner of a small walkway leading between two large estates, half-shrouded in darkness. The Gor gestured to him, then disappeared down the walkway between the high walls that bordered the estates. Kole followed.

Redwyn was halfway down the walkway, struggling with Darvin's weight. He glanced back at the sound of their approach.

"By the Empress's grace. My arms were about to fall off. They breed you country folk big, don't they?"

Kole took Darvin's weight again as the sound of the approaching militia grew louder in the avenue behind them. Juragar said something to Redwyn in his strange tongue. The priest nodded.

"I couldn't agree more." He looked at Kole. "I'm in a running mood. How about you?"

CHAPTER
44

THE CITY BECAME a blur for Kole, half-glimpsed through alleyways and side streets. They cut through a market square that was eerie in its silence. The canvas awnings of empty stalls flapped in the cool night breeze. There was almost no one on the streets—no one but them and their pursuers and the occasional stray cat. Was it always like this at night, or were the horns of the Hallowed Order driving people back to their homes, where they wouldn't get mixed up in things they wanted no part of?

Kole didn't know. He just staggered on. Pain stabbed at his reforged leg with every step, making him thankful whenever they had to pause and wait for a patrol to pass.

Redwyn led the way—he seemed familiar with the city—while Juragar watched their rear, his black eyes surveying every dark corner and rooftop. The Gor had his hook-and-chain wrapped around his wrist while his other hand clutched the scabbard of the curved sword at his belt to keep it from rattling.

The roads began to slope downward as they got closer to the docks. The buildings here were less grand and more tightly packed.

Redwyn paused at the end of an alley and peered out. Suddenly, he jerked his head back in and gestured for them to be still.

A few moments later Kole heard the hurried stomp of boots on cobblestones. He held his breath.

"You militiamen take Artur Street," came a man's voice. "We'll take the crossroads. Sound the alarm if you see anything."

"Of course, Sergeant-Armsman." There was a hint of sarcasm in the reply. If the armsman who'd been giving the orders heard it, he didn't say anything.

There was more tromping of boots, less hurried this time. Someone was coming closer.

"Pompous assholes," a voice muttered.

"Quiet. They'll hear."

"What are they going to do? Have me flogged? Those bald pricks don't have the authority. It's not their city."

"Try telling them that."

The two militiamen appeared in the street outside the alley. Each wore a faded green gambeson and a bowl-shaped helmet. The hafts of their spears tapped on the cobbles as they walked.

They didn't appear to be in any great hurry. The older of the two, a round-faced man with an unkempt gray beard, pulled a flask from some hidden pocket and took a swig.

The younger man was more nervous. He was no older than twenty, and his gambeson was far too big for him. He kept glancing behind him, though Kole didn't know whether he was more afraid of fugitives or the Hallowed Order.

Kole remained still and silent, trying to press himself even deeper into the dark of the alley.

Something touched his leg and he only just managed to stifle a gasp. He glanced down to see a stray cat rubbing itself against his ankle and purring.

At last the militiamen moved on, the older one still grumbling about the Hallowed Order giving them commands. Their footsteps faded and Redwyn peeked out of the alley again. He gestured, and they hurried on.

"What happens when we get to the ports?" Kole whispered to Redwyn as they moved. "Do you know somewhere we can hide?"

"It's too late for hiding, my friend. We drew blood from the Hallowed Order. They will tear this city apart to find us. They will drag us back to the Blackspire in chains and have their Sanctifiers take us apart piece by piece. A fate I would rather avoid, if at all possible. We flee the city tonight."

"You have a ship?"

"Me? No. But I have a friend who has a ship. A very new friend, granted. But all who follow the will of the Dreaming Empress are bound by friendship."

"This friend will leave tonight? With the Hallowed Order on our heels?"

"I very much hope so. Or our flight is going to be a short one."

The smell of salt and fish grew stronger as they neared the docks. So did the amount of activity—the docks never slept.

Slipping between tightly-packed warehouses, they finally reached the dockside. There were more lamps burning here than Kole had seen in any other part of the city. He suddenly felt exposed.

Most of the people working the docks were too busy to pay them any attention. Many of the ships at the dockside were dark and quiet, with only the occasional grumpy-looking sailor on sentry duty. Other ships blazed with lantern light as they were loaded or unloaded. Stevedores shouted to each other as cranes swung nets filled with crates and barrels into place.

Further down the dockside was a large tavern filled to bursting with drunk sailors. Someone inside was playing a stringed instrument, and many of the tavern's patrons were singing along. As far as Kole could tell, each man and woman was singing an entirely different set of lyrics.

There were guards about, but they weren't militiamen. Most seemed to be sailors or ex-sailors—stocky men and women with wide gaits and permanent scowls. They marched up and down the dockside with cudgels in hand, no doubt there to threaten away any would-be thieves and put a stop to drunken brawls before they got out of hand. The ports were the beating heart of Locket—city folk of all classes made their living from the trade that these ships brought. Kole supposed everyone wanted to ensure that things stayed that way.

"Calm, now," Redwyn said. "Let's look like we belong."

Kole glanced from the white-robed priest to a drunk-looking Darvin and then to the Gor, who had made his hook-and-chain weapon vanish. The four of them were hard to miss.

But as they started making their way along the dockside, Kole began to realize that their uniqueness was actually helping them blend in. Even at this hour the ports were filled with many different kinds of people. Not just Sundarins and Nizaani and Ashashi but peoples he'd never seen before—people with skin tones of a deep red and people with bright blue feathers woven into their hair. One woman he passed was covered from head-to-toe in gray cloth, with tinted spectacles concealing even her eyes.

There were several priests of Ur about—bare-foot men and women with wild hair and canvas robes accepting sacrifices and tributes from sailors due to depart come the morning.

Kole saw other priests as well. One stood near the tavern, shouting mad ramblings at the tavern's drunken patrons, who were all ignoring him. Further on, they passed a pair of dark-skinned men in the same white robes as Redwyn. The men touched their fingertips to their foreheads and murmured something to Redwyn as they continued on.

"The Empress smiles on us," Redwyn said. "We are here. Observe."

He gestured to a small, two-masted ship docked between a much larger merchant carrack and a Sundarin whaler. It was made from ghostly-white timber, and on its stern something was written in red paint. Kole couldn't read the foreign script. There were lanterns lit on deck, and figures hurrying about.

"What does it say?" Kole asked Redwyn, pointing to the writing on the stern.

"*The Butterfly That Touches Down Lightly.*"

"That's the ship's name?"

Redwyn nodded. "Quickly. We have company."

The priest gestured with his chin further down the dockside. There, pushing their way through a chain of stevedores loading carts, was a group of four militiamen. They were coming closer.

Redwyn led them quickly up the creaking gangway of the *Butterfly*. When he reached the top, Kole saw the deck was busy with activity. There were some two dozen sailors hurrying about their work, which mostly seemed to consist of tying and untying ropes. He had little concept of how a ship like this worked. Though Kole had grown up in a fishing town, he'd never been on anything larger than a rowboat before—and that only a couple of times, when he and Arabeth had "borrowed" one of the fisher-folk's boats after dark.

As Kole helped Darvin off the gangplank, Redwyn tried to catch the attention of a passing sailor. The woman hurried on about her work, muttering something about being busy.

Before Redwyn could flag down another sailor, someone boomed "Ho! Priest! You're here!" from across the foredeck.

Weaving his way effortlessly between the bustling sailors came the biggest man Kole had ever seen. He was around Kole's height, with a girth so tremendous it was stunning to behold. The man's size was made all the more overwhelming by the gaudy clothes he was dressed in. A huge collar of white lace surrounded his neck like a gigantic wilting flower. The lace was yellowed with age and old stains. He wore a red coat with mismatched buttons and too many pockets, with more lace spilling out of the sleeves.

It had been patched and repaired in a dozen places, the fact made obvious by the golden thread used to stitch it. White hose clung to his thick legs, leaving little to the imagination.

The huge man stopped before them, thick fingers absentmindedly twirling the ends of his long mustache. "Four of you! You didn't tell me there'd be four of you. Perhaps the country boys might make a nice snack for the cargo, eh?"

He threw his head back and laughed riotously. The man's accent had a strange cadence, rising and falling as he gestured expansively.

"My apologies, Captain—" Redwyn began, but the big man cast the apology away with a grand sweep of his hand.

"I jest! I jest! Your timing is exquisite. The priests of Ur just left, and I even had a Nizaani confession-taker drop by a few hours ago to cleanse the crews' sins. She had to work double-time to fit everyone in. Truth be told I think she cut a few corners, but no matter! Now we have our very own holy man aboard. A priest of the Sleeping Empress!"

"Dreaming Empress," Redwyn corrected him.

"Yes, yes! The Dreaming Empress. Even better. You know, I never met a god I didn't like. That's what I always say. Never met a god I didn't like." He laughed again, clutching his belly.

Redwyn smiled. "Captain—"

The man threw an arm around Redwyn's shoulders and spun to face the crew. "Did you hear that?" he boomed. "Our voyage is blessed by the Dreaming Empress!"

A half-hearted cheer went up, then the crew immediately returned to their duties.

Beside Kole, Juragar gave a grunt. Kole turned and saw the Gor looking over at the dockside. Two of the militiamen were interrogating a stevedore while the other two continued to push their way through the crowd in the direction of the *Butterfly*.

Juragar saw Kole looking and gestured with his chin down the way they'd come. There, further down, Kole could make out a pair of Hallowed Order armsmen emerging from a side street.

Juragar leaned close to Redwyn and said something in a low voice. With a nod, Redwyn extracted himself from the flamboyant captain's embrace. "I am honored, Captain. And I will be delighted to share the Word of the Empress with you on our journey. How long until we can depart?"

"Only minutes, good priest. I got your message. A nighttime departure through the Bay of Barbarians! Thrilling! I'm glad we have a godly man like you aboard to keep us safe."

"Well—"

"And these are your friends?" He gestured to Darvin. "That one had a little too much of the Kraken's Piss, eh? I know that feeling." Chuckling, he addressed Kole and the others. "May the blessings of all amiable gods be upon you, friends! I am Tleli Tecatoa Tochtil, Captain of the *Butterfly*. You can call me Toch, or Captain Toch, if you prefer."

From across the deck, one of the crew called for the captain. The big man bowed an apology to Kole and the others.

"Introductions must wait, I'm afraid. Get comfortable. We're almost ready to cast off."

"Captain," Kole spoke up as Toch was about to turn away. "We're still waiting on a friend of mine."

"Another? Priest, you didn't tell me you were bringing the whole circus with you! What does this one do, juggle hoops?" Captain Toch glanced down at the dockside. "I cannot delay our departure. Unless perhaps you'd like to ask those militiamen down there to be sporting and search some other ships first." He shook his head. "I'm transporting some...delicate cargo. More delicate than you fugitives. No delays." He began to turn away again.

"My friend has gold," Kole said.

Toch paused, then turned slowly back. "How much gold?"

"Enough to buy a five minute delay."

"Ha! You don't know how highly I value my time!" He twisted the end of his mustache in thought. "Eh, I'll do what I can. Maybe ask the priest here to pray your friend has light feet."

The crewman called out to Toch again, and the big man swept away. "I come! I come!"

Kole looked back at the dockside, still holding Darvin upright. Where was Mara? What was taking her so long? Surely she was still alive. Surely she hadn't...

Redwyn appeared alongside Kole, helping take Darvin's weight. "Let me take your friend below deck. He looks tired."

He was right. Darvin was barely able to hold his head upright. Blinking, the boy tried to focus on Kole. "We're on a boat," he murmured.

"That's right."

"Hate fishing almost as much as I hate hunting."

Something about that made Kole laugh. "Go with Redwyn."

"Who's Redwyn?"

"I am," Redwyn said. "Let's find you a hammock. You ever sleep in a hammock before?"

As he helped Darvin away, Redwyn glanced at Juragar and said something in his northern tongue. With no expression on his face, the Gor nodded and stayed where he was.

It wasn't until Redwyn and Darvin had disappeared among the busy crew that Kole realized he had forgotten to thank Redwyn. If it weren't for the two of them, Kole would be on his way to his own execution right now, and Darvin...only the gods knew what they would have done to Darvin.

Kole glanced over at Juragar. The Gor had wiped the blood off his cheek, but a faint pink stain still marred his stony white skin. Juragar turned his black eyes toward Kole, staring back at him.

Kole swallowed. "Thank you," he said, putting a hand over his heart and bowing his head. He wasn't sure how much of his language Juragar understood. "Thank you."

The Gor stared at him unblinking for a moment. Then, placing a hand over his own heart, Juragar bowed his head in imitation of Kole.

The militiamen on the dockside were marching past the carrack alongside the *Butterfly* now. Down the other end of the docks, the Order armsmen had spread out to question a gang of stevedores unloading a ship. One of the stevedores rubbed his chin then pointed down the docks in their direction.

The deck creaked behind Kole and Captain Toch reappeared beside him. "Do you see your friend?"

Kole shook his head.

"Looks like more friends want to introduce themselves." Toch looked down at the approaching militiamen. "Time to depart."

Kole shook his head again, his throat too tight to speak. He couldn't leave. Not without Mara.

But if he didn't...

One of the militiamen on the dock looked up toward the deck of the *Butterfly*. "You there! Are you in charge of this vessel?"

"Eh?" Toch called back, cupping his hand around his ear. With his other hand he gestured to a pair of nearby crewmen.

"Are you in charge of this ship?" the militiaman shouted louder, enunciating each word.

Captain Toch threw up his hands and gesticulated wildly as he began to jabber in some foreign tongue. The militiaman, growing frustrated, gestured for his companions to follow him. One of them pointed up at Juragar, whose pale skin shone even in the dim light. Gripping their spears in both hands, the militiamen began to march up the gangway.

"Cast off!" Toch barked. "We depart at haste!"

A group of sailors rushed forward with hatchets, hacking at the mooring lines. Two more crew cut free the ropes that secured the gangplank.

The militiamen saw what was happening. The two at the rear leapt back to the dockside, while the two in front tried to charge forward to reach the ship.

They were too slow. Toch kicked the gangplank free and it toppled into the water, taking the militiamen with it. The huge captain threw back his head and roared with laughter.

A horn rang out. At first Kole thought the alarm was meant for them. But the sound was coming from one of the alleys leading off the docks. Shouts and the tromping of boots grew loud enough that Kole could hear them even over Captain Toch's laughter.

A figure burst from the alley, knocking aside a drunk stumbling away from the tavern. As the figure stepped into the lamplight, Kole grabbed the ship's railing and shouted.

"Mara!"

She turned toward the sound of his voice. One side of her face was smeared with blood, sealing her right eye shut. She was blowing hard, all color drained from her skin.

Toch shouted an order to his crew. A triangular sail snapped open, and up on the quarterdeck the ship's pilot spun the wheel.

"Wait!" Kole shouted, pointing. "My friend!"

Limping, Mara ran toward the *Butterfly*, pushing aside anyone that got in her way.

More figures appeared in the alley, pursuing her. An armsman, two militiamen who'd joined the chase, and Knight-Captain Pruska.

Despite her armor, Pruska was leading the chase. Still, Mara had some ground on them.

She could make it. She had to make it.

"Bring us close to the dock." There was a note of begging in Kole's voice. "Captain, please! My friend can jump."

Below, two militiamen were reaching down to help their companions scramble out of the water. The Order armsmen further down the dock seemed to have heard the commotion—they were approaching quickly, swords drawn and crossbows at the ready.

Toch eyed the scene, then shrugged. "Eh, why not? We are blessed, are we not? Pilot! Ease us back in!"

The pilot swore and began shouting orders at the men working the sails.

"Clear the way!" Knight-Captain Pruska's voice rang out, scattering the bystanders that filled the dockside. "Armsmen, move to intercept!"

The *Butterfly* drifted back toward the dock. The two militiamen trying to get out of the water shouted in alarm and dropped back into the bay, paddling furiously to prevent themselves getting crushed between the ship and the dock. Kole stretched his arm out.

"Run, Mara! You can make it!"

Pruska was gaining ground on the limping Mara, but there was still time. She was nearly there.

"Armsman Ceran," Pruska called. "Bring her down!"

The dark eyes of Pruska's helmet were pointed off down the dockside. Kole followed her gaze and saw an Order armsman brace himself as he raised his crossbow.

"No!" Kole roared.

The armsman squeezed the trigger lever.

For an instant Kole wasn't on the deck of the *Butterfly*. He was back in Hale's Crossing, breathing in smoke, listening to the screams of its terrified townsfolk. He was watching as an arrow soared through the air toward his father.

It's happening again. How is it happening again?

The crossbow string twanged. The bolt whistled through the air. And he was back, back in a present that seemed a cruel mirror of the past.

Mara gasped as the crossbow bolt penetrated her side. She stumbled.

No! He wouldn't let it happen. Not again.

The song of Flesh crooned in his head, a seductive melody, begging for his embrace. A simple incantation and all could be made right. He could pluck the bolt from Mara's side and heal her as he'd healed his own leg. He could grant her the strength she'd need to leap to the ship.

He could ensure Knight-Captain Pruska would pursue him no more. He could tear the skin from her body and turn her veins into snakes that would eat her from the inside out. He could destroy her so utterly that no one would recognize her corpse.

He let the song fill his head. It was so warm, so comforting. So right. All he had to do was open his mouth.

Mara looked up at him with the eye that wasn't sealed with blood. She shook her head.

Kole roared in frustration, pushing away the song of sorcery. The power was in his grasp—the power to save her! The power to fix everything!

And yet he couldn't. Again, he couldn't. Not without spreading the plague to Juragar and Captain Toch and half the crew of the *Butterfly*. Not without damning them all.

Perhaps this was some cruel joke by Mara's dead gods. Perhaps they were laughing even now, laughing at him as they slept their endless sleep.

Mara staggered closer to the ship, the Order armsmen closing in behind her. Even if they didn't reach her first, Kole saw now that she didn't have the strength to leap to the ship. Maybe she never did.

Cringing in pain, she shrugged her pack from her shoulders. Taking one last step, she hurled the bag toward him.

Kole reached out, leaning perilously over the railing. He caught a strap with his fingertips.

The weight of the pack pulled him down and he began to topple over the railing. Juragar grabbed him, hauling him back.

From the dockside, Pruska barked another order. Kole caught a glimpse of crossbows pointing in his direction before Juragar threw him to the deck.

Crossbow bolts whistled overhead. One sailed past Toch's head. The captain just frowned, planting his hands on his hips.

"That's hardly sporting!" he barked. "Very well. Time for us to leave. Pilot! Depart!"

"Aye, Captain!" came the response, a note of frustration in the pilot's voice. She spun the wheel back the other way while the crew pushed off the dockside with barge poles.

With crossbow bolts still flying overhead, Kole wriggled out from beneath Juragar and peeked over the railing. The armsmen had closed in around Mara. She was wounded and flagging, but none of them seemed to want to be the first to attack her. She lashed out with her hammer at any who came too close.

The ship was pulling away from the dock. Kole was struck by a sudden urge to leap overboard and try to help Mara. He touched the hilt of the naked sword tucked through his belt.

He didn't draw it, though. He didn't leap over the side. He just stayed where he was, feeling the weight of her backpack in his hand as they pulled away.

The crossbow bolts stopped flying. The armsman surrounding Mara moved to attack. She fought off the first strike, and the second.

The knot of warriors was growing smaller as the *Butterfly* sailed away from the dock. The armsmen closed in tighter, and Kole could no longer make out Mara within the melee.

The dark eye holes of Knight-Captain Pruska's beaked helmet turned away from the skirmish, toward the ship. Kole could feel her gaze.

She lifted her sword in a mocking salute. And then, just before the dockside passed out of sight, she strode in and joined the fray.

PART V
MERCY

CHAPTER
45

THE *BUTTERFLY THAT TOUCHES DOWN LIGHTLY* cut through the night, sailing on a sea of black glass. Though the moon was out and only a few clouds drifted across the sky, the darkness ahead seemed as complete as anything Kole had experienced in the temple of Gnothea.

Kole sat on the deck, his back against the railing, blind to the movements of the crew around him. Toch had disappeared off somewhere, still jovially shouting orders.

Mara's pack sat in front of him. He didn't know how long he stared at it for. Then, slowly, he opened it and looked inside.

There was a purse tucked down the side, containing a portion of the coin she'd received selling the scepters to Medicus Gery. It was heavy. Kole opened it. It was filled mostly with gold, with some silver mixed in as well.

It was substantially more money than he'd ever held in his life.

He thought of the two gold coins Angok had paid him to come with the freebooters into the swamp. There was something funny about it all, but he couldn't bring himself to laugh.

He returned the purse to the bag and took out the two tomes that gave the pack most of its weight. He opened the larger book first, the one he always found Mara poring over whenever she had a free moment. The pages were thin and silky and in good condition for a book so old and so well-used. Red and blue and gold inks had been used to illuminate the borders of each page. The patterns were beautiful and yet somehow incomprehensible. It was difficult for the eye to follow them around the page. He felt like he should be able to gather some meaning from the patterns, but every time he thought he nearly had it, the meaning slipped away again.

The text itself was densely written in ancient pictographs. There were no spaces, no punctuation, nothing to break up the endless text.

Sighing, Kole closed the book and picked up the Thesis. Though the locked tome was smaller than the other book, it seemed denser somehow. He turned it over in his hands.

"What am I supposed to do now?" he whispered.

He knew what Mara would want from him. She'd want him to take the Thesis to the Citadel, to the Wayfarers. She'd sacrificed herself to give him that chance.

But how? He was cut loose. He didn't know where to find this Citadel of hers. All the other Wayfarers he knew of were dead, and Mara was... Dead? Captured? He didn't even know that.

What was he supposed to do? He could barely keep himself from using his sorcery. Mara had promised him help—she'd promised that at the Citadel he'd find people who could help him make sense of what had happened to him.

He felt a surge of anger toward Mara, knowing it was irrational and not caring. Why in the hells had she come back for him? What foolishness had possessed her?

This whole gods-damned journey she'd made it clear that the Thesis was everything. It was all that truly mattered. She believed that it held some clue that might slow humanity's descent into oblivion.

So when it mattered most, why had she betrayed that belief? How could she have been so stupid, so arrogant?

He'd known his fate. He'd accepted it. He was a sorcerer. He'd known since he left the temple of Gnothea that he would face a headsman if he was ever caught.

When the Hallowed Order had finally found him, it had almost been a relief. He would die, but Mara would get away. She'd get back to her Citadel. And maybe all this would've been for something.

But now...now he was lost, left holding an impossible burden. Instead of facing a headsman's blade he would simply wander until his was either caught again or he somehow destroyed himself.

His fingers tightened around the Thesis. He was gripped by an urge to hurl the damned thing into the bay. It was worthless now, anyway. Just a reminder of all that had gone wrong.

Not only that, said a voice that sounded too much like Mara's.

He dragged his hand across his face, fighting back the tears that prickled at his eyes. The anger left him feeling cold and drained. He suddenly became aware of how cool the sea air was. Shivering, he returned the Thesis to the pack.

He looked up to see Juragar standing at the railing beside him. Had the Gor been there ever since they left the dock? If so, he hadn't made a sound.

Juragar stood with his legs apart, one hand gripping the railing. Sea spray had dampened his cloak. Though there was no expression on his strange face, Kole got the impression he was uncomfortable on the swaying deck of the ship. There weren't many oceans where he was from.

Kole pushed himself to his feet and stood alongside Juragar.

"I think it helps if you look at the horizon," Kole said, looking out at the dark. "Wherever that is."

The Gor just stared at him.

Kole sighed and glanced back toward Locket. The city lights were dim specks in the distance now. He thought perhaps if he concentrated he could get some sense of Mara, of whether she was still alive.

He couldn't, of course, no more than he could know if his family still survived. There was a deep, aching loneliness in his bones. He hadn't realized how tightly he'd been holding onto Mara until she was ripped away from him.

Kole glanced over at Juragar. He had to remind himself once again how young the Gor was. He was only a few years older than Kole, maybe less.

Redwyn had said that Juragar had been cast out of his tribe for some perceived impurity. He'd been left to wander the desert with only carrion birds for company.

And now he was here, farther from home than Kole was. He couldn't even speak the language of those around him—or chose not to.

Did he feel alone? When he was fighting those Hallowed Order armsmen, had he felt the same fear Kole had felt?

Juragar noticed Kole looking at him and turned to stare back again. His black eyes shone in the lamplight.

Kole nodded. After a moment, the Gor nodded back.

Over Juragar's shoulder, Kole saw a distant light blinking. It seemed to be coming from the walls of Locket.

From the crow's nest of the *Butterfly* came a shout. "Captain! The city is signaling. Two patrol ships are moving to intercept!"

Kole spun toward the prow of the ship. There, off in the dark, Kole could see distant lanterns burning as the shapes of two ships came about.

"By all the gods, you lot really pissed them off, didn't you?" Captain Toch's voice boomed from the quarterdeck.

Kole swallowed. "Can you outrun them?"

"Not in this wind. The *Butterfly* is nimble, but she's no racehorse."

"We'll have to dump the cargo," the pilot said.

"Have you lost your senses? That cargo is worth more than you!"

"Better than losing our heads," the pilot retorted.

Kole stared out at the black sea. It was strange, but for a moment he thought he heard a whisper on the wind. There were no words, but the whisper seemed somehow inviting. Begging, almost.

"North," Kole said, staring out into the darkness. "What's north of here?"

He'd been speaking more to himself than anyone else, but Captain Toch heard him.

"North!" the man boomed. "By the gods, you are a gutsy one." He rubbed his chins, glancing from the approaching patrol ships to the dark sea off to port. "But perhaps a little butterfly can go where a racehorse cannot. Very well! Cut north!

The pilot—a Nizaani woman with colored beads shining in her hair—stared at him in horror. "No. Not at night. We'll be wrecked in minutes."

Toch laughed and slapped her on the shoulder. "Not with a fine pilot at the helm and the gods smiling down on us. Someone fetch the priest! Get him on deck. We're going to need him."

A manic grin spread across the captain's face.

"We're taking the coastal route!"

Kole knew only a little about the Tattered Coast. It had once been a great landmass that bordered the Sea of Reavers, a rich and fertile land during the time of the old empire.

Not anymore. During the Outbreak, mad sorcerers—or perhaps some terrible magical catastrophe—had ripped apart a huge swathe of the coast, shattering it into a thousand thousand pieces. Now those fragments stood like so many teeth, jutting out from the wild sea.

Monsters lived in those roiling waters, so the stories went. He'd never believed them before.

After all he'd seen, he wasn't so skeptical anymore.

The Tattered Coast was a place where ships went to die. The endless islands and jutting rocks were bad enough. But supposedly there were many more fragments of the earth's bones hidden just below the surface of the white waters, waiting to tear holes in the hull of any ship foolish enough to try to navigate the maze.

And Captain Toch was sailing them into that place. In the dark.

Kole couldn't see the Tattered Coast yet. The darkness was too heavy to penetrate. But he thought he could sense the Coast's teeth ahead, just waiting to chew the *Butterfly* to splinters.

Several members of the crew shouted protestations when Toch announced his plan. For a few moments, Kole thought there might be a mutiny within hours of their departure.

"My friends!" Toch shouted from the quarterdeck. "Do you think me a melancholy man? Answer truthfully! Is that what you think? Am I a man given to thoughts of self-destruction? Has the pressure of captaincy at last driven me over the edge?"

He stared out at the crew, daring them to speak. Even those who'd been shouting before were quiet now.

"Ah, so I didn't hire fools after all!" he said. "I doubted myself for a moment. Answer me this, then. Have we not navigated the edges of the Coast before, dodging corsairs and greedy tariff-hunters?"

"Not at night!" someone shouted.

"Correct, friend! Never at night. For who would do such a thing? Who would be brave enough to slip a hand beneath the Coast's skirts and into her britches in the dead of night?"

He made a rude gesture with his hands, earning laughs from several sailors.

"What about you, Harlow?" Toch pointed at one of the sailors closest to him. "I never took you for a coward. Are you a coward, Harlow?"

"No, Captain."

"You're partial to a little nighttime dalliance, aren't you, Harlow? Don't lie to me, now!"

The sailor grinned sheepishly. "Yes, Captain."

"Yes! But I know who is a coward," Toch announced. "Shipmaster Yaan of the *Feathered Arrow*! He tries to flirt with Mistress Coast from time to time. Yet every time she rebuffs him. Captain Aileen of the *Grinning Demon* thinks she can dance her way into the Coast's graces. Her crew wouldn't go within a hundred yards of the Coast's edges."

Toch held out his hands to the crew. "But there are no cowards on the

Butterfly. This is not suicide, friends. This is an adventure. Tonight, we do what no ship has done before. Tonight, we do not flirt with the Coast. We ravish her!"

The crew laughed and cheered. A moment later, Redwyn was brought up on deck. It was hard to tell in the lantern light, but Kole thought that even the normally optimistic priest looked a little pale at the thought of Toch's mad plan.

Toch didn't seem to notice. "Ah, and now we have a priest to officiate! For once we're done with the Coast, she will surely wish to marry us. Friend priest, come up here and share your Word with the crew. Preach! Give us the blessing of your god! As for the rest of you, back to work!"

As the two patrol ships pursued them through the night, Redwyn was hurried to the prow of the ship, facing back toward the crew. And as the crew worked, Redwyn spoke.

"For ten thousand days She wore those shackles," Redwyn shouted to be heard over the wind and the flapping of the ship's two triangular sails. "Slave, they called Her, from the hour She was put upon this earth. Born out of the ashes of the old world, eating nothing but dust and drinking nothing but sand, She labored beneath the burning sun for ten thousand days. And though She often felt the kiss of the slaver's lash, it could not bleed Her. It could not break Her. That which is perfect cannot be broken by the cruelty of petty men."

The *Butterfly* skimmed across the dark sea, dancing on the swells. A wave crashed against the prow, sending up a spray that soaked Redwyn. He only paused for a breath before continuing. The priest had one arm wrapped around a rope to hold himself in place as the ship rocked.

The lights of the two pursuing ships were growing brighter. They were coming at them from the right, cutting off any chance of abandoning Toch's mad plan and sailing out into open sea.

Juragar stood next to Kole, clinging to the railing. Kole knew how he felt. He was beginning to wonder if he'd ever walk straight again.

"Rocks!" cried the man in the crow's nest. "Ten degrees to port!"

Kole saw them now: dark shadows looming out of the sea. The roar of the water grew louder as the sea crashed against the huge, jagged rocks. The biggest stretched twenty feet above the surface of the water, while uncountable smaller rocks lay scattered about like a row of crooked teeth in the maw of some great sea beast.

"Hard to starboard!" Toch shouted. "Reef the sails. Find us an opening, crow!"

"Aye, Captain." There was doubt in the voice of the man in the crow's nest.

The ship tilted to the side as it began to turn. They were soon running nearly parallel to the line of massive rocks and chunks of earth that marked the border of the Tattered Coast.

It was becoming clear to Kole just how far the Coast stretched. The dark shadows that blocked the stars stretched from horizon to horizon. Some were large enough that all of Hale's Crossing could be set atop them, dozens of feet above the boiling sea.

"Port, twenty degrees!" screamed the crow. "Rocks in the water!"

The ship lurched again and Kole caught a glimpse of a low rock as sharp as a knife blade go sweeping past the starboard side of the ship. They now had several huge cliffs off to their left as they weaved between some of the smaller rocks on the outskirts of the Coast.

Their course was taking them toward the path of the pursuing ships. On the wind Kole could hear the distant shouts of their crews.

"Where's our opening, crow?" Toch called. He sounded like a man out enjoying a brisk gallop through the countryside.

"I...I can't see one. It's too dark!"

"Then let's get ourselves some light! Where's my ex-wife? Get up here, Cotzl!"

The closest of the patrol ships was turning to avoid crashing into the rocks. In a minute they'd be alongside the *Butterfly*, within bowshot.

From below deck a strongly-built woman emerged, struggling to drag a large trunk up the stairs. She was dressed in similar gaudy attire to Toch, though with considerably less lace. Her curled white hair was clearly a wig. Sweat was ruining the blush she'd applied to her cheeks.

Painted eyes darted around and settled on Kole. "You don't look like you're doing much," she said in the same accent as Toch's. "Help me with this."

Kole was glad to have instructions to follow. It took his mind off the terror and the nausea. Leaving Juragar leaning over the railing, he rushed over and picked up the other end of the trunk.

They carried it quickly toward the prow of the ship, where Redwyn was still shouting his sermon to the crew.

"Set it down here," the woman said—Cotzl, Kole presumed. "Don't go running off. I might have use of you."

The woman snapped open the latches on the trunk and threw open the lid.

Kole quickly saw that most of the weight came from the trunk itself. It was made of thick timber and covered in waxed leather. Inside, packed in straw, were a dozen paper tubes as long as his forearm. Each was tied to a long wooden stake.

Cotzl removed one of the tubes, handed it to Kole, and carefully closed the trunk.

"What is this?" Kole asked as she took a nearby lantern from its hook. "Is this the cargo you're smuggling?"

She laughed at that—a laugh that rivaled Toch's. "No, farmboy! Just a little Nizaani firestick. Point it up and over there, will you?"

"Like this?" Kole held the thing upright by the wooden stake.

"Perfect. You'll make a good fencepost one day."

Toch called out. "Where's that light, Cotzl?"

"Coming, dear."

There was a short string trailing from the base of the paper tube— Cotzl took hold of it, swung open the door of the lantern, and touched the end of the string to the candle flame inside. The string caught and Kole realized it was some sort of matchrope.

Kole watched the string rapidly shrink as the flame burnt through it. "What should I—"

Fire burst from the bottom of the paper tube, blindingly bright. The flame singed his hands and he dropped the stake in surprise.

In a flash of red light the tube soared into the air. The light played across the surface of the towering rocks as it flew ever higher, past the *Butterfly*'s masts, past the jagged cliff tops.

As it flew, Kole caught glimpses of what lay beyond the first row of rocks and cliffs. More cliffs, stretching for miles in every direction. He saw water churning around the bases of the looming cliffs, slowly whittling them away like a woodsman felling a tree with a bread knife.

He tore his eyes from the Tattered Coast and looked out over the starboard side of the ship. In the light of the soaring firestick he could see the shapes of the crew on the nearest patrol ship. Crossbow bolts started splashing into the water and thudding into the side of the *Butterfly*.

Just as the firestick reached its highest point, it burst. For a few seconds the red light became like a second moon filling the sky.

"There!" the man in the crow's nest shouted, pointing. "Forty degrees to port! Through the arch!"

The huge stone arch was topped with a crooked slab of land. The ruin of some ancient stone hall sat at the edge, half of it crumbled away into the water below. Gulls, awakened by the firestick, squawked and took flight from their nests amid the ruin.

The *Butterfly* turned hard toward the arch. Forgetting his singed hands, Kole grabbed hold of the railing. With wide eyes he stared at the rapidly approaching walls of the arch.

They wouldn't fit. The masts would catch. They'd be dashed against the rocks and swallowed by the dark sea.

"Steel your hearts, friends!" Captain Toch called from the quarter-deck as the red light began to fade. Beside him, the pilot wrestled with the wheel, weaving between the smaller rocks in their path. "Let the gods guide us through the eye of the needle! Inspire us, priest!"

Kole glanced back to see that their pursuers were turning away, unwilling to risk themselves chasing the smaller *Butterfly* into the Coast. They fired one more ineffectual volley of crossbow bolts and then were out of range.

Redwyn's voice was growing hoarse, but he shouted all the louder. His eyes were wide and he faced the crew as if unwilling to look at what they were sailing into.

"And how the storm did rage!" he shouted as he was thrown about by the lurching ship. "Those red sands were whipped about on a divine wind strong enough to tear flesh from bones. Those who pursued the Empress's Chosen screamed as they died, their screams joining the wind's howl. Atop the plateau the Chosen huddled, watching the sands approach. The children cried and the men wailed and the women wept, not wanting to die so soon after being freed from their shackles by the dream of She they called Empress."

A wild gust of wind caught the sails, propelling them even faster toward their doom. Sailors shouted. Some pulled at ropes to adjust the sails, while others clutched at whatever handhold they could get and stared enraptured at Redwyn.

Something scraped against the side of the *Butterfly*. The ship groaned but didn't slow. The trunk full of firesticks began to slide across the deck.

"Grab it!" Cotzl said.

Without thinking, Kole let go of the railing with one hand and grabbed the handle of the trunk. For a moment he thought he was going to be torn in two by the pull of the trunk's weight, but then the ship lurched to the other side and it ceased its slide.

The arch loomed. Kole glimpsed the man in the crow's nest scurrying down the rigging.

"But the Dreaming Empress spoke, bidding them be calm," Redwyn shouted. "For they were Her people, and no storm would harm them. And when she reached out her arms, it was as if she could encompass them all, all six hundred blessed souls who had broken their chains and fled with slave-hunters on their heels. The tears ceased and the people quieted. Because they could feel the warmth of the Dreaming Empress's embrace, and they knew that no harm would come to them."

The *Butterfly* entered the arch.

A jagged spike of stone that jutted from the inner edge of the arch smashed into the railing, showering the crew in splinters. The very tip of the main mast snapped off as it struck the top of the arch.

And then they were through, into calmer water. The wind left the sails and the ship began to slow. Quiet descended.

"And when at last the storm subsided," Redwyn croaked. "The Chosen of the Dreaming Empress looked out from the plateau. Their pursuers had been reduced to polished bone by the wrathful sands. But they were safe. They were whole. They knelt before the Dreaming Empress. And when they rose, they were free."

The crew were silent. Kole released both the trunk and the railing and sat down on the damp deck, suddenly exhausted.

The fragments of the Tattered Coast rose about the *Butterfly* on all sides. Wide rivers of dark water ran between them, offering several routes for the ship to take.

Captain Toch exhaled loudly. "I told you. We are blessed, are we not? Trim the sails. Let's take it slow now. Check for leaks. We'll go a little deeper and then lay anchor until morn. Let's not test the gods too much."

With silent nods, the crew went about their work. There were no cheers now—just a sense of tired relief.

Kole picked himself up and went over to Redwyn. The priest was sitting down on the deck, his robes soaking wet. His face was drawn, but he offered a tired smile as Kole approached.

"How did you do that?" Kole asked. "How did you get your god to help us?"

Redwyn shook his head, a nervous laugh on his lips.

"I'm not sure I did."

CHAPTER
46

PLEASE, DEATHBRINGER.

Kole woke with a start and nearly threw himself out of the hammock. The *Butterfly* creaked around him. Someone snored in the neighboring hammock. There was only limited sleeping space on the *Butterfly*, so Kole had had to share with the crew. After all the nights he'd spent sleeping on the cold ground recently, the hammock in the cramped, humid crew quarters was almost as good as Medicus Gery's feather bed.

After a small struggle, Kole clambered to the floor. For the first night in days he hadn't dreamed of the temple of Gnothea—instead, he dreamed of the scene he'd viewed in the great mirror at the top of the ruined vox tower. He dreamed of the figure in heavy purple robes, with its gnarled hands clutching a ring of keys. He'd dreamed of a clifftop city fallen into ruin. And he dreamed of the man in his wooden throne—the man who'd become part of that throne.

In the dream, that man had whispered to him from cracked, bark-like lips. "Please, Deathbringer."

It had been a strangely intense dream. More real than the worst of the nightmares he often had about the temple or the burning of Hale's Crossing. Even now it lingered, so strong he had the sense that the man in the throne was here among the swaying hammocks and sleeping sailors.

Please, Deathbringer.

He turned, but of course there was no one there. No one awake, anyway. Rubbing his head, Kole dressed and left the sleeping quarters, hoping that some morning sun might burn away the night's dreams.

In the morning light, the Tattered Coast took on a strange beauty. The *Butterfly* was setting sail again when he came up on deck. Captain Toch—looking none the worse for wear—had found time to change into a deep purple coat that was even more moth-eaten than the one he'd been wearing yesterday. It had clearly been designed for a smaller man—large white panels had been sewn in to accommodate Toch's extra girth. He was happily giving orders as the crew raised anchor and set off slowly between the towers of earth and rock that surrounded them.

Kole found Redwyn on deck, a steaming mug in his hands. He leaned against the railing, looking up at the hunks of shattered land. Now that it was morning, Kole could see that many of the earthen cliffs had a glassy sheen, much like the fractured section of hill he'd seen near the old vox tower. It was as if the sorcery that had shattered the land had also cauterized it.

He joined Redwyn at the railing. The priest gave him a tired smile. "Beautiful, isn't it?"

Kole looked up at the pillars of earth. "In a way. Terrifying, too."

"That it is." Redwyn took a sip from his mug and nodded. "That it is."

Captain Toch strode past, bidding them a fine morning as he moved among the crew. He was going to each man and woman, slapping shoulders and exchanging words.

"He's a strange man, isn't he?" Kole said to Redwyn.

"Who? Our captain?" Redwyn smiled. "Perhaps you seem strange to him."

"Maybe." Kole chewed on a piece of hard tack he'd brought up for his breakfast. "Why does he dress like that, though?"

"You don't like bright colors?"

"It's not the colors. It's just all so…"

"Old?"

Kole nodded. "If he owns a ship, surely he can afford some new clothes."

"But then they wouldn't be the clothes of his people."

"His people don't have tailors?"

"Not anymore. His people have fallen."

Kole frowned. "What do you mean?"

"Their nation used to exist far to the east, across the Sea of Reavers, beyond the Nizaani Isles. But now they are no more. Their cities have collapsed. Those of their people who remain are scattered. They hold to the past, taking pride in it. Those clothes were probably his grandfather's, or his great-grandfather's. He wears their clothes so that they may live again."

Kole looked over at the captain. He was laughing grandly at something a young crewman had said to him.

"I think he might be a little mad."

Redwyn smiled. "Aren't we all?"

"I wanted to thank you. For saving us. I'm still not sure I understand why you did it."

"We owed you," Redwyn said.

"Not that much."

Redwyn shrugged. "We are not misers, carefully weighing out the cost of each favor." He paused, his face growing serious. "Do you want the honest truth? Twice in my life I have felt something...divine. Twice I believe the Dreaming Empress has put her hand on my shoulder to guide me. The first time was in the wastes when I found Juragar, just before the vultures were about to make a meal of him. The second was last night, when Mara arrived at the Diving Kraken. She burst through that tavern door like a ray of golden sunshine. She was looking for sellswords. She found Juragar and myself instead."

Too bad this Dreaming Empress didn't see fit to protect Mara when it really mattered. He bit back the remark before he could speak it aloud.

"I must say," Redwyn said, "I'm very glad I didn't ask Juragar to try to kill her back at the tower. Especially now I've seen her fight."

Kole stared. "You were going to kill her?"

Redwyn shrugged, smiling. "If necessary. The Dreaming Empress hates to see innocents chained. And the Hallowed Order takes great delight in doing just that. We worried you and your young friend were prisoners."

"But you didn't attack Mara."

"No. Call it a hunch."

Kole didn't know what to say. He just kept thinking about the look Mara gave him before she turned to fight and the *Butterfly* carried him away.

"She may yet live," Redwyn said, looking at him.

"That might be worse," Kole whispered. "Maybe being killed would be better than being captured alive by the Hallowed Order." His throat tightened. "It was my fault. She shouldn't have come back for me."

"She thought it was worth the risk."

"I just...I don't understand why."

"Maybe you will, in time. Or not. We cannot always know the heart of another. Sometimes we cannot even know our own heart."

Kole shot him a look. "You're full of wisdom, aren't you?" he said sarcastically.

Redwyn grinned and plucked at his white robe. "It comes with the uniform."

Darvin was awake when Kole went to take him breakfast and his medicine. It wasn't until Kole was in the room that he realized Darvin might not want to be served food by a corpse dragger. So few people knew what he really was that he was almost starting to forget himself.

Or maybe it was just that he wanted to forget.

Perhaps Darvin had forgotten as well, or perhaps his condition had stripped him of the strength to care. Kole helped him into a chair and then Darvin wolfed down the biscuit and orange slices that Kole had brought him. After he'd had something to line his stomach, Kole showed Darvin the medicines Gery had given him and explained the doses she'd told him Darvin needed. Darvin made a face as he swallowed the bitter concoctions, but he didn't complain.

Darvin grew more lucid with some food and medicine in him. He rubbed his head, and Kole noticed how wasted the muscles in his hand were. Despite their attempts to feed him, Darvin had lost a lot of weight since the temple.

"How do you feel?" Kole asked.

"Sore. Confused." He frowned and looked around the small cabin. The sway of the ship seemed to be disorienting him. "I feel like I'm slipping in and out of dreams. Every time I open my eyes I'm somewhere different." He rubbed his eyes. "There was a girl."

"A girl?"

"Yeah. A Sundarin girl. She gave me medicine."

"Khahra. A physik's apprentice."

"Yeah? Is she here?"

"No."

"Shame," Darvin said. "She was pretty."

"I nearly stabbed her once."

"What? Why?"

"I was having a nightmare. Then I woke up, and she was there, and I just..." He mimed swinging a sword.

Darvin laughed, then the laugh became a hacking cough. He doubled over, clutching at his chest until the coughing fit passed. He wiped his mouth. "You're a real ladies' man, Felmen."

"It isn't as if she would've been interested in you after she spent two days emptying your bedpan."

"You never know." He rubbed his chest and looked around the cabin again. "Where are we going?"

"Godsmouth. Hopefully."

"Godsmouth," he echoed. "Why?"

Kole took a deep breath. He'd been putting this off for so long. Until now Darvin had been in no condition to hear the truth, and Kole had been thankful for that.

"Felmen," Darvin said. "Something…something happened, didn't it? Something happened back home."

Kole nodded. Swallowing, he began to tell him what had happened since they left the temple.

Darvin was silent as he listened to the story. Kole only left out one major detail—the fact that he was a sorcerer. There was no point in terrifying him. Maybe Darvin already knew, but Kole didn't think so.

Kole wasn't sure how much of the story Darvin absorbed. His eyes clouded when Kole told him about the burning of Hale's Crossing and he didn't seem to listen to much after that. Darvin asked only one question: whether his ma was safe. When Kole said he didn't know, Darvin lapsed back into silence.

"I want to be by myself for a bit," Darvin said when Kole finished the story. Kole said he'd be back later with his second dose of medicine.

Darvin didn't answer. Kole wasn't sure he'd heard.

For four more days the *Butterfly That Touches Down Lightly* weaved slowly through the Tattered Coast. They traveled only when they had good light. Since the island cliffs around them kept the sunlight out until well into the morning, the amount of time they actually spent traveling was limited.

Whenever they were sailing, Captain Toch had crew members at the prow thrusting bargepoles into the water, testing for hidden rocks. The *Butterfly* had sustained some damage to its hull as it entered the Tattered Coast, and though the crew had repaired the leaks as best they could, they wanted to avoid causing any further damage to the ship.

The ship seemed to be well-provisioned, at least. The crew supplemented their food supplies with fish and saltwater eels they caught whenever they were anchored. Most nights Captain Toch or one of his officers brought out some rum for the crew to share, which kept spirits high.

There was no sign of pursuit. Toch was certain there wouldn't be—not until they were long gone.

"The *Butterfly* is an exploration ship, you see," Toch told him one night. "Small crew, shallow hull, highly maneuverable. One of the last of its kind. Belonged to my uncle, and my grandfather before him. May all kind gods guard their souls. Those floating bricks the Free Lady sent after us would never dare to brave these waters."

"Won't they just wait for us to leave and catch us then?" Kole asked.

"Eh, they can try!" Toch laughed. "Let them try to patrol the whole Coast! If we come out and run into them, we'll just duck back in and try again somewhere else."

The man seemed so confident it was hard to doubt him.

"Please, Deathbringer."

Kole woke with a stabbing sensation in his reforged leg. The pains were becoming more frequent—almost as frequent as the dreams that haunted him. He hadn't thought it possible, but the intensity of the dreams was growing stronger each night. Even now he could taste the air in that ruined throne room—a taste of dust and salt and things long dead.

As the image of the man in the throne filled his head, another spasm of pain went through his leg. Gritting his teeth to keep himself from crying out and waking the sleeping sailors, he lay back in his hammock and massaged his calf. Tight muscles twitched and spasmed. He could feel the heat of his skin through his trousers. The flesh prickled at the touch.

Kole didn't know what time it was. Not even a crack of light entered the sleeping cabin, so dawn had to be a long way off.

He tried to go back to sleep, but the pain in his leg wouldn't subside. At last he clambered out of his hammock and limped blindly out to find somewhere private he could examine his leg.

Even at night, it was a challenge to find privacy on a ship this small. The deck was out—there were always several crew members on watch at any given time. Kole lit a lantern and made his way into the ship's hold, where he thought he might be able to find a quiet space.

He hadn't ventured into the hold before. It wasn't forbidden, but for the first few days he'd found the rolling of the ship easier to deal with when he had a window nearby, or better yet the open space of the deck. At last, though, the faint seasickness that had afflicted him since leaving port was finally subsiding.

When he reached the hold, he decided it had been a good idea to come here. There were many large crates and barrels lashed to the floor of the hold, giving him plenty of dark corners to ensconce himself. It might even be a good place to come down and do some drawing.

There was a strange mix of smells in the hold. Stale liquor mingled with the scents of dried meat and citrus fruits from the provisions. There was another smell coming from some of the crates—spice, perhaps—and something dirty and foul coming from the far end of the hold. Kole put himself as far away from that smell as possible, finding a much more pleasant spot next to a crate of oranges.

Putting down his lantern, he sat and rolled up the leg of his trousers.

His leg was weeping. Patches of clear, sticky fluid stuck to his trousers as he pulled the fabric away from the skin. Tendons bulged and twitched against the thin, purple skin. He'd lost more muscle mass, giving his calf an almost skeletal look.

Swallowing, he touched his calf. It was burning hot and tingled to the touch. He brought his finger to his face, smelling the sticky fluid that had wept from his pores. At first he didn't smell much over the scent of the oranges next to him, but then he caught a whiff of something faint.

Decay.

Gods. It was getting worse. He felt around his leg and cringed as he touched an open sore on the back of his knee.

What was happening to him? Was the sorcery failing? Would the leg become like it had been in the temple—nothing but crushed meat?

He needed to do something. He needed to fix it. He'd done it once, he could do it again. Maybe this time, when he spoke the incantation, he'd see where he went wrong.

But how? He couldn't use sorcery on the ship. There was a chance the sorcerous miasma would penetrate the gaps in the timbers to infect the crew who moved about above him. Or perhaps the miasma would linger for a while, tainting the food and water in the hold.

Or maybe not. There was so much about it he didn't understand. Still, he couldn't risk someone coming down into the hold while he was casting the spell. Even if he didn't infect them, the sailors would undoubtedly kill him if they learned what he was.

As if in response to his thoughts, he heard a snort from the other end of the hold. He jerked the leg of his trousers down to conceal his weeping leg and picked up his lantern.

"Is someone there?" he called out.

There was another snort. Was some drunk sailor asleep down here?

Slowly, he peeked out from his corner of the hold. He could see no one from where he was. But the light of his lantern didn't reach to the far end of the hold, and there were plenty more dark hollows between the lashed-down stacks of crates.

Maybe it was time he returned to bed. But as he headed for the stairs he heard another snort. It was followed by a high-pitched grunt and a scrabbling of feet on wood.

The ship probably has rats, Kole tried to convince himself.

His curiosity began to tug at him. He keenly felt the lack of a weapon— he'd left his stolen sword next to his hammock. Glancing around, Kole found a pole hook used for moving cargo nets around. He grabbed it and limped to the back of the hold.

Kole could no longer convince himself it was a drunk sailor. His lantern light fell on a series of large wooden crates lashed to the rear wall. Each was as tall as he was, and as he neared he noticed they were iron-banded with hinges on the side, so that the front of each crate formed a kind of door. There was a panel at head-height in each of the doors that looked like it could slide open.

Holes had been drilled around the top of each crate. *Air holes*, he realized.

One of the crates was moving.

It rattled in place as someone or something moved about inside. There were a few more high-pitched grunts and something that sounded like nails scratching on the inside of the crate.

They're transporting livestock for trade. He couldn't convince himself of that either.

Not wanting to see but unable to stop himself, Kole edged forward. He reached for the sliding panel.

"Watch your fingers," came a voice from behind him.

Kole spun, nearly dropping his lantern. At the bottom of the stairs was Cotzl, Captain Toch's ex-wife. Kole had only occasionally seen her about the ship in the last few days. She would appear at mealtimes for a few seconds before vanishing again. Maybe this was where she came to hide.

Even at this hour, the woman's face was plastered with makeup and a tattered white wig was set atop her head. She was holding a lantern of her own, along with a bucket.

"What's in the crate?" Kole asked.

"Take a look," Cotzl said. "Just watch your fingers." She went to one of the water barrels and filled up the bucket.

Whatever was in the crate gave another snort. Kole stared at it.

"This is the cargo Toch mentioned, isn't it? The cargo you're smuggling."

"We smuggle many things," she said.

He turned back to the crate. Swallowing, he lifted his lantern and slid back the panel.

Golden eyes flashed at him from the darkness. There was a hunched shape inside, a foot shorter than Kole. A foul scent wafted out. With a screeching snarl, the thing threw itself at the small opening.

Kole staggered back as a pointed snout tipped with a pink nose tried to push through the gap. A pair of long, yellowed teeth snapped at him. When they found only the wood of the crate, the creature pulled back its snout, whiskers twitching. It brought a beady eye to the hole and stared out at him.

Cotzl was chuckling to herself as Kole gaped. Putting down her lantern, she slid the panel closed again, causing the creature inside to shriek and go quiet.

"Ratmen," Kole whispered. "They're real."

"Of course they're real," Cotzl said. "Haven't you ever heard of the Ratwood?"

He looked at the rest of the crates lashed to the wall. "You're transporting ratmen."

"Among other things." She patted the largest of the crates. "This is our prize specimen. A tundra strider from Deep Sundar. We slip sedatives into her food to keep her docile."

"But...why?"

"You don't want to see a female tundra strider in a rage."

"No, I mean...why are you smuggling them? *Where* are you smuggling them?"

"The pits of Godsmouth are always hungry for new monsters. The ratmen will provide a moderately entertaining fight for the warm-up bouts, but the Godsmouth nobles really want to see their champions set against something more...exotic. The strider should fetch us a nice fee. It has been years since the nobles saw one fight. The Nizaani firesticks were the key to capturing her, you see. The light and sound disorients the beasts for a time."

Kole was having trouble wrapping his head around what she was saying. "You're allowed to bring monsters into Godsmouth?"

She laughed. "Oh, by the gods, no. The whole enterprise is highly illegal. Arena combat included. But you have to understand that the nobles of Godsmouth are not like the nobles of other places. There is something depraved about their nature. But they pay handsomely to feed that depravity."

Kole nodded though he still wasn't sure he fully understood. He watched in silence as Cotzl began opening smaller hatches near the base of each crate to pour water into bronze basins attached to each hatch. Most of the other monsters seemed to be asleep, except for the one ratman that Kole had seen. He could hear it snuffling around inside its crate, its tail slapping against the sides.

"Darvin is not going to believe this," he said.

CHAPTER
47

IT DOWN BEFORE YOU pull a muscle, farmboy," the sailor growled. She was stout and muscular and brown-skinned, with a pattern of dots tattooed along each forearm.

Darvin didn't sit. He lifted his chin, glaring at the sailor. "Why don't you go climb some ropes, boat girl? Tie a fucking knot while you're at it."

It was their fourth day in the Tattered Coast—four days since they'd last seen open sea. Despite the extra rum rations Toch was handing out every night, the mood on the ship was starting to sour. The Coast no longer seemed beautiful—it had become a never-ending maze. Kole had heard some of the crew muttering that they were lost, that they'd never find a way out.

Toch was always quick to put down such talk.

Darvin hadn't been idle since they'd entered the Tattered Coast. With each passing day his strength was returning. At some stage he'd convinced one of the crew to lend him a bow and a quiver full of hunting arrows, and now whenever they were anchored he could be found shooting at a target he'd set up at the rear of the quarterdeck.

He'd struggled at first, his muscles atrophied from disuse, but now he was hitting his target reliably and was growing frustrated that Toch wouldn't let him set up a second target further down the ship.

"By all the gods, boy," Toch had boomed. "This is a working ship, not an archery range! I don't want to be pulling broadheads out of my crew each time they go on deck!"

Judging from the bow and quiver lying beside Darvin, he'd been practicing again when the argument broke out.

"I might be able to tie some *fucking knots*," the tattooed sailor said to Darvin, "if you weren't on my deck getting in my way all the time."

"Oh, I'm sorry." Darvin bowed mockingly. "This is your deck? I didn't realize. Should I call you Captain? Or Your Majesty?"

Kole edged over to the railing, where Redwyn was eating an orange slice as he watched the argument unfold. A few other sailors idled nearby, apparently enjoying the disruption from their usual routine.

"What are they arguing about?" Kole whispered to Redwyn.

"What they're arguing about isn't important," Redwyn said. "It's the underlying reason for the argument that I'm more interested in."

"And what is that underlying reason?"

"My money is on unresolved sexual tension." Redwyn cut another slice of fruit and handed it to Kole. "Orange?"

Kole took the offering and sat down on the deck next to Redwyn. The sailors weren't the only ones in need of distraction.

"You've got an awful big mouth for an invalid getting by on Toch's charity," the tattooed sailor said.

Kole saw a muscle twitch in Darvin's cheek. "Charity? Last I checked, we were paying you knuckleheads. You remember? Big bag of gold? Or did the sea breeze blow that memory right out of that hollow head of yours?"

"The deck is for folk who are working. Not little farmboys pretending they know their way around a bow."

"Oh, I know my way around a bow. I've been hunting since I was three years old." Darvin snatched up his borrowed bow. "Stick an apple in that fat mouth of yours and I'll prove it."

The tattooed sailor grinned nastily, revealing a silver tooth. "Is that what you hunt up north?" she barked at Darvin. "Apples?"

A few of the rubbernecking crew laughed. Darvin glared at them all.

Kole wiped the orange juice from his chin. He bent over to whisper to Redwyn again. "Maybe we should stop them."

"Why? The crew are enjoying themselves."

"They won't be laughing when Darvin shoots her."

The sailor gestured to the quiver of arrows resting next to Darvin. "Well go on then, little hunter. You want to take up space on deck, then pull your weight. Hunt us some lunch, why don't you?"

"Gladly." Darvin snatched an arrow from the quiver. "You'll keep the crew fed for a week."

"I was thinking something a little gamier."

The sailor pointed overhead. Circling far overhead was some sort of gull, or maybe a cormorant. To Kole it looked like a speck against the cloudy sky.

"Unless," the sailor drawled, "that's too difficult a shot for someone in your condition."

Narrowing his eyes, Darvin drew back the string and sighted along the arrow into the sky.

A few seconds passed. Kole could see Darvin's muscles begin to tremble.

"What are you waiting—?" the sailor began.

Darvin's bowstring twanged. The arrow sailed into the sky. Darvin didn't even watch it go. He lowered his bow and locked eyes with the tattooed sailor.

Something fell from the sky and landed in the water alongside the ship with a splash. Kole jumped to take a look, along with several of the crew who'd been watching the argument unfold.

The cormorant was a big one. It splashed about in the water, not quite dead, Darvin's arrow in its shoulder. Its blood stained the sea around it.

Darvin appeared at Kole's side. Kole glanced over at him, expecting to see smug satisfaction on the boy's face. But as Darvin stared down at the wounded bird, Kole could see no pride there. Darvin just looked pale, as if the exertion had made him sick. And...was that regret?

"By the gods!" Captain Toch's voice rang out from the other end of the ship. "What is so important that my entire crew has decided to gawk instead of working?"

Toch bounded over as a few of the sailors hurriedly returned to their duties. The huge captain leaned out over the railing.

"Ho! Was that you, boy?" he said to Darvin. "Are you trying to anger the gods? Shooting down cormorants! Don't you know that's bad luck?"

Without looking at the captain, Darvin nocked another arrow and loosed it at the wounded bird. This time he got it in the breast. The cormorant went still.

Darvin turned back toward the tattooed sailor. She was staring at him with a hand on her hip. A hint of admiration sparkled in her eyes.

"There's lunch," Darvin said as he walked away. "You fish it out."

That evening they dropped anchor in a still bay formed by several towering islands. It had been raining since the afternoon, and now a small waterfall poured down one cliff edge, a rainbow forming in the spray.

To distract himself from the pain in his leg—and to take his mind off the ratmen trapped in the hold—Kole spent the rainy afternoon as he spent much of his time on the ship: poring over Mara's old book. The illuminations fascinated him, though the deeper meaning he was sure they held continued to elude him.

He kept studying the tome nonetheless. Each page seemed to have its own unique patterns illuminating the edges, each of which, he suspected, formed part of some greater whole. Some days he tried to replicate the illuminations in his sketchbook. They were always more complex than they first appeared. Sometimes if he looked too deeply he began to grow queasy, although perhaps that was just seasickness.

Mostly, though, the book just gave him a strange sort of comfort. It made him feel like Mara was still nearby.

Most of the crew came belowdecks as soon as their work was done, few of them willing to brave the rain if they weren't on watch. The ship was soon filled with the sounds of laughter and conversation and arguments. Redwyn was off giving a sermon to some of his new converts, so Kole, Darvin, and Juragar found a corner to take their dinner.

"Hey, Felmen," Darvin said after several minutes of silence. "You know anything about Godsmouth?"

"Not really."

"Me neither." He took a swig of his rum, then wiped his mouth with his sleeve. "What in the hells are we supposed to do when we get there?"

Kole had been worrying over that himself. Mara had given him the Thesis. But what was he supposed to do with it? He knew no one in Godsmouth—certainly no other members of the Wayfarers. If what Mara said was true, they would be hard to find. The Hallowed Order had a strong presence in Godsmouth, after all.

And even if he did find one of their members, could he be sure they would help him? Mara wasn't here to vouch for them. Without her, who knew how the Wayfarers would react, especially once they discovered what Kole really was.

Perhaps they should just flee. Find another ship in Godsmouth and sail far away from the Hallowed Order. Or they could head north, past the Windless Peaks, to Ashashi lands.

But whenever he considered it, he pictured the look on Mara's face the last time he'd seen her.

He couldn't run. It wouldn't do him any good anyway.

He glanced at Juragar. The man looked back at him. Did he understand what they were saying? Did it matter if he did?

Kole lowered his voice so that the sailors nearby would not overhear. "Mara mentioned a scholar in Godsmouth," he said, searching his memory for the name. "Sygil Fairider. I think that was her name. Mara said she may be able to translate the tome Quintus found in the temple."

"And what good does that do us?"

"I don't know. But Mara said the book was important. Maybe if we find Fairider we'll find others who can help us."

Darvin leaned back, chewing some smoked fish. He had refused any of the roasted cormorant he'd killed.

"Didn't you say that book was locked?" Darvin said. "Bit hard to read a locked book, isn't it? Even for some fancy scholar."

Kole didn't have an answer for that.

"You think those Hallowed Order bastards are after the book too?" Darvin asked.

He thought of Knight-Captain Pruska and the look in her eyes when he'd accused her of something similar.

"I don't know," he said slowly. "It's possible."

"Maybe we should destroy it, then?"

"I can't."

"Why not?"

"I just can't."

Darvin shrugged. The rain outside was getting heavier—it hammered against the deck overhead. The ship bobbed and rocked in the water. Though it was warm and humid within the ship, Kole pulled his cloak around him.

Darvin was quiet for a few seconds as he finished off the last of his fish. He stared down at the fish bone in his hands. With his thumb, he rubbed the small scar on the back of his index finger—the scar Knight-Captain Pruska's dagger had left.

"I think I hear her voice, sometimes," he said suddenly. "When I'm dreaming."

"Who? Mara?"

He shook his head. "The Hallowed Order woman."

"Pruska."

Darvin nodded. "I was pretty out of it back there at the physik's house. I don't remember what she looks like. But that voice…"

His face tightened and something cracked. Kole glanced down and saw that Darvin had snapped the fish bone between his hands.

"She was there, wasn't she?" There was a quiet menace in his voice. "At Hale's Crossing. She was running things."

Kole nodded.

Darvin looked up at him. "You saw her face?"

"At the physik's house. Yes."

"You see her again, you point her out to me."

"What for?"

"If I can," he said coldly, "I'm going to put an arrow between her eyes."

Juragar stood suddenly, dropping his food at his feet. The movement made Kole flinch.

"What is it?" he said.

Juragar cocked his head to the side, black eyes darting back and forth.

A couple of nearby sailors glanced over. "What's wrong with the Gor? Seasick?"

Kole ignored them. "Juragar?"

The Gor glanced down at them. Though his features hadn't moved, Kole thought he could sense the barest hint of a frown on Juragar's face. He lifted a hand and made a small circular motion with his finger.

Kole didn't understand, but Darvin sat up straight and gripped the empty crate he was sitting on. "He's right. Do you feel that?"

"Feel what?"

Darvin called to the sailors. "Hey! Is the ship supposed to be rotating like this?"

The sounds of conversation died. There was a moment's pause as the more sober of the sailors frowned.

"Ur's throbbing cock," one of them swore, leaping to his feet. "One of the anchor cables must have snapped."

"We're adrift?" Kole said, on his feet his well. He could feel the rotation of the ship now as it bobbed in the swell.

"No," said another sailor. "There are two anchors. The other—"

The whole ship seemed to jerk, then the swaying grew suddenly worse. He felt the ship being swept to the side by the swell.

"There goes the other one!" came the nervous cry of one of the younger sailors.

"All hands on deck!" barked one of Toch's officers. "You four, fetch the spare anchor."

From somewhere up on deck, almost drowned out by the hammering of the rain, came a short scream, quickly silenced. It was followed by the rapid ringing of a bell.

"To arms!" someone above shouted. "To arms!"

CHAPTER
48

WORD IN HAND, Kole followed the sailors up onto the deck. Lantern flames guttered in the pouring rain. The shapes of men and women dashed through the haze as the *Butterfly* listed dangerously to one side. People were shouting, though much of it was drowned out by the downpour. Someone was still ringing a bell.

The water that had seemed so still a few hours ago now churned beneath the ship, throwing it about. The shadows of cliffs were growing larger even as Kole watched.

A horrible crunch set the whole ship shuddering. Kole was nearly thrown from his feet.

"Man the sails or we're sunk!" shouted a nearby woman. He recognized her as the pilot who'd sailed them into the Coast several days before. She dashed toward the quarterdeck as more sailors ran to drop one of the sails.

Kole stared around at the confusion, unsure of what to do. Juragar and Darvin appeared beside him. Juragar bore his chain weapon while Darvin had retrieved his borrowed bow. He had an arrow nocked.

"Where's the captain?" Darvin looked about wildly. "Are we under attack?"

Kole didn't know. It was hard to see in the dark and rain.

The bell suddenly stopped ringing. A panicked shout rose up from the direction the pilot had gone.

Juragar took off toward the scream, staggering as the deck rocked beneath him. After a moment's hesitation, Kole followed.

Out of the corner of his eye he saw movement from the starboard-side railing. As Juragar ran for the stairs to the quarterdeck, something came over the railing behind him.

Its limbs twisted and writhed as it pulled itself over the railing and dropped to the deck. It stood roughly the size of Juragar, with two legs and two arms and a head set atop a thin torso.

But it was not human. Not entirely.

The creature's skin had a translucent reddish hue. Dark veins snaked beneath the surface. A short, angular tail protruded from the base of its spine, and from its narrow head came a spiny fin that ran down the back of the creature's neck. It was entirely hairless and its skin seemed strangely oily.

The creature wore no clothing except for some sort of thin, woven rope it had looped around its chest. In its hand it gripped a short pole topped with a spear tip that seemed to be made entirely of rust.

Dripping rain and seawater onto the already wet deck, the thing took a step forward on strange webbed feet and raised its spear to throw at Juragar's back.

Kole screamed wordlessly and charged at the creature. It spun toward him in alarm and he got his first look at the thing's face.

Wet, bulging eyes stared unblinkingly at him. It had no nose, just a pair of slitted nostrils set above a maw filled with pointed teeth.

It let out a croaking snarl and brought its rusted spear toward Kole.

Driven by horror and disgust, all of the sword forms that Angok and Mara had taught him fled his mind. He just batted the speartip aside and stabbed forward wildly.

The blade punctured the thin skin of the creature's chest with ease, punching through ribs that seemed more like cartilage than bone. Dark purple blood spilled from the wound.

The creature breathed salty, stinking breath in his face. Its spear slipped from its clawed and webbed hands. With its last breath, the thing tried to snap at him with its long pointed teeth.

Kole jerked back in alarm, pulling the sword from its chest. The creature slumped, gasped, and fell to the deck, its dark blood spreading across the wet deck.

The whole thing had taken no more than two or three seconds. Juragar turned, his chain weapon spinning. Kole stared at his sword, at the blood staining it.

"What in the nine hells was that?" Darvin shouted, appearing beside Kole. "What is that thing?"

Kole didn't know how to answer. He suddenly felt like he was in a dream. The sway of the ship, the blood on his sword, the creature dying in front of him—none of it seemed real.

From the other side of the ship came a shout. More of the creatures were climbing out of the sea and leaping over the railing, rusted weapons in hand.

"Repel boarders!" an officer shouted, panic in his voice. Several members of the crew drew their own weapons and charged at the invaders, screaming.

"Felmen!" Darvin cried, drawing his bow and loosing an arrow in Kole's direction. Kole flinched as the arrow sailed past him. It buried itself in the chest of another creature that was climbing over the railing next to him.

The creature slipped, a horrible choking sound leaving its throat. But it wasn't dead. It drew a rusted knife from the rope harness around its bare chest.

As it prepared to leap at Kole, a chain whipped around its neck. Juragar jerked on the chain, pulling the thing toward him. It stumbled, and as it fell the Gor drew his curved sword and stabbed it through the back.

Kole had no time to thank the others. More webbed hands appeared on the railing and four more of the creatures began to climb onto the deck. Juragar went into battle like a tornado, his hook-and-chain never slowing.

The creature nearest Kole crested the railing. Kole charged to meet it, blood rushing in his ears.

He brought his sword down on the hand of the thing as it tried to climb onto the deck. The blade bit into flesh, severing fingers and catching in the wood of the railing. The creature let out a gurgling cry and stabbed at him with the spear it held in its other hand.

Kole jerked back, the spear tip cutting into his damp tunic but only scratching the skin. He yanked the sword free of the railing and slashed at the spear, trying to bat it away.

Though he kept it from stabbing him again, the creature managed to pull itself over the railing with what remained of its other hand. With a throaty hiss, the creature advanced on him, spear raised.

Juragar was engaged with two of the monsters nearby, and on Kole's other side Darvin was backing away, drawing and loosing arrows as fast as he could. All along the sides of the ship sailors were fighting off the sea creatures as they climbed aboard. Other crew members were desperately working the sails, trying to follow orders being bellowed from the quarterdeck.

Kole heard Captain Toch's voice from somewhere down the ship. "Send these foul monsters back to the depths!"

The horrifying creature advanced on Kole. He wanted to run, but there was nowhere to run to. The sword felt slippery in his hand. He tried to remember the forms he'd learned on those evenings in camp.

As the creature lifted its spear to throw, a haze swept over his mind. He could hear hearts beating—not just his own but Darvin's as well, and Juragar's, and even the strange slow-beating hearts of the creatures from the sea.

The *Butterfly* crashed against some rock hidden underwater, a glancing hit that made the ship groan and shudder. Both Kole and the creature stumbled back toward the railing.

Kole regained his feet first and saw his chance. As the creature bumped up against the railing, he moved in, ducked beneath the creature's clumsy spear strike, and slashed at its belly.

Steel bit through flesh. Blood and viscera bubbled from the wound. Before the creature could stab at him again, Kole brought the sword around and stabbed it up through the creature's chin.

It died immediately. Fish-like eyes stared at him blankly. Kole yanked his sword free. The dead thing slumped back over the railing and fell into the churning sea.

As the pounding of blood in his ears faded, Kole became suddenly aware of the sounds of battle all around him. Weapons clashed. Men and women were screaming. Someone was crying. The creatures gurgled—almost as if they were calling to each other.

He glimpsed knots of fighting up and down the length of the ship. A woman slipped on the wet deck and took a rusty knife blade through her abdomen. As she screamed, her attacker grabbed her and pulled her over the side of the ship.

Near the mainmast, a trio of sailors were trying to push back a group of the sea creatures so that their companions working the sails could keep the ship from being dashed against the cliffs. Further along, Captain Toch was laughing, the shadow of his great figure thrusting and slashing at two of the creatures with his sword.

None of it was like the sparring practice he'd had with Angok and Mara, or even the brief fight he'd had with the ganger back in Locket. This was more like the temple.

This was chaos.

He glimpsed movement at the railing beside him and turned in time to see a jagged knife plunge into the meat of his left arm. The creature holding the blade had climbed up to the ship's railing in silence. Now it gurgled at him in triumph.

He didn't feel the pain at first. Not until the creature ripped the knife out. He felt it then.

Howling, he tried to bring his sword to bear. This monster was smaller than the last he'd faced. Quicker, too. It got in close and Kole was only able to hammer the sword's crossguard against the creature's shoulder.

The thing stabbed at him with the knife again. Kole caught the creature's wrist with his left hand, his wounded arm screaming as he fought to keep the rusted knife from driving into his chest.

Darvin was shouting something that Kole couldn't make out. As the ship rocked, he threw his weight at the creature, trying to unbalance it against the railing.

But the thing twisted and they both hit the railing together. Kole still had the monster's knife hand in a death grip as he bashed it with the pommel of the sword.

Snarling, its inhuman face just inches from Kole's, the creature tried to force him over the edge. Despite himself, Kole glanced down at the sea.

The water frothed white as it swirled around jagged rocks. The *Butterfly* had drifted from its anchorage. It was only due to the work of the crew that they hadn't already smashed into one of the cliffs that surrounded them. Near the prow, Kole glimpsed a slack anchor cable being dragged through the water.

Another half-dozen of the cursed monsters were climbing up the side of the ship. They seemed to need no ropes or nets. With the short claws on the tips of their webbed feet and hands, they pulled themselves up the hull of the *Butterfly*.

He didn't have the energy to wonder why the creatures had sabotaged the ship and attacked them. All his strength was spent fighting for his life. The monster snapped its teeth at him, straining against him. He could feel its salty breath on his cheek.

He kicked out, risking his balance to get himself some breathing room. His boot hit spongy flesh. The creature gurgled with pain, the strength momentarily leaving its knife arm.

It was the chance he needed. He shoved the creature along the deck away from him.

The creature staggered back, snarling. Over its shoulder, Kole glimpsed Darvin pulling back his bow with shaking arms. The boy was pale, rain pouring down his face. He looked close to collapse from the panic and strain.

Darvin loosed at the same moment the creature threw itself toward Kole. The arrow plunged into its shoulder. The creature didn't seem to notice. Its bulbous eyes were fixed on Kole as it leapt.

Kole brought the point of his sword up and let the creature impale itself. The blade punched through the left side of its chest. But the creature didn't slow.

It slammed into Kole, its weight throwing him backward into the railing. It dropped its knife and sank the points of its short claws into Kole's shoulders.

Kole's stomach lifted into his throat as he teetered on the edge of the railing, the creature on top of him. He felt the void beneath him, the crashing waves.

Out of the corner of his eye he saw Juragar stretching out a pale hand toward him while simultaneously fending off another of the monsters.

Then the ship rocked to the side and Kole felt the balance tip. His feet left the deck.

"Felmen!" Darvin shouted.

Locked in a deadly embrace, Kole and the monster plunged over the side.

CHAPTER
49

E SEEMED TO FALL for hours. Through the dark and the rain he plummeted, locked together with the creature. Kole stared up at the clouded night sky and thought of the smoke that had filled Hale's Crossing the last time he saw his home.

They hit the water and the cold sucked the breath from Kole's lungs. He gasped, nearly breathing in seawater.

But he didn't stop falling. His cloak dragged at him. The monster pulled him down, its claws digging into his shoulders. Though it was badly wounded, with an arrow in its shoulder and Kole's sword though its chest, the creature was not yet dead. It thrashed, kicked, swimming deeper into the freezing sea.

Even wounded, even dragging Kole's weight with it, the thing swam impossibly fast. For a few seconds he could still make out the creature's shape, but then they were too far down, too deep in the dark, and Kole could no longer see anything.

The salt water burned his wounds. Still gripping the sword that was embedded in the creature's chest, he tried to struggle free of the creature's grip.

He couldn't.

It's trying to drown me, he realized. The thought horrified him.

Deeper they went. Kole's lungs began to burn. He tried to wrench the sword free of the creature, but it was wedged between them. He flailed, unable to see what he was hitting.

As the panic began to take over, some part of Kole's mind reached out. He began to sense things again—the creature's slow heartbeat, the flow of its blood through its veins. The sorcery in his head began to sing its seductive tune again.

He wanted to laugh. He was alone at last—alone where none but the dying monster could possibly be infected by his sorcery. And yet in the water he couldn't speak the incantations that might save him. He couldn't even breathe.

His reforged leg spasmed in pain as he kicked, trying to fight their descent. But the creature was too strong in the water, too perfectly designed for the sea.

His sense of the creature grew stronger. He could read its flesh—he could see how it had been pieced together, its body twisted and altered by the will of insane sorcerers. What madness had driven them to create such things?

Though he was blind, he could see the creature now, as if it were an impossibly complex machine. He could see its life draining away. He could see where the machine was broken.

Kole wrapped his hand around the arrow stuck in the creature's shoulder.

He shoved it deeper, twisting. He could sense pain flooding the creature's body. Deeper again he pushed it, until the arrow scraped bone.

Then he yanked it free.

Through the water Kole heard something that might have been a gurgle of pain. It didn't stop the creature from swimming.

It did stop, though, when Kole plunged the arrow point into the monster's eye.

The creature released Kole's shoulders. He twisted in the water, planting his boot in the center of the creature's chest. Gripping the hilt of his sword, he pulled.

The sword came free and Kole could sense the monster's foul blood mixing with the water. The flame of its life was dimming.

Kole began to swim. His wet cloak tried to pull him deeper. With clumsy hands he unfastened it and let it drift away.

With the weight gone, he kicked his legs. It was so dark. Where was the surface? Gods, how far down had the creature taken him?

His chest burned. His muscles burned. Everything burned. He kicked desperately, not knowing if he was swimming up or down. He began to see light again, but it was just colored spots dancing in his eyes as his mind began to shut down. He fought down a desperate desire to inhale.

Something sparkled in front of him. He didn't know if it was real or not. He swam toward it anyway. The water became wilder, pushing him this way and that.

He broke the surface of the water and gulped for air. He'd only just filled his lungs when a wave crashed over him, pushing him back under.

He found the surface again and this time managed to dive underneath the next wave coming for him. A dark cliff rose up to one side of him, offering him no land to clamber onto.

As the waves battered him, he cast around in the water. *The ship. Where's the ship?*

There. He could see its lights in the distance, about to disappear behind another cliff. It had gone so far. The mainsail was open, allowing the pilot to steer through the rocks instead of being dashed against them.

He could still hear the distant sounds of fighting. Shadows moved about on deck.

"Hey!" Kole spluttered. He waved his arms to signal the ship and only then realized he was still holding the sword. "Wait!"

He started to swim toward the ship despite the protests of his weary muscles. It was no use. The ship slid out of sight through the maze of cliffs.

The weight of despair descended on him, heavier than his waterlogged clothes. With the lights of the ship gone, darkness was everywhere. He could hardly distinguish the waves from the cliffs.

He nearly stopped swimming and let the sea take him. He wasn't sure why he didn't. It wasn't strength or bravery. Simple desperation, maybe. The need to survive just a few minutes longer, no matter the cost.

He tried to swim in the direction the ship had gone, the waves tossing him about like one of Arabeth's dolls. He knew all it would take was one good wave and a rock he hadn't noticed to leave him with broken bones.

A dark shape came bobbing along toward him. He clutched his sword, wondering if it was another of the sea monsters come to finish him off.

But as it came closer he saw it was just part of a broken wooden crate. It must've been lost overboard during the fighting.

Perhaps the gods really were watching over him. Paddling as fast as he could, he caught the broken crate before it was swept away.

He couldn't put all his weight on the piece of flotsam, but by clinging to it he could finally stop treading water. He wedged his sword into a gap between the planks and panted, catching his breath and giving his exhausted muscles a chance to recover.

Now that he was still, the cold set in. The rain hadn't let up. The wind that blew through the Coast wasn't as strong as that on the open sea, but at night it had an icy chill to it.

Shivering, he started to kick again, trying to steer himself away from the cliffs and jagged rocks.

The ship will come back, he kept trying to tell himself. But he didn't believe it. They were too busy fighting for their lives. Even if they fought off the monsters, Toch was unlikely to venture back and risk another attack. Not for a passenger who'd already caused them too much trouble.

He lost track of how long he bobbed on the surface of the water, clinging to that broken crate. An hour? Two? After some time the rain subsided to a light drizzle and the waves grew smaller.

His head was growing fuzzy with the cold. He was tired. His grip on the crate weakened and without noticing he began to slip deeper into the water.

Please, Deathbringer.

He jerked out of the haze and scrambled back up out of the water, grabbing for the crate with numb fingers.

The voice had seemed so close this time.

He was losing it. He had to get out of this water. The cold would be the death of him.

But where? All around him were nothing but towering cliffs. There was no way he could climb the sorcery-smoothed sides. And the smaller jagged rocks that jutted out of the sea offered no flat surface large enough to stand on, let alone shelter from the wind and rain.

So he floated on, letting the currents take him. At least he didn't feel so cold anymore. He just felt tired. So tired. If he rested his head on the crate, maybe he could close his eyes, just for a moment.

No, he told himself. *Don't.*

But he couldn't hold his head up anymore. His eyelids drooped.

As he floated around another cliff face, he lifted his head again, blinking. There was something in the darkness ahead of him. Not another cliff. It almost looked like...

An island. It couldn't be. He screwed up his eyes, opened them again. It was too dark to make out more than the hint of a shadow. He couldn't see how big it was, how far it stretched. It seemed to slope out of the water at an angle. Other shapes reached up toward the sky—broken arches and the corners of ruined buildings. Kole got the impression that it stretched out and away from him, rising out of the sea like a mountain. The top was lost to the darkness.

There were rocks or maybe more ruins rising from the water around the island. It would be a treacherous approach.

But from what little he could see, the slope looked climbable. The ruins might provide some degree of shelter from the elements. It was a chance.

Hope surged in Kole's heart, warming him. That hope was doused when he realized the current was taking him past the island.

"No," he murmured.

He willed strength into legs he could no longer feel. The frozen joints slowly thawed. He began to kick.

At first he didn't know if it was making any difference. But no—little by little, the island was coming closer, even as the current tried to sweep him past it. He put an arm in the water and started paddling, clinging to the broken crate by only the fingers of his left hand.

The island loomed closer. It was big. Bigger than Hale's Crossing, bigger than he could make out in the dark. The water began to get rougher again as he approached. The pieces of stone that jutted from the water were definitely ruins—he could see that now. It was as if a town—or maybe even a city—had toppled half into the water.

A wave came out of nowhere, throwing him toward a broken pillar worn smooth by the water. He twisted, just managing to get the crate between him and the pillar before he collided.

The crate smashed against the stone a moment before Kole did. It meant he only broke a rib instead of his neck. Sharp pain stabbed through his chest.

The sword, he thought through the pain. *Get the sword!*

He spotted glinting steel sinking below the water and grabbed the hilt before it could disappear entirely. Getting to land was only the first step. A blade might help him make a fire or build a shelter.

Or keep the monsters away.

He clung to the broken pillar as another wave crashed against him. As soon as it had passed, he pushed off the stone and swam for the shore.

Desperation kept him moving despite the pain of his injuries. Another wave came at him. Water splashed into his mouth and rushed up his nose. He coughed and spluttered as he kicked against the current.

A wave slammed into his back, pushing him under. He spun head over heels, blind in the darkness. Something hard smashed into his shoulder. He twisted about and broke the surface again as the wave receded.

His foot touched something solid. He could reach the bottom. Kole nearly cried. Still coughing the water from his lungs, he crawled out of the sea onto hard stone.

His fingers found the well-worn edges of ancient paving stones. Patches of lichen covered what Kole assumed had once been a narrow street. He could make out the shapes of ruined buildings to either side of him, crooked shadows in the dark.

He wanted so badly to collapse to the ground and sleep, but he knew that would kill him as surely as the sea. He needed shelter. He needed warmth.

Groaning, he picked himself up, putting aside the pain of the broken rib and the wound in his arm and the throbbing of his reforged leg and the innumerable cuts and bruises that covered his body. Dripping wet, he staggered along the ancient street, searching for a building that was still intact enough to offer him some shelter.

He found it two hundred yards up the street, where he hoped the sea wouldn't reach even at high tide. It was a small two-story building with a weed-choked courtyard in the center. Pillars held aloft balconies that looked down into the courtyard. The bottom story was overgrown with plant life, but the upper story seemed usable—even the window shutters and slate roof were still in place.

Kole carefully climbed the steps, praying that they wouldn't collapse beneath him. They held.

Most of the furniture inside the upper story was rotten beyond use, but even in the dark it was clear to Kole that this had once been someone's home.

Safe at last from the biting wind and rain, he stripped off his soaking clothes. He smashed an ancient wooden chair and piled the wood into a brick fireplace. Shivering violently, he struck his sword blade against the stone again and again until sparks flew and a small fire sputtered to life.

With a strangled cheer, he sat down at last, huddled close to the tiny flame. Only then did he turn his attention to his injuries.

His rib hurt like the hells. Broken ribs could pierce a man's lungs, he knew. He could still breathe, though—even if it hurt to inhale. Maybe that meant his lungs were intact

He examined the cuts in his shoulders where the monster had dug its claws in. His toes and fingers had started to go blue, but now that he was in front of the fire the warmth was slowly coming back to them. They prickled with pain, though it was bearable.

His reforged leg looked worse than ever. The skin was broken in several places, oozing fluid.

But it was the wound in his arm he was most worried about. The creature had sunk its rusted blade deep into the meat of his upper arm, and the gash was long. It made him dizzy just to look at it.

The blade that had stabbed him had been filthy. If he left the wound like this, he might lose the arm entirely.

All he had to bind his wound were his damp clothes. He reached for his trousers, intending to tear a strip off the cuff, but he paused.

You already have everything you need.

As he stared at the wound, words in a language he didn't fully understand bubbled up out of the depths of his mind. Instinctively, he shifted them around in his head until they began to feel right, until they formed a complete whole.

He could do it. He could repair the gash, knit the flesh back together. He had an incantation that would work. And there was no one around to be infected by the miasma.

More words came to him as well, whole strings of them. Words that would set his broken rib and close over the claw marks in his shoulders. Words that might even reverse the decay of his reforged leg.

He swallowed nervously. In the temple he had thought he knew what he was doing. He'd used his sorcery to put his crushed leg back together.

But something had clearly gone wrong. The flesh had broken down again. Maybe the bones would be next. He'd made a mistake, or maybe the sorcery that infected him was so corrupted it was unable to heal him fully. Would the same thing happen to his broken rib and the gash in his arm?

There was still so much he didn't understand about his own power. Mara had warned him against using it—not just to protect those around him, but also for his own sake. What if something even worse happened this time? What if he altered himself irrevocably?

This may be your only chance. Your only chance to practice without endangering anyone else.

That didn't matter. He'd made a promise to Mara.

And if the wound gets infected and you die here on this island, what other promises will you end up breaking?

He looked down at his reforged leg. He was tired. Tired of hating what he was—tired of fearing it.

He was a sorcerer. And it was time for him to learn what that really meant.

Kole emptied his mind and let the incantation take form once again.

He began to speak.

CHAPTER
50

KOLE RAN HIS HAND over his upper arm, marveling at it. There was only a little puckering and some faint white lines to suggest that he'd been injured only an hour ago. The pain had faded as well, along with the ache from his healed rib.

Until now, part of him had wondered if he'd hallucinated the healing of his leg in the temple. He'd been scared out of his wits, after all. Perhaps it had never really been seriously injured in the first place.

But he'd done it again. He'd sung the incantation that had formed in his mind, instructing his body to reshape itself. He'd called on the Lore of Flesh, pouring his own will into the words.

And his flesh had answered. He'd watched the muscles knit back together, then the fat, then the skin. It was somehow both horrifying and beautiful at the same time.

When he'd finished and caught his breath, he repaired his rib as well. The words had poured out of him, warm and liquid and sweet.

Despite his exhaustion, he still wanted more. For so long he'd been resisting the urge to use his sorcery. Now, at last, he was free to test the bounds of what he could do. He turned his attention back to his reforged leg.

Could he fix whatever had gone wrong last time?

He began slowly at first, knitting together the open sores, stimulating the atrophied muscles to grow once again. Then he delved deeper, clearing away the rot that had set in, trying to bolster the strength of the bones. He hadn't realized how brittle the bones of his leg had become until he started probing with his sorcery. There were holes everywhere, pockets of decay. It was a miracle he hadn't broken the leg during his struggle in the water.

He did his best to reverse the decay. But there was only so much he could do. The leg seemed to resist his healing. He poured more energy into the incantations, drawing on what little reserves he had left.

But something was still wrong. He could patch over the injuries in his leg, but they did not truly heal in the way his rib had.

It was like a bad forgery. Over time the ink would run. It would lose its meaning. The effects of the spell would fade once again.

By the time he'd finished casting his spells he was so dizzy he could barely move. He would have vomited if there was anything left in his stomach. He could taste hot blood in his mouth. Even in the dark, everything seemed too bright.

Trembling, he lay down in front of the small fire. Though his body was exhausted, his mind kept working.

He needed some way to fix the spell. To keep the ink from running. There was a way—he was sure of it.

Maybe there was a hole in his knowledge. Some piece of grammar he needed to learn, some quirk of syntax. He did not truly understand the language he spoke when he cast a spell, though he could grasp an incantation's overall meaning.

He needed a teacher. Or failing that, a guidebook. Some piece of the past that might give him what he needed.

The Citadel. That was his best chance of finding the information he needed. He would try to get there. If he ever got off this island.

If he didn't live out the rest of his days in a drowned city.

Please, Deathbringer.

Kole opened his eyes. He was standing in darkness. Not the dark of the sea at night—a blackness so pure it hurt.

The darkness was warm, the air still. He breathed deep.

Something metallic rattled behind him. He turned in place. Someone was standing there, draped entirely in tattered purple robes. The figure's hood was up, their head turned so that Kole couldn't see their face. A pair of gnarled hands—the only skin he could see—picked through a huge ring filled with hundreds of keys.

He'd seen this figure before, he knew. In a vision? Or a mirror? He couldn't remember. Trying to think was like wading through mud.

"Who are you?" Kole asked. His voice echoed strangely.

"Ask not the dead," came a voice from behind him. "For they do not know themselves."

Kole turned again. The man who'd spoken was smiling at him. He had a regal bearing, bright eyes. Young, no more than thirty.

Or perhaps he was decrepit and withered, with skin the color of dead bark. Kole wasn't quite sure from one moment to the next.

Where the man stood, dark vines—or roots, perhaps—stretched out across the floor. If there was a floor.

"Who should I ask, then?" Kole said.

"Yourself. Anyone. I do not know. I have forgotten."

The man's words seemed to hold little meaning. "I don't understand."

"I did, once. Perhaps that too I have forgotten."

Kole chewed on the words. They were thick. Bitter.

"Are you mad?" he asked.

The man smiled. "Quite mad, I think."

Kole nodded. That was a relief. He could understand madness.

"I knew you would come," the man told him. "I saw it. I called to you, and you came."

"How?"

The man just looked up and said nothing. Kole followed his gaze, but there was only more of the same darkness.

"What do you want?" Kole asked.

"This." The man gestured around.

"What is this?"

"Oblivion. I think. I hope. I have never truly experienced it myself, though I have long wished to."

A dull ache was growing behind Kole's eyes.

"The Keeper holds the eagle's pearl," the man said. "I will give it to you. I will give you whatever you desire if you grant me what I seek. Make your way through the city. Pay heed to the Starseeker. He will guide you. All other roads lead to the people. The people are lost. We are all of us lost."

His smile slipped, and for an instant he was withered and wretched, bent like a lone tree on a plain. Then he was himself again, young and smiling. He seemed royal somehow, though Kole couldn't say what the man was wearing or even what he really looked like.

"The palace stands, cradled by thorns. Inside, find me. Find me."

A tear ran down the man's smiling cheek, thick and brown like sap.

"Please, Deathbringer."

◆ ◆ ◆

Kole woke to the sound of gurgling.

The strange dream sat thick in his head, like it had been thrust into his mind. His head ached. Everything ached.

But the gurgling brought him out of sleep and set his heart pounding. He knew that sound. It was coming from the street.

Sword in hand, he crawled silently past the burnt-out fire to the shuttered window. Lifting his head, he peeked through the crack between the ancient shutters.

The rain had stopped and predawn light was reaching across the sky. Kole could now see the ruined city stretching away from him, sloping back down toward the sea. Once, it must have been grander than Locket. Now the sea was slowly claiming everything, eroding the ancient buildings and spreading tendrils of barnacle-like growths along the streets.

There were creatures moving in the street outside—the same creatures that had attacked the *Butterfly*. They gurgled to each other as their webbed feet slapped against the ancient paving stones.

There were eight of them. One was wounded. It trailed behind the others, limping and struggling to keep up. The others seemed to be ignoring its gurgles.

Three of the sea creatures were bent-backed, each carrying a person. Sailors from the *Butterfly*.

The sailors were dead. Even in the gloom Kole could see that. One man still had a broken spear through his chest. Another, Kole suspected, was the woman he'd seen disemboweled and dragged overboard during the battle. Her entrails dragged along the street behind the creatures.

What were the creatures doing with them? He thought of the creatures' sharp, tearing teeth and imagined them biting into the flesh of the dead sailors—

Kole covered his mouth, suppressing the urge to retch. Guilt was stirring up his insides.

The *Butterfly* never would have had to flee Locket if not for the attention Kole had brought to them at the docks. And worse, it had been Kole who had inadvertently suggested that they sail north into the Coast. These sailors—and however many more—would not have died if Kole hadn't listened to that voice on the wind.

The group of sea creatures disappeared down a side street. Was this their home? Did they have a nest or a lair here? Or a village? How sophisticated were they? They seemed to be able to communicate and work together, at least.

Kole dressed and sat by the cold fireplace, scrubbing his salt-crusted hair with his hands. He didn't know what to do. Should he just hide in this ruined house forever? Should he go in search of rescue?

Did he even want to be rescued? Did he deserve it?

Sighing, he picked himself up and glanced around the room. Now that it was getting light, he could see that this must have been some sort of living room. There was an ancient painting hanging in a gilded frame above the fireplace. The damp had partly eaten away at the corners of the picture, but what remained showed a nude woman standing atop a mountain, plucking a feather from the air. Kole stood staring at it for a long time, trying to make sense of it. Though the subject matter seemed still and serene, there was an urgency to the brush strokes, as if the artist had been racing to finish it before the inspiration vanished forever.

When the painting's true meaning—if it had any—continued to elude him, Kole set about exploring the rest of the house's upper floor. Perhaps there was something useful to be found here.

The fireplace shared a chimney with a cooking stove on the other side of the wall. There, in the kitchen, ancient crockery was stacked on shelves. A few bowls and silver forks sat in a washbasin, grime spread across the unwashed porcelain. He found drawers filled with more silver cutlery and picked up a knife. It was too blunt to be much use as a weapon, but he pocketed it anyway. He also picked up an ancient glass jar that might serve as a water bottle if he ever found something to drink.

Beyond the kitchen was a dining room. A crystal chandelier hung above a collapsed table. A badly decayed cushion sat on one the chairs. When Arabeth was little, she used to sit on a similar cushion at their own table back home. He thought of her as a small girl sitting there, peeking up over the edge of the table, refusing to eat her parsnips no matter how much Ma and Da begged and shouted and cajoled. The memory made his heart ache.

The last room he found was was a bedroom. It held two small beds— the beds of children. A carved wooden seahorse sat in one corner, large enough for a child to ride.

Colored balls were suspended from the ceiling on wires. Several more had fallen and shattered on the floor. They seemed to be made of some thin ceramic. Though they were strangely beautiful, he couldn't determine what they were supposed to represent. One was even surrounded by a thin band of rings that seemed to glisten in the light from the windows.

He stood among the ghosts of the past until he could bear it no longer. With his thirst starting to make his head pound, he headed downstairs to the weed-choked courtyard.

In the center of the courtyard was a stone statue that had toppled off its perch long ago. It seemed to have been some sort of seashell—a clam, perhaps. It had landed by chance so that it formed a bowl. A puddle of rainwater had collected in the bottom.

Kole plunged his cupped hands into the water and greedily drank. It tasted clean enough, at least, and soon he'd quenched his thirst. There was even enough rainwater left to half-fill the glass jar he'd taken from the kitchen.

His stomach growled, but there was no food here. Sword in hand, Kole made his way through a wide archway and peeked out at the street. The sun was slowly rising above the city, causing long shadows to reach up the street. There was a black stain along the ancient pavers—a streak of blood and filth left behind by the disemboweled sailor. Other than that, there was no sign of the creatures.

He still didn't know what to do. Stay here and he would starve. Leave and he might be caught by the creatures—and he shuddered to think what would happen to him then.

He ducked back inside the archway, trying to get up the nerve to venture out. He was so gods-damned sick of being scared all the time.

As he glanced around, looking for another exit to the courtyard that might take him somewhere less exposed than the street, he noticed a set of doors he hadn't seen before. They were set into a wall on the far side of the courtyard, so overgrown with vines and weeds that they were nearly invisible. As he made his way over he saw that they belonged to an outbuilding set into the corner of the courtyard, nestled beneath an overhanging balcony.

There was a small window alongside the doors. Kole tore away some weeds, wiped off the dust, and peered inside. He stared.

The exhaustion is getting to you, he told himself. *You're seeing things.*

He rubbed his eyes and looked again. But nothing had changed. He could still see it.

A boat.

Kole hurried down the street, dragging the boat and its cart behind him.

He had to be quick. He needed the tide with him if he was to get away from this place and be out of sight of the island before the creatures spotted him.

He was sweating hard despite the cool sea breeze. The cart was meant to be pulled by a horse, not a man. The muscles in his reforged leg were knotted up in agony. The squeaking of one of the cart wheels seemed to echo down the narrow street, making Kole cringe. If the creatures heard...

It was a risk he had to take. He was lucky to find the boat and its cart in such good condition. Perhaps Ur had taken pity on him.

The boat, as near as he could tell, was intact. It was small, not much bigger than the two-man fishing boats back home. There were oars and even a small sail that could be unfolded—not that he was confident in its use.

No matter. If he could find a way through the sunken ruins and jagged stones that surrounded the dead city, he'd have a chance. Get to the mainland, find civilization.

He came around a corner and caught sight of the sparkling waters ahead. He couldn't have timed it better if he'd tried. The tide was just beginning to turn. He could ride it out.

He had almost nothing in the way of supplies. Nothing but the half-full jar of rainwater. If he didn't reach land within a day or two he'd be in trouble. But it was too late to worry about that now. He slowed, turning the back of the cart toward the water that lapped at the sunken street ahead.

Please let it float, he prayed as he unlashed the ancient boat from its cart. The building that had housed the boat and cart had been sealed for centuries, untouched by the elements. He'd looked the vessel over and found no holes, no loose timbers. But he wouldn't know for sure until he tested it.

He glanced at the street behind him. The ruins of the tall, terraced homes stretched away. Nothing moved. There was still no sign of the creatures.

Moving so quickly he nearly slipped on the slick paving stones, he made his way around the cart and found a hinged section that could be lowered to form a ramp for the boat. The hinges squealed even louder than the cart's squeaky wheel. Kole didn't slow. With protesting muscles he dragged the boat down from the cart and waded into the water with it.

The boat floated.

If he had his coin purse with him he would have emptied it into the sea as tribute to Ur. The god—if he existed—was being uncharacteristically generous. Kole pushed the boat out and clambered in.

Ahead, the sea churned around the ancient pillars and well-worn ruins that jutted out of the water. This would be the most dangerous part. Taking a deep breath, he picked up the oars and sat down facing back toward the city.

As he floated away, he got his first good look at the city in daylight. It sloped upward away from him, thousands of tiled rooftops peeking out from behind their neighbors, hundreds of narrow streets winding through them all.

A steep slope rose up toward the highest point of the city. There, atop a plateau accessible via a gigantic stone bridge, was the ruin of a walled palace. The walls were completely covered in greenery—vines, maybe, or ivy. He couldn't tell at this distance. The tallest of the palace's towers had fallen, leaving only a stump behind.

Though it was a pitiful ruin now, it had once been something glorious. Kole knew because he'd seen it before.

He'd seen it in his dreams. He'd seen it in the mirror at the old vox tower.

Please, Deathbringer.

He shook his head, pushing the intrusive voice away. His head was aching again.

It didn't matter that he recognized the place. He was leaving. This was his chance.

But he stared up at the ruined palace, hesitating. There was someone up there. He knew it. A man had communicated with him through the vox tower. He'd shown Kole this place. He'd called him here. Which could only mean one thing.

There was a sorcerer in that palace.

Wasn't this what Kole had been desperate for? Someone who had experience with sorcery, who knew first-hand how it worked? Someone to teach Kole how to control his power?

No. He remembered what Mara had told him on their journey to Locket. If there was a sorcerer up there, he was mad. And a mad sorcerer was dangerous.

Kole recalled the dream he'd had last night, the dreams he'd had every night since entering the Tattered Coast. Someone spoke to him in those dreams, but they were the ramblings of a madman. If he heeded them he would only put himself in more danger.

Maybe if things had been different he would have risked it. But Mara was gone now. Captured or worse. She'd entrusted the Thesis to him. He needed to ensure it got to Sygil Fairider in Godsmouth. He couldn't leave Darvin to do that on his own.

Please, Deathbringer.

Gritting his teeth, he took hold of the oars and dipped their blades into the water. He looked up at the palace one last time.

A memory flashed before his eyes. He wasn't sure if he'd remembered it himself or if someone had put it there. It was a memory from something he'd seen in the mirror at the vox tower: The robed figure picking through a huge ring of keys. The figure selected a key and held it up. The strange key had a white gem at the tip and a carving of an eagle in flight at its base.

The Keeper holds the eagle's pearl, came another memory, unbidden. *I will give it to you. I will give you whatever you desire if you give me what I seek.*

Kole pictured that key in his mind. Alongside it he saw the Thesis, and the image of an eagle etched in brass upon the cover. He saw the pearl-like stone that formed the heart of the lock that kept the Thesis bound.

It wasn't possible. He was far from Notte's Mire, far from the temple they'd found the Thesis. Why would the key that unlocked it be here, of all places?

It was a trick. It had to be. The sorcerer in the palace was showing him what he wanted to see.

But what if it was true? Could he really leave without finding out for sure? Didn't he owe it to Mara to at least take the chance, no matter how slim?

He was floating slowly away from the island, toward the sunken ruins that surrounded it. If he did nothing, the tide would carry him out. He wouldn't even have to make the choice himself. All he had to do was sit in the boat and let the sea take him.

Please, Deathbringer.

He looked down at the boat. Ur hadn't taken pity on him, he realized now. This was all a cosmic joke. The god of the Sea of Reavers had been mocking him the whole time.

Uttering a curse, Kole turned the boat around and rowed back to shore.

CHAPTER
51

KOLE STOOD BEFORE the fallen statue of a man. Once, the statue would have been three times his height. But it had broken off at the ankles and now it lay on the cracked paving stones, tangled with wildflowers that had pushed themselves up from the earth below.

The statue depicted an old man with a well-trimmed beard and a head full of curls. He had been holding some long, cylindrical contraption to his eye, pointing with his other hand as he aimed the device at the sky.

Now that the statue had fallen, his outstretched arm seemed to be pointed toward a narrow side street branching off the main avenue where Kole had found himself. The side street was half-blocked with rubble and so narrow that he wouldn't have even realized it was a street if not for the madman's words whispering in his head.

Pay heed to the Starseeker. He will guide you.

Kole looked up at the palace. He was close now, close enough that he could better see the approach to the palace—the huge bridge that stretched over a section of the city, sending great pillars down among the buildings nestled at the base.

The bridge—like the rest of the city—was leaning at an angle. It seemed intact, though his view of it was incomplete.

Kole thought that if he followed the main avenue he was on, it would wind around and meet the bridge. That seemed the most obvious route.

But in his dream, the madman had told him the Starseeker would guide him. And the Starseeker was pointing at the rubble-strewn side street.

Assuming this statue was the Starseeker, of course. And assuming Kole was interpreting the madman's words correctly.

He sighed. He'd followed the lions' path. He might as well continue following the madman's directions. If—as Kole suspected—the side street reached a dead end, he could always return and make his way to the bridge.

He climbed over the base of the Starseeker's statue and picked his way through the rubble at the entrance to the side street. The loose rocks scraped against the paving stones as he squeezed through. He prayed the sound didn't attract any of the creatures who dwelt in this place.

Once he'd clambered past the rubble it was easier going. The street was only wide enough to fit three people across. Through long broken windows he caught glimpses of furniture and faded artwork, collapsed bookshelves with their contents destroyed by rain pouring through holes in the walls. It felt like there were ghosts here—memories of the people who had once lived in the city. A sense of melancholy seemed to cling to the place.

The street wound its way downhill. Kole was sure he was going the wrong way. He needed to go up, not down. But he followed a little longer until at last the narrow street opened up.

He'd come out at the bottom of a dip. Smaller buildings sat clustered in the small valley, beneath the shadow of the great bridge that stretched overhead. Across from Kole there was a steep rise up toward the cliff top where the palace perched.

Kole looked up at the bridge overhead and saw what he had been unable to see before. A crack stretched across the width of the bridge, revealing sky through the broken section. He could also see the webs of other cracks stretching out across the crumbling masonry. Chunks of the bridge looked like they might collapse the moment any weight was placed on them.

Glad of his choice not to take the bridge, he turned his attention back to the steep slope across from him. Despite the sharp incline, the slope was vibrant with greenery. But as he studied the slope, he thought he could make out an old path winding its way from the valley floor up to the side of the palace. A servants' road, maybe.

His aching muscles groaned at the thought of the climb.

Please, Deathbringer.

"All right, all right," he muttered, pressing the heel of his hand against his forehead. "I'm coming."

◆ ◆ ◆

It was past noon by the time he finally reached the palace walls. Hunger pangs came at him in waves. He'd seen some wild berries on the climb up, but they were unfamiliar and he hadn't been brave enough to try eating them. He was beginning to wish he'd taken the risk.

The palace walls were covered nearly entirely by a blanket of thick, thorny brambles. The thorns were longer and more viciously curved than any other he'd seen before.

They couldn't possibly be natural. Not growing all the way up the wall like that. He gave one of the branches an experimental chop with his sword. The blade stuck halfway into the branch and he spent the next five minutes trying to pull it out without slicing his hands on the thorns.

The path that had led up the slope ended at the base of a guard tower halfway along the western wall. Through the net of bramble branches was a tunnel through the wall, blocked by a recessed door.

The madman's words came to him again. *The palace stands, cradled by thorns. Inside, find me.*

Kole's doubts were growing. He didn't think he'd like what he found inside. If he could get inside.

He could try to climb the brambles. He wouldn't make it a third of the way up before the thorns opened up his wrists and his blood fed the brambles.

As he stared at the wall, a screeching note echoed across the valley. Kole spun, moving to hide. It was too late.

Near the base of the bridge were a small group of the horrible sea creatures. One was gesturing across the valley toward Kole, while another was blowing into what looked like a large spiked shell. The sound it made rang across the valley—and undoubtedly the whole island.

Clutching weapons, the other creatures rushed for a road that led into the valley. Another, more distant screech responded from somewhere else on the island.

He'd been found. It wouldn't be long before the creatures started up the winding servants' road. And with the bridge broken, he knew of no other ways to escape the rise that the palace sat atop.

Fight, he told himself. *Not with a sword. You don't need a sword anymore.*

Incantations came to him unbidden. He was free now, free to test his power against these creatures. They'd been made by flesh sorcery. They could be unmade.

His head swam. He felt suddenly light-headed. He remembered trying to use sorcery against the knight that had pursued him outside Hale's Crossing. Even before the knight broke that crystal and sucked the sorcery from his lips, his spell had been failing. Attacking the flesh of another required keen skill and a great deal of will.

Perhaps, if he was lucky, he'd be able to use his sorcery to bring down the first few creatures that attacked him. He could blind them, melt their bones, crush the air from their lungs.

But it would cost him dearly. He was already weak. How many of them were there? He couldn't fight an entire island of the creatures.

Inside, find me. Inside.

As the closest band of creatures rushed to the base of the valley, Kole turned to the wall. He looked at the brambles and the recessed servants' door at the base of the guard tower.

He didn't need to fight, he realized. He studied the twisting brambles, let the thought of them fill his mind.

The brambles were alive. Old, but alive. He could sense the trace of sorcery that had been left behind in the branches. They had not grown naturally. Someone had made them thicker, stronger, taller. A flesh sorcerer, like him.

Kole spoke the incantation that formed in his head. He could feel the strength draining from him as he forced his will upon the brambles. It felt different than when he'd worked sorcery upon himself. Something was fighting him. The plants themselves, or whatever sorcery had been used to create them. He poured more of his energy into the words, trying to overcome the resistance by brute force.

The words were coming easier now, easier than they had been when he'd first spoken them at the temple of Gnothea. His tongue was getting used to the intricacies of the strange language. As he spoke, the brambles around the door finally responded.

They withered, pulling back as if their growth had been reversed. The thorns shrank and turned away from the doorway. The curtain of brambles parted.

Gasping for breath, Kole finished the incantation. He felt as drained as he had reforging his leg in the temple.

He pushed through the gap in the curtain of brambles. Thorns caught in his clothes and sliced at his forearms.

He made it into the tunnel and turned back. Though he was near his limit, he couldn't leave the gap in the brambles open. The creatures would follow him inside, where there would be no escape. He had to ensure they couldn't get in.

Gathering his strength, he began another incantation, reversing the changes he'd made. The brambles responded, shifting back into position, their cruel thorns extending.

Kole slumped against the doorway, exhausted. It was several minutes before he was able to breathe smoothly again.

He turned to the servants' door. It had an iron handle and a lock that seemed like it took a large key. He tried the door, expecting it to be locked, but to his surprise it opened. The rusted hinges screeched in protest. Putting his shoulder against the door, he forced it open enough to squeeze through.

An arched passage led beneath the guard tower to the other side of the wall. Kole passed through and stepped out into a wide courtyard in front of the palace.

There was someone waiting for him.

Kole jerked his sword up, stifling a cry. The figure was as still as a scarecrow.

The person—or whatever it was—stood bent over, clad in heavy, tattered robes. The filth that coated the robes was so thick that the only reason Kole knew they were actually purple was because he'd seen them in his visions.

The figure was hunched so low that its hood entirely covered its face. Even then, it stood half a head taller than Kole. The hands that emerged from the billowed sleeves were so thin as to be skeletal. Kole could see the outline of every bone protruding against the waxy skin.

In both hands the thing clutched a huge iron ring holding hundreds of keys. The ring looked heavy enough to use as a weapon.

Kole stood with his sword pointed at the robed figure, trying to calm his pounding heart. He'd automatically fallen into the basic guard stance that Angok and Mara had taught him.

The figure didn't move an inch. The breeze seemed not to touch its heavy robes. It stood in the shadow of the palace, face turned to the dirt.

Kole swallowed. "Are you…are you real?"

For several seconds the thing was silent. Then, slowly, one hand released the ring of keys.

It creaked as it moved, and Kole was reminded of the sound of ropes creaking aboard the *Butterfly*. As it lifted its hand, he became aware of how absurdly long its fingers were. Cracked fingernails the color of bleached bone stretched from the tip of each finger.

It gestured once, *Come*. And then it turned slowly in place and began to shuffle toward the front of the palace, its robes trailing in the dirt behind it.

Kole felt a pressing desire to be somewhere else, anywhere else. He stood frozen in place, sword still raised. From across the valley he heard another distant screech from the sea creatures.

The robed figure paused and without turning back gestured to him again. Then it continued its slow shuffle.

Making his mind up, Kole followed.

The courtyard stretched from the front of the palace to the gatehouse in the center of the southern wall. It had once been paved, but someone or something had torn up a swathe of the paving stones to reveal the earth beneath. Neat lines had been hoed in the dirt and several different vegetables were being grown—carrots, it looked like, as well as cabbages and pumpkins and something that could have been potatoes. Everything looked surprisingly healthy.

Rusted scraps of armor had been discarded against one wall, though Kole didn't know what had happened to the people wearing them. He wasn't sure he wanted to know.

The robed figure led Kole past the vegetable garden and up the wide steps to the palace's main doors. One of the two large doors was already open just wide enough for the figure to pass through. Above the doors was the remnant of a sunbleached banner that depicted something that might have been a tree.

The figure passed through the opening in the doors, and Kole followed.

The suffocating smell of rotting plant matter wafted over him. Covering his mouth and nose, he waited for his eyes to adjust to the darkness inside the palace.

They were in a great entrance hall. The carpet that had been laid across the tiled floor was filthy and rotted through. The statues that had once lined the hall had all been knocked to the floor and shattered. Dirt and mulch collected in the alcoves and at the bases of the large, mural-covered pillars.

Vines—no, roots—stretched out in every direction, covering walls, piercing windows, climbing up pillars. The smallest roots were the width of Kole's thigh, the largest were as thick as tree trunks. Looking at them,

Kole was suddenly reminded of the great snake-like abomination in the temple at Gnothea. His head spun for a moment before he got himself under control.

The robed figure was making its way toward a carpeted staircase leading off the entrance hall. Though there were roots all over the floor—including some that had broken open cracks in the tiles to reach the earth below—the robed figure seemed to know exactly how to navigate the maze. Kole followed so he wouldn't be left behind.

The air was moist and heavy. As they made their way up the staircase, Kole caught sight of an open area at the far end of the entrance hall set beneath a ceiling of dirt-streaked glass.

A huge tree with a white trunk and a handful of wilted pink blossoms stretched its branches up toward whatever little light came through the filthy glass ceiling. Kole thought for a moment that the roots that filled the palace originated with the tree, but he quickly saw that wasn't true. In fact, there were roots snaking through the branches of the tree, twisting around the trunk, strangling it. Those roots seemed to be coming from above, over one of the large balconies that overlooked the tree.

The robed figure led Kole up the stairs, along balconies and down passages. The figure was painfully slow, and the route it was taking seemed circuitous. Perhaps the other paths had been blocked by the press of all the roots. The further they went, the thicker and denser the roots seemed to become. Some had even punched holes through walls and floors, while others had pulled down chandeliers in their endless expansion.

At last they came to a wide doorway whose doors had been torn down by the press of roots. As Kole followed the figure through the doorway, he realized they'd reached their destination. Kole had seen this room before.

It was a throne room. A dozen windows lined each side of the hall, all choked with roots. Dirt crunched beneath Kole's boots. There was a mosaic on the floor, he knew, but it was entirely covered with a layer of mulch.

In the center of the room was something he hadn't seen in his vision: a long dining table that seemed to have been woven by a thousand tiny branches and roots. There was a single chair as well, grown in the same way. A few shoots of green sprouted from the table and chair, as if they were not finished growing.

Food was laid out on the table. Raw vegetables sat in ancient bowls—the same types of vegetables he'd seen growing outside. Dirt still clung to them, as if they'd only just been harvested and no one had thought to wash them. The only part of the meal that showed any sign of additional preparation was in a large bronze pot that sat in the center of the table. It was some sort of thick, congealed soup. It looked like it had been sitting there for some time.

Despite how unappetizing it looked, Kole's stomach growled at the sight of the food. He tore his eyes away from it and followed the robed figure past the table toward the rear of the throne room. His heart hammered in his chest, his throat growing dry. He'd had some inkling of what he was going to find here. But the truth was more horrifying than he'd imagined.

In his visions he'd seen the man fused with the wooden throne, made part of it. And that was what he saw now. Except neither the man nor the throne had stopped growing, stopped aging.

His face was still human—nearly human, at least. His skin had taken on a white-brown hue and had a texture like the bark of a birch tree. The bark-like skin had peeled away in patches, revealing something dark beneath, neither flesh nor wood. Moss and dried sap clung to the corners of the man's cracked lips.

He was blind. His eyes had become knots with green shoots sprouting from them. He had no arms or legs either, nothing left with which to interact with the world.

He no longer sat in that wooden throne that looked like it had been grown. There was only the barest hint that this tangle of roots and branches had once been a throne at all. It now filled the whole rear of the throne room, a great mass of fleshy branches and leaves punching into the wall and floor and stretching up to the domed ceiling overhead. Innumerable roots spilled from what had once been the man's upper torso, splitting and splitting and spreading their network through the whole palace.

All the rest of the man's body was now either part of the mass or hidden by it. In a few more decades, Kole thought the man would be subsumed entirely by the growth, and there would be nothing to suggest he had once been human.

Kole stared, horrified and nauseated and filled with pity. He forced himself forward, swallowing.

"You came," the man said. "I knew you would come."

His voice was like the creaking of old boughs. He spoke slowly, the words stretched out agonizingly. As his lips moved, a bead of sap oozed from one of the cracks in them.

"Who are you?" Kole breathed.

"I am the throne. I am the palace. I am the city."

Kole swallowed. "Do you have a name?"

"A…name…" The sound of his exhalation was like wind whistling through branches. "Not anymore. It is lost. All lost."

"You were a lord? A king?"

The man's face creaked as his brow creased. "A prince. And a scholar. Like those before me. They are lost too. Their names. Their deeds. All lost."

The robed figure shuffled toward the table. Picking up a filthy, blackened silver spoon, it began to stir the pot of vegetable soup. The Scholar-Prince seemed to cringe at the sound of the spoon tapping the side of the pot.

"Eat," the Prince said. "Sit. You are weak."

Despite the churning in his stomach, Kole was desperately hungry. His use of sorcery the night before had left him drained. He lowered himself into the chair that seemed to be woven from hundreds of small roots. It was fixed to the broader root network, so there was no way to pull it closer to the table.

He brushed the dirt off a carrot and took a bite. It was surprisingly good. He wolfed it down and reached for another.

The robed figure was ladling soup into a bowl. He shuffled toward the Scholar-Prince.

"No, later," the Scholar-Prince begged. "I shall eat later. I—"

The figure wrapped its long, skeletal fingers around the Prince's jaw. Yanking his mouth open, it began to pour the soup down the Prince's throat. The Prince spluttered and struggled, but the figure kept pouring.

"Hey!" Kole shouted, getting to his feet. The robed figure took no notice of him.

Kole rushed to the figure's side. By the time he got there the bowl was empty. Soup dripped down the Prince's chin. Fresh scratches weeped sap where the figure had grabbed his jaw. The Prince was still choking and spluttering.

"What are you doing?" Kole grabbed the figure's thin arm through the robe, pulling the thing toward him.

For the first time he got a glimpse of the shadowed face inside the hood.

It was the face of a grinning corpse.

Waxy skin was pulled tight over a skull. Shriveled eyes peered out from sockets that were far too large.

He recoiled, releasing the robed figure. Horrified, he staggered back.

"Keeper," the Scholar-Prince rasped. "Leave him."

The robed figure turned away from Kole and shuffled to the corner, leaving a stink of decay in the air behind it. The ring of keys rattled beneath its robes.

Kole stared after the figure, trying to keep down the little he'd eaten. "What is it?"

The Prince's coughing slowly subsided. "It is my Keeper," he rasped.

"It's dead."

"Blessedly so."

Warily, Kole sat back down at the table. He picked up another carrot. He wasn't hungry anymore, but he took a bite anyway. He had to keep his strength up.

"It listens to you?" he asked the Prince, still eying the robed corpse.

"Sometimes."

"But it forced you to eat."

"My Keeper places some commands above others. It is bound to keep me alive."

Kole hesitated. "How…how long have you been alive?"

"The stars spin and spin and spin. And still I live."

Kole stared at the Prince, trying to imagine what he had once been. "Who did this to you?"

"They all went mad. The people. The city. Mad. I did too, but it took longer. So much longer. It was a relief when it happened."

"A sorcerer did this. Someone with the plague."

"Plague… Yes. Yes, I think so."

"Why?"

"You are not mad. You would not understand their reasons."

"You do?" he asked.

"I understand that there are no reasons. I realized that when my eyes went. I could think, then, at last. Truly think."

Kole rubbed his head. He wanted a drink, but the only fluid he could see was the foul soup the Keeper had forced on the Prince.

"You talked to me. At the vox tower."

"Yes." The Scholar-Prince drew out the word.

"How?"

"Look above. Can you see?"

Kole looked up at the darkened ceiling above the Prince's form. The rear of the chamber was circular, and at its zenith was a dome half-covered with reaching branches. As he studied the grimy surface, he realized the ceiling there was actually a mirror—or a lens—ringed with brass and gold. It was much like the mirror at the vox tower.

"You're a sorcerer," Kole said.

"Starlight once bathed me," the Prince agreed.

The Lore of Starlight. Aetherlight. He remembered what Mara had told him about the lore. Aetherlight sorcery was concerned with thoughts and dreams and divination. Kole's basic grasp of sorcery had allowed him to act as a receiver at the vox tower, but it was the Prince's skill as an Aetherlight sorcerer that had allowed him to reach out to Kole, to bring their minds together.

A thought occurred to him. "You said you didn't go mad when everyone else did."

"No. I was lucky." He made a strange creaking noise. It was only after a few seconds that Kole realized he was laughing.

Another one like me, Kole realized. Whether or not the Prince had been a sorcerer before the Outbreak, the plague should have turned him mad. But it didn't. At least not right away.

Knight-Captain Pruska had been telling him the truth. There were others like him—other sorcerers who through luck or blood did not suffer the same madness that had destroyed people like Mertyn Walter.

Perhaps Mertyn got the better end of the deal. Look at the Prince. Is this what your future holds?

Kole ignored the voice. "If you're a sorcerer, then you can teach me. You can help me learn how to control my sorcery."

The creaking laughter grew stronger. "You would learn from a madman?"

"I have to learn somehow. Please."

"Lost," the Prince whispered, his laughter fading. "Too much has been lost. My mind is full of holes. I do not even know myself anymore. How can I teach you when the words I need slip from my grasp like laughing carp?"

Kole balled his hands into fists at his side. Here was a sorcerer at last—perhaps even one from before the Outbreak. And yet still Kole was no closer to truly understanding his own powers. He was gripped by a sudden urge to scream, to overturn bowls and tear ancient paintings from the walls.

Exhaling, he tried to collect himself. There might still be knowledge to be found here. There had to be.

"What happened to the others?" he asked finally.

"Others?"

"The people who used to live in this city."

"You have met them, have you not? Their descendants, at least."

Kole paused. "The creatures. The creatures who attacked the ship."

"The city was sinking. Some thought to survive it. Those who had not already destroyed themselves. So they changed. Changed and changed until they lost what it was they had been." He gave that creaking laugh again. "I sympathize."

Kole found he couldn't share in the mad Prince's humor. "Why have you brought me here?"

"You brought yourself here. A long journey, full of pain. And yet it is not over. This is but a moment. You have so much more to do."

"You want something from me."

"Yes. Yes. And there are things you want from me, do you not?" A tongue, strange because of how human it was, licked the sap leaking from his bark-like lips. "Come closer, so we may speak."

As he said it, Kole could've sworn the Scholar-Prince's face twitched toward the Keeper standing motionless in the corner of the throne room.

Kole pushed aside his plate and rose. Reluctantly he approached the Prince, stepping over the roots that littered the floor. Some of the smaller ones he had no choice but to stand on, but the Prince seemed not to notice.

"A Flesh sorcerer," the Prince said. "I have waited countless rotations for a Flesh sorcerer to come to my city. Would that it had been sooner."

"What do you want from me? If you want me to reverse what's been done to you, I don't think I can. I'm not skilled enough."

"None alive are," the Prince agreed. "I want you to retrieve something for me."

"What?"

"Something I have spent many long years creating. A blade."

"You want me to fetch a sword for you?" Kole looked at the place where the man's sword arm should be. Only roots stretched from his shoulder now.

"Yes."

"Is it far away?"

"Not at all," the Prince said. "It is here, within the palace. It grows like a tumor within the Tree of Knowledge."

Kole remembered the huge tree growing on the ground floor of the palace, strangled by roots.

"The sword grows?" he asked.

"Yes."

Kole frowned. "Why not have your Keeper get it?"

"He cannot," the Prince said. "He will not. It is not his place. He is bound to me. Bound to my protection. My life."

"Why do you need a Flesh sorcerer, then?"

"That will become clear." The ghost of a mad smile touched his lips.

"This tree. Is it dangerous?"

"Perhaps," the Prince said. "Though not in the way you fear."

"I don't like this."

"No?"

"You're speaking in riddles."

"Am I?" the Prince frowned. "Forgive me."

Kole sighed. This man had become a pitiful thing. Kole wasn't sure he could trust what he said.

"Do this thing for me," the Prince said before Kole could speak, "and I will aid you."

"How? Can you get me off this island?"

"No. But that is not why you came here, is it? You know what I can offer you. Ask."

Kole took a breath. "In the mirror at the vox tower you showed me your Keeper. It had a key. A strange key with a carved eagle at one end and a pearl at the tip."

The corner of the Scholar-Prince's lip twitched into a smile. "Yes."

"Does it...does it open what I think it opens? Will it unlock the Thesis?"

"The two are bound, the book and the key. You have but to bring them together and its secrets will be unlocked."

Kole glanced at the robed corpse in the corner. "How does he have a key? We found the Thesis in a temple far from here."

"He was once a Keeper of many things. Old knowledges. Old treasures. All lost beneath the waves now. Now he only keeps me."

"The Thesis. What is it?"

"I do not know. Perhaps I used to. I remember a great gathering, and arguments, and the gifting of keys to the greatest of scholars from across the Empire. I remember bold men and women who each thought disaster could be averted. I was one of them. Fools, all of us. Is the book a wish, perhaps? A contingency?"

"What sort of contingency?"

"A contingency against the end of the world, perhaps." He laughed, creaking like brittle wood about to break. "Too little, too late."

"I hope not."

He looked again at the Keeper. The corpse had hidden the keys beneath its robes, but they were there. What if Kole just took them? Could the corpse stop him?

"I would not try," the Prince said. "He is very protective of his keys."

Kole stared. "Can you hear my thoughts?"

"Only the loud ones."

Swallowing, Kole tried to quieten his thoughts. He had no idea if it was working.

"If I get you this sword, you'll tell your Keeper to give me the key."

"Yes."

"And there are no traps protecting this sword. No monsters."

"Only those you bring with you," the Prince said.

Damned riddles again. Kole wanted to tear his hair out.

This was foolish. What was he going to do with the key anyway? The Thesis was still on the *Butterfly*—if the ship had not been sunk. The Scholar-Prince couldn't help Kole get off the island. So what did it matter?

Mara would think it matters.

That was his thought, not the Prince's. Although who could tell?

"All right," he said finally. "How do I get to this sword?"

CHAPTER
52

THE TREE WAS DYING.

It still strove for the sunlight filtering through the filthy palace windows above. A handful of pink, bell-shaped blossoms hung limply from the lower branches.

Slowly, though, the life was being leeched from it. The Scholar-Prince's roots were wrapped around its white trunk, strangling it and sucking the nutrients from the soil at its base. Kole was amazed the tree had survived this long.

He didn't know what kind of tree it was. It was certainly no species he'd ever seen before. The Prince had called it the Tree of Knowledge. It had been created by both Flesh and Aetherlight sorcerers working together. It was a relic of the ancient past, perhaps the last of its kind.

And Kole was going to be the one to kill it.

He had to clamber over roots to reach the tree. Dozens of low-hanging branches drooped down to catch in his hair and tickle his neck as he reached the trunk. He could almost believe the branches were moving on their own despite the still air inside the palace. Whenever he turned to glance at the branches, though, they hung unmoving.

He spared a glance for the scattered pink blossoms hanging from some of the branches. Before Kole had left the throne room, the Scholar-Prince had warned him not to touch the flowers. At least Kole thought that was what he was trying to say. The Prince's words never made as much sense as they seemed to at first.

Still, Kole kept his distance from the hanging flowers. Perhaps they were poisonous.

Taking a deep breath, he moved toward the trunk. The Prince's roots reached down from a balcony overlooking the tree, tangling in its upper branches and twisting around the trunk. Two roots, smaller than most of the others, had burrowed into the trunk through a fold in the bark, forcing their way inside over the course of years. The bark around the invading roots had turned a sick gray color.

Kole could sense the sorcery in the tree, though it was not like the traces of sorcery he could sense in the wall of thorns that surrounded the palace or in the magic-tainted blood of the monsters who'd attacked the *Butterfly*. This was something quieter, almost dormant.

Inside, the Prince had said. *The sword grows inside. A parasite, an unwanted child. The two are entwined.*

He stared at the point where the Prince's roots had invaded the tree. He didn't understand the sorcery at work here. It went far beyond his own crude spells. Far beyond his primitive, instinctual knowledge. This was the work of a master artisan.

But he didn't need to understand it. The true work had already been completed, like a statue of bronze prepared by a master sculptor. All that remained was to crack open the mold.

As he looked at the tree, he felt a stab of regret for what he was about to do.

The tree is dying no matter what you do, he told himself. He was simply cutting its life short a little earlier.

Clearing his mind, he opened himself up to the song in his head. It came easier each time. As he did so, his senses were flooded by the complexities of the sorcery woven into the tree. It was as he'd suspected—the skill used in crafting the Tree of Knowledge went far beyond anything he understood. That sorcery sustained it even now, centuries after those who tended it had died.

Overwhelmed, Kole shut out the information. Raising his hands toward the tree to help him focus, he began to speak an incantation. The words reached out, wrapped around the tree's soul, and squeezed. It was a simple thing, like stepping on a man's throat.

All at once, the tree's dormant life flame sputtered in alarm. The sorcery in its being began to twist and writhe, attempting to fight him off.

Kole spoke faster, pouring more of his will into the incantation. He found himself wishing he'd eaten more when he had the chance. This was going to leave him more drained than he'd realized.

The tree's extremities began to wither. A pink blossom crumpled in on itself and dropped from the branch. The flower was dust by the time it hit the ground.

The sound of snapping wood filled the chamber as cracks began to spread outward from the place where the Prince's roots invaded it. More dying flowers fell.

He could feel the tree's dormant sorcery weakening. It was growing easier to overpower the tree's life force.

Kole realized there were tears running down his cheeks, though he couldn't say what he was crying for. For all its strangeness, it was still just a tree. It had no thoughts, no sentience of its own. This was no different than taking an axe to it.

He pushed harder, determined to end the tree's existence quickly rather than drawing it out. The cracks in the tree widened, and a large vertical split opened up down the center of the trunk. Inside, Kole caught a glimpse of the Prince's roots wrapped around something as brown and smooth as polished wood.

His strength was fading fast, though the tree no longer fought him. He reached the crescendo of his incantation. Words he didn't fully understand poured out of him.

And then, with one last ear-splitting crack, it was done. Shriveled, broken, the last flicker of life left the tree. All he could feel in its place was the cold emptiness of death.

Kole fell to his knees, panting. He closed his mind to his sorcery, shutting out the sense of death that had swept over him. He wanted to vomit.

Is this all you are? A murderer of things you could never understand?

He spat the taste of bile into the dirt and rose on quivering legs. *It's just a tree,* he told himself. *If the Thesis really was worth Quintus's life, Angok's life, Catgut's life, then it was certainly worth the life of a damned tree.*

He looked at what had he had wrought. The trunk was split almost entirely in two. There, wrapped in roots in the rotten core of the tree, something remained.

The sword trapped inside the tree was smooth and dark and so perfect that Kole found it difficult to believe that it had not been crafted by the hands of a master smith. But it was not made of iron or steel or bronze. It was made from the heart of the tree itself.

The hilt of the wooden sword stretched up toward the ceiling. It was a long hilt, long enough for two hands to grip it. The tip of the sword's wide blade was still embedded in the trunk of the tree. As Kole stepped closer, he saw the razor-sharp edges of the blade. How could wood possibly be sharpened to that keen an edge?

He stepped over a root, reaching for the hilt. It would be an effort, but he thought he could pull the sword free now.

Strange, though. As he got closer, he thought the sword almost looked like—

A shriveled pink blossom fell from the dead branch above and landed on the skin of his forearm. It sat there for a moment, seeming to stick to the tiny hairs on his arm.

He quickly tried to brush the flower away with his other hand. The petals turned to ash as he touched it. The black dust settled on his skin.

It began to itch. Then it began to burn. And then, all of a sudden, it seemed as if he were floating.

Stars swam in his eyes. He fell, but he never hit the ground.

CHAPTER
53

OMEONE WAS SHAKING HIM.

"Wake up, fish brains. Gods, you snore like a wild boar."

Groaning, Kole opened his eyes and blinked at the orange light that came slanting in through the open window.

He groaned again and rolled away from the light. The pillow was pulled from beneath his head.

"Go away," he mumbled.

The mattress shifted beneath him as someone climbed onto the bed. A heel dug into his ribs, shoving him toward the edge of the bed.

"Up, come on. Or I'm getting a bucket of water to tip on your head."

"All right, all right." He slowly sat up, rubbing his eyes. He felt groggy, like he'd stayed up far too late drawing by candlelight the night before.

Slowly, the room came into focus. Someone was sitting on the bed next to him, still jabbing him in the ribs with her foot.

He looked over at her. She was small and pale, her dark hair falling in a tangle around her cheeks. Her dress was streaked with dirt and dotted with spikeseeds. She'd been out on her nightly adventures again.

"Arabeth," he said. Something about his sister's name seemed strange in his head, though he wasn't sure why. Maybe he'd been dreaming about her. A bad dream, he thought.

She frowned quizzically at him. "What? Why are you looking at me like that?"

"I...I don't..." He rubbed his head. He must have been deep in sleep.

He was having trouble getting his bearings. "Never mind. What time is it?"

"Dawn," she said.

He groaned. "I'm going back to sleep."

She stuck her toes into his ribs again. "No you're not. Da wants you."

Da. There was that feeling again. It must have been a nightmare he'd been having. He had a flash of a memory—Da yelling at him to run. But then it was gone.

"What for?" he asked.

"Old man Tarem carked it. Stayed out fishing too late and fell in. Washed up on the shore this morning. You should've heard the fisherfolk screaming about it. They won't go out on the water until Tarem's dealt with. Da's heading down there now."

He wasn't surprised Tarem was dead. The old man was a drunkard and a terrible fisherman. No doubt he'd had one too many, fallen out of the boat, and drowned. The only thing Kole was surprised about was that it had taken this long to happen.

Kole hauled himself out of bed and got dressed. "What are you going to do?"

"I'm going to sleep," Arabeth said.

"Lucky for some."

Kole stuffed a cold pork sausage in his mouth as he hurried out of the house, his corpse-handling gear slung over his shoulder. Ma was already up as well, though she looked bleary-eyed at being woken so early. She was kneading some dough in the kitchen when Kole left. That made Kole hurry. The sooner Tarem's body was dealt with, the sooner Kole could come home for some fresh bread.

Hale's Crossing seemed more lively than it usually did at this time of morning—must have been all the commotion at the shore. Mrs. Tannith was out on the step of her general store, gossiping with the young women taking down the string of colored lanterns across the boardwalk now that Lampnight was over for another year. Kole couldn't quite remember how the festival had turned out, but that was no surprise. He wasn't invited to the festivities, after all.

The women all grew quiet as he passed, lips twitching in disgust as they watched him hurry on toward the shore. Kole opened his mouth to say something, then stopped himself. What was he doing? He kept his head down instead, walking on in silence.

He turned away before he reached the Empty Net Inn and hurried down the boardwalk that led to the shore. Just back from the waterside he could see a small crowd gathered, mostly fisherfolk impatient to get out on the water.

Ahead of him, loitering beside the bait store, Kole caught sight of three young people talking and laughing among themselves. Kole's heart sank. He quickened his pace, hoping they wouldn't see him.

He wasn't so lucky.

"Hey, corpse dragger!" Darvin Rike called out. "You're late."

Ignoring them, Kole tried to continue on, but Darvin and his two friends sauntered out from beside the bait store, blocking his way.

"Took your time, didn't you?" Darvin said. "Still scrubbing that sorcerer's taint off? Or just the smell of rotten apples?"

Wolfun and Tilda laughed while Darvin gave Kole a sour grin.

Something about this was wrong. All wrong.

"You're not...like this," Kole said to Darvin. "Not anymore."

"What in the hells are you talking about, corpse dragger?"

"Darvin..." Kole took a step toward the boy. Darvin jerked away as if Kole was threatening him.

"What do you think you're doing?" Darvin snapped. "Did you just try to touch me?"

"Gross," Tilda said, spitting on the boardwalk at Kole's feet.

He looked at her, and for a brief second her face seemed swollen, her eyes bulging and bloodshot. Then he blinked, and she was sneering at him again.

"What are you looking at, freak?"

He ignored her and turned to broad-shouldered Wolfun. For a moment he remembered the boy with iron spikes piercing his head and chest, his mouth hanging open in a silent scream.

"You're dead," Kole said.

The boy puffed out his chest. "That a threat, corpse dragger?"

"Kole!" a voice called out.

Through a gap in the crowd of fisherfolk, Kole saw his da. He was in his corpse-handling apron, wearing gloves that stretched up to his elbow.

Da's dark eyes swept over Darvin and the other two. He frowned.

"We have work to do," Da called. "Come on."

"Yeah, corpse dragger," Darvin whispered. "Daddy's calling. We'll see you later, huh?"

Darvin jerked his head at his friends. Tilda spat at Kole's feet again and then they all strutted off down the boardwalk. Kole stared after them, trying to make sense of the images that kept flashing through his head.

"Kole!" Da called again.

"Coming!"

Pulling his own apron over his head, Kole quickly hurried toward the shore. The crowd of fisherfolk parted as he approached, none willing to come too close to him.

Old man Tarem's body was swollen and waterlogged. He lay on the muddy shore, not far from the water's edge. Da was laying out a linen sheet so the man could be wrapped. After the funerary rites, the body would be burned and Tarem's name would be entered into the town records.

Da gave Kole a concerned look as he tugged on his gloves. "That Rike boy bothering you again?"

"He's not so bad," Kole said. "He's just…"

Just what? Why was he feeling sympathy for Darvin Bloody Rike, after all the huntsman's son had put him through?

"Get on with it, corpse draggers," one of the fishermen snapped. "We've got fish to catch."

Several other fisherfolk grumbled in agreement.

Da smiled politely, keeping his eyes on old Tarem. "Don't let us delay you. We'll stay out of your way."

"We ain't heading out when there's a corpse laying about. Ain't healthy."

"Of course," Da said. He met Kole's eyes, shrugging slightly and giving a wry smile. They both knew the fisherfolk just wanted an excuse to gawk.

The smell of smoke touched Kole's nostrils. *Fire*, he thought, his heart lurching. *The town burns.* He stood up straight, spinning around to find the source of the smell.

A fisherwoman stared at him, lowering the pipe that she was smoking. Twin streams of smoke spilled from her nostrils.

"What?" she said.

"Kole," Da said softly. He was crouched at old Tarem's side. "I need your help with this."

Frowning, Kole turned back to Da and looked down at the body.

"This isn't right," he whispered to himself.

"What isn't right?" Da asked.

Kole hesitated, lifting his eyes to meet Da's. "Me. I'm not right. I don't belong here. Not anymore. Things have changed. I've changed."

Da studied him a second, then rose, stripping off his gloves. "Give it time."

"I don't think I have time."

Da smiled sadly. "It's not perfect here. But it's not so bad. You can stay, you know. For as long as you'd like."

"I can't." Kole shook his head. "I'm sorry."

Da nodded. "It's all right, son. I understand."

The crowd of fisherfolk around them had gone still. A silence settled over the world. Not even the waves lapping at the shore made a sound. There was nothing, nothing but Kole and his da.

"I'm going to find you." Kole's voice broke. "You and Ma and Arabeth. If I can, and if you're alive, I'll find you."

Da laid both his hands on Kole's shoulders. "I know you will. That's the kind of man you are."

"I'm sorry that I left." He could feel wet tears on his cheeks. "I'm sorry I didn't say goodbye."

"Say it now, then."

Pink blossoms began to fall around them, floating on a still breeze.

"Goodbye, Da," he said.

Da just smiled.

Reaching out, Kole plucked a blossom from the air. As soon as he touched it, it began to melt in his palm. Hale's Crossing grew fuzzy, distant. The fisherfolk around him faded like smoke.

Kole wanted to hold onto Da, just for a few seconds more. But he too was dissolving, turning to ash like the world around him.

The last thing to go was Da's smile.

CHAPTER
54

OLE WAS FALLING when he woke. The corpse of the Tree of Knowledge loomed above him. He got his hands beneath him and collapsed against the roots strangling the dead tree.

He could still see petals falling around him, but when he blinked and rubbed his eyes, they were gone. So was Hale's Crossing. So was Da. He was back in the palace of the Scholar-Prince, amid the decay of the past.

The weight of all he'd lost pressed down on him. Tears rolled down his cheeks, though whether he was crying for his family or himself he couldn't say.

He sat there in the dirt before the dead tree for several minutes, trying to cling to the feeling of Da's hands on his shoulders, the grin on Arabeth's face. The vision the flower had given him seemed far more real than any dream.

He looked down at his arms. There was no sign of the flower that had touched his skin. No sign of any of the pink flowers that had once clung to the tree.

There was no going back, not even if he wanted to.

Shakily, he stood. In the back of his head he heard Mara's words as the freebooters had led him away from Hale's Crossing and into the swamp.

Hold to the past, boy, but not too tightly. We can only go forward.

Drying his eyes, he approached the corpse of the tree he had killed.

The sword embedded in the broken trunk had a soft shine to it, as if the dark wood had been lacquered and polished. There was nothing ornate about the sword, though the grain of wood made it seem like lines of gold were streaked through the blade.

Clambering up onto one of the larger roots that ran across the floor, Kole took hold of the long hilt with both hands. He expected to have to wrench the blade free, but to his surprise it slipped out of the trunk at the slightest pull, like a well-oiled blade leaving its scabbard.

He stepped back into the dirt, holding the sword in both hands. He could no longer deny what he'd suspected when he first glimpsed the weapon inside the tree.

It was a headsman's sword. Not just any headsman's sword: his sword. A perfect replica of the great two-handed sword he'd wielded at Mertyn Walter's execution.

He studied the rounded point and the wide, heavy blade. Gods, even the weight was right. How was that possible? How could wood feel so much like steel?

He touched the edge with his thumb. There was a flash of pain, then blood welled from a slice on the pad of his thumb. The sword was even sharper than he'd thought. He had no doubt that it could take a man's head off just as easily as the sword he'd spent so many hours wielding against tree stumps and straw dummies.

With nothing to wrap the sword's blade, Kole rested the flat against his shoulder and turned back toward the stairs, leaving the dead tree behind. The Scholar-Prince was going to explain to him what in the hells was going on.

Kole touched the rounded tip of the wooden sword to the filthy mosaic floor. The Scholar-Prince's lips twisted at the sound.

"You have retrieved the blade."

"Why did you make this?" Kole demanded.

"Is it right?" the Prince asked, ignoring his question. "Is it as you remember?"

"You know it is."

"Good. I am glad. For it is yours."

Kole shook his head. "I don't want this." He looked down at the sword. "I never wanted this."

"And yet it is still yours. You know that. You can feel it, can you not?"

Kole threw the headsman's sword to the floor in front of the Prince's body of knotted roots. "Now it's yours. All I want is what you promised me. I want the key to the Thesis."

Though the Prince was blind, he seemed to regard Kole for several seconds. Then his cracked lips parted again. "Keeper. The key."

The robed corpse in the corner stirred. As it shuffled over to Kole, it pulled the huge iron ring from beneath its robes and picked through the keys. At last it found the strange key with a pearl at its tip and a carved eagle at the other end. It looked just as it had in the mirror at the old vox tower.

The Keeper removed the key from the ring and pressed it into Kole's hand. The Keeper's cold, dead flesh brushed Kole's palm and he fought back the urge to recoil.

You're no stranger to dead things, he told himself.

Kole looked down at the key. It seemed to weigh more than it should. There was ancient grime caught in the crevices of the eagle's outstretched wings. Was the Prince right? Would it really open the Thesis? Or was it just some old relic, the key for some noble's trinket box?

"There is one more thing I can do for you, should you wish it," the Prince said. "If you will do me a small kindness in return."

Kole closed his fist around the key, squeezing it tight.

I did it, Mara. I hope it was worth it.

"What is it you can do for me?" he asked as he slipped the key into his pocket.

With his head, the Prince seemed to gesture skyward. "I can help you see."

Kole looked up at the mirror mounted high above the ancient throne. Roots wound around its edges.

"I've already seen enough." Kole began to turn away.

"The tree showed you what might have been," the Prince said. "I can show you what is."

Kole paused and looked up again at the mirror. "What do you mean? You can show me other places? People?"

"Indeed."

"Can you show me...can you show me my family? If they still live?"

"I can promise nothing. Starlight is fickle and uneven. Sometimes it shines bright, and other times it winks out. But I can try."

Kole swallowed. "And what kindness would you have me do in return?"

The blind Scholar-Prince smiled. "I ask only for that which should have been mine long ago." He strained against his own roots. "I ask that you pick up that sword and at last end my pitiful existence."

CHAPTER
55

HE RATTLE OF KEYS interrupted Kole before he could respond. He spun away from the Scholar-Prince. Something heavy came arcing toward him.

With a cry, Kole threw himself back. The Keeper slammed the huge ring of keys to the floor where Kole had been standing a moment earlier. Without slowing, the Keeper lifted the ring of keys and came at him again.

Kole fumbled for the sword at his belt, pulling the naked steel free. The Keeper swung again and Kole dodged back, the heavy keys raking through the air in front of his face.

"What are you doing?" Kole yelled to the Prince. "Call this thing off!"

"I cannot," the Prince said regretfully. "Above all else the Keeper is bound to keep me alive. At last I have spoken my true wish. The Keeper will do all it can to keep me from achieving it."

Kole threw himself over a waist-high root. The robed corpse kept coming. It made no sound except the rattle of its keys and the whisper of its robes against the floor.

"I won't do it!" Kole yelled. "I'm not your executioner." He turned to shout at the Keeper. "You hear me? I'm no threat to your master!"

The Keeper didn't slow. If it heard him, it either didn't believe him or didn't care.

"For too long we have lingered, my Keeper and I." The Prince had to speak louder to make himself heard over the clank of keys. "Look at me! Look at what I have become! I have lost my sight. I have lost my mind!

Please, Deathbringer. Destroy us both!"

With a roar of frustration, Kole ducked under another of the Keeper's swings and slashed at the corpse's side with his sword. The steel sliced into the thick fabric and bit into the thing's dead flesh.

The Keeper didn't seem to notice. It brought its ring of keys arcing back around.

Kole tried to step back, but his sword was stuck in the Keeper's ribs. Panicking, he let go of the hilt.

Not soon enough. The heavy iron ring smashed into his reforged leg. Blinding pain swept upward from his knee. He felt weak bones break.

Kole was thrown backward by the force of the blow. He landed against a root, all the wind going out of his lungs in an instant.

And still the Keeper didn't stop.

Dizzy from pain and dragging his broken leg behind him, Kole scrambled over the root as the corpse trudged closer. Its hood had fallen back, revealing the horrible dead face within. Patches of hair still clung to the corpse's ancient scalp. With an eyeless gaze and a rictus grin, it advanced.

Gasping for air, Kole pushed himself up, limping toward the throne. He got two steps before he collapsed to the floor again. He began to crawl.

"Forgive me!" the Scholar-Prince wailed. "Forgive me, Deathbringer. It has been so long. I only ask for the death that time has not seen fit to grant me."

Kole blocked out the sound. His leg was in agony. A cold sweat washed over him. He felt like he was back in the temple, the leg crushed beneath stone once more. All his attempts to heal it had been reversed in a single blow.

As he crawled, he heard iron keys scraping along the floor behind him. He glanced back to see the Keeper approaching once more.

"Do something," he gasped, crawling toward the Prince.

"My Keeper will not heed me. Not in this. Not now I have revealed my true desire. You must end his suffering. End us both!"

Kole turned toward the approaching Keeper. The corpse grabbed the hilt of the sword still embedded in its side, tugged it free, and tossed the weapon away.

The song of Flesh filled Kole's head. He had to use sorcery. It was the only way.

Pushing the pain from his mind, he reached out with his senses. He could feel the Prince's life force spread across the whole palace. He could feel his own panicked heartbeat and the terrible damage that had been done to his reforged leg.

But when he reached out toward the Keeper, there was just emptiness. Cold. Nothing.

No. Not nothing. Something else—a mocking reflection of life.

As the Keeper shuffled closer, Kole could sense sorcery driving the corpse. It was Flesh sorcery, the same language he knew, the same song that sang inside his head.

But it did not sound like he'd heard it before. It had been reversed, inverted. A song made from the space between the notes. The sorcery was wrapped around the shadow of what had once been a man, woven through his body to give it a life it no longer truly possessed.

Kole knew instantly that he could not stop the Keeper with an incantation. The corpse had no life for Kole to manipulate, and he simply did not have the strength to tear down the sorcery that powered the corpse.

But as he quickly studied the strange, inverted sorcery, he began to understand how it worked. He could see how it clung to the dead flesh, preserving it, replacing its life flame with something else.

Kole looked down at himself, turning his senses inward once more. And at last he realized why he'd never been able to fully heal the leg that had been crushed in the temple of Gnothea.

The leg was dead.

It had been dead since the rock first crushed it. He'd acted quickly enough to bring the shattered bones back together, repair the damaged flesh, knit blood vessels back together. That had been enough to sustain it for a time.

But it could not undo what had already been done. Not entirely. Not forever. He had been trying—and failing—to give life to something that was already dead.

Now, though, he could see another solution.

He spoke an incantation. The Keeper paused at the sound of his sorcery, then continued its approach.

Kole's shattered bones snapped back into place. The pain of it was almost enough to suck the words from his throat, but he could not stop.

As soon as the bones had fixed themselves back together, he ceased his incantation. Through a tear in his trousers he could see that the flesh was still swollen and bloody. Blackened sores marred the skin. He didn't have time to repair the broken blood vessels or knit the muscles back together.

It didn't matter. The leg wouldn't need blood anymore. It wouldn't need muscle. Preparing another incantation in his head, he began to speak again.

This time the song was different. No longer beautiful. No longer in harmony with nature.

Now every note seemed off. Every word reversed and twisted. He was no longer rewriting his own nature. He was defying it.

The skin of his leg wrinkled and tightened as the last hints of life went out of it. A sickening gray spread outward from the shattered knee. Blood stopped dripping from the cuts that the keys had opened up. The pain went, and so did any other feeling.

And as the leg died, Kole wove something else into the bones and flesh. A shadow of life, a pale imitation. Like a puppet's strings.

The Keeper raised the ring of keys. Without a flicker of expression on its dead face, the corpse swung the iron ring toward Kole's head.

He rolled, tugging on the threads of sorcery woven through his dead leg. The leg responded. It was a jerky, unnatural movement, but it was enough.

The keys smashed into the floor, cracking mosaic tiles. Kole was on his feet. Both his feet. For the first time in days he could stand without pain.

As the Keeper came for him again, he picked up the wooden headsman's sword in both hands and charged.

The Keeper was caught off guard by his sudden aggression. The corpse brought its ring of keys up to defend itself.

With all his strength, Kole brought his sword sweeping down.

The heavy blade sliced through the Keeper's wrist. The ring of keys clattered to the floor, the Keeper's severed hand still clutching it.

The Keeper staggered back in silence. It turned its eyeless gaze toward the stump emerging from the sleeve of its robe. For a moment, the thing almost seemed confused.

Shouting, Kole planted his feet and swung the sword once more.

The blade cleaved through the Keeper's neck. The corpse's head tumbled to the floor. A moment later, the rest of the body followed.

Kole planted the tip of the sword against the tiled floor, leaning on it for support. He drew wheezy breaths. Sweat dripped into his eyes.

The Keeper's body lay motionless, its internal sorcery dispelled. Kole began to tremble.

He reached down to touch his leg. It was like touching a week-old shank of beef. Dry and cold and withered. There was no sensation. Nothing at all.

There never would be again.

He straightened, still trembling, and looked at the Scholar-Prince.

"You did it," the Prince rasped.

Kole wanted to vomit. He couldn't look at the Keeper's severed head.

"Forgive me," the Prince said. "I beg of you. And forgive him. My Keeper was not always this way. He cared for me once, really and truly."

Tasting blood, Kole dragged a hand across his mouth. He'd bitten his lip sometime during the fight. He couldn't remember doing it.

The Prince exhaled. "Please, Deathbringer. It is time."

"I can't do it," Kole said.

"You…you can't? Are you injured?"

He glanced down at his dead leg. "No. Not anymore."

"Then you must help me. Please, Deathbringer. I beg of you. Set me free."

He couldn't keep his hands from shaking. "I'm not an executioner. Not anymore."

"You have killed before."

"Not a human."

"I am not human. Am I?" The Prince sounded unsure.

"You saw what happened to Mertyn Walter. You saw it in the mirror." His throat grew tight. "I tried, and I failed."

"This time you will succeed. I have crafted the instrument you need. I am sorry to ask this of you, but—"

"I won't do it!" Kole barked. He threw the sword down. "I left all that behind. It was taken from me. And you know what? Sometimes I'm glad. Because for the first time in my life people look at me with something other than disgust in their eyes. I don't want to be a headsman. I'm tired of death."

"A man is not just who he seeks to be. Nor is he only what he once was."

Kole shook his head, turning away. "I'm sorry."

He couldn't stay here. Not for another second. Tugging on the sorcerous strings that animated his dead leg, he began to walk away.

"Deathbringer, please!" the Scholar-Prince called. "I have waited centuries for you to come! You were supposed to end my suffering! Do not let me linger here among the corrupted descendants of those I once watched over. Do not leave me breathing in the dust of my failure. Deathbringer, please. Have mercy!"

Kole froze. *Mercy.* How many times had Da used that word? Kole always thought he understood, but…

The Scholar-Prince made a jerky, rasping sound. Kole glanced back and realized the Prince was weeping. Beads of sticky sap poured from the knots that had taken over his eyes.

Mercy. Not an execution. A mercy.

He looked at the pitiful man, looked at what he had become. Now that the Keeper could no longer force feed him, the Prince would eventually wither away on his own. But how long would that take? Another four hundred years?

He turned back. "You said you would try to show me my family."

"Yes! Yes! I will try. Please."

Kole's heart started to pound again as he returned to the Prince. With a creaking of wood, the Scholar-Prince turned his face skyward. The tears of sap dried on his cheeks.

"Quiet now." There was an edge of desperation in the Scholar-Prince's voice. "I must search."

The Prince began to sing. It was the same language that Kole himself used in his own incantations. He recognized the structure, the melody. But the words themselves seemed somehow foreign to him. It was like listening to someone speak in an accent so thick it could not be understood.

Kole looked up at the mirror set high above the throne. For several long minutes he could see nothing through the grime that tarnished its surface. Something dark flashed across the reflection and then was gone.

The Prince was trembling like a tree in the breeze. Finally, his head flopped back, the cracks in his bark-like skin deeper than they had been.

There was a panicked shake in his voice when he spoke. "Forgive me, Deathbringer. I thought I had them. But they are being hidden from my sight. The Void is too strong for me to penetrate."

Void. Kole remembered the crystal that the Hallowed Order knight had crushed outside Hale's Crossing. If the Prince's sorcery was being blocked by something similar, it was likely that Ma and Da and Arabeth were still in the custody of the Hallowed Order. Had they been taken somewhere well-protected from the intrusions of sorcery? Some sort of prison? The Blackspire itself?

The Scholar-Prince was weeping again, quietly this time. "Please," he kept whispering. "Please."

Mercy. That word came to him again.

"Mara," he said suddenly. "Can you show me Mara?"

The Prince's weeping faded. "I can try."

He knew it was a long shot. Most likely Mara was in the Hallowed Order's custody as well. She might be just as invisible to the Prince as

Kole's family. But he had to try.

"Do it," Kole said. "Please."

"If…if I try, you will give me what I ask?"

Mercy. He picked up the wooden sword he'd thrown in front of the Prince.

"Yes," Kole whispered. "If your death is what you desire, I will grant it."

"It is," the Prince said. "Oh, it is."

The Prince turned his head toward the mirror once more. The song of his sorcery filled the chamber.

For the first few seconds there was nothing, just as Kole had suspected. He opened his mouth to tell the Prince that it was all right; he need not waste his energy anymore.

But then something appeared on the surface of the mirror. Within a pool of black stood two figures in brown robes. Their heads were lowered as they worked on something on the long table in front of them.

The image shifted and Kole could see what was on the table. His knees buckled.

Mara lay between the two ashers, eyes closed. She was nude except for the sheet of white linen that the ashers were slowly wrapping around her.

Her body was covered in bruises and cuts, but the worst by far was the ragged slash across her throat. It was that wound, Kole knew immediately, that had killed her.

Dead. It can't be.

There was a screaming in his head, but when he opened his mouth he found he could make no sound. He wanted to look away from the image. He couldn't.

Dead. All dead.

It was just Kole and Darvin now. They were the only two still alive of all those who had gone into Notte's Mire.

If Darvin *was* still alive. If he hadn't become a feast for those monsters that had climbed out of the sea.

"Enough," Kole managed to croak. "That's enough."

The Scholar-Prince brought his incantation to an end. The image of Mara and the ashers vanished.

"I am sorry, Deathbringer," the Prince said softly. "She was important to you."

"She saved me. She died for me."

"There are worse fates than to die for another."

Kole rubbed his eyes. He'd hoped…he'd hoped…

"Deathbringer," the Prince said. "I am spent. Will you grant me your mercy?"

Kole nodded numbly. The Prince had held up his end of the bargain. He'd shown Kole exactly what he asked to see.

He hefted the sword and stepped up to the the tangle of roots and branches that had once been the ruler of this city.

The Prince started weeping again, but they were tears of relief.

"Is there anything you would like to say?" Kole asked. "Anything you would like to be remembered?"

"I was a good prince, I think. I hope I was. I tried to be, at least."

"That's all we can do," Kole said.

The Prince smiled. "Yes." He bent his neck forward as far as it would go. "Thank you, Deathbringer."

Kole was trembling again as he lifted the sword above his head. A cold sweat broke out across his forehead. His heart lurched sickeningly. He remembered the sword getting caught in Mertyn Walter's neck, and the horrible sound the man had made after.

One strike, delivered with all your strength. Find the spot where the sword should fall. The blade will take care of the rest.

He exhaled slowly, letting his fears bleed from his mind. He found the spot at the back of the Prince's neck.

And he swung hard, just as Da had taught him.

CHAPTER
56

HE SCHOLAR-PRINCE'S BODY burned well.

In hindsight, that should not have been a surprise to Kole. The Prince had been more tree than man by the end.

Kole had not added all of the Prince's many roots and branches to the pyre he'd built at the top of the broken palace tower. That would have been an impossible task. The roots stretched through most of the palace, and many of them were two or three feet thick.

But Kole had spent some time cutting the Prince's core free of the tangle to prepare it for the fire. He didn't know what funerary rites the Prince would have enjoyed if he'd died in his own time, but he deserved something at least. Everyone did.

The Keeper lay beside the Prince on the pyre. The blaze consumed them both, sending smoke high into the orange sky.

Exhausted, Kole sat down and leaned against a slab of ruined stone. The broken tower stood open to the sky, giving Kole a perfect view of the lost city below as the sun slowly sank behind the endless cliffs of the Tattered Coast.

Though he was sitting well back from the pyre, the heat from the fire was still uncomfortable. He suspected he would welcome it once the sun's rays were gone.

The strange wooden sword the Prince had crafted for him lay across his knees, wrapped in a faded tapestry he'd found tucked in an old storage room. The artist inside him objected at using an ancient piece of artwork as a makeshift scabbard, but the last thing he needed was to cut himself open carrying the blade around naked.

The sword had done its job admirably. The blade parted the Prince's head from his shoulders in an instant, and in that same instant his soul was freed from the prison of his body.

A mercy. Just as Da had said.

Kole wasn't sure what to do with the sword now. He'd strongly considered throwing it onto the fire along with the Prince and his Keeper. It had served the purpose the Prince had crafted it for.

But that felt wrong. It had been a gift from the Prince. And though some part of Kole still hated what the sword represented, he couldn't deny that it felt right in his hands. It was made for him, after all.

He would keep it a little longer, at least. He might find a use for it.

Through his trouser pocket he felt the weight of the pearl-tipped key the Keeper had given him. He wondered where the Thesis was now. At the bottom of the churning waters along with the *Butterfly*? Or had the ship survived the attack?

There was only one course of action open to Kole now. Only one he was willing to take.

Godsmouth. He had to get there.

If the *Butterfly* had survived the attack, if they made it out of the Tattered Coast, they would make for Godsmouth. Darvin knew the importance of the Thesis. He would keep it safe. Kole had to believe that.

Perhaps Darvin would even find the scholar Mara had mentioned and deliver the Thesis to her. But Sygil Fairider would need the key if she was to divine the book's secrets. So Kole had to get there too.

He'd found a cliffside path winding down from the palace to the water below. In the morning Kole would gather together what wood and supplies he could and fashion a raft to get him off this island. It would be safer than trying to sneak back through the city to where he'd left the ancient sailboat.

He didn't fancy his chances on the rough waters. But what choice did he have? Stay here for all eternity, trapped like the Scholar-Prince? The thought sent a shiver down his spine.

With the last of the day's light, Kole looked down toward the dead city. He could make out clusters of figures moving like ants along the ancient paved streets. The creatures that had attacked the *Butterfly* seemed to have three or four nests across the city—different tribes, perhaps. Kole watched them all scurry about until the last of the sun's light finally disappeared behind the cliffs.

Kole sighed. He supposed he'd better go inside and find some place to spend the night, but the idea of sleeping among the roots and decay brought a chill to his bones. He would stay out here a little longer, until the fire began to die.

He looked down over the shadow of the city once more. From somewhere behind him, far in the distance, came a faint whistle. A flickering red light appeared overhead, pushing back the deepening dark.

For a moment Kole could see the distant creatures in the city once more among the shadows of the ruins. They stood frozen, staring up at the sky. And then, as one, they scattered, fleeing for the cover of the ruins.

Kole clambered to his feet and rushed to the edge of the broken tower. Soaring into the sky was the blazing light of a Nizaani firestick.

Triangular sails sliced out from behind a cliff. In the light of the firestick, the shape of the *Butterfly That Touches Down Lightly* was unmistakable.

A distant shout was carried on the wind, followed by the ringing of a bell. Kole thought he could make out someone on deck pointing toward the blazing pyre behind Kole.

His strength left him and he clutched the ruined tower wall to keep himself from collapsing. He didn't know whether to laugh or cry, so he did both.

Three days later the *Butterfly That Touches Down Lightly* found a way out of the Tattered Coast.

As Captain Toch had predicted, there were no patrols waiting for them. The Coast was simply too large for any reasonable blockade. So the *Butterfly* had slipped quietly out into the open sea and continued eastward.

That evening, after they dropped anchor, the crew conducted funerary rites for those who had died in the creatures' attack.

Kole helped prepare the four crew members who had died of their injuries while still on the ship. Some of the crew had seemed uneasy learning they were sharing their ship with a corpse dragger, but most did not react as badly as Kole had feared. Out of necessity, sailors seemed to have a different relationship with death than those who spent most of their time on land. Toch, in fact, seemed pleased to have a real live corpse man involved in the funeral.

Another three crew members had been taken overboard by the creatures—the same three dead sailors that Kole had seen being carried away by the monsters in the lost city. For them, their belongings had been wrapped in the same manner as the other bodies and set on deck alongside them.

The crew gathered on deck, many still sporting injuries from the battle. As Toch began to wax lyrical about the exploits of the fallen, Kole lingered at the back of the crowd with Darvin, Redwyn, and Juragar.

Darvin picked at a scab on his cheek. He'd taken a nasty cut from one of the creatures after Kole went overboard. It would leave a scar, which Darvin seemed quite proud of.

When at last Captain Toch had finished heaping praise upon the dead, he called Redwyn up to give a sermon. Kole only half listened. His mind kept being drawn back to the palace atop the lost city.

As Redwyn spoke to the crowd, Darvin sidled up next to Kole. "This is almost as bad as listening to old Preacher Gameson, huh?"

"Nothing is as bad as Preacher Gameson's sermons," Kole whispered back. "That man spat like a fountain. The one time I was glad I had to stand at the back."

"Patience, piety, purposefulness." Darvin mimicked the preacher's tone, spitting with every word. "That's what the gods love."

Kole stifled a laugh. Darvin grinned and picked at his scar. His gaze wandered and Kole caught him looking at one of the female sailors near the front of the crowd—the same woman who'd goaded him into shooting down the cormorant several days ago.

Kole had heard rumors that after the creatures had been dispatched, Darvin and the woman had started a passionate affair, though the sailor was ten years his senior. In the days since it had become a game among the rest of the crew for someone to interrupt the two of them whenever they tried to find somewhere private.

After a while, Darvin glanced back at Kole. "You ever going to tell me how you got that weird sword?" he asked.

"Maybe," Kole said. "Someday."

"What happened to you on that island, Felmen?"

Kole shook his head and said nothing. It wasn't that he wanted to keep it a secret. He just wasn't sure how to explain it. What could he say about the Scholar-Prince, or the Keeper, or what the Tree of Knowledge had shown him, or what he'd done to his leg?

Kole's hand moved automatically toward the key that sat in his pocket. He had not yet tested to see if it would unlock the Thesis. He just couldn't quite bring himself to do it. What if it didn't work? What if it had all been for nothing?

Darvin stared at him a moment longer, then shrugged. "All right, then. Be that way." He stared eastward out at the sea. "Godsmouth's not far now, huh?"

"Toch says another three or four days." Once they got their bearings they'd know for sure.

Despite the deaths of the crew members, Toch was excited to reach Godsmouth. During the battle his men had captured two of the sea creatures and secured them in the hold alongside the ratmen and tundra strider. Apparently these particular creatures had never been caught alive before, and Toch was envisioning grand pit battles involving a glass-sided artificial lake. The profits, he assured them all, would be astounding.

"You think that Hallowed Order woman will be in Godsmouth?" Darvin asked. "The one who caught us in Locket?"

"We're going to Godsmouth to find the scholar. We have to give her the Thesis. That's all we're there for."

"That's what you're there for, maybe," Darvin said. "I've got other plans."

It was just bluster, Kole hoped. Darvin had to realize he couldn't go up against the Hallowed Order in their own city with nothing more than a bow and arrow.

But when he met Darvin's eyes, he wasn't so sure.

Darvin frowned back at him. "Your eyes," he said.

"What?"

"Were they always…?" He shook his head. "Never mind. Must have been the light. They just looked red for a second."

Before Kole could respond, Redwyn finished addressing the crew. Toch gestured grandly.

"Young Kole! A hand, if you will. It's time for our brothers and sisters to return home."

With one last glance at Darvin, Kole made his way to the front of the crowd. One by one, Toch and Kole together picked up the dead crew members and the empty shrouds and threw them overboard. The bodies and shrouds were all weighted with stones, so they soon disappeared below the swell.

When it was done, Toch turned back to the crowd and threw up his hands.

"Two barrels tonight!" he shouted. "Drink your fill! Remember your fallen companions! Think about what you plan to spend your gold on! For tomorrow, my friends, we sail for Godsmouth!"

A cheer rose up. Someone started playing a fiddle. The crew were soon dancing and singing and fighting and weeping. Kole spotted Darvin dancing with the woman who'd goaded him into shooting down the cormorant. After a few minutes the two of them disappeared belowdecks. A couple of giggling sailors sneaked after them.

Kole found Redwyn standing alone at the prow, staring out at the sea. The priest smiled at Kole as he approached.

"It's always a strange feeling, going home," Redwyn said. "When you're away you remember it as it was when you left. But it doesn't stay that way. Nothing does."

"What's it like?" Kole asked. "Godsmouth."

"Terrible. Magnificent. Indescribable." He shrugged. "You have to experience it for yourself."

Kole was quiet a few seconds. "She's dead," he said finally.

Redwyn didn't ask who or how he knew. He just bowed his head.

"I am sorry, Kole. Really I am."

"Thank you."

"When Mara found Juragar and myself at the Diving Kraken, she asked me to tell you something if she didn't make it. Perhaps you can make more sense of it than me."

Kole swallowed. "What did she say?"

"'The path is clear.' Does that mean anything to you?"

The path is clear. They were the same words Quintus had spoken before he threw the sphere that had destroyed the abomination in the temple.

"I don't know," Kole said. "Maybe."

"Think on it a while. Then get yourself a drink. If you don't hurry there will be none left. You know what sailors are like." He laid a hand on Kole's shoulder. "I better find Juragar. He hates being left alone at a party."

Kole nodded. "Goodnight, Redwyn."

"*Badi haa*, my friend."

As Redwyn left, Kole stood staring out at the sea. Behind him he could feel three dozen hearts beating, full of life. But he focused eastward, toward Godsmouth.

"The path is clear," he murmured to himself.

And it was.

EPILOGUE

ASHER PYKE WAS FUMING.

It just wasn't fair. He shouldn't have been working here in the furnace room of Locket's Grand Crematorium, broiling in his heavy robes. This was a job for young ashers, and Pyke was anything but young.

He'd done his time here already. He'd spent years shoveling bodies into the huge furnaces. He'd spent nearly as long carrying corpses through the Dead Road, and the same again embalming and dressing the bodies once they arrived. His back and his hips and his knees had all been ruined by long years spent hauling the dead about.

He'd earned his job on the Crematorium's upper floor, sweeping and cleaning and directing mourners to the appropriate service. It was his right after a lifetime laboring in the Crematorium.

A right that had been taken from him. The Nametaker, in her pettiness, had stripped him of his duty and cast him back to the basement to work the furnaces like some novice asher.

A penance, she'd called it, for disloyalty. Disloyalty! As if she herself had not allowed outsiders—and a horse!—to walk the Dead Road.

Yes, he'd told the Hallowed Order what she'd done. What else was he supposed to do? The Hallowed Order had been all over Locket, searching for the fugitives from up north. They worried the corruption might spread to the city.

And the Nametaker had simply allowed people she did not know to circumvent the Order's checkpoints! She did not care what corruption these outsiders might bring to the city, to say nothing of the Dead Road itself.

And for what? A bribe? Some golden artifact? Did she have no honor as an asher?

Pyke had to admit he'd smirked when he found out the Hallowed Order had confiscated the artifact. He thought that smirk, more than his "disloyalty," had been what damned him to the furnace room. The Nametaker could be a vindictive woman.

Trying to ignore the ache at the small of his back, Pyke gestured to his much younger partner to help him lift the next body in line. The other asher—Naith or Nerith or some such, he could never remember—took the shoulders while Pyke took the ankles. Grunting, they lifted the wrapped body onto the metal slab that would soon feed the corpse into the fires.

Pyke groaned, pressing a hand against his back. At least the day's work was nearly done. He gestured for the other asher to conduct the rites. The noise was so bad in here he could barely think, let alone go through the mind-numbing rituals. The six brass furnaces roared endlessly, drowning out the sound of all the ashers working them.

Naith or Nerith or whatever it was plucked the piece of parchment from the rope that held the shroud closed. Her eyes moved silently across the words, then she opened her mouth to begin the rites.

A flash of light filled the chamber, bright enough to make the furnace fires seem like candle flames. Pyke cried out and staggered, his eyes burning. A dozen other ashers echoed him.

Blind, he groped for something to hold onto. His hand found the metal slab that fed into the furnace. He rubbed his eyes, blinking until the burning pain finally subsided and the furnace room came back into focus.

Ashers called to each other and helped up those who had fallen. There was rumble of nervous conversation over the sound of the furnaces.

A scream rang out, loud enough to make Pyke slap his hands over his ears. He looked around, searching for the source. Had some foolish asher burned themselves in the confusion?

He stopped and stared at the body that he and his partner had lifted onto the slab.

It was sitting up.

Still screaming, the body began to thrash. The ropes that bound it came loose. An arm jerked free of the shroud, pulling the linen off its head.

It was a woman. Her hair was cropped close at the sides and left longer on the top. A thick knot of scar tissue ran across her throat. As she tugged more of the linen away, Pyke saw other healed injuries marring her nude, well-muscled torso. In Pyke's dazed state he thought she looked vaguely familiar.

Still flailing, the woman toppled off the slab and landed on her hands and knees. She pressed her forehead against the stone floor, her scream becoming a sob.

"How many times?" she moaned, slamming her fist against the floor. "How many times must I return?"

Pyke gaped, frozen in place. This wasn't possible. All bodies were embalmed and stored for the requisite five day period before they were brought to the furnace room. Had someone made a mistake?

He wasn't the only one staring. The other ashers had all gathered round. None spoke.

"Name," the woman rasped.

No one moved.

The woman sat up and glared at them all. "What is my name?"

Pyke's partner was the first to move. Trembling, she picked up the piece of parchment she'd dropped.

"M...Mara," the asher read. "No other names given."

"Mara," the woman echoed. She blinked and looked around.

Pyke suddenly realized where he'd seen her before. She was one of those who had walked the Dead Road!

He knew no good would come from outsiders being allowed on the Dead Road. It went against the natural order of things. And now look! The dead were returning to life!

"This is Locket?" the woman asked.

Pyke's partner nodded shakily. "Yes."

Grabbing at the metal slab she'd been lying on moments before, the woman hauled herself to her feet. The rest of the shroud fell away, though the woman seemed not to notice her nakedness. She touched her fingertips to the scar across her throat, then jerked her hand away.

She stared at Pyke. Her eyes burned so intensely he couldn't look at them.

"Where are my belongings?" she asked. "I have a journey to make."

About the Author

Chris R. Underwood's obsession with fantasy began more than two decades ago with a dog-eared copy of *The Hobbit*. Many suspect that Chris actually is a hobbit, given that he is a short, curly-haired, hairy-footed homebody.

Chris lives in Auckland, New Zealand with his partner and daughter. Find out more or get in touch at:

www.chrisrunderwood.com